Before becoming a full-time writer, Michael Robotham was an investigative journalist in Britain and Australia. He is the pseudonymous author of ten bestselling non-fiction titles, involving prominent figures in the military, the arts, sport and science. He currently lives on Sydney's northern beaches with his wife and three daughters.

THE SUSPECT

Michael Robotham

timewarner
books

A *Time Warner* Book

First published in Great Britain in 2004
by Time Warner Books

Copyright © Michael Robotham 2004

A CIP catalogue record for this book
is available from the British Library.

HARDBACK ISBN 0 316 72552 8
C-FORMAT ISBN 0 316 72620 6

Typeset by Palimpsest Book Production Limited,
Polmont, Stirlingshire
Printed and bound in Great Britain by
Clays Ltd, St Ives plc

Time Warner Books UK
Brettenham House
Lancaster Place
London WC2E 7EN

www.TimeWarnerBooks.co.uk

To the four women in my life:
Vivien, Alexandra, Charlotte and Isabella

Acknowledgements

For his counsel, wisdom and sanity I thank Mark Lucas and all the team at LAW. For her belief ahead of all others, I thank Ursula Mackenzie and those who took the gamble with her.

For their hospitality and friendship I thank Elspeth Rees, Jonathan Margolis and Martyn Forrester – three of many friends and family who have answered my questions, listened to my stories and shared the journey.

Finally, for her love and support I thank Vivien who had to live with all my characters and my sleepless nights. A lesser woman would have slept in the guest room.

Book One

*'I did that,' says my memory.
'I could not have done that,' says my pride, and remains
inexorable. Eventually – the memory yields.*

Friedrich Nietzsche
Beyond Good and Evil

1

From the pitched slate roof of the Royal Marsden Hospital, if you look between the chimney pots and TV aerials, you see more chimney pots and TV aerials. It's like that scene from *Mary Poppins* where all the chimneysweeps dance across the rooftops twirling their brooms.

From up here I can just see the dome of the Royal Albert Hall. On a clear day I could probably see all the way to Hampstead Heath, although I doubt if the air in London ever gets that clear.

'This is some view,' I say, glancing to my right at a teenager crouched about ten feet away. His name is Malcolm and he's seventeen today. Tall and thin, with dark eyes that tremble when he looks at me, he has skin as white as polished paper. He is wearing pyjamas and a woollen hat to cover his baldness. Chemotherapy is a cruel hairdresser.

The temperature is 3°C, but the wind chill has chased it below zero. Already my fingers are numb and I can barely feel my toes through my shoes and socks. Malcolm's feet are bare.

I won't reach him if he jumps or falls. Even if I stretch out and lean along the gutter, I will still be six feet short of catching him. He realises that. He's worked out the angles. According to his oncologist, Malcolm has an exceptional IQ. He plays the violin and speaks five languages – none of which he'll speak to me.

For the last hour I've been asking him questions and telling him stories. I know he can hear me, but my voice is just background noise. He's concentrating on his own internal dialogue, debating whether he should live or die. I want to join that debate, but first I need an invitation.

The National Health Service has a whole raft of guidelines for dealing with hostage situations and threatened suicides. A critical incident team has been pulled together, including senior members of staff, police and a psychologist – me. The first priority has been to learn everything we can about Malcolm that might help us identify what has driven him to this. Doctors, nurses and patients are being interviewed, along with his friends and family.

The primary negotiator is at the apex of the operational triangle. Everything filters down to me. That's why I'm out here, freezing my extremities off, while they're inside drinking coffee, interviewing staff and studying flip charts.

What do I know about Malcolm? He has a primary brain tumour in the right posterior temporal region, dangerously close to his brain stem. The tumour has left him partially paralysed down his left side and unable to hear from one ear. He is two weeks into a second course of chemotherapy.

He had a visit from his parents this morning. The oncologist had good news. Malcolm's tumour appeared to be shrinking. An hour later Malcolm wrote a two-word note that said, 'I'm sorry'. He left his room and managed to crawl on to the roof through a dormer window on the fourth floor. Someone must have left the window unlocked, or he found a way of opening it.

There you have it – the sum total of my knowledge about a teenager who has a lot more to offer than most kids his age.

4

I don't know if he has a girlfriend, or a favourite football team, or a celluloid hero. I know more about his disease than I do about him. That's why I'm struggling.

My safety harness is uncomfortable under my sweater. It looks like one of those contraptions that parents strap on to toddlers to stop them running off. In this case it's supposed to save me if I fall, as long as someone has remembered to fix the other end. It might sound ridiculous, but that's the sort of detail that sometimes gets forgotten in a crisis. Perhaps I should shuffle back towards the window and ask someone to check. Would that be unprofessional? Yes. Sensible? Again yes.

The rooftop is speckled with pigeon droppings and the slate tiles are covered in lichen and moss. The patterns look like fossilised plants pressed into the stone, but the effect is slick and treacherous.

'This probably makes no difference, Malcolm, but I think I know a little about how you're feeling,' I say, trying once more to reach him. 'I have a disease too. I'm not saying that it's cancer. It's not. And trying to make comparisons is like mixing apples with oranges, but we're still talking about fruit, right?'

The receiver in my right ear begins to crackle. 'What in Christ's name are you doing?' says a voice. 'Stop talking about fruit salad and get him inside!'

I take the earpiece out and let it dangle on my shoulder.

'You know how people always say, "It'll be fine. Everything is going to be OK"? They say that because they can't think of anything else. I don't know what to say either, Malcolm. I don't even know what questions to ask.

'Most people don't know how to handle someone else's disease. Unfortunately, there's no book of etiquette or list of do's and don't's. You either get the watery-eyed, I-can't-bear-it-I'm-going-to-cry look or forced jokiness and buck-up speeches. The other option is complete denial.'

Malcolm hasn't responded. He's staring across the rooftops as if looking out of a tiny window high up in the grey sky. His pyjamas are thin and white with blue stitching around the cuffs and collar.

Between my knees I can see three fire engines, two ambulances and half a dozen police cars. One of the fire engines has an extension ladder on a turntable. I haven't taken much notice of it until now, but I see it slowly turning and begin to slide upwards. Why would they be doing that? At the same moment, Malcolm braces his back against the sloping roof and lifts himself. He squats on the edge, with his toes hanging over the gutter, like a bird perched on a branch.

I can hear someone screaming and then I realise that it's me. I'm yelling the place down. I'm wildly gesticulating for them to get the ladder away. I look like the suicidal jumper and Malcolm looks totally calm.

I fumble for the earpiece and hear pandemonium inside. The critical incident team is shouting at the chief fire officer, who is shouting at his second-in-command, who is shouting at someone else.

'Don't do it, Malcolm! Wait!' I sound desperate. 'Look at the ladder. It's going down. See? It's going down.' Blood is pounding in my ears. He stays perched on the edge, curling and uncurling his toes. In profile I can see his long dark lashes blinking slowly. His heart is beating like a bird's within his narrow chest.

'You see that fireman down there with the red helmet?' I say, trying to break into his thoughts. 'The one with all the brass buttons on his shoulders. What do you think my chances are of gobbing on his helmet from here?'

For the briefest of moments, Malcolm glances down. It's the first time he's acknowledged anything I've said or done. The door has opened a chink.

'Some people like to spit watermelon seeds or cherry pips. In Africa they spit dung, which is pretty gross. I read some-

6

where that the world record for spitting Kudu dung is about thirty feet. I think Kudu is a kind of antelope but don't quote me on that. I prefer good old-fashioned saliva and it's not about distance; it's about accuracy.'

He's looking at me now. With a snap of my head I send a foaming white ball arcing downwards. It gets picked up by the breeze and drifts to the right, hitting the windscreen of a police car. In silence I contemplate the shot, trying to work out where I went wrong.

'You didn't allow for the wind,' Malcolm says.

I nod sagely, barely acknowledging him, but inside I have a warm glow in a part of me that isn't yet frozen. 'You're right. These buildings create a bit of a wind tunnel.'

'You're making excuses.'

'I haven't seen you try.'

He looks down, considering this. He's hugging his knees as if trying to stay warm. It's a good sign.

A moment later a globule of spit curves outwards and falls. Together we watch it descend, almost willing it to stay on course. It hits a TV reporter squarely between the eyes and Malcolm and I groan in harmony.

My next shot lands harmlessly on the front steps. Malcolm asks if he can change the target. He wants to hit the TV reporter again.

'Shame we don't have any water bombs,' he says, resting his chin on one knee.

'If you could drop a water bomb on anyone in the world, who would it be?'

'My parents.'

'Why?'

'I don't want to have chemo again. I've had enough.' He doesn't elaborate. It isn't necessary. There aren't many treatments with worse side effects than chemotherapy. The vomiting, nausea, constipation, anaemia and overwhelming fatigue can be intolerable.

7

'What does your oncologist say?'

'He says the tumour is shrinking.'

'That's good.'

He laughs wryly. 'They said that last time. The truth is they're just chasing cancer all around my body. It doesn't go away. It just finds somewhere else to hide. They never talk about a cure; they talk about remission. Sometimes they don't talk to me at all. They just whisper to my parents.' He bites his bottom lip and a carmine mark appears where the blood rushes to the indentation.

'Mum and Dad think I'm scared of dying, but I'm not scared. You should see some of the kids in this place. At least I've had a life. Another fifty years would be nice but, like I said, I'm not scared.'

'How many more chemo sessions?'

'Six. Then we wait and see. I don't mind losing my hair. A lot of footballers shave their hair off. Look at David Beckham; he's a tosser, but he's a wicked player. Having no eyebrows is a bit of a blow.'

'I hear Beckham gets his plucked.'

'By Posh?'

'Yeah.'

It almost raises a smile. In the silence I can hear Malcolm's teeth chattering.

'If the chemo doesn't work my parents are going to tell the doctors to keep trying. They'll never let me go.'

'You're old enough to make your own decisions.'

'Try telling *them* that.'

'I will if you want me to.'

He shakes his head and I see the tears starting to form. He tries to stop them, but they squeeze out from under his long lashes in fat drops that he wipes away with his forearm.

'Is there someone you can talk to?'

'I like one of the nurses. She's been really nice to me.'

'Is she your girlfriend?'

He blushes. The paleness of his skin makes it look as though his head is filling with blood.

'Why don't you come inside and we'll talk some more? I can't raise any spit unless I get something to drink.'

He doesn't answer, but I see his shoulders sag. He's listening to that internal dialogue again.

'I have a daughter called Charlie who is eight years old,' I say, trying to hold him. 'I remember when she was about four, we were in the park and I was pushing her on a swing. She said to me, "Daddy, do you know that if you close your eyes really tightly, so you see white stars, when you open them again it's a brand new world". It's a nice thought, isn't it?'

'But it's not true.'

'It can be.'

'Only if you pretend.'

'Why not? What's stopping you? People think it's easy to be cynical and pessimistic, but it's incredibly hard work. It's much easier to be hopeful.'

'I have an inoperable brain tumour,' he says incredulously.

'Yes, I know.'

I wonder if my words sound as hollow to Malcolm as they do to me. I used to believe all this stuff. A lot can change in ten days.

Malcolm interrupts me. 'Are you a doctor?'

'A psychologist.'

'Tell me again why should I come down?'

'Because it's cold and it's dangerous and I've seen what people look like when they fall from buildings. Come inside. Let's get warm.'

He glances below at the carnival of ambulances, fire engines, police cars and media vans. 'I won the spitting contest.'

'Yes, you did.'

'You'll talk to Mum and Dad?'

'Absolutely.'

He tries to stand, but his legs are cold and stiff. The paralysis down his left side makes his arm next to useless. He needs two arms to get up.

'Just stay there. I'll get them to send up the ladder.'

'No!' he says urgently. I see the look on his face. He doesn't want to be brought down in the blaze of TV lights, with reporters asking questions.

'OK. I'll come to you.' I'm amazed at how brave that sounds. I start to slide sideways in a bum shuffle – too frightened to stand. I haven't forgotten about the safety harness, but I'm still convinced that nobody has bothered to tie it off.

As I edge along the gutter, my head fills with images of what could go wrong. If this were a Hollywood movie Malcolm will slip at the last moment and I'll dive and pluck him out of mid-air. Either that or I'll fall and he'll rescue me.

On the other hand – because this is real life – we might both perish, or Malcolm could live and I'll be the plucky rescuer who plunges to his death.

Although he hasn't moved, I can see a new emotion in Malcolm's eyes. A few minutes ago he was ready to step off the roof without a moment's hesitation. Now he wants to live and the void beneath his feet has become an abyss.

The American philosopher William James (a closet phobic) wrote an article in 1884 pondering the nature of fear. He used an example of a person encountering a bear. Does he run because he feels afraid, or does he feel afraid after he has already started running? In other words, does a person have time to think something is frightening, or does the reaction precede the thought?

Ever since then scientists and psychologists have been locked in a kind of chicken-and-egg debate. What comes first – the conscious awareness of fear or the pounding heart and surging adrenalin that motivates us to fight or flee?

I know the answer now, but I'm so frightened I've forgotten the question.

I'm only a few feet away from Malcolm. His cheeks are tinged with blue and he's stopped shivering. Pressing my back against the wall, I push one leg beneath me and lever my body upwards until I'm standing.

Malcolm looks at my outstretched hand for a moment and then reaches slowly towards me. I grab him by the wrist and pull him upwards until my arm slips around his thin waist. His skin feels like ice.

The front of the safety harness unclasps and I can lengthen the straps. I pass them around his waist and back through the buckle, until the two of us are tethered together. His woollen hat feels rough against my cheek.

'What do you want me to do?' he asks in a croaky voice.

'You can pray the other end of this is tied on to something.'

2

I was probably safer on the roof of the Marsden than at home with Julianne. I can't remember exactly what she called me, but I seem to recall her using words like irresponsible, negligent, careless, immature and unfit to be a parent. This was after she hit me with a copy of *Marie Claire* and made me promise never to do anything so stupid again.

Charlie, on the other hand, won't leave me alone. She keeps bouncing on the bed in her pyjamas, asking me questions about how high up it was, whether I was scared and did the firemen have a big net ready to catch me?

'At last I have something exciting to tell for news,' she says, punching me on the arm. I'm glad Julianne doesn't hear her.

Each morning when I drag myself out of bed I go through a little ritual. When I lean down to tie my shoes I get a good idea of what sort of a day I'm going to have. If it's early in the week and I'm rested, I will have just a little trouble getting the fingers of my left hand to cooperate. Buttons will find buttonholes, belts will find belt-loops and I can even tie a Windsor knot. On my bad days, such as this one, it is a different story. The man I see in the mirror will need two hands to shave and will arrive at the breakfast table with bits of toilet paper stuck to his neck and chin. On these mornings Julianne will say to me, 'You have a brand new electric shaver in the bathroom.'

'I don't like electric shavers.'

'Why not?'

'Because I like lather.'

'What is there to *like* about lather?'

'It's a lovely sounding word, don't you think? It's quite sexy – *lather*. It's decadent.'

She's giggling now, but trying to look annoyed.

'People *lather* their bodies with soap; they *lather* their bodies with shower gel. I think we should *lather* our scones with jam and cream. And we could *lather* on suntan lotion in the summer . . . if we ever have one.'

'You are silly, Daddy,' says Charlie, looking up from her cereal.

'Thank you, my turtle dove.'

'A comic genius,' says Julianne as she picks toilet paper from my face.

Sitting down at the table, I put a spoonful of sugar in my coffee and begin to stir. Julianne is watching me. The spoon stalls in my cup. I concentrate and tell my left hand to start moving, but no amount of willpower is going to budge it. Smoothly I switch the spoon to my right hand.

'When are you seeing Jock?' she asks.

'On Friday.' *Please don't ask me anything else.*

'Is he going to have the test results?'

'He'll tell me what we already know.'

'But I thought—'

'He didn't say!' I hate the sharpness in my voice.

Julianne doesn't even blink. 'I've made you mad. I like you better silly.'

'I am silly. Everyone knows that.'

I see right through her. She thinks I'm doing the macho

thing of hiding my feelings or trying to be relentlessly positive, while really I'm falling apart. My mother is the same – she's become a bloody armchair psychologist. Why don't they leave it to the experts to get it wrong?

Julianne has turned her back. She's breaking up stale bread to leave outside for the birds. Compassion is her hobby.

Dressed in a grey jogging suit, trainers and a baseball cap over her short-cropped dark hair, she looks twenty-seven, not thirty-seven. Instead of growing old gracefully together, she's discovered the secret of eternal youth whereas I need two tries to get off the couch. Monday is yoga, Tuesday is Pilates, Thursday and Saturday are circuit training. In between times she runs the house, raises a child, teaches Spanish lessons and still finds time to try to save the world. She even made childbirth look easy, although I would never tell her that unless I developed a death wish.

We have been married for sixteen years and when people ask me why I became a psychologist, I say, 'Because of Julianne. I wanted to *know* what she was really thinking.'

It didn't work. I still have no idea.

Sunday morning is normally *my* time. I bury myself under the combined weight of four newspapers and drink coffee until my tongue feels furry. After what happened yesterday I'm going to avoid the headlines, although Charlie is insisting we cut them out and make a scrapbook. I guess it's pretty cool being 'cool' for once. Up until yesterday she's regarded my job as more boring than cricket.

Charlie's rugged up in jeans, skivvy and a ski jacket because I've promised she can come with me today. After gulping down her breakfast, she watches me impatiently – convinced that I'm drinking my coffee too slowly.

When it's time to load up the car, we carry the cardboard boxes from the garden shed and put them next to my old Metro. Julianne is sitting on the front steps with a cup of coffee resting on her knees. 'You're both mad, you know that?'

'Probably.'

'And you'll get arrested.'

'And that's going to be your fault.'

'Why is it my fault?'

'Because you won't come with us. We need a getaway driver.'

Charlie pipes up. 'C'mon, Mum. Dad said you used to.'

'That's when I was young and foolish and I wasn't on the committee at your school.'

'Do you realise, Charlie, that on my second date with your mother she was arrested for scaling a flag-pole and taking down the South African flag.'

Julianne scowls. 'Don't tell her that!'

'Did you really get arrested?'

'I was cautioned. It's not the same thing.'

There are four boxes on the roof racks, two in the boot and two on the back seat. Fine beads of sweat, like polished glass, are decorating Charlie's top lip. She slips off her ski jacket and tucks it between the seats.

I turn back to Julianne. 'Are you sure you won't come? I know you want to.'

'Who's going to post bail for us?'

'Your mother will do that.'

Her eyes narrow, but she puts her coffee cup inside the door. 'I'm doing this under protest.'

'Duly noted.'

She holds out her hand for the car keys. 'And I'm driving.'

She grabs a jacket from the coat rack in the hallway and pulls the door shut. Charlie squeezes herself between the boxes on the back seat and leans forward excitedly. 'Tell me the story again,' she says as we swing into light traffic along Prince Albert Road, alongside Regent's Park. 'And don't leave anything out just because Mum's here.'

*   *   *

I can't tell her the whole story. I'm not even sure of all the details myself. At the heart of it is my great aunt Gracie – the *real* reason I became a psychologist. She was my maternal grandmother's youngest sister and she died at the age of eighty, having not set foot outside her house in nearly sixty years.

She lived about a mile from where I grew up in West London, in a grand old detached Victorian house with miniturrets on the roof, metal balconies and a coal cellar underneath. The front door had two rectangular panes of leadlight. I would press my nose against them and see a dozen fractured images of Aunt Gracie bustling down the hallway to answer my knock. She would open the door just wide enough to let me slip inside and then close it again quickly.

Tall and almost skeletal, with clear blue eyes and fair hair gone streaky white, she always wore a long black velvet dress, with a string of pearls that seemed to glow against the black material.

'Finnegan, come! COME! Joseph's here!'

Finnegan was a Jack Russell without a bark. His voice box had been crushed in a fight with a neighbourhood Alsatian. Instead of barking, he huffed and puffed as though auditioning to play the big bad wolf in a pantomime.

Gracie talked to Finnegan as though he were a person. She read him stories from the local paper, or asked him questions about local issues. She would nod her agreement whenever he responded with a huff, or a puff, or a fart. Finnegan even had his own chair at the table and Gracie would slip him morsels of cake and admonish herself in the same breath for 'feeding an animal from the hand'.

When Gracie poured the tea she half filled my cup with milk because I was too young to have full-strength brew. My feet could barely touch the floor when I sat on the dining chairs. If I sat back, my legs stuck straight out underneath the white lace tablecloth.

Years later, when my feet could reach the floor and I had

to bend down to kiss Gracie on the cheek, she continued to add half a cup of milk to my tea. Maybe she didn't want me to grow up.

If I'd come straight from school, she made me sit next to her on the chaise longue, clutching my hand in her own. She wanted to know everything about my day. What I learned in class. What games I played. What fillings I had in my sandwiches. She soaked up the details as though picturing every footstep.

Gracie was a classic agoraphobic – terrified of open space. She once tried to explain it to me, having grown sick of fobbing off my questions.

'Have you ever been afraid of the dark?' she asked.

'Yes.'

'What did you fear would happen if the lights went out?'

'That a monster would get me.'

'Did you ever see this monster?'

'No. Mum says that monsters don't exist.'

'She's right. They don't. So where did your monster come from?'

'Up here.' I tapped my head.

'Exactly. I have a monster too. I know he's not supposed to exist, but he won't go away.'

'What does your monster look like?'

'He is ten feet tall and he carries a sword. If I try to leave the house he's going to cut my head off.'

'Are you making that up?'

She laughed and tried to tickle me, but I pushed her hands away. I wanted an honest answer.

Tiring of this conversation, she screwed shut her eyes and tucked loose strands of white hair into her tightly wrapped bun. 'Have you ever watched one of those horror films where the hero is trying to get away and the car won't start? He keeps turning the key and pumping the accelerator, but the engine just coughs and dies. And you can see the villain coming. He's got a gun or a knife. And you keep saying to yourself, "Get out of there! Get out! He's coming!".'

I nod, wide-eyed. 'Well, you take that fear,' she said, 'and you multiply it by a hundred and then you'll know how I feel when I think about going outside.'

She stood and walked out of the room. The discussion had ended. I never raised the subject again. I didn't want to make her sad.

I don't know how she lived. Cheques would arrive periodically from a law firm, but Gracie would place them on the mantelpiece, where she could stare at them each day until they expired. I guess they were part of her inheritance, but she wanted nothing to do with her family's money. I didn't know the reason . . . not then.

She worked as a seamstress – making wedding gowns and bridesmaid's dresses. I would often find the front room draped in silk and organza, with a bride-to-be standing on a stool and Gracie with her mouth full of pins. It was not a place for young boys – not unless they fancied modelling a dress.

The rooms upstairs were full of what Gracie called her 'collectibles'. By this she meant books, fashion magazines, reels of cloth, cotton bobbins, hatboxes, bags of wool, photograph albums, soft toys and a treasure trove of unexplored boxes and trunks.

Most of these 'collectibles' had been recycled or purchased by mail order. The catalogues were always open on the coffee table and each day the mailman brought something new.

Not surprisingly, Gracie's view of the world was rather limited. The TV news and current affairs programmes seemed to magnify conflict and pain. She saw people fighting, wilderness vanishing, bombs falling and countries starving. While these weren't the reasons she ran away from the world, they were certainly no incentive to go back.

'It scares me just seeing how small you are,' she told me. 'It's not a good time to be a child.' She glanced out the bay window and shuddered as though able to see a terrible fate awaiting me. I only saw an overgrown and unkempt garden with white butterflies flitting between the gnarled branches of the apple trees.

'Don't you ever want to go outside?' I asked her. 'Don't you want to look up at the stars or walk along a riverbank or admire the gardens?'

'I stopped thinking about it a long while ago.'

'What do you miss most?'

'Nothing.'

'There must be something.'

She thought for a moment. 'I used to love the autumn, just as the leaves turn and begin to fall. We used to go to Kew Gardens and I'd run along the thoroughfares, kicking up the leaves and trying to catch them. The curled leaves would slip from side to side, like miniature boats riding the air until they settled into my hands.'

'I could blindfold you,' I suggested.

'No.'

'What if you put a box over your head? You could pretend you were inside.'

'I don't think so.'

'I could wait until you were asleep and push your bed outside?'

'Down the stairs?'

'Mmmm. Bit tricky.'

She put her arm around my shoulders. 'Don't you worry about me. I'm quite happy here.'

From then on we had a sort of running joke. I kept suggesting new ways to get her outside and new pastimes like hang-gliding and wing-walking. Gracie would react in mock horror and tell me I was the *real* lunatic.

'So what about her birthday?' says Charlie impatiently. We're driving through St John's Wood, just passing Lord's cricket ground. The traffic lights gleam brightly against the dullness of the outer walls.

'I thought you wanted the whole story?'

'Yes, but I'm not getting any younger.'

Julianne gets a fit of the giggles. 'She gets the sarcasm from you, you know.'

'OK,' I sigh. 'I'll tell you about Gracie's birthday. She never admitted her age, but I knew she was going to be seventy-five because I found some dates by looking through her photo albums.'

'You said she was beautiful,' says Charlie.

'Yes. It's not easy to tell from old photographs because nobody ever smiled and the women looked plain scary. But Gracie was different. She had twinkling eyes and always looked as though she was about to giggle. And she used to cinch her belt a little tighter and stand so the light shone through her petticoats.'

'She was a flirt,' says Julianne.

'What's a flirt?' asks Charlie.

'Never mind.'

Charlie frowns and hugs her knees, resting her chin on the patched knees of her jeans.

'It was pretty difficult to plan a surprise for Gracie because, of course, she never left the house,' I explain. 'I had to do everything when she was asleep—'

'How old were you?'

'Sixteen. I was still at Charterhouse.'

Charlie nods and begins pinning her hair up high on her head. She looks exactly like Julianne when she does that.

'Gracie didn't use her garage. She had no need of a car. It had big wooden doors that opened outwards, as well as an internal doorway into the laundry. First I cleaned the place up, clearing away the junk and washing down the walls.'

'You must have been very quiet.'

'I was.'

20

'And you put up fairy lights?'

'Hundreds of them. They looked like twinkling stars.'

'And then you got the big sack.'

'That's right. It took me four days. I had to carry the hessian sack over my shoulder and ride my bike. People must have thought I was a street sweeper or a park ranger.'

'They probably thought you were crazy.'

'Absolutely.'

'Just like we're crazy?'

'Yep.' I sneak a glance at Julianne, who isn't biting.

'What happened next?' asks Charlie.

'Well, on the morning of her birthday, Gracie came downstairs and I made her close her eyes. She held my arm and I walked her through the kitchen, into the laundry and then the garage. As she opened the door an avalanche of leaves came tumbling out around her waist. "Happy Birthday," I said. You should have seen her face. She looked at the leaves and then back at me. For a moment I thought she was angry, but then she gave me this beautiful smile.'

'I know what happened next,' says Charlie.

'Yes. I've told you before.'

'She ran into all those leaves.'

'Yep. We both did. We threw them in the air and kicked up our knees. We had leaf fights and made leaf mountains. And eventually, we were both so exhausted we collapsed on to a bed of leaves and stared up at the stars.'

'But they weren't really stars, were they?'

'No, but we could pretend.'

The entrance to Kensal Green Cemetery is in Harrow Road and is easy to miss. Julianne follows the narrow road and parks in a circle of trees as far from the caretaker's cottage as possible. Glancing out the windscreen, I see neat rows of gravestones intersected by paths and beds of flowers.

'Is this against the law?' whispers Charlie.

'Yes,' says Julianne.

'Not exactly,' I counter as I start unloading boxes and handing them to Charlie.

'I can take two,' she announces.

'OK, I'll take three and we'll come back for the rest. Unless Mum wants to—'

'I'm fine just here.' She hasn't moved from behind the wheel.

We head off, keeping close to the trees at first. Long fingers of lawn stretch between the graves. I walk cautiously, not wanting to tread on any flowers or knock my shins on one of the smaller headstones. The sounds of Harrow Road disappear and are replaced by snatches of birdsong and the periodic roar of intercity express trains.

'Do you know where we're going?' asks Charlie from behind me, puffing slightly.

'It's over towards the canal. Do you want a rest?'

'I'm OK.' Then her voice takes on a doubtful tone. 'Dad?'

'Yes?'

'You know how you said that Gracie loved kicking up leaves?'

'Yes.'

'Because she's dead, she can't really kick these up, can she?'

'No.'

'I mean, she can't come back to life. Dead people don't do that, do they? Because I've seen scary cartoons about zombies and mummies that come back from the dead, but that doesn't really happen, does it?'

'No.'

'And Gracie is in heaven now, isn't she? That's where she's gone.'

'Yes.'

'So what are we doing with all these leaves?'

It's at times like these I normally direct Charlie to Julianne. She sends her straight back to me, saying, 'Your father is a psychologist. He knows these things.'

Charlie is waiting.

'What we're doing is sort of symbolic,' I say.

22

'What does that mean?'

'Have you ever heard people say, "It's the thought that counts"?'

'You always say that when somebody gives me a present that I don't like. You say I should be grateful, even if the present sucks.'

'That's not quite what I mean.' I try a new approach. 'Aunt Gracie can't really kick up these leaves. But wherever she is, if she's watching us now I think she'll be laughing. And she'll really appreciate what we're doing. That's what counts.'

'She'll be kicking up leaves in heaven?' adds Charlie.

'Absolutely.'

'Do you think she'll be outside or will heaven have an inside place?'

'I don't know.'

I set my boxes on the ground and unload Charlie's arms. Gracie's headstone is a simple square of granite. Someone has left a muddy shovel leaning against the brass plaque. I have visions of gravediggers taking a tea break, except nowadays they use machines instead of muscle. I toss the shovel to one side and Charlie gives the inscription a polish with the sleeve of her ski jacket. I creep up behind her and dump a box full of leaves on top of her head.

'Hey! That's not fair!' Charlie scoops a big handful and stuffs them up the back of my jumper. Soon there are leaves tumbling all over the place. Gracie's headstone disappears completely under our autumnal offering.

Behind me somebody loudly clears his throat and I hear Charlie give a little yelp of surprise.

The caretaker is silhouetted against the pale sky, with his hands on his hips and legs akimbo. He's wearing a pea-green jacket and a pair of muddy Wellingtons that appear to be too big for his feet.

'Do you mind explaining what you're doing?' he asks in a monotone. He steps closer. His face is flat and round with a wide forehead and no hair. It brings to mind Thomas the Tank Engine.

'It's a long story,' I say feebly.

'You're desecrating a grave.'

I laugh at how ridiculous he sounds. 'I hardly think so.'

'You think this is funny? This is vandalism. This is a crime. This is littering—'

'Fallen leaves aren't technically litter.'

'Don't play games with me,' he stutters.

Charlie decides to intervene. With breathless eloquence, she explains, 'It's Gracie's birthday, but we can't give her a party because she's dead. She doesn't like going outside. We brought her some leaves. She likes kicking up leaves. Don't worry; she's not a zombie or a mummy. She's not going to come back from the dead. She's in heaven. Do you think there are trees in heaven?'

The caretaker looks at her with utter dismay and takes a few moments to realise that her last question is directed at him. Rendered almost speechless, he makes several unsuccessful attempts to speak before his voice deserts him. Having been totally disarmed, he crouches to be at her eye-level.

'What is your name, Missy?'

'Charlie Louise O'Loughlin. What's yours?'

'Mr Gravesend.'

'That's pretty funny.'

'I guess so.' He smiles.

He looks at me with none of the same warmth. 'Do you know how many years I've been trying to catch the bugger who spreads leaves all over this grave?'

'Around fifteen?' I suggest.

'I was going to say thirteen, but I'll take your word for it. You see, I worked out when you come. I made a note of the date. I nearly caught you two years ago but you must have come in a different car.'

'My wife's.'

'And then last year it was my day off – a Saturday. I told young Whitey to watch out for you but he thinks I'm fixating. He says I shouldn't get so worked up over a pile of leaves.'

His nudges the offending mound with the toe of his boot. 'But I take my job very seriously. People come here and try to do all sorts of things, like planting oak trees on graves or leaving kid's toys behind. If we let 'em do what they like, where will it end?'

'It must be a hard job,' I say.

'Too bleedin' right!' He glances at Charlie. 'Pardon me language, Missy.'

She giggles.

Over his right shoulder, on the far side of the canal, I notice flashing blue police lights as two cars pull up to join another already parked on the towpath. The lights reflect off the dark water and strobe against the trunks of winter trees that stand like sentries above the gravestones.

Several policemen are staring into a ditch beside the canal. They look frozen in place until one of them begins sealing off the area, wrapping blue and white police tape around the trees and fence posts.

Mr Gravesend has fallen silent, unsure of what to do next. His planning had involved catching me, but didn't extend any further than that. Moreover, he hadn't expected Charlie to be here.

I reach into the pocket of my overcoat and produce a Thermos. In my other pocket there are two metal mugs. 'We were just about to have a hot chocolate. Would you like to join us?'

'You can use my cup,' says Charlie. 'I'll share.'

He considers this, wondering if the offer can be construed as a bribe. 'So it's come to this,' he says in a clear, soft voice. 'Either I have you arrested or I have a hot chocolate.'

'Mum said we'd get arrested,' pipes Charlie. 'She said we were mad.'

'You should have listened to your mum.'

I hand the caretaker a mug and give the other to Charlie.

'Happy birthday, Aunt Gracie,' she says. Mr Gravesend mumbles an appropriate-sounding response, still stunned by the speed of his capitulation.

At that moment I notice two boxes approaching, swaying on black leggings and sneakers.

'That's my mum. She's our look-out,' observes Charlie.

'Not her strong suit,' Mr Gravesend replies.

'No.'

Julianne drops the boxes and lets out a startled squeak, not unlike Charlie's reaction.

'Don't worry, Mum, you're not going to be arrested again.'

The caretaker raises his eyebrows and Julianne smiles feebly. Hot chocolate is shared around and we make small talk. Mr Gravesend gives us a commentary on the writers, painters and statesmen buried in the cemetery. He makes them sound like personal friends, although most have been dead a century.

Charlie is kicking through the leaves until she suddenly goes still. She gazes down the slope towards the canal. Arc lights have been turned on and a white marquee is being set up beside the water. A flashgun fires time after time.

'What's happening?' she asks, wanting to go down and see. Julianne gently reaches out and pulls her close, draping her arms around her shoulders.

Charlie looks at me and then at the caretaker. 'What are they doing?'

Nobody answers. Instead we watch in silence, weighed down by an emotion that goes beyond sorrow. The air has grown colder. It smells of dampness and decay. The shuddering screech of steel in the distant freight yard sounds like a cry of pain.

There is a boat on the canal. Men in yellow fluorescent vests peer over the sides, shining torches into the water. Others walk in a slow line along the banks with their heads down, searching inch by inch. Occasionally one of them stops and bends down. The others wait rather than break the line.

'Have they lost something?' asks Charlie.

'Shush,' I whisper.

Julianne's face is bleak and raw. She looks at me. It's time to leave.

At that moment a coroner's van pulls up next to the marquee. The back doors open and two men in boiler suits pull out a stretcher on a collapsible trolley.

Over my right shoulder a police car appears through the cemetery gates, with flashing lights but no siren. A second car follows.

Mr Gravesend is already walking back towards the car park and the caretaker's cottage.

'Come on, we better go,' I say, tipping out the cold dregs of the chocolate. Charlie still doesn't understand but realises that it's time to be quiet.

I open the car door and she slips inside, escaping the cold. Across the bonnet, eighty yards away, the caretaker is in conversation with the police. Arms are pointed towards the canal. A notebook is produced. Details are taken.

Julianne is in the passenger seat. She wants me to drive. My left arm is trembling. I grip the gear lever to make it stop. As we pass the police cars, one of the detectives glances up. He is middle-aged with pockmarked cheeks and a punch-worn nose. He's wearing a crumpled grey overcoat and a cynical expression, as though he's done this before and it never gets any easier.

Our eyes meet and he looks straight through me. There's no light, no story, no smile in his eyes. He arches an eyebrow and cocks his head to one side. By then I'm gone, still gripping the gearshift and struggling to find second gear.

As we reach the entrance, Charlie peers through the back window and asks if we're coming back next year.

3

I walk to work every weekday morning across Regent's Park. At this time of year, when the temperature drops, I wear non-slip shoes, a woollen scarf and a permanent frown. Forget about global warming. As I get older the world gets colder. That's a fact.

The sun is like a pale yellow ball floating in the greyness and joggers slip past me with heads down and their trainers leaving patterns on the wet asphalt. The gardeners are supposed to be planting bulbs for the spring, but their wheel-barrows are filling with water. I can see them smoking ciga-rettes and playing cards in the toolshed.

As I cross Primrose Hill Bridge, I peer over the side at the canal. A lone narrow boat is moored against the towpath and mist curls from the water like wisps of smoke.

What were the police looking for? Who did they find?

I watched the TV news last night and listened to the radio this morning. Nothing. I know it's just morbid curiosity, yet a part of me feels as though I've been a witness – if not to the crime then the aftermath. It's like when you watch those *Crimewatch* shows and the police ask for people to come forward if they have any information. It's always someone else. It's never someone we know.

A soft rain slips down and clings to my jacket as I start walking again. The Post Office Tower is etched against the darkening sky. It is one of those landmarks that allow people to navigate a city. Streets will disappear into dead ends or twist and turn without reason, but the tower rises above the eccentricities of urban planning.

I like this view of London. It still looks quite majestic. It's only when you get close up you see the decay. But then again, I guess you could say the same about me.

My office is in a pyramid of white boxes on Great Portland Street designed by an architect who drew inspiration from his childhood. From ground level it doesn't look finished and I'm always half expecting a crane to turn up and hoist a few more boxes into the gaps.

As I walk up the front steps I hear a car horn and turn. A bright red Ferrari pulls on to the pavement. The driver, Dr Fenwick Spindler, raises a gloved hand to wave. Fenwick looks like a lawyer but he runs the psychopharmacology unit at London University Hospital. He also has a private practice with a consulting room next to mine.

'Good morning, old boy,' he shouts, leaving the car in the middle of the pavement so that people have to step around it on to the road.

'Aren't you worried about the parking police?'

'Got one of these,' he says, pointing to the doctor's sticker on the windscreen. 'Perfect for medical emergencies.'

Joining me on the steps, he pushes open the glass door. 'Saw you on the TV the other night. Jolly good show. Wouldn't have caught me up there.'

'I'm sure you would have—'

'Must tell you about my weekend. Went shooting in Scotland. Bagged a deer.'

'Do you *bag* deer?'

29

'Whatever,' he waves dismissively. 'Shot the bastard right through the left eye.'

The receptionist triggers a switch to open the security door and we summon a lift. Fenwick examines himself in the internal mirrors, brushing specks of dandruff from the bunched shoulders of an expensive suit. It says something about Fenwick's body when a hand-tailored suit doesn't fit him.

'Still consorting with prostitutes?' he asks.

'I give talks.'

'Is *that* what they call it nowadays?' He guffaws and rearranges himself via a trouser pocket. 'How do you get paid?

He won't believe me if I tell him I do it for nothing. 'They give me vouchers. I can redeem them for blowjobs later. I have a whole drawer full of them.'

He almost chokes and blushes furiously. I have to stop myself laughing.

Fenwick, for all his obvious success as a doctor, is one of those people who tries desperately hard to be somebody else. That's why he looks vaguely ridiculous behind the wheel of a sports car. It's like seeing Bill Gates in board shorts or George W. Bush in The White House. It just doesn't look right.

'How's the you-know-what?' he asks.

'Fine.'

'I haven't noticed it at all, old boy. Come to think of it, Pfizer is trailing a new drug cocktail. Drop by and I'll give you the literature . . . '

Fenwick's contacts with drug companies are renowned. His office is a shrine to Pfizer, Novatis and Hoffmann-La Roche; almost every item donated, from the fountain pens to the espresso machine. The same is true of his social life – sailing in Cowes, salmon fishing in Scotland and grouse shooting in Northumberland.

We turn the corner and Fenwick glances inside my office. A middle-aged woman sits in the waiting room clutching an orange torpedo-shaped lifebuoy.

'I don't know how you do it, old boy,' Fenwick mutters.

'Do what?'

'*Listen* to them.'

'That's how I find out what's wrong.'

'Why bother? Dish out some anti-depressants and send her home.'

Fenwick doesn't believe there are psychological or social factors in mental illness. He claims it is completely biological and therefore, by definition, treatable with drugs. It is just a matter of finding the right combination.

Every morning (he doesn't work after midday) patients march one by one into his office, answer a few perfunctory questions before Fenwick hands them a scrip and bills them £140. If they want to talk symptoms, he wants to talk drugs. If they mention side effects he changes the dosage.

The strange thing is that his patients love him. They come in *wanting* drugs and they don't care which ones. The more pills the better. Maybe they figure they're getting value for money.

Listening to people is considered to be old-fashioned nowa-days. Patients expect me to produce a magic pill that cures everything. When I tell them that I just want to talk, they look disappointed.

'Morning, Margaret. Glad to see you made it.'

She holds up the lifebuoy.

'Which way did you come?'

'Putney Bridge.'

'It's a good solid bridge that one. Been around for years.'

She suffers from Gephyrophobia – a fear of crossing bridges. To make matters worse, she lives south of the river and has to walk her children to school across the Thames every day. She carries the lifebuoy just in case the bridge falls down or is swept away by a tidal wave. I know that sounds irrational but simple phobias are like that.

'I should have gone to live in the Sahara,' she says, only half joking.

I tell her about Eremikophobia, the fear of sand or deserts. She thinks I'm making it up.

Three months ago Margaret panicked mid-crossing while walking her kids to school. It took an hour before anybody realised. The children were crying, still clutching her hands. She was frozen by fear, unable to speak or nod. Passers-by thought she might be a 'jumper'. In reality Margaret was holding up that bridge with sheer willpower.

We've done a lot of work since then, trying to break the thought loop that accompanies her irrational fear.

'What do you believe is going to happen if you cross the bridge?'

'It's going to fall down.'

'Why would it fall down?'

'I don't know.'

'What is the bridge made of?'

'Steel and rivets and concrete.'

'How long has it been there?'

'Years and years.'

'Has it ever fallen down?'

'No.'

Each session lasts fifty minutes and I have ten minutes to write up my notes before my next patient arrives. Meena, my secretary, is like an atomic clock, accurate to the last second.

'A minute lost is a minute gone for ever, ' she says, tapping the watch pinned to her breast.

Anglo-Indian, but more English than strawberries and cream, she dresses in knee-length skirts, sensible shoes and cardigans. And she reminds me of the girls I knew at school that were addicted to Jane Austen novels and always daydreaming about meeting their Mr Darcy.

Sadly, I'm losing her soon. She and her cats are off to open a Bed & Breakfast in Bath. I can just imagine the place – lace doilies under every vase, moggy figurines and the toast soldiers in neat ranks beside every three-minute egg.

Meena is organising the interviews for a new secretary. She has narrowed them down to a shortlist but I know I'll have trouble deciding. I keep hoping that she'll change her mind. If only I could purr.

Mid-afternoon, I glance around the waiting room. 'Where's Bobby?'

'He hasn't arrived.'

'Did he call?'

'No.' She tries not to meet my eyes.

'Can you try to find him? It's been two weeks.'

I know she doesn't want to make the call. She doesn't like Bobby. At first I thought it was because he didn't turn up for appointments, but it's more than that. He makes her nervous. Maybe it's his size or the bad haircut or the chip on his shoulder. She doesn't really know him. Then again, who does?

Almost on cue, he appears in the doorway with his odd-legged shuffle and an anxious expression. Tall and overweight, with flax-brown hair and metal-framed glasses, his great pudding of a body is trying to burst out of a long overcoat made shapeless by its bulging pockets.

'Sorry I'm late. Something came up.' He glances around the waiting room, still unsure whether to step inside.

'Something came up for two weeks?'

He makes eye contact with me and then turns his face away.

I'm used to Bobby being defensive and enclosed, but this is different. Instead of keeping secrets he's telling lies. It's like closing the shutters in front of someone and then trying to deny they exist.

I take a quick inventory – his shoes are polished and his hair is combed. He shaved this morning, but the dark shadow has returned. His cheeks are red from the cold but at the same time he's perspiring. I wonder how long he spent outside, trying to get up the courage to come and see me.

'Where have you been, Bobby?'

'I got scared.'

'Why?'

He shrugs. 'I had to get away.'

'Where did you go?'

'Nowhere.'

I don't bother pointing out the contradiction. He's full of them. Restless hands look for somewhere to hide and escape into his pockets.

'Do you want to take off your coat?'

'It's OK.'

'Well, at least sit down.' I nod towards my office. He walks through the door and stands in front of my bookshelves, perusing the titles. Most of them are texts on psychology and animal behaviour. Eventually he stops and taps the spine of a book, *The Interpretation of Dreams* by Sigmund Freud.

'I thought Freud's views had been pretty much discredited these days.' He has the faintest hint of a northern accent. 'He couldn't tell the difference between hysteria and epilepsy.'

'It wasn't one of his best calls.'

I point to the chair and Bobby folds himself down into it, with his knees facing sideways towards the door.

Apart from my own notes, there is very little paperwork in his file. I have the original referral, neurological scans and a letter from a GP in north London. These mention 'disturbing nightmares' and a sense of being 'out of control'.

Bobby is twenty-two years of age, with no history of mental illness or habitual drug use. He has above average intelligence, is in good health and lives in a long-term relationship with Arky, his fiancée.

I have a basic history – born in London, educated at state schools, O-levels, night classes, odd jobs as a delivery driver and storeman. He and Arky live in a tower block in Hackney. She has a little boy and works at the candy bar in the local cinema. Apparently it was Arky who convinced him to seek help. Bobby's nightmares were getting worse. He woke screaming in the night, hurtling out of bed and crashing into walls as he tried to escape his dreams.

Before the summer we seemed to be getting somewhere. Then Bobby disappeared for three months and I thought he'd gone for good. He turned up five weeks ago, with no appointment or explanation. He seemed happier. He was sleeping better. The nightmares were less severe.

Now something is wrong. He sits motionless but his flicking eyes don't miss a thing.

'What's happened?'

'Nothing.'

'Is something wrong at home?'

He blinks. 'No.'

'What then?'

I let the silence work for me. Bobby fidgets, scratching at his hands as though something has irritated his skin. Minutes pass and he grows more and more agitated.

I give him a direct question to get him started. 'How is Arky?'

'She reads too many magazines.'

'Why do you say that?'

'She wants the modern fairytale. You know all that bullshit they write in women's magazines – telling them how to have multiple orgasms, hold down a career and be a perfect mother. It's all crap. Real women don't look like fashion models. Real men can't be cut out of magazines. I don't know what I'm supposed to be – a new age man or a man's man. You tell me! Am I supposed to get drunk with the boys or cry at sad films? Do I talk about sports cars or this season's colours? Women think they want a man but instead they want a reflection of themselves.'

'How does that make you feel?'

'Frustrated.'

'Who with?'

'Take your pick.' His shoulders hunch and his coat collar brushes his ears. His hands are in his lap now, folding and unfolding a piece of paper, which has worn through along the creases.

'What have you written?'

'A number.'

'What number?'

'Twenty-one.'

'Can I see it?'

He blinks rapidly and slowly unfolds the page, pressing it flat against his thigh and running his fingers over the surface. The number '21' has been written hundreds of times, in tiny block figures, fanning out from the centre to form the blades of a windmill.

'Do you know that a dry square piece of paper cannot be folded in half more than seven times,' Bobby says, trying to change the subject.

'No.'

'It's true.'

'What else are you carrying in your pockets?'

'My lists.'

'What sort of lists?'

'Things to do. Things I'd like to change. People I like.'

'And people you don't like?'

'That too.'

Some people don't match their voices and Bobby is one of them. Although a big man, he seems smaller because his voice isn't particularly deep and his shoulders shrink when he leans forward.

'Are you in some sort of trouble, Bobby?'

He flinches so abruptly the legs of his chair leave the floor. His head is shaking firmly back and forth.

'Did you get angry with someone?'

Looking hopelessly sad, he bunches his fists.

'What made you angry?'

Whispering something, he shakes his head.

'I'm sorry, I didn't hear that.'

He mouths the words again.

'You'll have to speak up a little.'

Without a flicker of warning he explodes: 'STOP FUCKING WITH MY HEAD!'

The noise echoes in the confined space. Doors open along the corridor and the light flashes on my intercom. I press the button. 'It's OK, Meena. Everything's fine.'

A tiny vein throbs at the side of Bobby's temple, just above his right eye. He whispers in a little boy voice, 'I had to punish her.'

'Who did you have to punish?'

He gives the ring on his right index finger a half turn and then turns it back again as if he's tuning the dial on a radio, searching for the right frequency.

'We're all connected – six degrees of separation, sometimes less. If something happens in Liverpool or London or Australia, it's all connected . . . '

I won't let him change the subject. 'If you're in trouble, Bobby, I can help. You have to let me know what happened.'

'Whose bed is she in now?' he whispers.

'I beg your pardon?'

'The only time she'll sleep alone is in the ground.'

'Did you punish Arky?'

More aware of me now, he laughs at me. 'Did you ever see *The Truman Show*?'

'Yes.'

'Well, sometimes I think I'm Truman. I think the whole world is watching me. My life has been created to someone else's expectations. Everything is a façade. The walls are plywood and the furniture is papier mâché. And then I think that if I could just run fast enough, I'd get around the next corner and find the back-lot of the film set. But I can never run fast enough. By the time I arrive, they've built another street . . . and another.'

4

In real estate terms we live in purgatory. I say this because we haven't quite reached the leafy nirvana of Primrose Hill; yet we've climbed out of the graffiti-stained, metal-shuttered shit-hole that is the southern end of Camden Town.

The mortgage is huge and the plumbing is dodgy but Julianne fell in love with the place. I have to admit that I did too. In the summer, if the breeze is blowing in the right direction and the windows are open, we can hear the sound of lions and hyenas at London Zoo. It's like being on safari without the mini-vans.

Julianne teaches Spanish to an adult education class on Wednesday evenings. Charlie is sleeping over at her best friend's house. I have the place to myself, which is normally OK. I reheat some soup in the microwave and tear a French loaf in half. Charlie has written a poem on the white board, next to the ingredients for banana bread. I feel a tiny flicker of loneliness. I want them both here. I miss the noise, the banter.

Wandering upstairs, I move from room to room checking on the 'work in progress'. Paint pots are lined up on the windowsill and the floors are covered in old sheets that look like Jackson Pollock canvases. One of the bedrooms has become a storeroom for boxes, rugs and bits of cat-scratched furniture. Charlie's old pram and high chair are in the corner, awaiting further instructions. And her baby clothes are sealed in plastic tubs with neat labels.

For six years we've been trying for another baby. So far the score stands at two miscarriages and innumerable tears. I don't want to go on – not now – but Julianne is still popping vitamin pills, studying urine samples and taking temperature readings. Our lovemaking is like a scientific experiment, with everything aimed at the optimum moment of ovulation.

When I point this out to her she promises to jump on my bones regularly and spontaneously as soon as we have another baby.

'You won't regret a single moment when it happens.'

'I know.'

'We owe it to Charlie.'

'Yes.'

I want to give her all the 'what ifs' but can't bring myself to do it. What if this disease accelerates? What if there is a genetic link? What if I can't hold my own child? I'm not being mawkish and self-obsessed. I'm being practical. A cup of tea and a couple of digestives aren't going to fix this problem. This disease is like a distant train, hurtling through the darkness towards us. It might seem like a long way off, but it's coming.

At six-thirty the cab arrives and we join the rush hour. Euston Road is backed up past Baker Street and there's no point trying to find a shortcut past an obstacle course of bollards, speed bumps and one-way signs.

The driver is complaining about illegal immigrants sneaking through the Channel Tunnel and making the traffic problems worse. Since none of them have cars I can't understand this, but I'm too depressed to argue.

Shortly after seven he drops me at Langton Hall in Clerkenwell – a squat red-brick building with white-trimmed windows and black down pipes. Apart from a light over the front steps, the building looks deserted. Pushing through the double doors, I cross a narrow foyer and enter the main hall. Plastic chairs are arranged in rough lines. A table to one side holds a hot-water urn beside rows of cups and saucers.

About forty women have turned up. They range in age from teens to late thirties. Most are wearing overcoats, beneath which some are doubtless dressed for work in high heels, short skirts, hotpants and stockings. The air is a technicolour stink of perfume and tobacco.

On stage Elisa Velasco is already speaking. A wisp of a thing with green eyes and fair hair, she has the sort of accent that makes northern women sound feisty and no-nonsense. Dressed in a knee-length pencil skirt and a tight cashmere sweater, she looks like a World War II pin-up girl.

Behind her, projected on to a white screen, is an image of Mary Magdalene painted by the Italian artist Artemisia Gentileschi. The initials PAPT are printed in the bottom corner and in smaller letters: 'Prostitutes Are People Too'.

Elisa spies me and looks relieved. I try to slip along the side of the hall without interrupting her, but she taps the microphone and people turn.

'Now let me introduce the man you have *really* come to hear. Fresh from the front pages, I'd like you to welcome Professor Joseph O'Loughlin.'

There are one or two ironic handclaps. It's a tough audience. Soup gurgles in my stomach as I climb the steps at the side of the stage and walk into the circle of brightness. My left arm is trembling and I grasp the back of a chair to keep my hands steady.

I clear my throat and look at a point above their heads.

'Prostitutes account for the largest number of unsolved killings in this country. Forty-eight have been murdered in the past seven years. At least five are raped in London every day. A dozen more are bashed, robbed or abducted. They aren't attacked because they're attractive, or asking for it, but because they're accessible and vulnerable. They are easier to acquire and more anonymous than almost anyone else in society.'

Now I lower my eyes and connect with their faces, relieved to have their attention. A woman at the front has a purple satin collar on her coat and bright lemon-coloured gloves. Her legs are crossed and the coat has fallen open to reveal a creamy thigh. The thin black straps of her shoes crisscross up her calves.

'Sadly, you can't always pick and choose your customers. They come in all shapes and sizes, some drunk, some nasty—'

'Some fat,' yells a bottle-blonde.

'And smelly,' echoes a teenager wearing dark glasses.

I let the laughter subside. Most of these women don't trust me. I don't blame them. There are risks in all their relationships, whether with pimps, punters or a psychologist. They have learned not to trust men.

I wish I could make the danger more real for them. Maybe I should have brought photographs. One recent victim was found with her womb lying on the bed beside her. On the other hand these women don't *need* to be told. The danger is ever present.

'I haven't come here tonight to lecture you. I hope to make you a little safer. When you're working the streets at night, how many friends or family know where you are? If you disappeared, how long would it take for someone to report you missing?'

I let the question drift across them like a floating cobweb from the rafters. My voice has grown hoarse and sounds too harsh. I let go of the chair and begin walking to the front of the stage. My left leg refuses to swing and I half stumble, before correcting. They glance at each other – wondering what to make of me.

41

'Stay off the streets and if you can't then take precautions. Operate a buddy system. Make sure someone is taking down the number plate when you get into a car. Only work in well-lit areas and organise safe houses where you can take clients rather than using their cars . . . '

Four men have entered the hall and taken up positions near the doors. They're clearly policemen in plain clothes. As the women realise I hear mutters of disbelief and resignation. Several of them glare angrily at me as though it's my doing.

'Everybody stay calm. I'll sort this out.' I carefully swing down from the stage. I want to intercept Elisa before she reaches them.

The man in charge is easy to spot. It's the detective I saw at Kensal Green Cemetery, with the lived-in face and crooked teeth. He's wearing the same rumpled overcoat, which is a culinary road map of stains and spills. His rugby club tie has a silver plate tiepin of the Tower of Pisa.

I like him. He isn't into clothes. Men who take too much care with their presentation can look ambitious but also vain. When he talks he looks into the distance as if trying to see what's coming. I've seen the same look on farmers who never seem comfortable focusing on anything too close, particularly faces. His smile is apologetic.

'Sorry to gatecrash your convention,' he says wryly, addressing Elisa.

'Well fuck off then!' She says it with a sweet voice and a poisonous smile.

'It's lovely to make your acquaintance, Miss, or should I say *Madam?*'

I step between them. 'How can we help you?'

'Who are you?' He looks me up and down.

'Professor Joseph O'Loughlin.'

'No shit! Hey, fellas, it's that guy from the ledge. The one who talked down that kid.' His voice rumbles hoarsely. 'I never seen anyone more terrified.' His laugh is like a marble dropped down a drain. Another thought occurs to him. 'You're that expert on hookers, aren't you? You wrote a book or something.'

'A research paper.'

He shrugs ambivalently and motions to his men, who separate and move down the aisles.

Clearing his throat, he addresses the room. 'My name is Detective Inspector Vincent Ruiz of the Metropolitan Police. Three days ago the body of a young woman was found in Kensal Green, West London. She died about ten days earlier. At this stage we have been unable to identify her, but we have reason to believe that she may have been a prostitute. You are all going to be shown an artist's impression of the young woman. If any of you recognise her, I would appreciate it if you could make yourself known to us. We're after a name, an address, an associate, a friend – anyone who might have known her.'

Blinking rapidly, I hear myself ask, 'Where was she found?'

'Buried in a shallow grave beside the Grand Union Canal.'

The images are like snapshot memories. I can still see the white marquee and the arc lights: the scene-of-crime tape and the strobing of the flashguns. A woman's body fresh from the earth. I had been there. I had watched her being uncovered.

The hall seems cavernous and echoing. Drawings are passed from hand to hand. The noise level rises. A languid wrist is thrust towards me. The sketch looks like one of those charcoal drawings you see tourists posing for in Covent Garden. She's young with short hair and large eyes. That describes a dozen women in the hall.

Five minutes later the detectives return, shaking their heads at Ruiz. The Detective Inspector grunts and wipes his misshapen nose on a handkerchief.

'You know this is an illegal gathering,' he says, glancing at the tea urn. 'It's an offence to allow prostitutes to assemble and consume refreshments.'

'The tea is for me,' I say.

He laughs dismissively. 'You must drink a lot of tea. Either that or you take me for an idiot.' He's challenging me.

'I know what you are,' I bristle.

'Well? Don't keep me in suspense.'

'You're a country boy who found himself in the big city. You grew up on a farm, milking cows and collecting eggs. You played rugby until some sort of injury ended your career, but you still wonder if you could have gone all the way. Since then it's been a struggle to keep the weight off. You're divorced or widowed, which explains why your shirts need a decent iron and your suit needs dry-cleaning. You like a beer after work and a curry after that. You're trying to give up smoking, which is why you keep fumbling in your pockets for chewing gum. You think gyms are for wankers, unless they have a boxing ring and punch bags. And the last time you took a holiday you went to Italy because someone told you it was wonderful, but you ended up hating the food, the people and the wine.'

I'm surprised by how cold and indifferent I sound. It's as though I've been infected by the prejudices swirling around me.

'Very impressive. Is that your party trick?'

'No,' I mumble, suddenly embarrassed. I want to apologise but don't know where to start.

Ruiz fumbles in his pockets and then stops himself. 'Tell me something, Professor. If you can work out all that just by looking at me, how much can a dead body tell you?'

'What do you mean?'

'My murder victim. How much could you tell me about her if I showed you her body?'

I'm not sure if he's being serious. In theory it might be possible, but I deal in people's minds: I read their mannerisms and body language; I look at the clothes they wear and the way they interact; I listen for changes in their voices and their eye movements. A dead body can't tell me any of this. A dead body turns my stomach.

'Don't worry, she won't bite. I'll see you at Westminster Mortuary at nine o'clock tomorrow morning.' He roughly tucks the address into the inside pocket of my jacket. 'We can have breakfast afterwards,' he adds, chuckling to himself.

Before I can respond he turns to leave, flanked by detectives. At the last possible moment, just before he reaches the door, he spins back towards me.

'You were wrong about one thing.'

'What's that?'

'Italy. I fell in love with it.'

5

Outside on the pavement, Elisa kisses me on the cheek. 'I'm sorry about that.'

The last of the police cars are disappearing, along with my audience.

'It's not your fault.'

'I know. I just like kissing you.' She tousles my hair, then makes a fuss about getting a brush from her bag and fixing it up again. She stands in front of me and pushes my head down slightly. From here I can see down her sweater to the swoop of her lace-covered breasts and the dark valley in between.

'People are going to start talking,' she teases.

'There's nothing to talk about.' The statement is too abrupt. Her eyebrows lift almost imperceptibly.

She lights a cigarette and then guillotines the flame with the lid of her lighter. For a fleeting moment I see the light reflect off the golden specks in her green eyes. No matter how Elisa styles her hair it always appears sleep-tousled and wild. She cocks her head to one side and looks at me intently.

'I saw you on the news. You were very brave.'

'I was terrified.'

'Is he going to be OK – the boy on the roof?'

'Yes.'

'Are you going to be OK?'

The question surprises me, but I don't know how to respond. I follow her back into the hall and help her stack the chairs. She unplugs the overhead projector and hands me a box of pamphlets. The same painting of Mary Magdalene is printed on the front fold.

Elisa puts her chin on my shoulder. 'Mary Magdalene is the patron saint of prostitutes.'

'I thought she was a redeemed sinner.'

Annoyed, she corrects me. 'The Gnostic Gospels call her a visionary. She's also been called the Apostle of Apostles because she brought them the news of the Resurrection.'

'And you believe all that?'

'Jesus disappears for three days and the first person to see him alive is a whore. I'd say that was pretty typical!' She doesn't laugh. It isn't meant to be funny.

I follow her back on to the front steps, where she turns and locks the door.

'I have my car. I can give you a lift home,' she says, fumbling for her keys. We turn the corner and I see her red Volkswagen Beetle on a parking meter.

'There is another reason I chose that painting,' she explains.

'Because it was painted by a woman.'

'Yes, but that's not all. It's because of what happened to the artist. Artemisia Gentileschi was raped when she was nineteen by her instructor, Tassi, although he denied touching her. During his trial he said Artemisia was a lousy painter, who invented the rape story because she was jealous. He accused her of being "an insatiable whore" and called all his friends to give evidence against her. They even had her examined by midwives to find out if she was still a virgin.' Elisa sighs dolefully. 'Not much has changed in four centuries. The only difference now is that we don't torture our rape victims with thumbscrews to find out if they're telling the truth.'

Turning on the car radio, she signals that she doesn't want to talk. I lean back in the passenger seat and listen to Phil Collins singing 'Another Day in Paradise'.

I first set eyes on Elisa in a grotty interview room at a children's home in Brentford in the mid-eighties. I had just been accepted as a trainee clinical psychologist with the West London Health Authority.

She walked in, sat down and lit a cigarette without acknowledging I was there. She was only fifteen years old, yet had a fluid grace and certainty of movement that caught the eye and held it for too long.

With one elbow propped on the table and a cigarette held a few inches from her mouth, she stared past me to a window high on the wall. Smoke curled into her unruly fringe of hair. Her nose had been broken at some point and a front tooth was chipped. Periodically she ran her tongue across the jagged edge.

Elisa had been rescued from a 'trick pad' – a temporary brothel set up in the basement of a derelict house. The doors had been rigged so they couldn't be opened from the inside. She and another adolescent prostitute had been imprisoned for three days and raped by dozens of men who were offered sex with underage girls. A judge had placed her into care, but Elisa spent most of her time trying to escape from the children's home. She was too old to be placed with a foster family and too young to live on her own.

In that first meeting she looked at me with a mixture of curiosity and contempt. She was accustomed to dealing with men. Men could be manipulated.

'How old are you now, Elisa?'

'You know that already,' she said, motioning to the file in my hands. 'I can wait while you read it, if you like.' She was teasing me.

'Where are your parents?'

'Dead, hopefully.'

According to the file notes Elisa had been living with her mother and stepfather in Leeds when she ran away from home just after her fourteenth birthday.

Most of her answers were the bare minimum – why use two words when one will do? She sounded cocky and indifferent but I knew she was hurting. Eventually I managed to get under her skin. 'How the hell can you know so little?' she yelled, her eyes glistening with emotion.

It was time to take a risk.

'You think you're a woman, don't you? You think you know how to manipulate men like me. Well, you're wrong! I'm not a walking fifty-quid note looking for a blowjob or a quick fuck in a back lane. Don't waste my time. I've got more important places to be.'

Anger flared in her eyes and then disappeared as they misted over. She started crying. For the first time she looked and acted her age. The story came tumbling out, in between her sobs.

Her stepfather, a successful businessman in Leeds, had made a lot of money buying flats and doing them up. He was a real catch for a single mum like Elisa's. It meant they could move out of their council flat and into a proper house with a garden. Elisa had her own room. She went to grammar school.

One night, when she was twelve, her stepfather came to her room. 'This is what grown-ups do,' he said, putting her legs over his shoulders and his hand over her mouth.

'He was nice to me after that,' she said. 'He used to buy me clothes and make-up.'

This went on for two years until Elisa fell pregnant. Her mother called her a 'slut' and demanded to know the name of the father. She stood over her, waiting for an answer, and Elisa glimpsed her stepfather in the doorway. He ran his forefinger across his throat.

She ran away. In the pocket of her school blazer she had

the name of an abortion clinic in south London. At the clinic she met a nurse in her mid-forties with a kind face. Her name was Shirley and she offered Elisa a place to stay while she recuperated.

'Hold on to your school uniform.'

'Why?'

'It might come in handy.'

Shirley was a mother figure to half a dozen teenage girls and they all loved her. She made them feel safe.

'Her son was a real dickhead,' said Elisa. 'He slept with a shotgun under his bed and he thought he could have sex with any of us. Wanker! The first time Shirley took me out to work, she was saying, "Go on, you can do it." I was standing on Bayswater Road wearing my school uniform. "It's OK, just ask them if they want a girl," she said. I didn't want to disappoint Shirley. I knew she'd be angry.

'Next time she took me out, I did some hand jobs but I couldn't do the sex. I don't know why. It took me three months. I was getting too tall for my school uniform but Shirley said I had the legs to get away with it. I was her "Little Pot of Gold".'

Elisa didn't call the men she slept with 'punters'. She didn't like any suggestion that they were gambling with their money. She was a sure thing. And she didn't treat them with contempt, even if many were cheating on their wives, fiancées and girl-friends. This was purely business, a simple commercial trans-action; she had something to sell and they wanted to buy it.

As the months went by she became desensitised. She had a new family now. Then one day a rival pimp snatched her off the street. He wanted her for a one-off engagement, he said. He locked her in the basement of a house and collected money at the door from the men who queued up. A river of skin, of all different colours, flowed across her body and leaked inside her. 'I was their "Little White Fucktoy",' she said as she stubbed out another cigarette.

'And now you're here.'
'Where nobody knows what to do with me.'
'What do you want to do?'
'I want to be left alone.'

6

The first law of the National Health Service is that dead wood floats. It is part of the culture. If somebody is incompetent or hard to get along with, promotion is an easier option than sacking.

The duty supervisor at Westminster Mortuary is bald and thickset with pouchy jowls. He takes an instant dislike to me. 'Who told you to come here?'

'I'm meeting Detective Inspector Ruiz.'

'I haven't been told. Nobody made an appointment.'

'Can I wait for him?'

'No. Only family of the deceased are allowed in the waiting room.'

'Where can I wait?'

'Outside.'

I catch his sour smell and notice the sweat stains under his arms. He has probably worked all night and is doing over-time. He's tired and he's cranky. I normally have sympathy for shift-workers – in the same way that I feel sorry for loners and fat girls who never get asked to dance. It must be a lousy job, looking after dead people.

I'm just about to say something when Ruiz arrives. The supervisor begins his spiel all over again. Ruiz leans across the desk and picks up the phone. 'Listen, you jumped up little shit! I see a dozen cars parked on expired meters outside. You're going to be really popular with all your workmates when they get clamped.'

A few minutes later I'm following Ruiz along narrow corridors with strip lights on the ceiling and painted cement floors. Occasionally we pass doors with frosted glass windows. One of them is open. I glance inside and see a stainless steel table in the middle of the room with a central channel leading to a drain. Halogen lights are suspended from the ceiling, alongside microphone leads.

Further along the corridor, we come across three lab technicians in green medical scrubs standing around a coffee machine. None of them looks up.

Ruiz walks fast and talks slowly. 'The body was found at 11.00 on Sunday morning, buried in a shallow ditch. Fifteen minutes earlier an anonymous call was made from a pay phone a quarter of a mile away. The caller claimed his dog had dug up a hand.'

We push through double plexiglass doors and dodge a trolley being wheeled by an orderly. A white calico sheet covers what I imagine to be a body. A box of test tubes full of blood and urine is balanced on top of the torso.

We reach an anteroom with a large glass door. Ruiz taps on the window and is buzzed in by an operator sitting at a desk. She has blonde hair, dark roots and eyebrows plucked to the thinness of dental floss. Around the walls are filing cabinets and white boards. On the far side is a large stainless steel door marked 'STAFF ONLY'.

I suddenly get a flashback to my medical training when I fainted during our first practical lesson working with a corpse. I came round with smelling salts waved under my nose. The lecturer then chose me to demonstrate to the class how to direct a 150mm needle through the abdomen to the liver to take a biopsy sample. Afterwards he congratulated me on a new university record for the most organs hit with one needle in a single procedure.

Ruiz hands the operator a letter.

'Do you want me to set up a proper viewing?' she asks.

'The fridge will be fine,' he replies, 'but I'll need an SB.' She hands him a large brown paper bag.

The heavy door unlocks with a hiss like a pressure seal and Ruiz steps aside to let me go first. I expect to smell formalde-hyde – something I came to associate with every body I saw in medical school. Instead there's the faint odour of antiseptic and industrial soap.

The walls are polished steel. A dozen trolleys are parked in neat rows. Metal crypts take up three walls and look like over-sized filing cabinets, with large square handles that can accom-modate two hands.

I realise Ruiz is still talking. 'According to the pathologist she'd been in the ground for nine or ten days. She was naked except for a shoe and a gold chain around her neck with a St Christopher's medallion. We haven't found the rest of her clothes. There is no evidence of a sexual assault . . . ' He checks the label on a drawer and grips the handle. 'I think you'll see why we've narrowed down the cause of death.'

The drawer slides open smoothly on rollers. My head snaps back and I lurch away. Ruiz hands me the brown paper bag as I double over and heave. It's difficult to throw up and gasp for breath at the same time.

Ruiz hasn't moved. 'As you can see, the left side of her face is badly bruised and the eye is completely closed. Someone gave her a real working over. That's why we released the drawing instead of a photograph. There are more than twenty stab wounds – not one of them more than an inch deep. But here's the real kicker – every last one was self-inflicted. The pathologist found hesitation marks. She had to work up the nerve to force the blade through.'

Raising my head, I glimpse his face reflected in the polished steel. That's when I see it: fear. He must have investigated dozens of crimes, but this one is different because he can't understand it.

My stomach is empty. Perspiring and shivering in the cold, I straighten up and look at the body. Nothing has been done to restore the poor woman's dignity. She is naked, stretched out with her arms against her sides and her legs together.

The dull whiteness of her skin makes her look almost like a marble statue, only this 'statue' has been vandalised. Her chest, arms and thighs are covered in slashes of crimson and pink. Where the skin is pulled taut the wounds gape like empty eye sockets. At other places they naturally close and weep slightly.

I have seen post-mortems in medical school. I know the process. She has been photographed, scraped, swabbed and cut open from her neck to her crotch. Her organs have been weighed and her stomach contents analysed. Bodily fluids, flakes of dead skin and dirt from beneath her fingernails have been sealed within plastic or beneath glass slides. A once bright, energetic, vibrant human being has become exhibit A.

'How old was she?'

'Somewhere between twenty-five and thirty-five.'

'What makes you think she was a prostitute?'

'It's been nearly two weeks and nobody has reported her missing. You know better than I do how prostitutes move around. They take off for days or weeks at a time and then turn up at a totally different red-light area. Some of them follow the conference trade; others work the truck stops. If this girl had a strong network of family or friends, somebody would have reported her missing by now. She could be foreign but we have nothing from Interpol.'

'I'm not sure how I can help?'

'What can *you* tell me about her?'

Although I can't bear to look at her swollen face I'm already collecting details. Her fair hair is cut short in a practical style that's easy to wash, quick to dry and doesn't need constant brushing. Her ears aren't pierced. Her fingernails are trimmed and well cared for. She has no rings on her fingers, or any sign that she normally wore them. She's slim and fair-skinned, with larger hips than bust. Her eyebrows have been tidily shaped and her bikini line had been waxed recently, leaving a neat triangle of pubic hair.

'Was she wearing make-up?'

'A little lipstick and eye-liner.'

'I need to sit down for a while and read the post-mortem report.'

'I'll find you an empty office.'

Ten minutes later, alone at a desk, I stare at a stack of ring-bound photograph albums and folders bulging with statements. Among the pile is the post-mortem report and results from blood and toxicology analysis.

I glance at the summary page.

CITY OF WESTMINSTER CORONER
Post-Mortem Report

Name: Unknown   Post-Mortem No: DX-34 468
DOB: Unknown   Death D/T: Unknown
Age: Unknown   Post-Mortem D/T: 10/12/2000 0915
Sex: Female

Anatomical Summary:

1. Fourteen lacerations and incised wounds to the chest, abdomen and thighs, penetrating to a depth of 1.2 inches. They range in width from 3 inches to half an inch.
2. Four lacerations to the upper left arm.

3. Three lacerations to the left side of the neck and shoulders.
4. The direction of the sharp force injuries tends to be downward and are a mixture of stabbing and incised wounds.
5. The hesitation marks are generally straight and accompany the deeper incisions.
6. Heavy bruising and swelling to the left cheekbone and left eye-socket.
7. Slight bruising to the right forearm and abrasions to the right tibia and right heel.
8. Oral, vaginal and rectal swabs are clear.

Preliminary Toxicology Study:
    Blood ethanol – none detected
    Blood drug screen – no drugs detected

Cause of Death:
    Post-mortem X-rays reveal air in the right ventricular chamber of the heart, indicating a massive and fatal air embolism.

I scan the report quickly, looking for particular details. I'm not interested in the minutiae of *how* she died. Instead I look for clues that relate to her life. Did she have any old fractures? Was there any evidence of drug use or sexually transmitted diseases? What did she have for her last meal? How long since she'd eaten?

Ruiz doesn't bother to knock.

'I figured you were milk, no sugar.'

He puts a plastic cup of coffee on the desk and then pats his pockets, searching for cigarettes that exist only in his imagination. He grinds his teeth instead. 'So what can you tell me?'

'She wasn't a prostitute.'

'Because?'

57

'The median age of girls becoming prostitutes is only sixteen. This woman was in her mid-twenties, possibly older. There are no signs of long-standing sexual activity or evidence of sexually transmitted diseases. Abortions are common among prostitutes, particularly as they're often coerced into not using condoms, but this girl had never been pregnant.'

Ruiz taps the table three times as though typing three ellipsis dots. He wants me to go on.

'Prostitutes at the high-class end of the scale sell a fantasy. They take great care with their appearance and presentation. This woman had short fingernails, a boyish hairstyle and minimal make-up. She wore sensible shoes and very little jewellery. She didn't use expensive moisturisers or paint her nails. She had her bikini line waxed modestly . . . '

Ruiz is moving around the room again, with his mouth slightly open and a puckered brow.

'. . . she took care of herself. She exercised regularly and ate healthy food. She was probably concerned about putting on weight. I'd say she was of average or slightly above average intelligence. Her schooling would have been solid; her background most likely middle class.

'I don't think she's from London. Someone would have reported her missing by now. This sort of girl doesn't go missing. She has friends and family. But if she came to London for a job interview, or for a holiday, people might not have expected to hear from her for a while. They'll start to get worried soon.'

Pushing back my chair a little, I lack the conviction to stand. What else can I tell him?

'The medallion – it's not St Christopher. I think it's probably St Camillus. If you look closely, the figure is holding a pitcher and towel.'

'And who was he?'

'The patron saint of nurses.'

The statement concentrates his attention. He cocks his head

to one side and I can almost see him cataloguing the information. In his right hand he flicks open a book of matches and closes it again. Open and then closed.

I shuffle the papers and glance at the full post-mortem report. A paragraph catches my attention.

There is evidence of old lacerations running the length of her right and left forearms and inside her upper thighs. The degree of scarring suggests an attempt at self-suturing. These wounds were most likely self-inflicted and point towards past attempts at self-harm or self-mutilation.

'I need to see the photographs.'

Ruiz pushes the ring-bound folders towards me and in the same breath announces, 'I have to make a phone call. We might have a lead on a missing woman. An X-ray technician in Liverpool hasn't heard from her flatmate in a fortnight. She matches the age, height and hair colour of our Jane Doe. And how's this for a coincidence, Sherlock? She's a nurse.'

After he's gone I open the first folder of photographs and turn the pages quickly. Her arms had been along her sides when I viewed her body. I couldn't see her wrists or inner thighs. A self-mutilator with multiple stab wounds, all self-inflicted . . . Surely it's only a coincidence.

The first photographs are wide-angle shots of open ground, littered with rusting forty-four-gallon drums, rolls of wire and scaffolding poles. The Grand Union Canal forms an immediate backdrop but on the far side I see a smattering of well-established trees and the headstones in between.

The photographs begin to focus down on to the banks of the canal. Blue and white police tape has been threaded around metal posts to mark out the area.

The second set of photographs shows the ditch and a splash of white that looks like a discarded milk container. As the camera zooms closer it reveals it to be a hand, with fingers outstretched, reaching upwards from the earth. Soil is scraped away slowly, sifted and bagged. The corpse is finally exposed, lying with one leg twisted awkwardly beneath her and her left arm draped over her eyes as though shielding them from the arc lights.

Moving quickly, I skim over the pages until I reach the post-mortem pictures. The camera records every smear, scratch and bruise. I'm looking for one photograph.

Here it is. Her forearms are turned outwards and lying flat against the dull silver of the bench top. Awkwardly, I stand and retrace my steps along the corridors. My left leg locks up and I have to swing it in an arc from back to front.

The operator buzzes me into the secure room and I stare for a few seconds at the same bank of metal crypts. Four across. Three down. I check the label, grasp the handle and slide the drawer open. This time I force myself to look at her ruined face. Recognition is like a tiny spark that fires a bigger machine. Memories roar in my head. Her hair is shorter. She has put on weight, but only a little.

Reaching for her right arm, I turn it over and brush my fingertips along the milky white scars. Against the paleness of her skin they look like embossed creases that merge and criss-cross before fading into nothing. She opened these wounds repeatedly, picking apart the stitches or slicing them afresh. She kept this hidden, but once upon a time I shared the secret.

'Need a second look?' Ruiz is standing at the door.

'Yes.' I can't stop my voice from shaking. Ruiz steps in front of me and slides the drawer shut.

'You shouldn't be in here by yourself. Should have waited for me.' The words are weighted.

I mumble an apology and wash my hands at the sink, feeling his eyes upon me. I need to say something.

'What about Liverpool? Did you find out who . . . ?'

'The flatmate is being brought to London by the local CID. We should have a positive ID by this afternoon.'

'So you have a name?'

He doesn't answer. Instead I'm hustled along the corridor and made to wait as he collects the post-mortem notes and photographs. Then I follow him through the subterranean maze until we emerge, via double doors, into a parking garage.

All the while I'm thinking, I should say something now. I should tell him. Yet a separate track in my brain is urging, It doesn't matter any more. He knows her name. What's past is past. It's ancient history.

'I promised you breakfast.'

'I'm not hungry.'

'Well I am.'

We walk under blackened railway arches and down a narrow alley. Ruiz seems to know all the back streets. He is remarkably light on his feet for a big man, dodging puddles and dog faeces.

The large front windows of the café are steamed up with condensation, or it could be a film of fat from the chip-fryer. A bell jangles above our heads as we enter. The fug of cigarette smoke and warm air is overpowering.

The place is pretty much empty except for two sunken-cheeked old men in cardigans playing chess in the corner and an Indian cook with a yolk-stained apron. It's late morning but the café serves breakfast all day. Baked beans, chips, eggs, bacon and mushrooms – in any combination. Ruiz takes a table near the window.

'What do you want?'

'Just coffee.'

'The coffee is crap.'

'Then I'll have tea.'

He orders a full English with a side order of toast and two pots of tea. Then he fumbles for a cigarette in his jacket pocket before mumbling something about forgetting his phone.

'I didn't take any pleasure from dragging you into this,' he says.

61

'Yes, you did.'

'Well, just a little.' His eyes seem to smile but there is no sense of self-congratulation. The impatience I noticed the previous night has gone. He's more relaxed and philosophical.

'Do you know how you become a Detective Inspector, Professor O'Loughlin?'

'No.'

'It used to be based on how many crimes you solved and people you banged up. Nowadays it depends on how few complaints you generate and whether you can stick to a budget. I'm a dinosaur to these people. Ever since the Police and Criminal Evidence Act came into force *my* sort of policeman has been living on borrowed time.

'Nowadays they talk about pro-active policing. Do you know what that means? It means the number of detectives they put on a case depends on how big the tabloid headlines are. The media run these investigations now – not the police.'

'I haven't read anything about this case,' I say.

'That's because everyone thinks the victim is a prostitute. If she turns out to be Florence bloody Nightingale or the daughter of a duke I'll have forty detectives instead of twelve. The Assistant Chief Constable will take personal charge because of the "complex nature of the case". Every public statement will have to be vetted by his office and every line of inquiry approved.'

'Why did they give it to you?'

'Like I said, they thought we were dealing with a dead prostitute. "Give it to Ruiz," they said. "He'll bang heads together and put the fear of God into the pimps." So *what* if any of them object. My file is so full of complaint letters that Internal Affairs have given me my own filing cabinet.'

A handful of Japanese tourists pass the window and pause. They look at the blackboard menu and then at Ruiz, before deciding to keep going. Breakfast arrives, with a knife and fork wrapped in a paper napkin. Ruiz squeezes brown sauce over his eggs and begins cutting them up. I try not to watch as he eats.

'You look like you got a question,' he says between mouthfuls.

'It's about her name.'

'You know the drill. I'm not supposed to release details until we get a positive ID and inform the next of kin.'

'I just thought . . . ' I don't finish the sentence.

Ruiz takes a sip of tea and butters his toast. 'Catherine Mary McBride. She turned twenty-seven a month ago. A community nurse, but you knew that already. According to her flatmate she was in London for a job interview.'

Even knowing the answer doesn't lessen the shock. Poor Catherine. This is when I should tell him. I should have done it straight away. Why do I have to rationalise everything? Why can't I just say things when they enter my head?

Leaning over his plate, Ruiz scoops baked beans on to a corner of toast. His fork stops in mid-air in front of his open mouth. 'Why did you say, "Poor Catherine"?'

I must have been speaking out loud. My eyes tell the rest of the story. Ruiz lets the fork clatter on to his plate. Anger and suspicion snake through his thoughts. 'You knew her.'

It's an accusation rather than a statement. He's angry.

'I didn't recognise her at first. That drawing last night could have been almost anyone. I thought you were looking for a prostitute.'

'And today?'

'Her face was so swollen. She seemed so . . . so . . . vandalised. It wasn't until I saw the scars that I was certain. She used to be a patient.'

Not satisfied. 'You lie to me again, Professor, and I'll put my boot so far up your arse your breath will smell of shoe polish.'

'I didn't lie to you. I just wanted to be sure.'

His eyes haven't left mine. 'And when were you thinking of telling me all this?'

'I would have told you.'

'Yeah. Sure.' He pushes his plate to the centre of the table. 'Start talking – why was Catherine a patient?'

'The scars on her wrists and thighs – she deliberately cut herself.'

'A suicide attempt?'

'No.'

I can see Ruiz struggling with this. Leaning closer, I try to explain how people react when overwhelmed by confusion and negative emotions. Some drink too much. Others over-eat or beat their wives or kick the cat. And a surprising number hold their hands against a hotplate or slice open their skin with a razor blade.

It's an extreme coping mechanism. They talk about their inner pain being turned outwards. By giving it a physical mani-festation they find it easier to deal with.

'What was Catherine trying to cope with?'

'Mainly low self-esteem.'

'Where did you meet her?'

'She worked as a nurse at the Royal Marsden Hospital. I was a consultant there.'

Ruiz swirls the tea in his cup, staring at it as though it might tell him something. Suddenly he pushes back his chair, hitches his trousers and stands.

'You're an odd fucker, you know that?' A five-pound note flutters on to the table and I follow him outside. A dozen paces along the footpath, he turns to confront me. 'OK, tell me this. Am I investigating a murder or did this girl kill herself?'

'She was murdered.'

'So she was *made* to do this – to cut herself all those times? Apart from her face there are no signs that she was bound, gagged, restrained or compelled to cut herself. Can you explain that?'

I shake my head.

'Well, you're the psychologist! You're supposed to understand the world we live in. I'm a detective and it's beyond my fucking comprehension.'

7

As far as I can recall I haven't been drunk since Charlie was born and Jock took it upon himself to get me absolutely hammered because apparently that is what intelligent, sensible and conscientious fathers do when blessed with a child.

With a new car you avoid alcohol completely and with a new house you can't afford to drink, but with a new baby you must 'wet the head' or, in my case, throw up in a cab going around Marble Arch.

I didn't even get drunk when Jock told me about my Parkinson's Disease. Instead I went out and slept with a woman who wasn't my wife. The hangover didn't last. The guilt won't go away.

Today I had two double vodkas at lunchtime – a first for me. I felt like getting drunk because I can't get the image of Catherine McBride out of my mind. It's not her face I see but her naked body, stripped of all dignity; denied even a modest pair of panties or a strategically placed sheet. I want to protect her. I want to shield her from public gaze.

Now I understand Ruiz – not his words but the look on his

face. This wasn't the terrible conclusion to some great passion. Nor was it an ordinary, kitchen sink killing, motivated by greed or jealousy. Catherine McBride suffered terribly. Each cut had sapped her strength like a banderillero's barbs in the neck of a bull.

An American psychologist called Daniel Wegner conducted a famous experiment on thought suppression in 1987. In a test that might have been created by Dostoevsky, he asked a group of people *not* to think about a white bear. Each time the white bear entered their thoughts they had to ring a bell. No matter how hard they tried, no person could avoid the forbidden thought for more than a few minutes.

Wegner spoke of two different thought processes counter-acting each other. One is trying to think of anything except the white bear, while the other is subtly pushing forward the very thing that we wish to suppress.

Catherine Mary McBride is my white bear. I can't get her out of my head.

I should have gone home at lunchtime and cancelled my afternoon appointments. Instead I wait for Bobby Moran who turns up late again. Meena gives him the curt, cold treatment. It's six o'clock and she wants to go home.

'I would hate to be married to your secretary,' he says, before checking himself, 'she's not your wife, is she?'

'No.'

I motion for him to sit down. His buttocks spread out to fill the chair. Tugging at the cuffs of his coat, he seems distracted and anxious.

'How have you been?'

'No thanks, I've just had one.'

I pause to see if he realises that his answer makes no sense. He doesn't react.

'Do you know what I just asked you, Bobby?'

'Whether I want a tea or coffee.'

'No.'

67

A brief flicker of doubt crosses his face. 'But you were going to ask me about the tea or coffee next.'

'So you were reading my mind?'

He smiles nervously and shakes his head. 'Do you believe in God?' he asks.

'Do you?'

'I used to.'

'What happened?'

'I couldn't find him. He's supposed to be everywhere. I mean, he's not supposed to be playing hide and seek.' He glances at his reflection in the darkened window.

'What sort of God would you like, Bobby – a vengeful God or a forgiving one?'

'A vengeful God.'

'Why?'

'People should pay for their sins. They shouldn't suddenly get forgiven because they plead they're sorry or repent on their deathbed. When we do wrong we should be punished.'

The last statement rattles in the air like a copper penny dropped on a table.

'What are you sorry for, Bobby?'

'Nothing.' He answers too quickly. Everything about his body language is screaming denial.

'How does it feel when you lose your temper?'

'Like my brain is boiling.'

'When was the last time you felt like this?'

'A few weeks ago.'

'What happened?'

'Nothing.'

'Who made you angry?'

'Nobody.'

Asking him direct questions is useless, because he simply blocks them. Instead I take him back to an earlier point and let him build up momentum like a boulder rolling down a hill. I know the day – 11 November – because he missed his appointment that afternoon. I ask him what time did he wake? What did he have for breakfast? When did he leave home? Slowly I move him closer to the moment where he lost control. He had taken the Tube to the West End and visited a jeweller in Hatton Garden. He and Arky are getting married in the spring. Bobby had arranged to pick up their wedding rings. He argued with the jeweller and stormed out. It was raining. He was running late. He stood on Holborn Circus trying to hail a cab.

Having got this far, Bobby pulls away again and changes the subject. 'Who do you think would win in a fight between a tiger and a lion?' he asks in a matter-of-fact voice.

'Why?'

'I'd like to know your opinion.'

'Tigers and lions don't fight each other. They live in different parts of the world.'

'Yes, but if they *did* fight each other, who would win?'

'The question is pointless. Inane.'

'Isn't that what psychologists do – ask pointless questions?' His entire demeanour has changed in the space of a single question. Suddenly, cocky and aggressive, he jabs his finger at me. 'You ask people what they'd do in hypothetical situations. Why don't you try me? Go on. "What would I do if I was the first person to discover a small fire in a movie theatre?" Isn't that the sort of question you ask? Would I put the fire out? Or go for the manager? Or evacuate the building? I know what you people do. You take a harmless answer and you try to make a sane person seem crazy.'

'Is that what you think?'

'That's what I *know.*'

He's talking about a Mental Status Examination. Clearly Bobby has been evaluated before, yet there's no mention of it in his medical history. Each time I put pressure on him, he reacts with hostility. It's time to crank it up a notch.

'Let me tell you what I *know*, Bobby. Something happened

that day. You were pissed off. You were having a bad day. Was it the jeweller? What did he do?'

My voice is sharp and unforgiving. Bobby flinches. His hackles rise. 'He's a lying bastard! He got the engraving wrong on the wedding bands. He misspelt Arky's name but he said it was my mistake. He said I gave him the wrong spelling. The bastard wanted to charge me extra.'

'What did you do?'

'I smashed the glass on his counter.'

'How?'

'With my fist.'

He holds up his hand to show me. Faint yellow and purple bruising discolours the underside.

'What happened then?'

He shrugs and shakes his head. That can't be all. There has to be something more. In our last session he had talked of punishing 'her' – a woman. It must have happened after he left the shop. He was on the street, angry, his brain boiling.

'Where did you first see her?'

He blinks at me rapidly. 'Coming out of a music store.'

'What were you doing?'

'Queuing for a taxi. It was raining. She took my cab.'

'What did she look like?'

'I don't remember her.'

'How old was she?'

'I don't know.'

'You say that she *took* your cab – did you say anything to her?'

'I don't think so.'

'What did you do?'

He flinches.

'Was she with anyone else?'

He glances at me and hesitates. 'What do you mean?'

'Who was she with?'

'A boy.'

'How old was he?'

'Maybe five or six.'

'Where was the boy?'

'She was dragging him by the hand. He was screaming. I mean, really screaming. She was trying to ignore him. He dropped like a dead weight and she had to drag him along. And this kid just kept screaming. And I started wondering, why isn't she talking to him? How can she let him scream? He's in pain or he's frightened. Nobody else was doing anything. It made me angry. How could they just stand there?'

'Who were you angry at?'

'All of them. I was angry at their indifference. I was angry at this woman's neglect. I was angry with myself for hating the little boy. I just wanted him to stop screaming . . . '

'So what did you do?'

His voice drops to a whisper. 'I wanted her to make him stop. I wanted her to listen to him.' He stops himself.

'Did you say anything to her?'

'No.'

'What then?'

'The door of the cab was open. She pushed him inside. The kid was thrashing his legs. She gets in after him and turns back to get the door. Her face is like a mask . . . blank, you know. She swings her arm back and, *bang!*, she elbows him right in the face. He crumples backwards . . . '

Bobby pauses and then seems about to continue. He stops himself. The silence grows. I let it fill his head – working its way into the corners.

'I dragged her out of the cab. I had hold of her hair. I drove her face into the side window. She fell down and tried to roll away, but I kept kicking her.'

'Did you think you were punishing her?'

'Yes.'

'Did she deserve it?'

'Yes!'

71

He's staring directly at me – his face as white as wax. At that moment I have an image of a child in a lonely corner of a playground, overweight, freakishly tall, the owner of nicknames like Jellyarse and Lardbucket; a child for whom the world is a vast and empty place. A child seeking to be invisible, but who is condemned to stand out.

'I found a dead bird today,' Bobby says absent-mindedly. 'Its neck was broken. Maybe it was hit by a car.'

'It's possible.'

'I moved it off the path. Its body was still warm. Do you ever think about dying?'

'I think everyone does.'

'Some people deserve to die.'

'And who should be the judge of that?'

He laughs bitterly. 'Not people like you.'

The session overruns but Meena has already gone home to her cats. Most of the nearby offices are locked up and in darkness. Cleaners are moving through the corridors, emptying bins and chipping paint off the skirting boards with their trolleys.

Bobby has also gone. Even so, when I stare at the darkened square of the window, I can picture his face, soaked in sweat and spotted with the blood of that poor woman.

I should have seen this coming. He is *my* patient, *my* responsibility. I know I can't hold his hand and make him come to see me, but that's no consolation. Bobby was close to crying when he described being charged, but he felt more sorry for himself than the woman he attacked.

I struggle to care about some of my patients. They spend ninety quid and gaze at their navels or whinge about things they should be telling their partners instead of me. Bobby is different. I don't know why. At times he seems totally incapacitated by awkwardness, yet he can startle me with his confidence and intellect. He laughs at the wrong places, explodes unexpectedly, and has eyes as pale and cold as blue glass.

Sometimes I think he's waiting for something – as though mountains are going to move or all the planets will line up. And once everything is in place he'll finally let me know what's really going on.

I can't wait for that. I have to understand him now.

8

Muhammad Ali has a lot to answer for. When he lit the flame
at the Atlanta Olympics there wasn't a dry eye on the planet.

Why were we crying? Because a great sportsman had been
reduced to this – a shuffling, mumbling, twitching cripple.
A man who once danced like a butterfly now shook like a
blancmange.

We always remember the sportsmen. When the body deserts
a scientist like Stephen Hawking we figure that he'll be able to
live in his mind, but a crippled athlete is like a bird with a
broken wing. When you soar to the heights the landing is harder.

It's Friday and I'm sitting in Jock's office. His real name is
Dr Emlyn Robert Owens – a Scotsman with a Welsh name
– but I've only ever known him by his nickname.

A solid, almost square man, with powerful shoulders and a
bull neck, he looks more like a former boxer than a brain
surgeon. His office has Salvador Dali prints on the walls, along
with an autographed photograph of John McEnroe holding
the Wimbledon trophy. McEnroe has signed it, 'You cannot
be serious!'

Jock motions for me to sit on the examination table and

then rolls up his sleeves. His forearms are tanned and thick. That's how he manages to hit a tennis ball like an Exocet missile. Playing tennis with Jock is eighty per cent pain. Everything comes rocketing back aimed directly at your body. Even with a completely open court he still tries to drill the ball straight through you.

My regular Friday matches with Jock have nothing to do with a love of tennis – they're about the past. They're about a tall, slender college girl who chose me instead of him. That was nearly twenty years ago and now she's my wife. It still pisses him off.

'How is Julianne?' he asks, shining a pencil torch into my eyes.

'Good.'

'What did she think about the business on the ledge?'

'She's still talking to me.'

'Did you tell anyone about your condition?'

'No. You told me I should carry on normally.'

'Yes. *Normally!*' He opens a folder and scribbles a note. 'Any tremors?'

'Not really. Sometimes, when I try to get out of a chair or out of bed, my mind says get up but nothing happens.'

He makes another note. 'That's called starting hesitancy. I get it all the time – particularly if the rugby's on TV.'

He makes a point of walking from side to side, watching my eyes follow him. 'How are you sleeping?'

'Not so well.'

'You should get one of those relaxation tapes. You know the sort of thing. Some guy talks in a really boring voice and puts you to sleep.'

'That's why I keep coming here.'

Jock hits me extra hard on my knee with his rubber hammer, making me flinch.

'That must have been your funny bone,' he says sarcastically. He steps back. 'Right, you know the routine.'

I close my eyes and bring my hands together – index finger to index finger, middle finger to middle finger, and so on. I almost manage to pull it off, but my ring fingers slide past each other. I try again and this time my middle fingers don't meet in the middle.

Jock plants his elbow on the desk and invites me to arm-wrestle.

'I'm amazed at how high-tech you guys are,' I say, squaring up to him. His fist crushes my fingers. 'I'm sure you only do this for personal satisfaction. It probably has nothing to do with examining me.'

'How did you guess,' says Jock as I push against his arm. I can feel my face going red. He's toying with me. Just once I'd like to pin the bastard.

Conceding defeat, I slump back and flex my fingers. There's no sign of triumph on Jock's face. Without having to be told I stand and start walking around the room, trying to swing my arms as though marching. My left arm seems to hang there.

Jock takes the cellophane wrapper from a cigar and snips off the end. He rolls his tongue around the tip and licks his lips before lighting up. Then he closes his eyes and lets the smoke leak through his smile.

'God, I look forward to my first one of the day,' he says. He watches the smoke curl towards the ceiling, letting it fill the silence as it fills the empty space.

'So what's the story?' I ask, getting agitated.

'You have Parkinson's Disease.'

'I already know that.'

'So what else do you want me to say?'

'Tell me something I don't know.'

He chomps the cigar between his teeth. 'You've done the reading. I'll bet you can tell me the entire history of Parkinson's – every theory, research program and celebrity sufferer. Come on, you tell me. What drugs should I be prescribing? What diet?'

I hate the fact that he's right. I can give him chapter and verse. In the past month I have spent hours searching the Internet and reading medical journals. I know all about Dr James Parkinson, the English physician who in 1817 described a condition he called 'shaking palsy'. I can tell him that 120,000 people are affected by Parkinson's in Britain. It's more common in people over sixty, but one in seven patients show symptoms before they turn forty. About three-quarters of sufferers will develop a tremor at the onset, while the others may never have one.

Of course I've gone looking for answers. What did he expect? Except there aren't any to find. All the experts say the same thing – that Parkinson's is one of the most baffling and complex neurological disorders.

'What about the tests you ran?'

'The results aren't back yet. I should get them by next week. Then we'll discuss a drug regime.'

'What drugs?'

'A cocktail.'

He's starting to sound like Fenwick.

Jock ashes his cigar and leans forward. He looks more like a CEO every time I see him. Soon he'll be wearing coloured braces and golfing socks. 'How's Bobby Moran doing?'

'Not so good.'

'What happened?'

'He kicked a woman unconscious for stealing his cab.'

Jock forgets and inhales suddenly, coughing violently. 'Charming! Another happy outcome.'

It had been Jock who'd originally sent Bobby to me. A local GP had referred him for neurological tests but Jock could find nothing physically wrong, so he'd passed him on. His exact words to me were: 'Don't worry, he's insured. You might actually get paid.'

Jock thinks I should have stuck to 'real medicine' when I had the chance instead of having a social conscience more expensive than my mortgage. Ironically, he used to be just like me at university. When I remind him of the fact he claims all the best-looking girls were left wing in those days. He was a summer-of-love socialist – anything to get his leg over.

Nobody ever dies of Parkinson's Disease. You die with it. That's one of Jock's trite aphorisms. I can just see it on a bumper sticker because it's only half as ridiculous as 'Guns don't kill people, people do'.

My reaction to this disease normally comes under the heading, 'Why me?' but after meeting Malcolm on the roof of the Marsden I feel rather chastened. His disease is bigger than mine. His conker wins.

I began to realise something was wrong about fifteen months ago. The main thing was the tiredness. Some days it was like walking through mud. I still played tennis twice a week and coached Charlie's soccer team. During our training games I managed to keep up with a dozen eight-year-olds and picture myself as Zinedine Zidane, the playmaker, dispatching through balls and doing intricate one-twos.

But then I started to find that the ball didn't go where I'd intended it to any more, and if I took off suddenly I tripped over my own feet. Charlie thought I was clowning around. Julianne thought I was getting lazy. I blamed turning forty-two.

In hindsight I can see that the signs were there. My hand-writing had become even more cramped and buttonholes had become obstacles. Sometimes I had difficulty getting out of a chair and when I walked down stairs I held on to the handrails.

Then came our annual pilgrimage to Wales for my father's seventieth birthday. I took Charlie walking on Great Ormes Head, overlooking Penrhyn Bay. At first we could see Puffin Island in the distance, until an Atlantic storm rolled in, swallowing it like a gigantic white whale. Bent against the wind, we watched the waves crashing over rocks and felt the sting of the spray. Charlie said to me, 'Dad, why aren't you swinging your left arm?'

'What do you mean?'

'Your arm. It's just sort of hanging there.'

Sure enough, it was flopping uselessly by my side.

By next morning my arm seemed to be OK. I didn't say anything to Julianne and certainly not to my parents. My father – a man awaiting the summons to be God's personal physician – would have castigated me for being a hypochondriac and made fun of me in front of Charlie. He has never forgiven me for giving up medicine to study behavioural science and psychology.

Privately, my imagination was running wild. I had visions of brain tumours and blood clots. What if I'd had a minor stroke? Was a major one coming? I almost convinced myself that I had pains in my chest.

It was another year before I went to see Jock. By then, he too had noticed something was wrong. We were walking into the locker room at the tennis club and I started drifting towards the right, forcing him to stop in mid-stride. He had also noticed my left arm hanging limply by my side. Jock made a joke about it but I sensed that he was watching me closely.

There are no diagnostic tests for Parkinson's. An experienced neurologist like Jock relies on observation. There are four primary symptoms – tremors or trembling hands, arms, legs, jaw and face; rigidity or stiffness of the limbs and trunk; slowness of movement; and postural instability or impaired balance and coordination.

The disease is chronic and progressive. It is not contagious, nor is it usually inherited. There are lots of theories. Some scientists blame free radicals reacting with neighbouring molecules and causing damage to tissue. Others blame pesticides or some other pollutant in the food chain. Genetic factors haven't been entirely ruled out because there seems to be a

79

slight genetic predisposition in families, and it may be that it's somehow age-related.

The truth is, it could be a combination of all – or none – of these things.

Perhaps I should be grateful. In my experience of doctors (and I grew up with one), the only time they give you a clear, unequivocal diagnosis is if you're standing in the surgery with, say, a glue-gun stuck to your head.

At four-thirty I'm outside trying to push against the early tide of people walking to underground stations and bus stops. I head towards Cavendish Square and hail a cab as it starts to rain again.

The desk sergeant at Holborn Police Station is pink-faced and freshly shaven, with his hair slicked down over his bald crown. Leaning on the counter, he dunks biscuits into a mug of tea, spilling crumbs on to the breasts of a page three girl. As I push through the glass door, he licks his fingers, wipes them down his shirt and slides the newspaper under the counter. He smiles and his cheeks jiggle.

I show him a business card and ask if I could possibly see the charge sheet for Bobby Moran. His good humour disappears.

'We're very busy at the moment – you'll have to bear with me.'

I look over my shoulder. The charge room is deserted except for a wasted teenage boy in torn jeans, trainers and an AC/DC T-shirt, who has fallen asleep on a wooden bench. There are cigarette burns on the floor and plastic cups copulating beside a metal bin.

With deliberate slowness, the sergeant saunters towards a bank of filing cabinets on the rear wall. A biscuit is stuck to the backside of his trousers and the pink icing is melting into his rump. I allow myself a smile.

According to the charge sheet, Bobby was arrested in central

London eighteen days ago. He pleaded guilty at Bow Street Magistrates' Court and was bailed to appear again on 24 December at the Old Bailey. Malicious wounding is a Section 20 offence – assault causing grievous bodily harm. It carries a maximum penalty of five years' jail.

Bobby's statement is typed over three pages, double-spaced, with the corrections initialled in the margins. He makes no mention of the little boy or his argument with the jeweller. The woman had jumped the queue. For her troubles, she suffered a fractured jaw, depressed cheekbone, broken nose and three busted fingers.

'Where do I find out about the bail conditions?'

The sergeant leafs through the file and runs his finger down a court document.

'Eddie Barrett has the brief.' He grunts in disgust. 'He'll have this downgraded to ABH quicker than you can say ring-a-ding-ding.'

How did Bobby get a lawyer like Eddie Barrett? He's the best-known defence solicitor in the country, with a genius for self-promotion and the ability to produce the perfect sound-bite.

'How much was the bail?'

'Five grand.'

Considering Bobby's circumstances, it seems an impossible sum.

I glance at my watch. It's still only five-thirty. Eddie's secretary answers the phone and I can hear Eddie shouting in the background. She apologises and asks me to wait. The two of them shout at each other. It's like listening to a Punch and Judy show. Eventually, she comes back to me. Eddie can give me twenty minutes.

It's quicker to walk than to take a taxi to Chancery Lane. Buzzed through the main door, I climb the narrow stairs to the third floor, weaving past the boxes of court documents and files that have been stacked in every available space.

81

Eddie is talking on the phone as he ushers me into his office and points to a chair. I have to move two files to sit down. Eddie looks to be in his late fifties but is probably ten years younger. Whenever I've seen him interviewed on TV he's put me in mind of a bulldog. He has the same swagger, with his shoulders barely moving and his arse swinging back and forth. He even has large incisor teeth which must come in handy when ripping strips off people.

When I mention Bobby's name Eddie looks disappointed. I think he was hoping for a medical malpractice case. He spins his chair and begins searching the drawer of a filing cabinet.

'What did Bobby tell you about the attack?'

'You saw his statement.'

'Did he mention seeing a young boy?'

'No.' Eddie interrupts tiredly. 'Look, I don't want to get off on the wrong foot here, Roseanne, but just explain to me why the fuck I'm talking to you? No offence.'

'None taken.' He's a lot less pleasant up close. I start again. 'Did Bobby mention he was seeing a psychologist?'

Eddie's mood improves. 'Shit, no! Tell me more.'

'I've been seeing him for about six months. I also think he's been evaluated before but I don't have the records.'

'A history of mental illness – better and better.' He picks up a ringing telephone and motions for me to carry on. He's trying to conduct two conversations at once.

'Did Bobby tell you why he lost his temper?'

'She took his cab.'

'It's hardly a reason.'

'You ever tried to get a cab in Holborn on a wet Friday afternoon?' he chuckles.

'I think there's more to it than that.'

Eddie sighs. 'Listen, Pollyanna, I don't ask my clients to tell me the truth. I just keep them out of jail so they can go and make the same mistakes all over again.'

'The woman – what did she look like?'

'A fucking mess in the photographs.'

'How old?'

'Mid-forties. Dark hair.'

'What was she wearing?'

'Just a second.' He hangs up the phone and yells to his secretary to get him Bobby's file. Then he rifles through the pages, humming to himself. 'Mid-thigh skirt, high heels, a short jacket . . . mutton dressed as lamb if you ask me. Why do you want to know?'

I can't tell him. It's only half an idea. 'What's going to happen to Bobby?'

'Right now he faces prison time. The CPS won't downgrade the charges.'

'Jail isn't going to help him. I can do you a psych report. Maybe I can get him into an anger management programme.'

'What do you want from me?'

'A written request.'

Eddie's pen is already moving. I can't remember the last time I could write that fluidly. He slides it across the desk.

'Thanks for this.'

He grunts, 'It's a letter, not a kidney.'

If ever a man had issues. Maybe it's a Napoleon complex, or he's trying to compensate for being ugly. He's bored with me now. The subject no longer interests him. I ask my questions quickly.

'Who put up the bail?'

'No idea.'

'And who phoned you?'

'He did.'

Before I can say anything else, he interrupts. 'Listen, Oprah, I'm due in court and I need a pee. This kid is *your* nutcase; I just defend the sorry fuck. Why don't you take a peek inside his head, see if anything rattles and come back to me? Have a terrific day.'

9

Julianne and Charlie are watching television downstairs. I'm sitting on the floor of the attic room, going through boxes of my old case notes looking for my files on Catherine McBride. I don't know why exactly. Maybe I'm hoping to bring her to life in my mind so I can ask her questions.

Ruiz doesn't trust me. He thinks I'm trying to hide something. I should have told him sooner and I should have told him everything. It won't make any difference. Nothing can bring Catherine back.

The notebooks are all labelled with a month and year, which makes them easy to find. There are two of them, with dark green covers and mottled spines where silverfish have been feasting.

Downstairs in the study, I turn on the light and begin reading the notes. The A4 pages are neatly ruled, with a wide margin showing the date and time of each appointment. Assessment details, medical notes and observations are all here.

How do I remember Catherine? I see her walking down the corridor of the Marsden dressed in a light blue uniform with dark blue trim on the collar and sleeves. She waves to

84

me and smiles. She has a key chain on her belt. Most nurses have short-sleeved tunics but Catherine wore hers long.

In the beginning she was just another face in the corridor or in the cafeteria. She was pretty in a genderless way, with her boyish haircut, high forehead and full lips. She nervously cocked her head from one side to the other, never looking at me with both eyes at once. I seemed to bump into her a lot – often just as I was leaving the hospital. Only later did I suspect that she was orchestrating this.

Eventually she asked if she could talk to me. It took me a few minutes to realise that she meant professionally. I made an appointment for her and she arrived the next day.

From then on she came to see me once a week. She would put a bar of chocolate on my desk and break up the pieces on the silver foil, like a child divvying up sweets. And in between smoking menthol cigarettes, she would let the chocolate melt under her tongue.

'Do you know this is the only office in the entire hospital where you can smoke?' she told me.

'I guess that's why I get so many visitors.'

She was twenty, materialistic, sensible and having an affair with someone on staff. I don't know who it was but I suspect he was married. Occasionally she would say 'we' and then, realising her mistake, change to the singular.

Very rarely did she smile. She would cock her head and look at me with one eye or the other.

I also suspected she had seen someone like me before. Her questions were so precise. She knew about history-taking and cognitive therapy. She was too young to have studied psychology so she must have been a patient.

She talked of feeling worthless and insignificant. Estranged from her family, she had tried to mend fences but feared that she would 'poison their perfect lives'.

As she spoke and sucked pieces of chocolate, she sometimes rubbed her forearms through her buttoned-down sleeves. I thought that she was hiding something but waited for her to find the confidence to tell me.

During our fourth session she slowly wound up her sleeves. Part of her was embarrassed to show me the scars, but I also sensed defiance and a hint of self-satisfaction. She wanted me to be impressed by the severity of her wounds. They were like a life-map that I could read.

Catherine had first cut herself aged twelve. Her parents were going through a hate-filled divorce. She felt caught in the middle, like a rag doll being pulled apart by two warring children.

She wrapped a hand-mirror inside a towel and smashed it against the corner of her desk. She used a shard to open up her wrist. The blood gave her a sense of wellbeing. She was no longer helpless.

Her parents bundled her into the car and drove her to hospital. Throughout the entire journey they argued over who was to blame. Catherine felt peaceful and calm. She was admitted to hospital overnight. Her cuts had stopped bleeding. She fingered her wrist lovingly and kissed her cuts goodnight.

'I had found something I could control,' she told me. 'I could decide how many times I cut, how deep I would go. I liked the pain. I craved the pain. I deserved it. I know I must have masochistic tendencies. You should see the men I end up with. You should hear about some of my dreams . . . '

She never admitted spending time in a psychiatric hospital or in group therapy. Much of her past she kept hidden, particularly if it involved her family. For long periods she managed to stop herself cutting. But with each relapse she punished herself by cutting even deeper. She concentrated on her arms and thighs, where she could hide the wounds under her clothing. She also discovered which creams and bandages helped minimise scarring.

When she needed stitches she chose Accident & Emergency

centres away from the Marsden. She couldn't risk losing her job. She would give a false name to the triage nurse and sometimes pretend to be foreign and unable to speak English.

She knew from past experience how nurses and doctors regard self-mutilators – as attention-seekers and time-wasters. Often they get stitched without anaesthetic. 'If you enjoy pain so much, have a little more,' is the attitude.

None of this changed Catherine's behaviour. When she bled she escaped the numbness. My notebooks repeat her words, 'I feel alive. Soothed. In control.'

Dark brown flecks of chocolate are stuck between the pages. She would break off pieces and drop them on the page. She didn't like me writing. She wanted me to listen.

To break the cycle of blood, I gave her alternative strategies. Instead of reaching for a blade I told her to squeeze a piece of ice in her hand, bite down on a hot chillie or rub liniment on her genitals. This was pain without the scarring or the guilt. Once we broke into her thought loop, it was possible to find new coping mechanisms, less physical and violent.

A few days later, on 15 July, Catherine found me in the oncology ward. She had a bundle of sheets in her arms and was looking anxiously from side to side. I saw something in her eyes that I couldn't recognise.

She motioned me to follow her into an alcove and then dropped the sheets. It took me a few moments to notice the sleeves of her cardigan. They were stuffed with paper towels and tissues. Blood leaked through the layers of paper and fabric.

'Please don't let them find out,' she said. 'I'm so sorry.'

'You have to go to A and E.'

'No! Please! I need this job.'

A thousand voices inside my head were telling me what I should do. I ignored every one of them. I sent Catherine ahead to my office while I collected sutures, needles and butterfly clips, bandages and antibiotic ointment. Behind drawn blinds and a locked door I stitched up her forearms.

'You're good at this,' she said.

'I've had some practice.' I applied the antiseptic. 'What happened?'

'I tried to feed the bears.'

I didn't smile. She looked chastened. 'I had a fight with someone. I don't know who I wanted to punish.'

'Your boyfriend?'

She blinked back tears.

'What did you use?'

'A razor blade.'

'Was it clean?'

She shook her head.

'OK. From now on, if you insist on cutting yourself, you should use these.' I handed her a packet of disposable scalpels in a sterilised container. I also gave her bandages, steri-strips and sutures.

'These are my rules,' I told her. 'If you insist on doing this, you must cut in one place . . . on the inside of your thigh.'

She nodded.

'I'm going to teach you how to suture yourself. If you find that you can't do this, then you must go to a hospital.'

Her eyes were wide.

'I am not going to take the cutting option away from you, Catherine. Nor am I going to tell your superiors. But you must do everything in your power to control this. I am placing my trust in you. You can repay my faith by not harming yourself. If you weaken you *must* call me. If you fail to do this and cut yourself then I am not going to blame you or think any less of you. At the same time, I will not run to you. If you harm yourself I will not see you for a week. This is not a punishment – it is a test.'

I could see her thinking hard about the ramifications. Her face still showed fear but her shoulders betrayed her relief.

'From now on we set limits for your self-harm and you take responsibility for it,' I continued. 'At the same time we're going to find new ways for you to cope.'

I gave Catherine a quick sewing lesson using a pillow. She made a joke about me making someone a fine wife. As she rose to leave she put her arms around me. 'Thank you.' Her body sank into mine and she clung to me so tightly I could feel her heart beating.

After she had gone I sat staring at the blood-soaked bandages in the wastepaper bin. I was trying to work out if I was completely insane. I could see the coroner, rigid with indignation, asking me why I had given scalpels to a young woman who enjoyed slicing herself open? He would ask me if I also favoured handing matches to arsonists and heroin to junkies.

Yet I could see no other way to help Catherine. A zero-tolerance approach would simply reinforce her belief that other people controlled her life and decided things for her. That she was worthless and couldn't be trusted.

I had given her the choice. Hopefully, before she took up the blade, she would think closely about her reasons and weigh the consequences. And she would also consider other ways that she might cope.

In the months that followed Catherine slipped up only once. Her forearms healed. My stitching job was remarkably neat for someone so out of practice.

The notes end there but there's more to the story. I still cringe in embarrassment when I remember the details because I should have seen it coming.

Catherine started taking a little extra care with her appearance. She made appointments to see me at the end of her shift and would have changed into civvies. She wore make-up and a splash of perfume. An extra button was undone on her blouse. Nothing too obvious – it was all very subtle. She asked what I did in my spare time. A friend had given her two tickets to the theatre. Did I want to go with her?

There is an old joke about psychologists being the experts you pay to ask questions your spouse asks you for nothing. We listen to problems, read the subtexts and build up self-esteem, teaching people to like who they really are.

For someone like Catherine, having a man really listen and care about her problems was enormously attractive, but sometimes it can be mistaken for something more intimate.

Her kiss came as a total surprise. We were in my office at the Marsden. I pushed her away too suddenly. She stumbled backwards and tripped, landing on the floor. She thought it was part of a game. 'You can hurt me if you want to,' she said.

'I don't want to hurt you.'

'I've been a bad, bad girl.'

'You don't understand.'

'Yes, I do.' She was unzipping her skirt.

'Catherine, you're making a mistake. You've misread the signs.'

The harshness in my voice finally brought her round. She stood beside my desk with her skirt at her ankles and her blouse undone. Pantyhose hid the scars on her thighs. It was embarrassing for both of us – but more so for her. She ran out with mascara leaking down her cheeks and her skirt clutched around her waist.

She quit her job and left the Marsden but the ramifications of that day have plagued me for the rest of my career. Hell hath no fury like a woman scorned.

10

Julianne is doing her stretching exercises in the spare bedroom. She does these yoga-like poses every morning with names that sound like Indian squaws: 'Babbling Brook' meets 'Running Deer'.

A veteran early riser, she is combat-ready by 6.30 a.m. Nothing like me. I've been seeing bloody and beaten faces all night in my dreams.

Julianne pads barefoot into the bedroom wearing just a pyjama top. She bends to kiss me.

'You had a restless night.'

Pressing her head against my chest, she lets her fingers go tap-dancing up my spine until she feels me shiver. She is reminding me that she knows every square inch of me.

'I didn't tell you about Charlie singing carols with the choir.'

'Bugger! I totally forgot.' It was Thursday morning in Oxford Street. 'I was with that detective.'

'Don't worry. She'll forgive you. Apparently young Ryan Fraser kissed her on the bus on the way home.'

'Cheeky sod.'

'It wasn't easy. Three of her friends had to help her catch him and hold him down.'

We laugh and I pull her on top of me, letting her feel my erection against her thigh.

'Stay in bed.'

She laughs and slides away. 'No. I'm too busy.'

'C'mon?'

'It's not the right time. You have to save your fellas.'

My 'fellas' are my sperm. She makes them sound like paratroopers.

She's getting dressed. White bikini pants slide along her legs and snap into place. Then she raises the shirt over her head and shrugs her shoulders into the straps of a bra. She won't risk giving me another kiss. I might not let her go next time.

After she's gone I stay in bed listening to her move through the house, her feet hardly touching the floor. I hear the kettle being filled and the milk being collected from the front step. I hear the freezer door open and the toaster being pushed down.

Dragging myself upright, I take six paces to the bathroom and turn on the shower. The boiler in the basement belches and the pipes clunk and gargle. I stand shivering on the cold tiles waiting for some sign of water. The showerhead is shaking. At any moment I expect the tiles to start coming loose from around the taps.

After two coughs and a hacking spit, a cloudy trickle emerges and then dies.

'The boiler is broken again,' yells Julianne from downstairs.

Great! Brilliant! Somewhere there is a plumber laughing at me. He's no doubt telling all his plumber mates how he pretended to fix a Jurassic boiler and charged enough to pay for a fortnight in Florida.

I shave with cold water, using a fresh razor, without cutting myself. It may seem like a small victory, but worth noting.

I emerge into the kitchen and watch Julianne make plunger

coffee and put posh jam on a piece of wholemeal toast. I always feel childish eating my Rice Krispies.

I still remember the first time I saw her. She was in her first year studying languages at London University. I was doing my postgraduate degree. Not even my mother would call me handsome. I had curly brown hair, a pear-shaped nose and skin that freckled at the first hint of sunlight.

I had stayed on at university determined to sleep with every promiscuous, terminally uncommitted first-year on campus, but unlike other would-be lotharios I tried too hard. I even failed miserably at being fashionably unkempt and seditious. No matter how many times I slept on someone's floor, using my jacket as a pillow, it refused to crumple or stain. And instead of appearing grungy and intellectually blasé, I looked like someone on his way to his first job interview.

'You had passion,' she told me later, after listening to me rail against the evils of apartheid at a rally in Trafalgar Square, outside the South African embassy. She introduced herself in the pub and let me pour her a double from the bottle of whisky we were drinking.

Jock was there – getting all the girls to sign his T-shirt. I knew that he would find Julianne. She was a fresh face – a pretty one. He put his arm around her waist and said, 'I could grow to be a better person just being near you.'

Without a flicker of a smile, she took his hand away and said, 'Sadly, a hard-on doesn't count as personal growth.'

Everybody laughed except Jock. Then Julianne sat down at my table and I gazed at her in wonderment. I had never seen anyone put my best friend in his place so skilfully.

I tried not to blush when she said I had passion. She laughed. She had a dark freckle on her bottom lip. I wanted to kiss it.

Five doubles later she was asleep at the bar. I carried her to a cab and took her home to my bed-sit in Islington. She slept on the futon and I took the sofa. In the morning she kissed me and thanked me for being such a gentleman. Then she kissed me again. I remember the look in her eyes. It wasn't lust. It didn't say, 'Let's have some fun and see what happens.' Her eyes were telling me, 'I'm going to be your wife and have your babies.'

We were always an odd couple. I was the quiet, practical one, who hated noisy parties, pub-crawls and going home for weekends. While she was the only child of a painter father and interior designer mother, who dressed like sixties flower children and only saw the best in people. Julianne didn't go to parties – they came to her.

We married three years later. By then I was house-trained – having learned to put my dirty washing in the basket, to leave the toilet seat down and not to drink too much at dinner parties. Julianne didn't so much 'knock off my rough edges' as fashion me out of clay.

That was sixteen years ago. Seems like yesterday.

Julianne pushes a newspaper towards me. There's a photograph of Catherine and the headline reads: 'Tortured Girl is MP's Niece'.

Junior Home Office minister Samuel McBride has been devastated by the brutal murder of his 27-year-old niece.

The Labour MP for Brighton-le-Sands was clearly upset yesterday when the Speaker of the House expressed the chamber's sincerest condolences at his loss.

Catherine McBride's naked body was found six days ago beside the Grand Union Canal in Kensal Green, West London. She had been stabbed repeatedly.

'At this moment we are concentrating on retracing Catherine's final movements and finding anyone who may have seen her in the days prior to her death,' said Detective Inspector Vincent Ruiz, who is leading the investigation.

'We know she took a train from Liverpool to London on the thirteenth of November. We believe she was coming to London for a job interview.'

Catherine, whose parents are divorced, worked as a community nurse in Liverpool and had been estranged from her family for a number of years.

'She had a difficult childhood and seemed to lose her way,' explained a family friend. 'Recently attempts had been made for a family reconciliation.'

Julianne pours another cup of coffee. 'It's quite strange, don't you think, that Catherine should turn up after all these years?'

'How do you mean, strange?'

'I don't know.' She shivers slightly. 'I mean, she caused us all those problems. You nearly lost your job. I remember how angry you were.'

'She was hurting.'

'She was spiteful.'

She glances at the photograph of Catherine. It's a shot of her graduation day as a nurse. She's smiling fit to bust and clutching a diploma in her hand.

'And now she's back again. We were there when they found her. What are the chances of that? Then the police asked you to help identify her—'

'A coincidence is just a couple of things happening simultaneously.'

She rolls her eyes. 'Spoken like a true psychologist.'

95

11

Bobby is on time for once. He is dressed in his work clothes – a grey shirt and trousers. The word Nevaspring is sewn into the breast pocket. Again I'm surprised at how tall he is.

I finish the last of my notes, struggling to loop each letter, and then look up to see if he's ready. That's when I realise he'll never be entirely ready. Jock is right – there is something fragile and erratic about Bobby. His mind is full of half-finished ideas, strange facts and snatches of conversation.

Years ago a café called 'Oddballs' opened in Soho, which was supposed to attract all the eccentrics who inhabit the West End of London – the wild-haired artists, drag queens, punks, hippies, gonzo journalists and dandies. It never happened. Instead, every table in the place was filled with ordinary office workers, who arrived en masse hoping to see the oddballs. They finished up looking at each other.

Bobby often talks about writing in his spare time and his stories are sometimes sprinkled with literary allusions.

'Can I see some of the things you've written?' I ask.

'You don't really mean that.'

'Yes, I do.'

He thinks about this. 'Maybe I'll bring one next time.'

'Did you always want to be a writer?'

'Ever since I read *Catcher in the Rye*.'

My heart sinks. I have visions of another aging angst-ridden teenager who thinks Holden Caulfield is Nietzsche.

'Do you relate to Holden?'

No. He's an idiot!'

I feel relieved. 'Why?'

'He's naïve. He wants to save the children from falling over the cliff into adulthood – to preserve their innocence. He can't. It's impossible. We all get corrupted in the end.'

'How were you corrupted?'

'Ha!'

'Tell me more about your parents, Bobby. When was the last time you saw your father?'

'I was eight years old. He went to work and didn't come home.'

'Why?'

Bobby changes the subject. 'He was in the air force. He wasn't a pilot. He kept them in the air. A mechanic. He was too young for the war but I don't think it bothered him. He was a pacifist.

'When I was growing up he used to quote Marx to me – telling me about religion being the opium of the masses. And most Sundays we took a bus from Kilburn to Hyde Park so he could heckle the lay preachers on their packing crate pulpits.

'This one preacher looked like Captain Ahab from *Moby Dick*, with long white hair tied back in a ponytail and a big booming voice. "The Lord will repay the wages of sin with eternal death," he said, looking directly at me.

'And Dad yelled back, "Do you know the difference between a preacher and a psychotic?" He paused and then answered, "It's the sound of the voice they hear." Everybody laughed except the preacher, who puffed up like a blowfish. "Is it true that you welcome all denominations, but you prefer tens and twenties?" said Dad.

"'You, sir, will go to hell," yelled the preacher.

"'And which way is that? Do I turn right or go straight on?"'

Bobby even has their voices down pat. He looks at me self-consciously, embarrassed to be so vocal.

'How did you get on with him?'

'He was my dad.'

'Did you do things together?'

'When I was young I used to ride on the crossbars of his bike, between his arms. He used to pedal really fast and make me laugh. One day he took me to see Queen's Park Rangers play at home. I sat on his shoulders and wore a blue and white scarf. Afterwards there were running fights between rival fans on Shepherd's Bush Green. Police on horseback charged the crowd but Dad wrapped his coat around me. I should have been scared but I knew that nothing was ever going to knock him down, not even those horses.'

He lapses into silence, scratching at his hands.

Every childhood has a mythology that materialises around it. We add our own desires and dreams until the stories become like parables that are more emblematic than edifying.

'What happened to your father?'

'It wasn't his fault,' he says defensively.

'Did he abandon you?'

Bobby explodes out of his chair. 'You know nothing about my father!' He's on his feet, sucking air between clenched teeth. 'You'll never know him! People like you destroy lives. You thrive on grief and despair. First sign of trouble you're there, telling people how they should feel. What they should think. You're like vultures!'

Just as suddenly the outburst dissipates. He wipes away white flecks of spit from his mouth and looks at me apologetically. He fills a glass with water and waits, with a strange calm, for my next question.

'Tell me about your mother.'

'She wears cheap perfume and she's dying of breast cancer.'

'I'm sorry to hear that. How old is she?'

'Forty-three. She won't let them give her a mastectomy. She's always been proud of her breasts.'

'How would you describe your relationship with her?'

'I heard the news from a friend in Liverpool. That's where she lives.'

'You don't visit her.'

'Ha!'

His face twists in frustration and he stops himself. 'Let me describe my mother to you . . .' He makes it sound like a challenge. 'She was a grocer's daughter. Isn't that ironic? Just like Margaret Thatcher. She grew up in a corner shop – having her nappies changed right next to the cash register. By the time she was four she could tot up a basket of groceries, take the cash and hand back the correct change.

'Every morning and afternoon, as well as Saturdays and public holidays, she worked in that shop. And she read the magazines on the rack and daydreamed about escaping and living a different life. When Dad came along – dressed in his air force uniform – he said he was a pilot. It's what all the girls wanted to hear. A quick shag behind the social club at RAF Marham and she was pregnant with me. She found out he wasn't a pilot soon enough. I don't think she cared . . . not then. Later it drove her crazy. She said she married him under false pretences.'

'But they stayed together?'

'Yeah. Dad left the air force and got a job working as a mechanic fixing buses for London Transport. Later he became a conductor on the number ninety-six to Piccadilly Circus. He said he was a "people person", but I think he also liked the uniform. He used to ride his bike to the depot and home again.'

Bobby lapses into silence, reliving the memories. Prompting

99

him gently, he tells me his father was an amateur inventor, always coming up with ideas for timesaving devices and gadgets.

'People talk about building a better mousetrap; well, he was doing stuff like that.'

'What did your mother think?'

'She said he was wasting his time and their money. One minute she'd be calling him a dreamer and laughing at all his "stupid inventions" and the next she'd be saying he didn't dream big enough and that he lacked ambition.'

Blinking rapidly, he looks at me with his odd pale eyes, as though he's forgotten his train of thought. Suddenly he remembers.

'She was the *real* dreamer, not Dad. She saw herself as a free spirit, surrounded by boring mediocrity. And no matter how hard she tried she could never live a bohemian lifestyle in a place like Hendon. She hated the place – the flat-front houses with their pebbledash façades, the net curtains, cheap clothes, greasy spoon cafes and garden gnomes. Working-class people talk about "looking after our own", but she scoffed at that. She could see only smallness, insignificance and ugliness.'

He's settled into a dull riff, as though he's told the story too often before.

'She'd get dressed up and go out most nights. I used to sit on the bed and watch her get ready. She'd try on different outfits – modelling them for me. She let me zip up the back of her skirts and smooth her stockings. She called me her Little Big Man.

'If Dad wouldn't take her out, she went by herself – to the pub, or the club. She had the sort of wicked laugh that told everyone she was there. Men would turn their heads and look at her. They found her sexy even though she was plump. Pregnancy had added pounds that she had never managed to shed. She blamed me for that. And when she went dancing

100

or laughed too hard she sometimes wet her pants. That was my fault, too.'

This last comment is delivered through gritted teeth. His fingers pick at the loose skin on the back of his hands, twisting it painfully, as though trying to tear it off. His body humbled, he begins again.

'She drank white sparkling wine because it looked like champagne. And the drunker she got, the louder she became. She used to start talking in Spanish because it sounded sexy. Have you heard a woman speaking Spanish?'

I nod, thinking of Julianne.

'It cramped her style if Dad took her out. Men won't flirt with a woman when her husband is standing at the same bar. By herself she had them all over her, putting arms around her waist, squeezing her arse. She stayed out all night and came home in the morning, with her knickers in her handbag and her shoes swinging from her fingertips. There was never any pretence of fidelity or loyalty. She didn't want to be the perfect wife. She wanted to *be* someone else.'

'What about your dad?'

A long minute passes before he finds the answer he wants. 'He grew smaller every day. Disappearing little by little. Death by a thousand cuts. That's how I hope she dies.'

The sentence hangs in the air but the silence isn't arbitrary. It feels as though someone has reached up and put a finger in front of the second hand on the clock.

'Why did you use that term?'

'Which one?'

'"Death by a thousand cuts".'

His smile is slight, involuntary and crooked. 'That's how I want her to die. Slowly. In pain. By her own hand.'

'You want her to kill herself?'

He doesn't answer.

'Do you ever imagine her dying?'

'I dream about it.'

101

'What do you dream?'

'That I'll be there.'

He stares at me, his pale eyes like bottomless pools.

Death by a thousand cuts. The ancient Chinese had a more literal translation: 'One thousand knives and ten thousand pieces'. The woman Bobby dragged from the cab was roughly the same age and wore the same sort of clothes as his mother. She also showed a similar coldness towards her son. Is this enough to explain his actions? I'm getting closer. The desire to understand violence has built-in brutality. Don't think of the white bear.

Another patient is waiting outside. Bobby slowly rises and turns towards the door.

'I'll see you on *Monday*,' I say, putting emphasis on the day. I want him to remember it. I want him to keep coming back.

He nods and reaches across to shake my hand. He's never done that before.

'Mr Barrett said you're going to help me.'

'I'm going to prepare a psych report.'

He nods. 'I'm not mad, you know.'

'I know.'

He taps his head. 'It was just a stupid mistake.'

Then he's gone. My next appointment, Mrs Aylmer, is already sitting down and telling me how many times she checks the locks before she goes to bed. I'm not listening. I stand at the window, watching Bobby emerge on to the street and walk towards the station. Every so often he checks his stride so as not to walk on the cracks in the pavement.

He stops when he spies a young woman walking towards him. As she passes, he turns his whole body to keep watching her. For a moment I think he's debating whether to follow her. He looks one way and then the other as though caught at a T-junction. Then, after several seconds, he skips over a crack and carries on.

* * *

102

I'm back in Jock's office, listening to him rattle off my results, which I don't understand. He wants to start me on medication as soon as possible.

There is no definitive test for Parkinson's. Instead they have lots of games and exercises that gauge the progression of the disease. Clicking a stopwatch, Jock makes me walk along a line of masking tape on the floor, turn and walk back again. Then I have to stand on one foot with my eyes closed.

When he brings out the coloured blocks I groan. It feels so childish – stacking blocks one on top of the other. First I use my right hand and then my left. My left hand is trembling before I start, but once I pick up a block it's OK.

Putting dots in a grid is more difficult. I aim for the centre of the square but the pen has a mind of its own. *It's a stupid test anyway.*

Afterwards Jock explains that patients like me, who present initially with tremors, have a significantly better prognosis. There are lots of new drugs becoming available to lessen the symptoms.

'You can expect to lead a full life,' he says, as though reading from a script. When he sees the look of disbelief on my face he attempts to qualify the statement. 'Well, maybe you'll lose a few years.'

He doesn't say anything about my quality of life.

'Stem-cell research is going to provide a breakthrough,' he adds, sounding upbeat. 'Within five or ten years they'll have a cure.'

'What do I do until then?'

'Take the drugs. Make love to that gorgeous wife of yours. Watch Charlie grow up.'

He gives me a prescription for Selegiline. 'Eventually you'll need to take Levodopa,' he explains, 'but hopefully we can delay that for maybe a year or more.'

'Are there any side-effects?'

'You might get a little nauseous and have trouble sleeping.'

'Great!'

Jock ignores me. 'These drugs don't stop the progression of the disease. All they do is mask the symptoms.'

'So I can keep it secret for longer.'

He smiles ruefully. 'You'll face up to this sooner or later.'

'If I keep coming here maybe I'll die of passive smoking.'

'What a way to go.' He lights up a cigar and pulls the Scotch from his bottom drawer.

'It's only three o'clock.'

'I'm working on British summer time.' He doesn't ask, he simply pours me one. 'I had a visit from Julianne last week.'

I feel myself blinking rapidly. 'What did she want?'

'She wanted to know about your condition. I couldn't tell her. Doctor–patient privilege and all that bollocks.' After a pause, he says, 'She also wanted to know if I thought you were having an affair.'

'Why would she ask that?'

'She thinks you've been telling lies.'

I take a sip of Scotch and feel it burn my oesophagus. Jock watches through a stream of smoke, waiting for an answer. Instead of feeling angry or at fault, I have a bizarre sense of disappointment. How could Julianne have asked Jock a question like that? Why didn't she ask me directly?

Jock is still waiting for an answer. He sees my discomfort and begins to laugh, shaking his head like a wet dog.

I want to say, 'Don't you look at me like that – you've been divorced twice and are still chasing women half your age.'

'It's none of my business, of course,' he says, gloating. 'But if she walks out on you I'll be there to comfort her.'

He's not joking. He'd be sniffing around Julianne in a flash.

I quickly change the subject. 'Bobby Moran – how much do you know about him?'

Jock rocks his tumbler back and forth. 'No more than you do.'

104

'There's no mention in the medical notes about any previous psychiatric treatment.'

'What makes you think there has been any?'

'He quoted a question to me from a Mental Status Examination. I think he's been evaluated before.'

'Did you ask him?'

'He wouldn't talk about it.'

Jock's face is a study of quiet contemplation, which looks as though it's been practised in the mirror. Just when I think he might add something constructive, he shrugs, 'He's an odd fucker, that's for sure.'

'Is that a professional opinion?'

He grunts. 'Most of my patients are unconscious when I spend time with them. I prefer it that way.'

12

A plumber's van is parked out front of the house. The sliding door is open and inside there are trays stacked one on top of the other, with silver and brass fittings, corners, S-bends and plastic couplings.

The company name is attached to the side panels on magnetised mats – D.J. Morgan Plumbers & Gas Fitters. I find him in the kitchen, having a cup of tea and trying to catch a glimpse of Julianne's breasts beneath her v-necked top. His apprentice is outside in the garden showing Charlie how to juggle a football with her knees and feet.

'This is our plumber, D.J.,' says Julianne.

Getting lazily to his feet, he nods a greeting without taking his hands from his pockets. He's in his mid-thirties, tanned and fit, with dark, wet-looking hair combed back from his forehead. He looks like one of those tradesmen you see on lifestyle shows, renovating houses or doing make-overs. I can see him asking himself what a woman like Julianne's doing with someone like me.

'Why don't you show Joe what you showed me?'

The plumber acknowledges her with the slightest dip of his

head. I follow him to the basement door, which is secured with a bolt. Narrow wooden steps lead down to the concrete floor. A low-wattage bulb is fixed to the wall. Dark beams and bricks soak up the light.

I have lived in this house for four years and the plumber already knows the basement better than I do. With a genial openness, he points out various pipes above our heads, explaining the gas and water system.

I contemplate asking him a question but know from experience not to advertise my ignorance around tradesmen. I am not a handyman; I have no interest in DIY, which is why I can still count to twenty on my fingers and toes.

D.J. nudges the boiler with his work boot. The inference is clear. It's useless, junk, a joke.

'So how much is this going to cost?' I ask after getting lost halfway through his briefing.

He exhales slowly and begins listing the things that need replacing.

'How much for labour?'

'Depends how long it takes.'

'How long will it take?'

'Can't say until I check all the radiators.' He casually picks up an old bag of plaster, turned solid by the damp, and tosses it to one side. It would have taken two of me to move it. Then he glances at my feet. I am standing in a puddle of water that is soaking through the stitching of my shoes.

Mumbling something about keeping costs down, I retreat upstairs and try not to imagine him sniggering behind my back. Julianne hands me a cup of lukewarm tea – the last of the pot.

'Everything OK?'

'Fine. Where did you find him?' I whisper.

'He put a flyer through the letterbox.'

'References?'

She rolls her eyes. 'He did the Reynolds' new bathroom at number seventy-four.'

The plumbers carry their tools outside to the van and Charlie tosses her ball into the garden shed. Her hair is pulled back into a ponytail and her cheeks are flushed with the cold. Julianne scolds her for getting grass stains on her school tights.

'They'll come out in the wash,' says Charlie.

'And how would you know?'

'They always do.'

Charlie turns and gives me a hug. 'Feel my nose.'

'Brrrrrr! Cold nose, warm heart.'

'Can Sam stay over tonight?'

'That depends. Is Sam a boy or a girl?'

'Daaaad!' Charlie screws up her face.

Julianne interrupts. 'You have football tomorrow.'

'What about next weekend?'

'Grandma and Grandpa are coming down.'

Charlie's face brightens as mine falls. I had totally forgotten. God's personal physician-in-waiting is giving a talk to an international medical conference. It will be a triumph, of course. He will be offered all sorts of honorary positions and part-time consultancies, which he will graciously refuse because travel wearies him. I will sit in silence through all of this, feeling as though I am thirteen again.

My father has a brilliant medical mind. There isn't a modern medical textbook that doesn't mention his name. He has written papers that have changed the way paramedics treat accident victims and altered the standard procedures of battle-field medics.

His father, my grandfather, was a founding member of the General Medical Council and its longest serving chairman. He established his reputation as an administrator rather than as a surgeon, but the name is still writ large in the history of medical ethics.

This is where I come in – or don't come in. After having three daughters, I was the long-awaited son. As such, I was expected to carry on the medical dynasty, but instead I broke the chain. In modern parlance that makes me the weakest link.

Perhaps my father should have seen it coming. My failure to play rugby with any passion or aptitude should have tipped him off. All I can say for sure is that my flaws have mounted steadily since then and he's come to regard me as his own personal failure.

He couldn't understand my affection for Gracie. I didn't even try to explain. She was like a dropped stitch in our family's history – just like Uncle Rosskend, who was a conscientious objector during the war, and my cousin Brian who was done for stealing lingerie from department stores.

My parents never talked about Gracie. I had to pick up bits and pieces from cousins and distant relations who each had a tiny piece of the puzzle. Eventually I had enough to get a general picture of what had happened.

Gracie had been a nurse during World War I and fell pregnant to a childhood sweetheart who didn't return from the fighting. She was seventeen, unmarried, heartbroken and alone.

'No man wants a woman with a baby,' her mother told her as she put her on a train for London.

Gracie glimpsed her baby only once. The good sisters at Nazareth House in Hammersmith erected a sheet halfway down her body to stop her seeing the birth, but she tore it down. When she saw the mewling infant, ugly and beautiful all at once, something broke inside her that no medical doctor could ever fix.

My second cousin Angelina says there are family photographs of Gracie in mental asylums and county hospitals. All I can say for sure is that she moved into her house in Richmond in the early twenties and was still there when I went to university.

My mother called me to tell me that Gracie had died. I was mid-way through my exams in my third year of medicine – the exams I failed. According to the coroner's report, the blaze

109

started in the kitchen and spread quickly through the ground floor. Even so, Gracie had ample opportunity to get out.

The firemen had seen her moving around upstairs before the fire had completely taken hold. They said she could have crawled out of a window on to the garage roof. But if that's the case, why couldn't the firemen have gone in the same way and saved her?

All the books, newspapers and magazines fed the flames – along with the tins of fabric paint and bottles of dye in the laundry. The temperatures were so great that her entire rooms of 'collectibles' were reduced to a fine white ash.

Gracie had always sworn that they would have to carry her out of there in a pine box. In the end they could have swept her into a dustpan.

I had already decided that I didn't want to be a doctor. I just wasn't sure of the alternatives. I had questions instead of answers. I wanted to find out why Gracie had been so frightened of the world. Mostly, however, I wanted to discover if somebody could have helped her.

In the four years that it took me to get my degree, my father never once missed an opportunity to call me 'Mr Psychologist' or to make cracks about couches and inkblot tests. And when my thesis on agoraphobia was published in the *British Psychological Journal*, he said nothing to me or to anyone else in the family.

A comparable silence has greeted every stage of my career since then. I finished my training in London and was offered a job with Merseyside Health Authority. Julianne and I moved to Liverpool – a city of snub-nosed ferries, mill chimneys, Victorian statues and empty factories.

We lived in a gaunt, reformatory-like building with a pebbledash front and barred windows. It was opposite the Sefton Park bus terminal and we were woken each morning by the coughing and hacking of diesel engines that sounded like an ageing smoker spitting phlegm into a sink.

I lasted two years in Liverpool and still regard it as a place that I escaped from – a modern-day plague city full of sad-eyed children, long-term unemployed and mad poor people. If it hadn't been for Julianne I might have drowned in their misery.

At the same time I'm grateful because it taught me where I belong. For the first time London felt like home. I spent four years at West Hammersmith Hospital and later moved to the Royal Marsden. When I became a senior consultant my name was painted on a polished oak board in the foyer of the Marsden, opposite the front door. Ironically, my father's name was being taken off the same board as he, in his own words, 'scaled down commitments'.

I don't know if the two incidents were linked. I don't care. I long ago stopped worrying about what he thinks or why he does things. I have Julianne and Charlie. I have my own family now. One man's opinion doesn't matter – not even his.

13

Saturday mornings and soggy sports fields seem to go together like acne and adolescence. That's how I remember the winters of my childhood – standing ankle-deep in mud, freezing my bollocks off, playing for the school's Second XV. God's personal physician-in-waiting had a bellow that rose above the howling wind. 'Don't just stand there like a cold bottle of piss,' he'd shout. 'Call yourself a winger! I've seen continents drift faster than you.'

Thank goodness Charlie is a girl. She looks really cute in her soccer gear, with her hair pulled back and shorts down to her knees. I don't know how I managed to become coach. My knowledge of the round ball game could fit on the back of a coaster, which is probably why the Tigers haven't won a game all season. You're not supposed to count the score at this age, or keep a league table. It's all about having fun and getting every child involved. Tell that to the parents.

Today we're playing the Highgate Lions and each time they score the Tigers trudge back to halfway, debating who gets to kick off.

'It isn't our strongest side,' I say apologetically to the

opposition coach. Under my breath I'm praying, 'Just one goal, Tigers. Just give us one goal. Then we'll show them a real celebration.'

At halftime we're down four nil. The kids are sucking on quarters of orange. I tell them how well they're playing. 'This team is undefeated,' I say, lying through my teeth, 'but you guys are holding them.'

I put Douglas, our strongest kicker, in goal for the second half. Andrew, our leading goal-scorer, is fullback.

'But I'm a striker,' he whinges.

'Dominic is playing up front.'

They all look at Dominic, who has only just worked out which direction we're running. He giggles and shoves his hand down his shorts, grabbing his scrotum.

'Forget about dribbling, or passing, or scoring goals,' I say. 'Just go out there and try to kick the ball as hard as you can.'

As the game restarts I have a posse of parents bending my ear about my positional changes. They think I've lost the plot. But there's a method to my madness. Soccer at this level is all about momentum. Once the ball is moving forward the whole game moves in that direction. That's why I want my strongest kickers at the back.

For the first few minutes nothing changes. The Tigers may as well be chasing shadows. Then the ball falls to Douglas and he hoofs it up field. Dominic tries to run out of the way, falls over and brings down both defenders. The ball rolls loose. Charlie is closest. I'm muttering under my breath, 'Nothing fancy. Just take the shot.'

Accuse me of favouritism. Call me biased. I don't care. What comes next is the most sweetly struck, curling, rising, dipping, swerving shot ever sent goal-wards by a size six foot-ball boot. Such are the scenes of celebration that any independent observer must be convinced that we've won.

Shell-shocked by our new strategy, the Lions fall apart. Even Dominic poaches a goal when the ball bounces off the back of his head and loops over the goalkeeper. The Tigers beat the Lions five goals to four.

Our finest endorsement comes from Julianne, who isn't what you'd call a dedicated football mum. I think she'd prefer Charlie to do ballet or to play tennis. Looking immaculate in a long black hooded coat and Wellingtons, she announces that she has never seen a more exciting piece of sport. The fact that she calls it a 'piece of sport' is testament to how little she watches football.

Parents are wrapping their children up warmly and putting muddy boots into plastic bags. As I gaze across the field I notice a man standing alone on the far side of the pitch with his hands in the pockets of an overcoat. I recognise the silhouette.

'What brings you out so early on a Saturday, Detective Inspector? It's not the exercise.'

Ruiz glances towards the jogging path. 'There's enough heavy breathers in this town already.'

'How did you know where to find me?'

'Your neighbours.'

He unwraps a boiled sweet and pops it into his mouth, rattling it against his teeth.

'How can I help you?'

'Do you remember what I told you at our breakfast? I said that if the victim turns out to be the daughter of someone famous I'll have forty detectives instead of twelve.'

'Yes.'

'Did you know your little nurse was the niece of a Tory MP and the grand-daughter of a retired county court judge?'

'I read about her uncle in the papers.'

'I got the hyenas all over me – asking questions and shoving cameras in my face. It's a media fucking circus.'

There's nothing I can say, so I stare past him towards London Zoo and let him keep talking.

'You're one of the bright boys, right? University education, post-graduate degree, consultancy . . . I thought you might be able to help me out on this one. I mean, you knew this girl, right? You worked with her. So I figured you might have an insight into what she might be mixed up in.'

'I only knew her as a patient.'

'But she talked to you. She told you about herself. What about friends or boyfriends?'

'I think she was seeing someone at the hospital. He might have been married because she wouldn't talk about him.'

'She mention a name?'

'No.'

'Do you think she was promiscuous?'

'No.'

'Why are you so sure?'

'I don't know. It's just a feeling.'

He turns and nods at Julianne, who is suddenly beside me, slipping her arm through mine. Her hood is up and she looks like a nun.

'This is Detective Inspector Vincent Ruiz, the policeman I told you about.'

Concern creases her forehead. 'Is this about Catherine?' She pushes back her hood.

Ruiz looks at her as most men do. No make-up, no perfume, no jewellery and she still turns heads.

'Are you interested in the past, Mrs O'Loughlin?'

She hesitates. 'That depends.'

'Did you know Catherine McBride?'

'She caused us a lot of grief.'

Ruiz's eyes dart to mine and I get a sinking feeling.

Julianne looks at me and realises her mistake. Charlie is calling her. She looks over her shoulder and then turns back to Ruiz.

'Perhaps I should talk to your husband first,' he says slowly. 'I can always catch up with you later.'

Julianne nods and gives my arm a squeeze. 'I'll take Charlie for a hot chocolate.'

'OK.'

We watch her leave, stepping gracefully between muddy puddles and patches of turf. Ruiz tilts his head to one side as though trying to read something written sideways on my lapels.

'What did she mean?'

My credibility is non-existent. He's not going to believe me.

'Catherine made an allegation that I sexually assaulted her under hypnosis. She withdrew the complaint within hours but it still had to be investigated. It was all a misunderstanding.'

'How do you misunderstand something like that?'

I tell him how Catherine had confused my professional concern for something more intimate – about the kiss and her embarrassment. Her anger.

'You turned her down?'

'Yes.'

'So she made the complaint?'

'Yes. I didn't even know until after it had been withdrawn, but there still had to be an inquiry. I was suspended while the hospital board investigated. Other patients were interviewed.'

'All because of one letter?'

'Yes.'

'Did you talk to Catherine?'

'No. She avoided me. I didn't see her again until just before she left the Marsden. She apologised. She had a new boyfriend and they were going up north.'

'You weren't angry with her?'

'I was bloody furious. She could have cost me my career.' Realising how harsh that sounds, I add, 'She was very fragile emotionally.'

Ruiz gets out his notebook and begins writing something down.

'Don't make too much of it.'

'I'm not making anything out of it, Professor, it's just infor-mation. You and I both collect pieces of information until two or three of them fit together.' Turning the pages of his

116

notebook, he smiles at me gently. 'It's amazing what you can find out these days. Married. One child. No religious affiliation. Educated at Charterhouse and London University. BA and MA in psychology. Taken into custody in 1980 for projecting the image of a swastika on South Africa House during a 'Free Mandela' demonstration in Trafalgar Square. Twice caught speeding on the M40; one outstanding parking ticket; denied a Syrian visa in 1987 because of a previous visit to Israel. Father a well-known doctor. Three sisters. One works for the United Nations refugee programme. Your wife's father committed suicide in 1994. Your aunt died in a house fire. You have private medical insurance, an overdraft facility of ten thousand pounds and your car tax is due for renewal on Wednesday.' He looks up. 'I haven't bothered with your tax returns, but I'd say you went into private practice because that house of yours must cost a bloody fortune.'

He's getting to the point now. This whole spiel is a message to me. He wants to show me what he's capable of.

His voice grows quiet. 'If I find that you've withheld information from my murder inquiry I'll send you to jail. You can practise some of your skills first-hand when you're two-up in a cell with a Yardie who wants you to give it up for Jesus.' He closes the notebook and slips it into his pocket. Blowing on his cupped hands, he adds, 'Thank you for your patience, Professor.'

14

Bobby Moran intercepts me as I cross the lobby. He looks even more dishevelled than normal, with mud on his overcoat and papers bulging from his pockets. I wonder if he's been waiting for sleep or something bad to happen.

Blinking rapidly behind his glasses, he mumbles an apology. 'I have to see you.'

I glance over his head at the clock on the wall. 'I have another patient—'

'Please?'

I should say no. I can't have people just turning up. Meena will be furious. She could run a perfectly good office if it weren't for patients turning up unannounced or not keeping appointments. 'That's not the way to pack a suitcase,' she'll say and I'll agree with her, even if I don't completely understand what she means.

Upstairs, I tell Bobby to sit down and set about rearranging my morning. He looks embarrassed to have caused such a fuss. He is different today – more grounded, living in the here and now.

'You asked me about what I dream.' He is staring at a spot on the floor between his feet.

'Yes.'

'I think there's something wrong with me. I keep having these thoughts.'

'What thoughts?'

'I hurt people in my dreams.'

'How do you hurt them?'

He looks up at me plaintively. 'I try to stay awake . . . I don't want to fall asleep. Arky keeps telling me to come to bed. She can't understand why I'm watching TV at four in the morning, wrapped in a duvet on the sofa. It's because of the dreams.'

'What about them?'

'Bad things happen in them – that doesn't make me a bad person.' He is perched on the edge of the chair, with his eyes flicking from side to side. 'There's a girl in a red dress. She keeps turning up when I don't expect to see her.'

'In your dream?'

'Yes. She just looks at me – right through me as though I don't exist. She's laughing.'

His eyes snap wide as though spring-loaded and his tone suddenly changes. Spinning around in his chair, he presses his lips together and crosses his legs. I hear a harsh, feminine voice.

'Now, Bobby, don't tell lies.'

– 'I'm not a blabbermouth.'

'Did he touch you or not?'

– 'No.'

'That's not what Mr Erskine wants to hear.'

– 'Don't make me say it.'

'We don't want to waste Mr Erskine's time. He's come all this way—'

– 'I know why he's come.'

'Don't use that tone of voice with me, sweetie. It's not very nice.'

Bobby puts his big hands in his pockets and kicks at the floor with his shoes. He speaks in a timid whisper, with his chin pressed to his chest.

– 'Don't make me say it.'

'Just tell him and then we can have dinner.'

– 'Please don't make me say . . . '

He shakes his head and his whole body moves. Raising his eyes to me, I see a flicker of recognition.

'Do you know that a blue whale's testicles are as large as a Volkswagen Beetle?'

'No, I didn't know that.'

'I like whales. They're very easy to draw and to carve.'

'Who is Mr Erskine?'

'Should I know him?'

'You mentioned his name.'

He shakes his head and looks at me suspiciously.

'Is he someone you once met?'

'I was born in one world. Now I'm waist deep in another.'

'What does that mean?'

'I had to hold things together, hold things together.'

He's not listening to me. His mind is moving so quickly that it can't grasp any subject for more than a few seconds.

'You were telling me about your dream . . . a girl in a red dress. Who is she?'

'Just a girl.'

'Do you know her?'

'Her arms are bare. She lifts them up and brushes her fingers through her hair. I see the scars.'

'What do these scars look like?'

'It doesn't matter.'

'Yes it does!'

Tipping his head to one side, Bobby runs his finger down the inside of his shirtsleeve, from his elbow to his wrist. Then he looks back at me. Nothing registers in his eyes. Is he talking about Catherine McBride?

'How did she get these scars?'

'She cut herself.'

'How do you know that?'

'A lot of people do.' Bobby unbuttons his shirt cuffs and slowly rolls the sleeve along his left forearm. Turning his palm face-up, he holds it out towards me. The thin white scars are faint but unmistakable. 'They're like a badge of honour,' he whispers.

'Bobby, listen to me.' I lean forward. 'What happens to the girl in your dream?'

Panic fills his eyes like a growing fever. 'I don't remember.'

'Do you know this girl?'

He shakes his head.

'What colour hair does she have?'

'Brown.'

'What colour eyes?'

He shrugs.

'You said you hurt people in your dreams. Did this girl get hurt?'

The question is too direct and confrontational. He looks at me suspiciously. 'Why are you staring at me like that? Are you taping this? Are you stealing my words?' He peers from side to side.

'No.'

'Well, why are you staring at me?'

Then I realise that he's talking about the 'Parkinson's Mask'. Jock had warned me of the possibility. My face can become totally unresponsive and expressionless like an Easter Island statue.

I look away and try to start again, but Bobby's mind has already moved on.

'Did you know the year 1961 can be written upside down and right-way up and appear the same?' he says.

'No, I didn't.'

'That's not going to happen again until 6009.'

'I need to know about the dream, Bobby.'

'*No comprenderas todavia lo que comprenderas en el futuro.*'

'What's that mean?'

121

'It's Spanish. You don't understand yet what you will under-stand in the end.' His forehead suddenly creases as though he's forgotten something. Then his expression changes to one of complete bafflement. He hasn't just lost his train of thought – he's forgotten what he's doing here. He looks at his watch.

'Why are you here, Bobby?'

'I keep having these thoughts.'

'What thoughts?'

'I hurt people in my dreams. That's not a crime. It's only a dream . . . '

We have been here before, thirty minutes ago. He has forgotten everything in between.

There is an interrogation method, sometimes used by the CIA, which is called the *Alice in Wonderland* technique. It relies upon turning the world upside down and distorting every-thing that is familiar and logical. The interrogators begin with what sound like very ordinary questions, but in fact are totally nonsensical. If the suspect tries to answer, the second interrogator interrupts with something unrelated and equally illogical.

They change their demeanour and patterns of speech in mid-sentence or from one moment to the next. They get angry when making pleasant comments and become charming when making threats. They laugh at the wrong places and speak in riddles.

If the suspect tries to cooperate he's ignored, and if he doesn't cooperate he's rewarded – never knowing why. At the same time, the interrogators manipulate the environment, turning clocks backwards and forwards, lights on and off, serving meals ten hours or only ten minutes apart.

Imagine this continuing day after day. Cut off from the world and everything he knows to be normal, the suspect tries to cling to what he remembers. He may keep track of time or try to picture a face or a place. Each of these threads to

122

his sanity is gradually torn down or worn down until he no longer knows what is real and unreal.

Talking to Bobby is like this. The random connections, twisted rhymes and strange riddles make just enough sense for me to listen. At the same time, I'm being drawn deeper into the intrigue and the lines between fact and fantasy have begun to blur.

He won't talk about his dream again. Whenever I ask about the girl in the red dress, he ignores me. The silence has no effect. He is totally contained and unreachable.

Bobby is slipping away from me. When I first met him I saw a highly intelligent, articulate, compassionate young man, concerned about his life. Now I see a borderline schizophrenic, with violent dreams and a possible history of mental illness.

I thought I had a handle on him, but now he's attacked a woman in broad daylight and confessed to 'hurting' people in his dreams. What about the girl with the scars?

Take a deep breath. Review the facts. Don't force pieces to fit the puzzle. One in fifteen people harm themselves at some point in their lives: that's two children in every classroom, four people on a crowded bus, twenty on a commuter train and two thousand at an Arsenal home game.

In my sixteen years as a psychologist I have learned unequivocally not to believe in conspiracies or to listen for the same voices my patients are hearing. A doctor is no good to anyone if he dies of the disease.

15

The school is beautiful: solid, Georgian and covered with wisteria. The crushed quartz driveway begins to curve as it passes through the gates and finishes at a set of wide stone steps. The parking area looks like a salesroom for Range Rovers and Mercedes. I park my Metro around the corner on the street.

Charlie's school is having its annual fund-raising dinner and auction. The assembly hall has been decked out with black and white balloons and the caterers have set up a marquee on the tennis courts.

The invitation said 'formal casual' but most of the mothers are wearing evening gowns because they don't get out very much. They are congregated around a minor TV celebrity who is sporting a sun-bed tan and perfect teeth. That's what happens when you send your child to an expensive private school. You rub shoulders with diplomats, game-show hosts and drug barons.

This is our first night out in weeks but instead of feeling relaxed I'm on edge. I keep thinking about Julianne's visit to see Jock. Somehow she knows I lied to her. When is she going to say something? Ever since the diagnosis I have descended into dark moods and withdrawn from people. Maybe I'm feeling guilty. More likely it's regret. This is my way of disinfecting those around me.

I am losing my body bit by bit. One part of me thinks this is OK. I'll be fine as long as I have my mind. I can live in the space between my ears. But another part is already longing for what I haven't yet lost.

So here I am – not so much at a crossroads as at a cul-de-sac. I have a wife who fills me with pride and a daughter who makes me cry when I watch her sleeping. I am forty-two years old and I have just started to understand how to combine intuition with learning and do my job properly. Half my life lies ahead of me – the best half. Unfortunately, my mind is willing but my body isn't able – or soon won't be. It is deserting me by increments. That is the only certainty that remains.

The fund-raising auction takes too long. They always do. The master of ceremonies is a professional auctioneer with an actor's voice that cuts through the chatter and small talk. Each class has created two art works – mostly brightly coloured collages of individual drawings. Charlie's class made a circus and a beachscape with coloured bathing huts, rainbow umbrellas and ice-cream stalls.

'That would look great in the kitchen,' says Julianne, putting her arm through mine.

'How much is the plumbing going to cost us?'

She ignores me. 'Charlie drew the whale.'

Looking carefully, I notice a grey lump on the horizon. Drawing isn't one of her strong suits, but I know she loves whales.

Auctions bring out the best and worst in people. And the only bidder more committed than a couple with an only child is a besotted and cashed-up grandparent.

I get to make one bid for the beach scene at £65. When

the hammer comes down, to polite applause, it has made £700. The successful bid is by phone. You'd think this was bloody Sotheby's.

We arrive home after midnight. The babysitter has forgotten to turn on the front porch light. In the darkness I trip over a stack of copper pipes and fall up the steps, bruising my knee.

'D.J. asked if he could leave them there,' apologises Julianne. 'Don't worry about your trousers. I'll soak them.'

'What about my knee?'

'You'll live.'

We both check on Charlie. Soft animals surround her bed, facing outwards like sentries guarding a fort. She sleeps on her side with her thumb hovering near her lips.

As I clean my teeth, Julianne stands beside me at the vanity taking off her make-up. She is watching me in the mirror.

'Are you having an affair?'

The question is delivered so casually it catches me by surprise. I try to pretend I haven't heard her but it's too late. I've stopped brushing. The pause has betrayed me.

'Why?'

She's wiping mascara from her eyelashes. 'Lately I've had the feeling that you're not really here.'

'I've been preoccupied.'

'You still want to be here, don't you?'

'Of course I do.'

She hasn't taken her eyes off me in the mirror. I look away, rinsing my toothbrush in the sink.

'We don't talk any more,' she says.

I know what's coming. I don't want to go in this direction. This is where she gives me chapter and verse about my inability to communicate. She thinks that, because I'm a psychologist, I should be able to talk through my feelings and analyse what's going on. Why? I spend all day inside other people's heads.

When I get home, the hardest thing I want to think about is helping Charlie with her times tables.

Julianne is different. She's a talker. She shares everything and works things through. It's not that I'm scared of showing my feelings. I'm scared of not being able to stop.

I try to head her off at the pass. 'When you've been married as long as we have you don't need to talk as much,' I say feebly. 'We can read each other's minds.'

'Is that so? What am I thinking now?'

I pretend I don't hear her. 'We're comfortable with each other. It's called familiarity.'

'Which breeds contempt.'

'No!'

She puts her arms around me, running her hands down my chest and locking them together at my waist. 'What is the point of sharing your life with someone if you can't communicate with them about the things that matter?' Her head is resting against my back. '*That's* what married couples do. It's perfectly normal. I know you're hurting. I know you're scared. I know you're worried about what's going to happen when the disease gets worse . . . about Charlie and me . . . but you can't stand between us and the world, Joe. You can't protect us from something like this.'

My mouth is dry and I feel the beginnings of a hangover. This isn't an argument – it's a matter of perception. I know that if I don't answer, Julianne will fill the vacuum.

'What are you so frightened of? You're not dying.'

'I know.'

'Of course it's unfair. You don't deserve this. But look at what you have – a lovely home, a career, a wife who loves you and a daughter who worships the ground you walk on. If that can't outweigh any other problems then we're all in trouble.'

'I don't want anything to change.' I hate how vulnerable I sound.

'Nothing *has* to change.'

127

'I see you watching me. Looking for the signs. A tremor here, a twitch there.'

'Does it hurt?' she asks suddenly.

'What?'

'When your leg locks up or your arm doesn't swing.'

'No.'

'I didn't know that.' She puts her fist in my hand and curls my fingers around it. Then she makes me turn so her eyes can fix on mine. 'Does it embarrass you?'

'Sometimes.'

'Is there any special diet you should be on?'

'No.'

'What about exercise?'

'It can help, according to Jock, but it won't stop the disease.'

'I didn't know,' she whispers. 'You should have told me.' She leans even closer, pressing her lips to my ear. The droplets of water on her cheeks look like tears. I stroke her hair.

Hands brush down my chest. A zipper undone; her fingers softly caressing; the taste of her tongue; her breath inside my lungs . . .

Afterwards, as we lie in bed, I watch her breasts tremble with her heartbeat. It is the first time we've made love in six years without checking the calendar first.

The phone rings.

'Professor O'Loughlin?'

'Yes.'

'This is Charing Cross Hospital. I'm sorry to wake you.' The doctor sounds young; I can hear the tiredness in his voice. 'Do you have a patient named Bobby Moran?'

'Yes.'

'The police found him lying on the walkway across Hammersmith Bridge. He's asking for you.'

16

Julianne rolls over and nestles her face into my pillow, pulling the bedclothes around her.

'What's wrong?' she asks sleepily.

'Problem with a patient.' I pull a sweatshirt over my T-shirt and go looking for my jeans.

'You're not going in, are you?'

'Just for a little while.'

It takes me fifteen minutes to reach Fulham at that hour of the morning. Peering through the main doors of the hospital, I see a black cleaner pushing a mop and bucket around the floor in a strange waltz. A security guard sits at the reception desk. He motions me to the Accident & Emergency entrance.

Inside the plastic swinging doors, people are scattered around the waiting room, looking tired and pissed off. The triage nurse is busy. A young doctor appears in the corridor and begins arguing with a bearded man who has a bloody rag pressed to his forehead and a blanket around his shoulders.

'And you'll be waiting all night if you don't sit down,' says the doctor. He turns away and looks at me.

'I'm Professor O'Loughlin.'

It takes a moment for my name to register. The cogs slip into place. The doctor has a birthmark down one side of his neck and keeps the collar of his white coat turned up.

A few minutes later I follow this coat down empty corridors, past linen trolleys and parked stretchers.

'Is he OK?'

'Mainly cuts and bruises. He may have fallen from a car or a bike.'

'Has he been admitted?'

'No, but he won't leave until he sees you. He keeps talking about washing blood from his hands. That's why I put him in the observation room. I didn't want him upsetting the other patients.'

'Concussion?'

'No. He's very agitated. The police thought he might be a suicide risk.' The doctor turns to look over his shoulder. 'Is your father a surgeon?'

'Retired.'

'I once heard him speak. He's very impressive.'

'Yes. As a lecturer.'

The observation room has a small viewing window at head-height. I see Bobby sitting on a chair, his back straight and both feet on the floor. He's wearing muddy jeans, a flannelette shirt and an army greatcoat. He tugs at the sleeves of the coat, picking at a loose thread. His eyes are bloodshot and fixed. They are focused on the far wall, as if watching some invisible drama being played out on a stage that no one else can see. He doesn't turn as I enter.

'Bobby, it's me, Professor O'Loughlin. Do you know where you are?'

He nods.

'Can you tell me what happened?'

'I don't remember.'

'How are you feeling?'

He shrugs, still not looking at me. The wall is more interesting. I can smell his sweat and the mustiness of his clothes. There is another odour – something familiar but I can't quite place it. A medical smell.

'What were you doing on Hammersmith Bridge?'

'I don't know.' His voice is shaking. 'I fell over.'

'What can you remember?'

'Going to bed with Arky and then . . . Sometimes I can't bear to be by myself. Do you ever feel like that? It happens all the time to me. I pace around the house after Arky. I follow her, talking about myself constantly. I tell her what I'm thinking . . . '

At last his eyes focus on me. Haunted. Hollow. I have seen the look before. One of my other patients, a fireman, is condemned to listening to the screams of a five-year-old girl who died in a blazing car. He rescued her mother and baby brother but couldn't go back into the flames.

Bobby asks, 'Do you ever hear the windmills?'

'What sound do they make?'

'It's a clanking metal noise, but when the wind is really strong the blades blur and the air starts screaming in pain.' He shudders.

'What are the windmills for?'

'They keep everything running. If you put your ear to the ground you can hear them.'

'What do you mean by everything?'

'The lights, the factories, the railways. Without the windmills it all stops.'

'Are these windmills God?'

'You know nothing,' he says dismissively.

'Have you ever seen the windmills?'

'No. Like I said, I hear them.'

'Where do you think they are?'

'In the middle of the oceans; on huge platforms like oilrigs. They pull energy from the centre of the Earth – from the core. We're using too much energy. We're wasting it. That's why we have to turn off the lights and save power. Otherwise we'll upset the balance. Take too much out from the centre and you have a vacuum. The world will implode.'

'Why are we taking too much energy?'

'Turn off the lights, left, right, left, right. Do the right thing.' He salutes. 'I used to be right-handed but I taught myself to use my left . . . The pressure is building. I can feel it.'

'Where?'

He taps the side of his head. 'I've tapped the core. The apple core. Iron ore. Did you know the Earth's atmosphere is proportionately thinner than the skin of an apple?'

He is playing with rhymes – a characteristic of psychotic language. Simple puns and wordplay help connect random ideas.

'Sometimes I have dreams about being trapped inside a windmill,' he says. 'It's full of spinning cogs, flashing blades and hammers striking anvils. That's the music they play in hell.'

'Is that one of your nightmares?'

His voice drops to a conspiratorial whisper. 'Some of us know what's happening.'

'And what is that?'

He rears back, glaring at me. His eyes are alight. Then a peculiar half smile passes over his face. 'Do you know it took a manned spacecraft less time to reach the moon than it did for a stagecoach to travel the length of England?'

'No. I didn't know that.'

He sighs triumphantly.

'What were you doing on Hammersmith Bridge?'

'I was lying down, listening to the windmills.'

'When you came into the hospital, you kept saying that you wanted to wash the blood off your hands.'

He remembers, but says nothing.

'How did you get blood on your hands?'

'It's normal enough to hate. We just don't talk about it. It's normal enough to want to hurt people who hurt us . . . '

He's not making any sense.

'Did you hurt someone?'

'You take all those drops of hate and you put them in a bottle. Drop, drop, drop . . . Hate doesn't evaporate like other liquids. It's like oil. Then, one day, the bottle is full.'

'What happens then?'

'It has to be emptied.'

'Bobby, did you hurt someone?'

'How else do you get rid of the hate?' He tugs at the cuffs of his flannelette shirt, which are stained with something dark.

'Is that blood, Bobby?'

'No, it's oil. Haven't you been listening to me? It's all about the oil.' He stands and takes two steps towards the door. 'Can I go home now?'

'I think you should stay here for a while,' I say, trying to sound matter-of-fact.

He eyes me suspiciously. 'Why?'

'Last night you suffered some sort of breakdown, or memory lapse. You might have been in an accident or had a fall. I think we should run some tests and keep you under observation.'

'In a hospital?'

'Yes.'

'In a general ward?'

'A psych ward.'

He doesn't miss a beat. 'No fucking way! You're trying to lock me up.'

'You'll be a voluntary patient. You can leave any time you want to.'

'This is a trick! You think I'm crazy!' He's yelling at me. He wants to storm out but something is keeping him here. Maybe he has too much invested in me.

I can't legally hold him. Even if I had the evidence I don't

133

have the power to section or detain Bobby. Psychiatrists, medical doctors and the courts have such a prerogative but not a humble psychologist. Bobby's free to go.

'And you'll still see me?' he asks.

'Yes.'

He buttons his coat and nods his approval. I walk with him down the corridor and we share a lift. 'Have you ever had absences like this before?' I ask.

'What do mean "absences"?'

'Gaps in your memory where time seems to disappear.'

'It happened about a month ago.'

'Do you remember which day?'

He nods. 'The hate had to be emptied.'

The main doors of the hospital are open. On the front steps Bobby turns and thanks me. There is that smell again. I know what it is now. Chloroform.

17

Chloroform is a colourless liquid, half again as dense as water, with an ether-like odour and a taste forty times sweeter than sugar cane. It is an important organic solvent, mainly used in industry.

The Scottish physician Sir James Simpson of Edinburgh was the first to use it as an anaesthetic in 1847. Six years later, the English physician John Snow gave it to Queen Victoria during the birth of Prince Leopold, her eighth child.

A few drops on a mask or a cloth are usually enough to produce surgical anaesthesia within a few minutes. The patient awakens in 10–15 minutes, groggy but with very little nausea or vomiting. It is highly dangerous and causes fatal cardiac paralysis in about one in 3000 cases . . .

Closing the encyclopaedia, I slip it back on to a shelf and scribble a note to myself. Why would Bobby Moran have chloroform on his clothes? What possible use would he have for an industrial solvent or an anaesthetic? I seem to remember that chloroform is sometimes used in cough medicines and anti-itching creams, but the quantities aren't enough to create the unique odour.

Bobby said he worked as a courier. Maybe he delivers industrial solvents. I will ask him at our next session, if Major Tom is in touch with ground control by then.

I can hear banging coming from downstairs in the basement. D.J. and his apprentice are still working on the boiler. Apparently our entire internal plumbing system was put together by a maniac with a fetish for bending pipes. The insides of our walls look like a modern sculpture. God knows how much it's going to cost.

In the kitchen, having poured a coffee, I sit next to Charlie at the breakfast bar. She props her library book against a box of cereal. My morning paper is resting against the orange juice.

Charlie is playing a game – mimicking everything I do. When I take a bite of toast, she does the same. When I sip my coffee, she sips her tea. She even cocks her head the same way I do when I'm trying to read newsprint that has disappeared into the fold of the paper.

'Are you finished with the marmalade?' she asks, waving her hand in front of my face.

'Yes. Sorry.'

'You were away with the pixies.'

'They send their regards.'

Julianne emerges from the laundry, brushing a stray strand of hair from her forehead. The tumble dryer is rumbling in the background. We used to have breakfast together – drinking plunger coffee and swapping sections of the morning paper. Now she doesn't stop for long enough.

She packs the dishwasher and puts my pill in front of me.

'What happened at the hospital?'

'One of my patients had a fall. He's OK.'

She frowns. 'You were going to do fewer emergency calls.'

'I know. Just this once.'

She takes a bite from a quarter of toast and starts packing Charlie's lunchbox. I smell her perfume and notice that she's wearing new jeans and her best jacket.

136

'Where are you off to?'

'I have my seminar on "Understanding Islam". You promised to be home by four o'clock for Charlie.'

'I can't. I have an appointment.'

She's annoyed at me. 'Someone has to be here.'

'I can be home by five.'

'OK, I'll see if I can find a sitter.'

I call Ruiz from the office. In the background I can hear the sound of industrial equipment and running water. He's beside a river or a stream.

The moment I announce myself I hear a telltale electronic click. I contemplate whether he's recording our conversation.

'I wanted to ask you something about Catherine McBride.'

'Yeah?'

'How many stab wounds were there?'

'Twenty-one.'

'Did the pathologist find any traces of chloroform?'

'You read the report.'

'There wasn't any mention of it.'

'Why do you want to know?'

'It's probably not important.'

He sighs. 'Let's do a deal. Stop ringing me up asking bull-shit questions and I'll waive that unpaid parking fine of yours.'

Before I can apologise for troubling him, I hear someone calling his name. He grunts a thanks-for-nothing and hangs up. The man has the communication skills of a mortician.

Fenwick is lurking in my waiting room, glancing at his gold Rolex. We're going to lunch in Mayfair at his favourite restaurant. It is one of those places that gets written up in the Sunday supplements because the chef is temperamental, handsome and dates a supermodel. It is also a known hangout for celebrities, according to Fenwick, but they never seem to show up

137

for me. I did see Peter O'Toole in there once. Fenwick referred to him as 'Peter' and sounded very chummy.

Today Fenwick is trying extra hard to be affable. On the walk to the restaurant he asks after Julianne and Charlie. Then he runs through the entire menu out loud, commenting on each dish as though I can't read. When I choose mineral water instead of wine he looks disappointed. 'I've sworn off alcohol at lunchtime,' I explain.

'How antisocial.'

'Some of us work in the afternoon.'

The waiter arrives and Fenwick delivers precise instructions as to how he wants his meal prepared, right down to suggesting oven temperatures and whether the meat should be tenderised in advance. If the waiter has any sense he'll make sure these instructions never reach the kitchen.

'Didn't anyone ever tell you not to upset the person preparing your food?' I ask.

Fenwick looks at me quizzically.

'Forget it,' I say. 'You obviously didn't work your way through university.'

'I had an allowance, old boy.'

Typical!

Fenwick glances around, looking for any familiar faces. I'm never quite sure what these lunches are about. Usually, he's trying to convince me to invest in a property deal or a start-up biotech company. He has absolutely no concept of money or, more importantly, how little most people earn and the size of their mortgages.

Fenwick is probably the last person I would normally ask for advice, but he's here and the conversation has reached a lull.

'I have a hypothetical question for you,' I say, folding and unfolding my napkin. 'If you had a patient who you suspected might have committed a serious crime, what would you do?'

Fenwick looks alarmed. He glances over his shoulder as if

worried someone might have overheard. 'Do you have any evidence?' he whispers.

'Not really . . . more a gut instinct.'

'How serious a crime?'

'I don't know. Perhaps the most serious.'

Fenwick leans forward and cups a hand over his mouth. He couldn't be more conspicuous. 'You must tell the police, old boy.'

'What about doctor–patient confidentiality? It lies at the heart of everything I do. If patients don't trust me, I can't help them.'

'It doesn't apply. Remember the Tarasoff precedent.'

Tarasoff was a university student who murdered his ex-girlfriend in California in the late sixties. During a therapy session he told a psychologist that he planned to kill her. The murdered girl's parents sued the psychologist for negligence and won their case.

Fenwick is still talking, his nose twitching nervously. 'You have a duty to divulge confidential information if a client communicates a plausible intention to do serious harm to a third party.'

'Exactly, but what if he's made no threat against a specific person?'

'I don't think that matters.'

'Yes, it does. We have a duty to protect *intended* victims from harm, but only if the patient has communicated the threat of violence and actually identified someone.'

'You're splitting hairs.'

'No, I'm not.'

'So we leave a killer roaming the streets?'

'I don't know if he's a killer.'

'Shouldn't you let the police decide?'

Maybe Fenwick is right, but what if I'm jumping to the wrong conclusion? Confidentiality is an integral part of clinical psychology. If I reveal details of my sessions with Bobby without his consent, I'm breaking about a dozen regulations. I could end up being disciplined by my association or facing a lawsuit.

How confident am I that Bobby is dangerous? He attacked the woman in the cab. Other than that I have his psychotic ramblings about windmills and a girl in a dream.

Fenwick drains his wine and orders another glass. He is actually enjoying this cloak and dagger stuff. I get the impression that people don't regularly seek his advice.

Our food arrives and the conversation ebbs and flows over familiar territory. Fenwick tells me about his latest investments and holiday plans. I sense that he's building up to something but can't find an opening in the conversation that moves us smoothly on to the subject. Finally, over coffee, he plunges in.

'There's something I'd like to ask you, Joe. I'm not the sort of chap who usually asks for favours, but I have one to ask of you.'

My mind is automatically working out how to say no. I can't think of a solitary reason why Fenwick might need my help.

Weighed down by the gravity of the request, he starts the same sentence several times. Eventually he explains that he and Geraldine, his long-time girlfriend, have become engaged.

'Good for you! Congratulations!'

He raises his hand to interrupt me. 'Yes, well, we're getting married in June in West Sussex. Her father has an estate there. I wanted to ask you . . . well . . . what I wanted to say . . . I mean . . . I would be honoured if you would acquiesce to being my best man.'

For a brief moment I'm worried I might laugh. I barely know Fenwick. We have worked in adjacent offices for two years, but apart from these occasional lunches we have never socialised or shared a round of golf or a game of tennis. I vaguely remember meeting Geraldine at an office Christmas party. Until then I had harboured suspicions that Fenwick might be a bachelor dandy of the old school.

140

'Surely there must be someone else . . . '

'Well, yes, of course. I just thought . . . well, I just thought . . .' Fenwick is blinking rapidly, a picture of misery.

Then it dawns on me. For all his name-dropping, social climbing and overweening pride, Fenwick hasn't any friends. Why else would he choose me to be his best man?

'Of course,' I say. 'As long as you're sure . . .'

Fenwick is so excited I think he's going to embrace me. He reaches across the table and grasps my hand, shaking it furiously. His smile is so pitiful that I want to take him home as I might a stray dog.

On the walk back to the office he suggests all sorts of things we can do together, including arranging a stag night. 'We could use some of your vouchers from your lectures,' he says sheepishly.

I am suddenly reminded of a lesson I learned on my first day at boarding school, aged eight. The very first child to introduce himself will be the one with the fewest friends. Fenwick is *that* boy.

18

Elisa opens the door wearing a Thai silk robe. Light spills from behind her, outlining her body beneath the fabric. I try to concentrate on her face but my eyes betray me.

'Why are you so late? I thought you were coming hours ago.'

'Traffic.'

She sizes me up in the doorway, as if not quite sure whether to let me inside. Then she turns and I follow her down the hall, watching her hips slide beneath her robe.

Elisa lives in a converted printing factory in Ladbroke Grove, not far from the Grand Union Canal. Unpainted beams and timber joists crisscross each other in a sort of bonsai version of a Tudor cottage.

The place is full of old rugs and antique furniture that she had sent down from Yorkshire when her mother died. Her pride and joy is an Elizabethan love seat with elaborately carved arms and legs. A dozen china dolls, with delicately painted faces, sit demurely on the seat as if waiting for someone to ask them to dance.

She pours me a drink and settles on to the sofa, patting a spot beside her. She notices me pause and pulls a face. 'I thought

142

something was wrong. Usually I get a kiss on the cheek.'

'I'm sorry.'

She laughs and crosses her legs. I feel something shred inside me.

'Christ, you look tense. What you need is a massage.'

She pulls me down and slides behind me, driving her fingers into the knotted muscles between my shoulder blades. Her legs are stretched out around me and I can feel the soft crinkle of her pubic hair against the small of my back.

'I shouldn't have come.'

'Why did you?'

'I wanted to apologise. It was my fault. I started something that I shouldn't have started.'

'OK.'

'You don't mind?'

'You were a good fuck.'

'I don't want you to see it like that.'

'What was it then?'

I contemplate this for a moment. 'We had a brief encounter.'

She laughs. 'It wasn't that *fucking* romantic.'

My toes curl in embarrassment.

'So what happened?' she asks.

'I don't think it was fair on you.'

'Or your wife?'

'Yes.'

'You never told me why you were so upset that night.'

I shrug. 'I was just thinking about life and things.'

'Life?'

'And death.'

'Jesus, not another one.'

'What do you mean?'

'A married guy who reaches his forties and suddenly starts pondering what it all means? I used to get them all the time. Talkers! I should have charged them double. I'd be a rich woman.'

143

'It's not like that.'

'Well, what is it?'

'What if I told you I had an incurable disease?'

She stops massaging my neck and turns me to face her. 'Is that what you're saying?'

Suddenly I change my mind. 'No. I'm being stupid.'

Elisa is annoyed now. She thinks she's being manipulated. 'You know what your problem is?'

'What's that?'

'All your life you've been a protected species. Somebody has always looked after you. First it was your mother, then boarding school, then university, and then you got married.'

'And your point is?'

'It's been too easy. Nothing bad has ever happened to you. Bad stuff happens to other people and you pick up the pieces, but *you've* never fallen apart. Do you remember the second time we ever met?'

I nod.

'Do you remember what you told me?'

Now I'm struggling. It was in Holloway Prison. Elisa had been charged with malicious wounding after she stabbed two teenage boys with a flick knife. She was twenty-three years old and by then had graduated to working for an escort agency in Kensington, being flown all over Europe and the Middle East.

One night she was called out to a hotel in Knightsbridge. She didn't know the client. As soon as she walked into the room she sensed something was wrong. Normally her clients tended to be middle-aged. This one was a teenager. There were a dozen empty beer bottles on the coffee table.

Before she could react, the bathroom door opened and six youths emerged. One of them was having an eighteenth birthday party.

'I'm not fucking all of you.'

They laughed.

144

After the first rape she stopped fighting. She pleaded with them to let her go and at the same time concentrated on reaching her coat pocket, stretching her hand out along the bed, moving it just a fraction at a time. The boys took her two at a time. The rest waited their turn – watching Manchester United play Chelsea on *Match of the Day*.

Elisa struggled to breathe. Snot ran from her nose, mingling with tears. She finally reached her coat and in the pocket her fingers closed around the knife.

Ryan Giggs had picked up the ball near the halfway line and made a run down the left . . . Hands gripped the back of Elisa's bobbing head. Steve Clarke was trying to force Giggs to go wider, but he cut inside and then out again . . . A belt buckle dug into her chest and her forehead slapped against a stomach . . . Mark Hughes made a run to the near post, drawing the two central defenders. Giggs floated in the cross. Cantona struck the volley first time. The net bulged. So did Elisa's cheeks.

Pulling her mouth free, she whispered, 'It's *over.*'

She drove the knife into the buttocks of the boy in front of her. His scream filled the room. Then she spun and stabbed the boy behind her in the thigh.

As he reared backwards, she rolled away, grabbed the neck of a beer bottle and smashed it across the corner of the bedside table. With the knife in one hand and the jagged bottle in the other, she faced them across the bed.

The blade was only two inches long so none of the wounds were deep. Elisa phoned the police from the hotel lobby. She worked out the odds and realised she had no other option. Then she went through the motions of giving a statement. The boys each had a lawyer present as they were interviewed. Their stories were identical.

Elisa was charged with malicious wounding while the youths were given a stern talking to by the station sergeant. Six young men – with money, privilege and a walk-up start in life – had raped her with absolute impunity.

While on remand in Holloway Prison she asked for me by name. Although older, she seemed just as fragile. She sat on a plastic chair with her head cocked to one side and her hair falling over one eye. Her chipped tooth had been fixed.

'Do you think that we determine how things turn out in our lives?' she asked me.

'Up to a point.'

'And when does that point end?'

'When something happens that we have no control over: a drunk driver runs a stop sign, or the lotto balls drop in the right order, or rogue cancer cells begin dividing inside us.'

'So we only have a say over the *little* things?'

'If we're lucky. You take the Greek playwright Aeschylus. He died when an eagle mistook his bald head for a rock and dropped a tortoise on it. I don't think he saw that coming.'

She laughed. A month later she pleaded guilty and was sentenced to two years in jail. She worked in the prison laundry. Whenever she became angry or bitter about what had happened, she opened a dryer door, put her head inside and screamed into the big warm silver drum, letting the sound explode into her head.

Is that what Elisa wants me to remember – my own pithy homily on why shit happens? She slips off the sofa and pads across the room, looking for her cigarettes.

'So you came here to tell me that we're not going to fuck any more.'

'Yes.'

'Did you want to tell me before or after we go to bed?'

'I'm being serious.'

'I know you are. I'm sorry.'

She lets the cigarette hang from her lips as she re-ties the sash of her robe. For a brief moment I glimpse a small, taut nipple. I can't tell if she's angry or disappointed. Maybe she doesn't care.

146

'Will you read my Home Office submission when I'm finished?' she asks.

'Of course.'

'And if I need you to give another talk?'

'I'll be there.'

She kisses my cheek as I leave. I don't want to go. I like this house with its faded rugs, porcelain dolls, tiny fireplace and four-poster bed. Yet already I seem to be disappearing.

My home is in darkness, except for a light downstairs leaking through the curtains of the sitting room. Inside the air is warm. The fire has been burning in the front room. I can smell the smokeless coal.

The last of the red embers are glowing in the grate. As I reach for the lamp switch my left hand trembles. I see the silhouette of a head and shoulders in the armchair by the window. Forearms are braced along the wide arms of the chair. Black shoes are flat on the polished wooden floor.

'We need to talk.' Ruiz doesn't bother to stand.

'How did you get in here?'

'Your wife said I could wait.'

'What can I do for you?'

'You can stop pissing me about.' He leans forward into the light. His face looks ashen and his voice is tired. 'I asked the pathologist about chloroform. They didn't look the first time. When someone has been stabbed that many times, you don't bother looking for much else.' He turns to stare at the fireplace. 'How did you know?'

'I can't tell you.'

'That's not the answer I want to hear.'

'It was a long shot . . . a supposition.'

'Suppose you tell me why?'

'I can't do that.'

He's angry now. His features are chiselled instead of worn down. 'I'm an old-fashioned detective, Professor O'Loughlin.

147

I went to a local comprehensive and straight into the force. I didn't go to university and I don't read many books. You take computers. I know bugger all about them but I appreciate how useful they can be. The same is true of psychologists.'

His voice grows quiet. 'Whenever I'm involved in an investigation, people are always telling me that I can't do things. They tell me I can't spend too much money, that I can't tap particular phones or search particular houses. There are thousands of things I *cannot* do – all of which pisses me off.

'I've warned you twice already. You deny me information that is relevant to my murder inquiry and I'll bring all of this,' he motions to the room, the house, my life, 'crashing down around your ears.'

I can't think of a sympathetic response to disarm him. What can I tell him? I have a patient called Bobby Moran who may, or may not, be a borderline schizophrenic. He kicked a woman unconscious because she looked like his mother – a woman he wants dead. He makes lists. He listens to windmills. His clothes smell of chloroform. He carries around a piece of paper with the number '21' written on it hundreds of times – the same number of stab wounds that Catherine McBride inflicted on herself . . .

What if I say all this – he'll probably laugh at me. There is nothing concrete linking Bobby to Catherine, yet I'll be responsible for a dozen detectives hammering on Bobby's door, searching through his past, terrifying his fiancée and her son.

Bobby will know I've sent them. He won't trust me again. He won't trust anyone like me. His suspicions will be vindicated. He reached out for help and I betrayed him.

I know he's dangerous. I know his fantasies are taking him somewhere terrible. But unless he keeps coming back to me I might never be able to stop him.

Bitterness and rancour hang in the air like the smell of smokeless coal. Ruiz is putting on his coat and walking towards the front door. My left arm is trembling. It's now or never. Make a decision.

'When you searched Catherine's flat – did she have a red dress?'

Ruiz reacts as though struck. He spins and takes a step towards me. 'How did you know that?'

'Is the dress missing?'

'Yes.'

'Do you think she might have been wearing it when she disappeared?'

'Possibly.'

He is framed in the open doorway. His eyes are bloodshot but his stare fixed. Fingers open and close into fists. He wants to rip me apart.

'Come to my office tomorrow afternoon. There's a file. You can't take it away. I don't even know if it will help, but I have to show it to someone.'

19

The blue manila folder is on the desk in front of me. It has a ribbon that twists around a flat circular wheel to seal it shut. I keep undoing it and doing it up again.

Meena glances nervously behind her as she enters the office. She walks all the way across to my desk before whispering, 'There is a very scary-looking man in the waiting room. He's asking for you.'

'That's OK, Meena. He's a detective.'

Her eyes widen in surprise. 'Oh! He didn't say. He just sort of—'

'Growled?'

'Yes.'

'You can show him in.' I motion her closer. 'In about five minutes, I want you to buzz me and remind me of an important meeting outside the office.'

'What meeting?'

'Just an important meeting.'

She frowns at me and nods.

With a face like an anvil, Ruiz ignores my outstretched hand and leaves it hanging in the air as though I'm directing traffic.

He sits down and leans back in the chair, spreading his legs and letting his coat flare out.

'So this is where you work, Prof? Very nice.' He glances around the room in what appears to be a cursory way, but I know he's taking in the details. 'How much does it cost to rent an office like this?'

'I don't know. I'm just one of the partners.'

Ruiz scratches his chin and then fumbles in his coat pocket for a stick of chewing gum. He unwraps it slowly.

'What exactly does a psychologist *do*?'

'We help people who are damaged by events in their lives. People with personality disorders, or sexual problems, or phobias.'

'Do you know what I think? A man gets attacked and he's lying bleeding on the road. Two psychologists pass by and one says to the other, "Let's go and find the person who did this – he needs help."'

His smile doesn't reach his eyes.

'I help more victims than I do perpetrators.'

Ruiz shrugs and tosses the gum wrapper into the bin. 'Start talking. How did you know about the red dress?'

I glance down at the file and undo the ribbon. 'In a few minutes from now, I'm going to get a phone call. I will have to leave the office, but you are quite welcome to stay. I think you'll find my chair is more comfortable than yours.' I open Bobby's file.

'When you're finished, if you wish to talk about anything I'll be over the road having a drink. I can't talk about any specific patient or case.' I tap Bobby's folder to stress the point. 'I can only talk in general terms about personality disorders and how psychotics and psychopaths function. It will be much easier if you remember this.'

Ruiz presses the palms of his hands together as if in prayer and taps his forefingers against his lips. 'I don't like playing games.'

151

'This isn't a game. We do it this way, or I can't help you.'

The phone rings. Meena starts her spiel but doesn't finish. I'm already on my way.

The sun is shining and the sky is blue. It feels more like May than mid-December. London does this occasionally – puts on a glorious day to remind people that it isn't such a bad place to live.

This is why the English are among the world's greatest optimists. We get one magnificent hot dry week and the memory will give us succour for an entire summer. It happens every time. Come spring we buy shorts, T-shirts, bikinis and sarongs in glorious expectation of a season that never arrives.

Ruiz finds me standing at the bar nursing a mineral water.

'It's your round,' he says. 'I'll have a pint of bitter.'

The place is busy with a lunchtime crowd. Ruiz wanders over to four men sitting in the corner by the front window. They look like office boys, but are wearing well-cut suits and silk ties.

Ruiz flashes his police badge under the level of the table.

'Sorry to trouble you, gents, but I need to commandeer this table for a surveillance operation on that bank over there.'

He motions out the window and they all turn in unison to look.

'Try to make it a little less obvious!'

They quickly turn back.

'We have reason to believe it is being targeted for an armed hold-up. You see that guy on the corner, wearing the orange vest?'

'The street sweeper?' one of them asks.

'Yeah. Well, he's one of my best. So is the shopgirl in that lingerie shop, next door to the bank. I need this table.'

'Of course.'

'Absolutely.'

'Is there anything else we can do?'

I see a twinkle in Ruiz's eye. 'Well, I don't normally do this

152

– use civilians undercover – but I am short of manpower. You could split up and take a corner each. Try to blend in. Look for a group of men travelling four-up in a car.'

'How do we contact you?'

'You tell the street sweeper.'

'Is there some sort of password?' one of them asks.

Ruiz rolls his eyes. 'It's a police operation, not a fucking Bond movie.'

Once they've gone, he takes the chair nearest the window and sets his glass on a coaster. I sit opposite him and leave my glass untouched.

'They would have given you the table anyway,' I say, unable to decide if he likes practical jokes or dislikes people.

'Did this Bobby Moran kill Catherine McBride?' He wipes foam from his top lip with the back of his hand.

The question has all the subtlety of a well-thrown brick.

'I can't talk about individual patients.'

'Did he admit to killing her?'

'I can't talk about what he may or may not have told me.'

Ruiz's eyes disappear into a narrow maze of wrinkles and his body tenses. Just as suddenly he exhales and gives me what I suspect is a smile. He's out of practice.

'Tell me about the man who killed Catherine McBride?'

The message seems to have reached him. Pushing Bobby out of my head, I try to reflect on Catherine's killer, based on what I know of the crime. I've had a week of sleepless nights thinking of little else.

'You are dealing with a sexual psychopath,' I begin, unable to recognise my own voice. 'Catherine's murder was a manifestation of corrupt lust.'

'But there were no signs of sexual assault.'

'You can't think in terms of normal rape or sex crime. This is a far more extreme example of deviant sexuality. This man is consumed by a desire to dominate and inflict pain. He fantasises about taking, restraining, dominating, torturing and killing. At least some of these fantasies will mirror almost exactly what happened.

'Think about what he did to her. He took her off the street or enticed her to go with him. He didn't seek a quick and violent sexual coupling in a dark alley and then silence his victim so she couldn't identify him. Instead he aimed to break her – to systematically destroy her willpower until she became a compliant, terrified plaything. Even that wasn't enough for him. He wanted the ultimate in control; to bend someone so completely to *his* will that she would torture herself . . . '

I'm watching Ruiz – waiting to lose him. 'He almost succeeded, but in the end Catherine wasn't entirely broken. She still had a spark of defiance left. She was a nurse. Even with a short blade she knew where to cut if she wanted to die quickly. When she could take no more she cut the carotid artery in her neck. That's what caused the embolism. She was dead within minutes.'

'How do you know that?'

'Three years at medical school.'

Ruiz is staring at his pint glass, as though checking to see if it is centred properly on the coaster. The chimes of a church bell are ringing in the distance.

I continue: 'The man you're looking for is lonely, socially inept and sexually immature.'

'Sounds like your basic teenager.'

'No. He isn't a teenager. He's older. A lot of young men start out like this, but every so often one emerges who blames someone else for his loneliness and his sexual frustration. This bitterness and anger grow with each rejection. Sometimes he'll blame a particular person. Other times he will hate an entire group of people.'

'He hates all women.'

'Possibly, but I think it's more likely he hates a particular sort of woman. He wants to punish her. He fantasises about it and it gives him pleasure.'

154

'Why did he choose Catherine McBride?'

'I don't know. Perhaps she looked like someone he wanted to punish. He may have been driven by opportunity. Catherine was available so he changed his fantasy to incorporate her looks and the clothes she wore.'

'The red dress.'

'Perhaps.'

'Could he have known her?'

'Quite possibly.'

'Motivation?'

'Revenge. Control. Sexual gratification.'

'I take my pick?'

'No, it's all three.'

Ruiz stiffens slightly. Clearing his throat, he takes out his marbled notebook. 'So who am I looking for?'

'Someone in his thirties or forties. He lives alone, somewhere private, but surrounded by people who come and go – a boarding house, perhaps, or a caravan park.

'He may have a wife or a girlfriend. He is of above average intelligence. He is physically strong, but mentally even stronger. He hasn't been consumed by sexual desire or anger to the point of losing control. He can keep his emotions in check. He is forensically aware. He doesn't want to be caught.

'This is someone who has managed to successfully separate areas of his life and isolate them completely from each other. His friends, family and colleagues have no inkling of what goes on inside his head.

'I think he has sadomasochistic interests. It's not the sort of thing that springs out of nowhere. Someone must have introduced him to it – although probably only a mild version. His mind has taken it to a level that far outstrips any harmless fun. His self-assurance is what amazes me. There were no signs of anxiety or first-time nerves . . . '

I stop talking. My mouth has gone slack and sour. I take a sip of water. Ruiz is gazing at me dully, sitting up straighter and occasionally writing notes. My voice rises above the noise again.

'A person doesn't suddenly become a fully fledged sadist overnight – not one this skilful. Organisations like the KGB spend years training their interrogators to be this good. The degree of control and sophistication was remarkable. These things come from experience. I don't think he started here.'

Ruiz turns and stares out of the window, making up his mind. He doesn't believe me. 'This is bullshit!'

'Why?'

'None of it sounds like your Bobby Moran.'

He's right. It doesn't make sense. Bobby is too young to have this degree of familiarity with sadism. He is too erratic and changeable. I seriously doubt that he has the mental skills and malevolence to dominate and control a person like Catherine so completely. The physical size, yes; but not the psychological strength. Then again, Bobby has constantly surprised me and I have only scratched the surface of his psyche. He has held details back from me or dropped them like a trail of bread-crumbs on a fairytale journey.

Fairytales? That's what it sounds like to Ruiz. He's on his feet and threading his way to the bar. People hurriedly step out of his way. He has an aura like a flashing light that warns people to give him space.

I'm already beginning to regret this. I should have stayed out of it. Sometimes I wish I could turn my mind off instead of always looking and analysing. I wish I could just focus on a tiny square of the world, instead of watching how people commu-nicate and the clothes they wear; what they put in their shop-ping trolleys; the cars they drive; the pets they choose; the magazines they read and the TV shows they watch. I wish I could stop looking.

Ruiz is back again with another pint and a whisky chaser. He rolls the liquid fire around in his mouth as if washing away a bad taste. 'You really think this guy did it?'

'I don't know.'

156

He wraps his fingers around the pint glass and leans back. 'You want me to look at him?'

'That's up to you.'

Ruiz exhales with a rustle of dissatisfaction. He still doesn't trust me.

'Do you know why Catherine came down to London?' I ask.

'According to her flatmate, she had a job interview. We found no correspondence – she probably had it with her.'

'What about phone records?'

'Nothing from her home number. She had a mobile, but that's missing.'

He delivers the facts without comment or embellishment. Catherine's history matches with the scant details she gave me during our sessions. Her parents had divorced when she was twelve. She hooked up with a bad crowd, sniffing aerosols and doing drugs. At fifteen she spent six weeks in a private psychiatric hospital in West Sussex. Her family kept it quiet for obvious reasons. Becoming a nurse had seemed to be the turning point. Although she still had problems, she managed to cope.

'What happened after she left the Marsden?' I ask.

'She moved back to Liverpool and got engaged to a merchant seaman. It didn't work out.'

'Is he a suspect?'

'No. He's in Bahrain.'

'Any other suspects?'

Ruiz raises an eyebrow. 'All volunteers are welcome.' He smiles wryly and polishes off his drink. 'I have to go.'

'What happens next?'

'I get my people digging up everything they can on this Bobby Moran. If I can link him to Catherine, I'll ask him very politely to help me with my inquiries.'

'And you won't mention my name?'

Ruiz looks at me contemptuously. 'Don't worry, Professor, your interests are paramount in my concerns.'

20

My mother has a pretty face, with a neat upturned nose and straight hair that she has worn in the same uniform style – pinned back with silver clips and tucked behind her ears – for as long as I can remember. Sadly, I inherited my father's tangle of hair. If it grows half an inch too long it becomes completely unruly and I look like I've been electrocuted.

Everything about my mother denotes her standing as a doctor's wife, right down to her box-pleated skirts, unpatterned blouses and low-heeled shoes. A creature of habit, she even carries a handbag when taking the dog for a walk.

She can arrange a dinner party for twelve in the time it takes to boil an egg. She also does garden parties, school fêtes, church jamborees, charity fundraisers, bridge tournaments, car boot sales, walkathons, christenings, weddings and funerals. Yet for all this ability, she has managed to get through life without balancing a chequebook, making an investment decision or proffering a political opinion in public. She leaves such matters to my father.

Every time I contemplate my mother's life, I am appalled by the waste and unfulfilled promise. At eighteen she won a mathematics scholarship to Cardiff University. At twenty-five she wrote a thesis that had American universities hammering at her door. What did she do? She married my father and settled for a life of cultivating convention and making endless compromises.

I like to imagine her doing a 'Shirley Valentine' and running off with a Greek waiter, or writing a steamy romantic novel. One day she is suddenly going to toss aside her prudence, self-discipline and correctness. She will go dancing barefoot in daisy fields and trekking through the Himalayas. These are nice thoughts. They're certainly better than imagining her growing old listening to my father rant at the TV screen or read aloud the letters he's written to newspapers.

That's what he's doing now – writing a letter. He only reads the *Guardian* when he stays with us, but 'that red rag', as he refers to it, gives him enough material for at least a dozen letters.

My mother is in the kitchen with Julianne, discussing tomorrow's menu. At some stage in the previous twenty-four hours it was decided to make Sunday lunch a family get-together. Two of my sisters are coming, with their husbands and solemn children. Only Rebecca will escape. She's in Bosnia working for the UN. Bless her.

My Saturday morning chores now involve moving a ton of plumbing equipment from the front hallway to the basement. Then I have to rake the leaves, oil the swing and get two more bags of coal from the local garage. Julianne is going to shop for the food, while Charlie and her grandparents go to look at the Christmas lights in Oxford Street.

My other chore is to buy a tree – a thankless task. The only truly well proportioned Christmas trees are the ones they use in advertisements. If you try to find one in real life you face inevitable disappointment. Your tree will lean to the left or the right. It will be too bushy at the base, or straggly at the top. It will have bald patches, or the branches on either side

159

will be oddly spaced. Even if you do, by some miracle, find a perfect tree, it won't fit in the car and by the time you strap it to the roof rack and drive home the branches are broken or twisted out of shape. You wrestle it through the door, gagging on pine needles and sweating profusely, only to hear the maddening question that resonates down from countless Christmases past: 'Is that really the best one you could find?'

Charlie's cheeks are pink with the cold and her arms are draped in polished paper bags full of new clothes and a pair of shoes.

'I got heels, Dad. Heels!'

'How high?'

'Only this much.' She holds her thumb and forefinger apart.

'I thought you were a tomboy,' I tease.

'They're not pink,' she says sternly. 'And I didn't get any dresses.'

God's personal physician-in-waiting is pouring himself a Scotch and getting annoyed because my mother is chatting to Julianne instead of bringing him some ice. Charlie is excitedly opening bags. Then she suddenly stops. 'The tree! It's lovely.'

'So it should be. It took me three hours to find.'

I have to stop myself telling her the whole story about my friend from the Greek deli in Chalk Farm Road, who told me about a guy who supplies trees to 'half of London' from the back of a three-ton truck.

The whole enterprise sounded pretty dodgy but for once I didn't care. I wanted to get a flawless specimen and that's what it is – a pyramid of pine-scented perfection with a straight trunk and evenly spaced branches.

Since getting home I have been wandering back and forth to the sitting room, marvelling at the tree. Julianne is getting slightly fed up with me saying, 'Isn't that a great tree?' and expecting a response.

God's personal physician-in-waiting is telling me his solution to traffic congestion in central London. I'm waiting for him to comment on the tree. I don't want to prompt him. He's talking about banning all delivery trucks in the West End except in designated hours. Then he starts complaining about shoppers who walk too slowly and suggests a fast and slow lane system.

'I found a tree today,' I interject, unable to wait. He stops abruptly and looks over his shoulder. He stands and examines it more closely, walking from side to side. Then he stands back to best appreciate the overall symmetry.

Clearing his throat, he asks, 'Is it the best one they had?'

'No! They had dozens of better ones! Hundreds! This was one of the worst; the absolute pits; the bottom of the barrel. I felt sorry for it. That's why I brought it home. I adopted a lousy Christmas tree.'

He looks surprised. 'It isn't *that* bad.'

'You're fucking unbelievable,' I mutter under my breath, unable to stay in the same room. Why do our parents have the ability to make us feel like children even when our hair is greying and we have a mortgage that feels like a Third World debt?

I retreat to the kitchen and make myself a gin and tonic, with an extra large slurp of gin that spills over the counter. My father has only been here for ten hours and already I'm hitting the bottle. At least reinforcements arrive tomorrow.

I was always running in my childhood nightmares – trying to escape a monster or a rabid dog or perhaps a Neanderthal second-rower forward with no front teeth and cauliflower ears. I would wake just before getting caught. It didn't make me feel any safer. That is the problem with nightmares. Nothing is resolved. We rouse ourselves in mid-air or just before the bomb goes off or stark naked in a public place.

I have been lying in the dark for five hours. Every time I think nice thoughts and begin drifting off to sleep, I jump

161

awake in a panic. It's like watching a trashy horror movie that is laughably bad, but just occasionally there is a scene that frightens the bejesus out of you.

Mostly I'm trying not to think about Bobby Moran, because when I do it leads me to Catherine McBride and that's a place I don't want to go. I wonder if Bobby is in custody, or if they're watching him. I have this picture in my head of a van with blacked out windows parked outside his place.

People can't really sense when they're being watched – not without some clue or recognising something untoward. However, Bobby doesn't operate on the same wavelength as most people. He picks up different signals. A psychotic can believe the TV is talking to him and will question why workmen are repairing phone lines over the road, or why there's a van with blacked out windows parked outside.

Maybe none of this is happening. With all the new technology, perhaps Ruiz can find everything he needs by simply typing Bobby's name into a computer and accessing the private files that every conspiracy theorist is convinced the government keeps on the nation's citizens.

'Don't think about it. Just go to sleep,' Julianne whispers. She can sense when I'm worried about something. I haven't had a proper night's sleep since Charlie was born. You get out of the habit after a while. Now I have these pills which are making things worse.

Julianne is lying on her side, with the sheet tucked between her thighs and one hand resting on the pillow next to her face. Charlie does the same thing when she's sleeping. They barely make a sound or stir at all. It's as though they don't want to leave a footprint in their dreams.

On Sunday morning the house is full of cooking smells and feminine chatter. I'm expected to set the fire and sweep the front steps. Instead, I sneak to the newsagents and collect the morning papers.

162

Back in my study, I set aside the supplements and magazines and begin looking for stories on Catherine. I'm just about to sit down when I notice one of Charlie's bug-eyed goldfish is floating upside down in the aquarium. For a moment I think it might be some sort of neat goldfish trick, but on closer inspection it doesn't look too hale and hearty. It has grey speckles on its scales – evidence of an exotic fish fungus.

Charlie doesn't take death very well. Middle-eastern kingdoms have shorter periods of mourning. Scooping up the fish in my hand, I stare at the poor creature. I wonder if she'll believe it just disappeared. She *is* only eight. Then again, she doesn't believe in Santa or the Easter Bunny any more. How could I have bred such a cynic?

'Charlie, I have some bad news. One of your goldfish has disappeared.'

'How could it just disappear?'

'Well, actually it died. I'm sorry.'

'Where is it?'

'You don't really want to see it, do you?'

'Yes.'

The fish is still in my hand, which is in my pocket. When I open my palm it seems more like a magic trick than a solemn deed.

Being very organised, Julianne has a whole collection of shoeboxes and drawstring bags that she keeps for this sort of death in the family. With Charlie looking on, I bury the bug-eyed goldfish under the plum tree, between the late Harold Hamster, a mouse known only as 'Mouse' and a baby sparrow that flew into the French doors and broke its neck.

By midday most of the family has assembled, except for my eldest sister Lucy and her husband Eric, who have three children whose names I can never remember, but I know they end with an 'ee' sound like Debbie, Jimmy or Bobby. God's personal physician-in-waiting had wanted Lucy to name her eldest boy after him. He liked the idea of a third generation 'Joseph'. Lucy held firm and called him something else – Andy, maybe, or Gary, or Freddy.

They're always late. Eric is an air-traffic controller and the most absent-minded person I have ever met. It's frightening. He keeps forgetting where we live and has to phone up and ask for directions every time he visits. How on earth does he keep dozens of planes apart in the air? Every time I book a flight out of Heathrow I feel like ringing up Lucy in advance and asking whether Eric is working.

My middle sister Patricia is in the kitchen with her new man, Simon, a criminal lawyer who works for one of those TV series that exposes miscarriages of justice. Patricia's divorce has come through and she's celebrating with champagne.

'I hardly think it warrants Bollinger,' says my father.

'Why ever not?' she says, taking a quick slurp before it bubbles over.

I decide to rescue Simon. Nobody deserves this sort of introduction to our family. We take our drinks into the sitting room and make small talk. Simon has a jolly round face and keeps slapping his stomach like a department store Santa.

'Sorry to hear about the old Parkinson's,' he says. 'Terrible business.'

My heart sinks. 'Who told you?'

'Patricia.'

'How did she know?'

Suddenly realising his mistake, Simon starts apologising. There have been some depressing moments in the past month, but none quite so depressing as standing in front of a complete stranger who is drinking my Scotch and feeling sorry for me.

Who else knows?

The doorbell rings. Eric, Lucy and the 'ee' children come bustling in, with lots of vigorous handshakes and cheek kisses. Lucy takes one look at me and her bottom lip starts to tremble.

164

She throws her arms around me and I feel her body shaking against my chest.

'I'm really sorry, Joe. So, so sorry.'

My chin is resting on the top of her head. Eric puts his outstretched hand on my shoulder as if giving me a Papal blessing. I don't think I have ever been so embarrassed.

The rest of the afternoon stretches out before me like a four-hour sociology lecture. When I get tired of answering questions about my health, I retreat to the garden where Charlie is playing with the 'ee' children. She is showing them where we buried the goldfish. I finally remember their names, Harry, Perry and Jenny.

Harry is only a toddler and looks like a miniature Michelin man in his padded jacket and woollen hat. I toss him in the air, making him giggle. The other children are grabbing my legs, pretending I'm a monster. I spy Julianne looking wistfully out the French doors. I know what she's thinking.

After lunch we retire to the sitting room and everyone says nice things about the tree and my mother's fruitcake.

'Let's play "Who Am I?"' says Charlie, whose mouth is speckled with crumbs. She doesn't hear the collective groan. Instead, she hands out pens and paper, while breathlessly explaining the rules.

'You all have to think of someone famous. They don't have to be real. It can be a cartoon character, or a movie star. It could even be Lassie . . . '

'That's my choice gone.'

She scowls at me. 'Don't let anyone see the name you write. Then you stick the paper on someone else's forehead. They have to guess who they are.'

The game turns out to be a scream. God's personal physician-in-waiting can't understand why everybody laughs so uproariously at the name on his forehead: 'Grumpy' from *Snow White and the Seven Dwarfs*.

I'm actually starting to enjoy myself when the doorbell rings and Charlie dashes out to answer it. Lucy and Patricia start clearing the cups and plates.

'You don't look like a policeman,' says Charlie.

'I'm a detective.'

'Does that mean you have a badge?'

'Do you want to see it?'

'Maybe I should.'

Ruiz is reaching into his inside jacket pocket when I rescue him.

'We've taught her to be careful,' I say apologetically.

'That's very wise.' He smiles at Charlie and looks fifteen years younger. For a brief moment I think he might ruffle her hair, but people don't do that so much nowadays.

Ruiz looks past me into the hall and apologises for disturbing me.

'Is there something I can do for you?'

'Yes,' he mumbles, and then pats at his pockets as though he's written a note to remind himself.

'Would you like to come in?'

'If that's OK.'

I lead him to my study and offer to take his coat. Catherine's notes are still open on my desk where I left them.

'Doing a little homework?'

'I just wanted to make sure I hadn't forgotten anything.'

'And had you?'

'No.'

'You could let me be the judge of that.'

'Not this time.' I close the notebooks and put them away.

Walking around my desk, he glances at my bookcases, studying the various photographs and my souvenir water pipe from Syria.

'Where has he been?'

'I beg your pardon?'

'You said that my murderer didn't start with Catherine, so where has he been?'

166

'Practising.'

'On whom?'

'I don't know.'

Ruiz is now at the window, looking across the garden. He rolls his shoulders and the starched collar of his shirt presses under his ears. I want to ask him what he's learned about Bobby but he interrupts me. 'Is he going to kill again?'

I don't want to answer. Hypothetical situations are perilous. He senses me pulling back and won't let me escape. I have to say *something*.

'At the moment he is still thinking about Catherine and how she died. When those memories begin to fade, he may go looking for new experiences to feed his fantasies.'

'How can you be so sure?'

'His actions were relaxed and deliberate. He wasn't out of control or consumed by anger or desire. He was calm, considered, almost euphoric in his planning.'

'Where are these other victims? Why haven't we found them?'

'Maybe you haven't established a link.'

Ruiz flinches and squares his shoulders. He resents the inference that he's missed something important. At the same time he's not going to jeopardise the investigation because of overweening pride. He *wants* to understand.

'You're looking for clues in the method and symbolism, but these can only come from comparing crimes. Find another victim and you may find a pattern.'

Ruiz grinds his teeth as though wearing them down. What else can I give him?

'He knows the area. It took time to bury Catherine. He knew there were no houses overlooking that part of the canal. And he knew what time of night the towpath was deserted.'

'So he lives locally.'

'Or used to.'

Ruiz is seeing how the facts support the theory, trying them

167

on for size, People are moving downstairs. A toilet flushes. A child cries in anger.

'But why would he choose such a public place? He could have hidden her in the middle of nowhere.'

'He wasn't hiding her. He *let* you have Catherine.'

'Why?'

'Maybe he's proud of his handiwork, or he's giving you a sneak preview.'

Ruiz grimaces. 'I don't know how you do your job. How can you walk around knowing sick fucks like that are on the loose? How can you live inside their heads?' His crosses his arms and jams his hands under his armpits. 'Then again, maybe you enjoy that sort of shit.'

'What do you mean?'

'You tell me. Is it a game for you, playing detective? Showing me one patient's file and not another's. Phoning up and asking me questions. Are you enjoying this?'

'I . . . I didn't ask to be brought into this.'

He enjoys my anger. In the silence I hear laughter downstairs.

'I think you had better leave.'

He regards me with satisfaction and physical superiority, before taking his coat and descending the stairs. Exhausted, I can visualise my energy draining away.

At the front door, Ruiz turns down the collar of his jacket and looks back at me. 'In the hunt, Professor, there are foxes and there are hounds and there are hunt saboteurs. Which one are you?'

'I don't believe in fox hunting.'

'Is that right? Neither does the fox.'

When all our guests have gone, Julianne sends me upstairs to have a bath. Some time later, I'm aware of her sliding into bed beside me. She turns and nestles backwards until her body moulds into mine. Her hair smells of apple and cinnamon.

168

'I'm tired,' I whisper.

'It's been a long day.'

'That's not what I'm getting at. I've been thinking about making a few changes.'

'Like what?

'Just changes.'

'Do you think that's wise?'

'We could go on a holiday. We could go to California. We've always talked of doing that.'

'What about your job . . . and Charlie's schooling?'

'She's young. She'll learn a lot more if we go travelling for six months than she will at school . . .'

Julianne turns around and props herself up on her elbow so she can look at me. 'What's brought this on?'

'Nothing.'

'When this all started, you said you didn't want things to change. You said the future didn't have to change.'

'I know.'

'And then you stopped talking to me. You give me no idea of what you're going through and then you spring this!'

'I'm sorry. I'm just tired.'

'No, it's more than that. Tell me.'

'I have this rackety idea in my head that I should be doing more. You read about people whose lives are packed with incident and adventure and you think, wow, I should do more. That's when I thought about going away.'

'While there's still time?'

'Yes.'

'So this *is* about the Parkinson's?'

'No . . . I can't explain . . . just forget it.'

'I don't want to forget it. I want you to be happy. But we don't have any money – not with the mortgage and the plumbing. You said so yourself. Maybe in the summer we can go to Cornwall . . . '

'Yeah. You're right. Cornwall would be nice.' As hard as I

169

try to sound enthusiastic, I know I don't succeed. Julianne slips an arm around my waist and pulls herself closer. I feel her warm breath on my throat.

'With any luck I might be pregnant by then,' she whispers. 'We don't want to be too far away.'

21

My head aches and my throat is scratchy. It could be a hang-over. It might be the flu. According to the papers half the country has succumbed to some exotic bug from Beijing or Bogotà – one of those places that nobody ever leaves without carrying a virulent germ.

The good news is that I have had no detectable side effects from taking Selegiline except for the insomnia, a pre-existing condition. The bad news is that the drug has had absolutely no effect on my symptoms.

I telephone Jock at seven a.m.

'How do you know it isn't working?' he says, annoyed at being woken.

'I don't feel any different.'

'That's the whole point. It doesn't make the symptoms go away – it stops them getting worse.'

'OK.'

'Just be patient and relax.'

That's easy for him to say.

'Are you doing your exercises?' he asks.

'Yes,' I lie.

'I know it's Monday but do you fancy a game of tennis? I'll go easy on you.'

'When?'

'I'll meet you at the club at six.'

Julianne will see right through this, but at least I'll be out of the house. I'm owed some leeway after yesterday.

My first patient of the day is a young ballet dancer with the grace of a gazelle and the yellowing teeth and receding gums of a devoted bulimic. Then Margaret arrives clutching her orange lifebuoy. She shows me a newspaper clipping about a bridge collapse in Israel. The look on her face says, 'I told you so!' I spend the next fifty minutes getting her to think about how many bridges there are in the world and how often they fall down.

By three o'clock I'm standing at the window, looking for Bobby among the pedestrians. I wonder if he's going to turn up. I jump when I hear his voice. He's standing in the doorway, rubbing his hands up and down his sides as if wiping something from them.

'It wasn't my fault,' he says.

'What?'

'Whatever it is you think I've done.'

'You kicked a woman unconscious.'

'Yes. That's all. Nothing else.' Light flares off the gold frames of his glasses.

'Hostility like that has to come from somewhere.'

'What do you mean?'

'You're an intelligent young man. You get the idea.'

It's time to confront Bobby, to see how he reacts under pressure.

'How long have you been my patient? Six months. You disappeared for half that time. You've been late for appointments, you've turned up unannounced and you've dragged me out of bed at four in the morning . . . '

He blinks rapidly. My tone of voice is so polite that he isn't sure whether I'm criticising him or not.

'... even when you *are* here, you change the subject and prevaricate. What are you trying to hide? What are you so frightened of?'

I pull my chair closer. Our knees are almost touching. It's like looking into the eyes of a beaten dog that doesn't know enough to turn away. Some aspects of his functioning I see so clearly – particularly his past – but I still can't see his present. What has he become?

'Let me tell you what I think, Bobby. I think you are desperate for affection, yet unable to engage people. This started a long while ago. I see a boy who is bright and sensitive, who waits each evening to hear the sound of his father's bicycle being wheeled through the front gate. And when his father comes through the door in his conductor's uniform, the boy can't wait to hear his stories and help him in the workshop.

'His father is funny, kind, quick-witted and inventive. He has grand plans for weird and wonderful inventions that will change the world. He draws pictures of them on scraps of paper and builds prototypes in the garage. The boy watches him working and sometimes at night he curls up to sleep among the wood shavings, listening to the sound of the lathe.

'But his father disappears. The most important figure in his life – the only one he truly cares about – abandons him. His mother, sadly, doesn't recognise or excuse his grief. She regards him as being weak and full of dreams, just like his father. He is never good enough.'

I keep a close eye on Bobby, looking for signs of protest or dissent. His eyes flit back and forth as though dreaming, but somehow he stays focused on me.

'... this boy is particularly perceptive and intelligent. His senses are heightened and his emotions are intense. He begins to escape from his mother. He's not old enough or brave enough to run away from home. Instead, he escapes into his mind. He creates a world that others never see or know exists.

173

A world where he is popular and powerful: where he can punish and reward. A world where nobody laughs at him or belittles him, not even his mother. She falls at his feet – just like all the others. He is Clint Eastwood, Charles Bronson and Sylvester Stallone all rolled into one. Redeemer. Revenger. Judge. Jury. Executioner. He can dispense his own brand of justice. He can machine gun the entire school rugby team or have the school bully nailed to a tree in the playground . . . '

Bobby's eyes glitter with connected memories and associated sounds – the light and dark that shade his past. The corners of his mouth are twitching.

'So what does he grow into, this boy? An insomniac. He suffers bouts of sleeplessness that jangle his nerves and have him seeing things out of the corner of his eye. He imagines conspiracies and people watching him. He lies awake and makes lists and secret codes for his lists.

'He wants to escape to his other world but something is wrong. He can't go back there because someone has shown him something even better, more exciting – real!'

Bobby blinks and pinches the skin on the back of his hand.

'Have you ever heard the expression, "One man's meat is another man's poison"?' I ask him.

He acknowledges the question almost without realising it.

'It could be a description for human sexuality and how each of us has different interests and tastes. This boy grows up and as a young man he tastes something that excites and disturbs him in equal measure. It is a guilty secret. A forbidden pleasure. He worries that it makes him a pervert – this sexual thrill from inflicting pain.'

Bobby shakes his head; his eyes magnified by each lens.

'But you needed a point of reference – an introduction. This is what you haven't told me, Bobby. Who was the special girlfriend who opened your eyes? What did it feel like when you hurt her?'

'You're sick!'

'And you're lying.' Don't let him change the subject. 'What was it like that first time? You wanted nothing to do with these games but she goaded you. What did she say? Did she make fun of you? Did she laugh?'

'Don't talk to me. Shut up! SHUT UP!'

He clutches the cuffs of his coat in his fists and covers his ears. I know he's still listening. My words are leaking through and expanding in the crevices of his mind like water turned to ice.

'Someone planted the seed. Someone taught you to love the feeling of being in control . . . of inflicting pain. At first you wanted to stop, but she wanted more. Then you noticed that you weren't holding back. You were enjoying it! You didn't want to stop.'

'SHUT UP! SHUT UP!'

Bobby rocks back and forth on the edge of the chair. His mouth has gone slack and he's no longer focused on me. I'm almost there. My fingers are in the cracks of his psyche. A single affirmation, no matter how small, will be enough for me to lever his defences open. But I'm running out of story. I don't have all the pieces. I risk losing him if I overreach.

'Who was she, Bobby? Was her name Catherine McBride? I know that you knew her. Where did you meet? Was it in hospital? There's no shame in seeking help, Bobby. I know you've been evaluated before. Was Catherine a patient or a nurse? I think she was a patient.'

Bobby pinches the bridge of his nose, rubbing the spot where his glasses perch. He reaches slowly into his trouser pocket and I suddenly feel a twinge of doubt. His fingers are searching for something. He has eighty pounds and twenty years on me. The door is on the far side of the room. I won't reach it before he does.

His hand emerges. I'm staring at it, transfixed. He is holding a white handkerchief, which he unfolds and lays in his lap. Then he takes off his glasses and slowly cleans each lens, rubbing the cloth between his thumb and forefinger. Maybe this slow-motion ritual is buying him time.

He raises the glasses to the light, checking for any smudges. Then he looks past them and stares directly at me. 'Do you make up this crap as you go along, or did you spend all weekend coming up with it?'

The pressure is dispelled like air leaking from a punctured raft. I have overplayed my hand. I want to ask Bobby where I went wrong, but he's not going to tell me. A poker player doesn't explain why he calls a bluff. I must have been near the mark, but that's a lot like NASA saying its Mars Polar Lander achieved its target because it crashed and went missing on the right planet.

Bobby's faith in me has been shaken. He also knows that I'm frightened of him, which is not a good basis for a clinical relationship. What in God's name was I thinking? I've wound him up like a clockwork toy and now I have to let him loose.

22

The white Audi cruises along Elgin Avenue, slowing as it passes me. I continue limping along the pavement, my tennis racket under one arm and a bruise the size of a grapefruit on my right thigh. Ruiz is behind the wheel. He looks like a man who is willing to follow me all the way home at four miles an hour.

I stop and turn towards him. He leans over to open the front passenger door. 'What happened to you?'

'A sporting injury.'

'I didn't think tennis was that dangerous.'

'You haven't played against my mate.'

I get in beside him. The car smells of stale tobacco and apple-scented air freshener. Ruiz does a U-turn and heads west.

'Where are we going?'

'The scene of the crime.'

I don't ask why. Everything about his demeanour says I don't have a choice. The temperature has fallen to just above freezing and a mist blurs the streetlights. Coloured lights are blinking in windows and plastic wreaths of holly decorate front doors.

We drive along Harrow Road and turn into Scrubs Lane. After less than half a mile the lane rises and falls over Mitre Bridge, where it crosses the Grand Union Canal and the Paddington rail lines. Ruiz pulls over and the engine dies. He gets out of the car and waits for me to do the same. The doors centrally lock as he walks away, expecting me to follow. My thigh is still stiff from Jock's well-aimed smash. I rub it gingerly and limp along the road towards the bridge.

Ruiz has stopped at a wire cyclone fence. Grabbing hold of a metal post, he swings himself upwards on to a stone wall flanking the bridge. Using the same post, he lets himself down the other side. He turns and waits for me.

The towpath is deserted and the nearby buildings are dark and empty. It feels a lot later than it is – like the early hours of the morning, when the world always seems much lonelier and beds much warmer.

Ruiz is walking ahead of me with his hands buried in his coat pockets and his head down. He seems full of pent-up rage. After about five hundred yards the railway tracks appear to our right. Maintenance sheds are silhouetted against the residual light. Rolling stock sits idle in a freight yard.

With barely any warning a train roars past. The sound bounces off the tin sheds and the stone walls of the canal, until it seems as though we're standing in a tunnel.

Ruiz has stopped suddenly on the path. I almost run into him.

'Recognise anything?'

I know exactly where we are. Instead of feeling horror or sadness, my only emotion is anger. It's late; I'm cold; and more than anything else I'm tired of Ruiz's snide glances and raised eyebrows. If he has something to say, get it over with and let me go home.

'You saw the photographs.'

'Yes.'

Ruiz raises his arm and for a moment I think he's going to

178

strike me. 'Look over there. Follow the edge of the building down.'

I trace the path of his outstretched hand and see the wall. A darker strip in the foreground must be the ditch where they found her body. Looking over his left shoulder, I see the silhouettes of the trees and the headstones of Kensal Green Cemetery. I remember standing on the ridge, watching the police uncover Catherine.

'Why am I here?' I ask, feeling empty inside.

'Use your imagination – you're good at that.'

He's angry, and for some reason I'm to blame. I don't often meet someone with his intensity – apart from obsessive-compulsives. I used to know guys like him at school; kids who were so ferociously determined to prove they were tough that they never stopped fighting. They had too much to prove and not enough time to prove it.

'Why am I here?'

'Because I have some questions for you.' He doesn't look at me. 'And I want to tell you some things about Bobby Moran.'

'I can't talk about my patients.'

'You just have to listen.' He rocks from foot to foot. 'Take my word for it, you'll find it fascinating.' He walks two paces towards the canal and spits into the water. 'Bobby Moran has no girlfriend or fiancée called Arky. He lives in a boarding house in north London with a bunch of asylum seekers waiting for council housing. He's unemployed and hasn't worked for nearly two years. There is no such company as Nevaspring – not a registered one at any rate.

'His father was never in the air force – as a mechanic, a pilot, or anything else. Bobby grew up in Liverpool, not London. He dropped out of school at fifteen. He did stints at night school and for a while worked as a volunteer at a sheltered workshop in Lancashire. We found no history of psychiatric illness or hospitalisation.'

Ruiz is pacing back and forth as he talks. His breath

179

condenses in the air and trails after him like he's a steam engine. 'A lot of people had nice things to say about Bobby. He is very neat and tidy according to his landlady. She does his washing and doesn't remember smelling chloroform on any of his clothes. His old bosses at the shelter called him a "big softie".

'That's what I find really strange, Professor. Nothing you said about him is true. I can understand you getting one or two details wrong. We all make mistakes. But it's as though we're talking about a completely different person.'

My voice is hoarse. 'It can't be him.'

'That's what I thought. So I checked. Big guy, six-two, overweight, John Lennon glasses – that's our boy. Then I wondered why he'd tell all these lies to a shrink who was trying to help him. Doesn't make sense, does it?'

'He's hiding something.'

'Maybe. But he didn't kill Catherine McBride.'

'How can you be so sure?'

'A dozen people at an evening class can verify his whereabouts on the night she disappeared.'

I don't have any strength left in my legs.

'Sometimes I'm pretty slow on the uptake, Prof. My old mum used to say that I was born a day late and never caught up. Truth is, I normally get there in the end. It just takes me a little longer than clever people.' He says it with bitterness rather than triumph.

'You see, I asked myself why Bobby Moran would make up all these lies. And then I thought, what if he didn't? What if *you* were telling the lies? You could be making this whole thing up to divert my attention.'

'You can't be serious?'

'How did you know that Catherine McBride cut her carotid artery to hasten her death? It wasn't mentioned in the postmortem.'

'I studied to be a doctor.'

'What about the chloroform?'

180

'I told you.'

'Yes, you did. I did some reading. Do you know that it takes a few drops of chloroform on a mask or a cloth to render a person unconscious? You have to know what you're doing when you play around with that stuff. A few drops too many and the victim's breathing is shut off. They suffocate.'

'The killer most likely had some medical knowledge.'

'I came up with that too.' Ruiz stamps his shoes on the bitumen, trying to stay warm. A stray cat, wandering along inside the wire fence, suddenly flattens itself at the sound of our voices. Both of us wait and watch, but the cat is in no hurry to move on.

'How did you know she was a nurse?' says Ruiz.

'She had the medallion.'

'I think you recognised her straight away. I think all the rest was a pretence.'

'No.'

His tone is colder. 'You also knew her grandfather – Justice McBride.'

'Yes.'

'Why didn't you say so?'

'I didn't think it was important. It was years ago. Psychologists often give evidence in the family division. We do evaluations on children and parents. We make recommendations to the court.'

'What did you make of him?'

'He had his faults but he was an honest judge. I respected him.'

Ruiz is trying hard to be cordial, but polite restraint doesn't come naturally to him.

'Do you know what I find really hard to explain?' he says. 'Why it took you so long to tell me about knowing Catherine McBride and her grandfather, yet you give me a crock of shit about somebody called Bobby Moran. No, sorry, that isn't right – you *don't* talk about your patients, do you? You just play little schoolboy games of show and tell. Well, two can play that game . . . ' He grins at me – all white teeth and dark eyes. 'Shall I tell you what I've been doing these last two weeks? I've been searching this canal. We brought in dredging equipment and emptied the locks. It was a lousy job. There was three feet of putrid sludge and slime. We found stolen bicycles, shopping trolleys, car chassis, hubcaps, two washing machines, car tyres, condoms and over four thousand used syringes. Do you know what else we found?'

I shake my head.

'Catherine McBride's handbag and her mobile phone. It took us a while to dry everything out. Then we had to check the phone records. That's when we discovered that the very last call she made was to your office. At 6.37 p.m. on the thirteenth of November. She was calling from a pub not far from here. Whoever had arranged to meet her hadn't turned up. My guess is that she called to find out why.'

'How can you be sure?'

Ruiz smiles. 'We also found her diary. It had been in the water for so long the pages were stuck together and the ink had washed away. The scene of crime boys had to dry it very carefully and pull the pages apart. Then they used an electron microscope to find the faint traces of ink. It's amazing what they can do nowadays.'

Ruiz has squared up to me, his eyes just inches from mine. This is his Agatha Christie moment: his drawing room soliloquy.

'Catherine had a note in her diary under November thirteenth. She wrote down the name of the Grand Union Hotel. Do you know it?'

I nod.

'It's only about a mile along the canal, near that tennis club of yours.' Ruiz motions with a sway of his head. 'At the bottom of the same page she wrote a name. I think she planned to meet that person. Do you know whose name it was?'

182

I shake my head.

'Care to hazard a guess?'

I feel a tightness in my chest. 'Mine.'

Ruiz doesn't allow himself a final flourish or triumphant gesture. This is just the beginning. I see the glint of handcuffs as they emerge from his pocket. My first impulse is to laugh, but then the coldness reaches inside me and I want to vomit.

'I am arresting you on suspicion of murder. You have the right to remain silent, but it is my duty to warn you that anything you do say will be taken down and may be used in evidence against you . . . '

The steel bracelets close around my wrists. Ruiz forces my legs apart and searches me, starting at my ankles and working his way up.

'Have you anything to say?'

It's strange the things that occur to you at times like this. I suddenly remember a line my father used to quote to me whenever I was in trouble: 'Don't say anything unless you can improve on the silence.'

Book Two

'We are often criminals in the eyes of the earth, not only for
having committed crimes, but because we know what crimes have
been committed.'

Hombre de la Máscara de Hierro
(The Man in the Iron Mask)

1

I have been staring at the same square of light for so long that when I close my eyes it's still there, shining inside my eyelids. The window is high up on the wall, above the door. Occasionally I hear footsteps in the corridor. The hinged observation flap opens and eyes peer at me. After several seconds, the hatch shuts and I go back to staring at the window.

I don't know what time it is. I was forced to trade my wrist-watch, belt and shoelaces for a grey blanket that feels more like sandpaper than wool. The only sound I can hear is the leaking cistern in the adjacent cell.

It has been quiet since the last of the drunks arrived. That must have been after closing time – just long enough for someone to fall asleep on the night bus, get into a fight with a taxi driver and finish up in the back of a police van. I can still hear him kicking at the cell door and shouting, 'I didn't fucking touch him.'

My cell is six paces long and four paces wide. It has a lavatory, a sink and a bunk bed. Graffiti have been drawn, scratched, gouged and smeared on every wall, although valiant attempts have been made to paint over them.

I don't know where Ruiz has gone. He's probably tucked up in bed, dreaming of making the world a safer place. Our first interview session lasted a few minutes. When I told him that I wanted a lawyer, he advised me, 'Get a bloody good one.'

Most of the lawyers I know don't make house calls at that time of night. I called Jock and woke him instead. I could hear a female voice complaining in the background.

'Where are you?'

'Harrow Road Police Station.'

'What are you doing there?'

'I've been arrested.'

'Wow!' Only Jock could sound impressed at this piece of news.

'I need you to do me a favour. I want you to call Julianne and tell her I'm OK. Tell her I'm helping the police with an investigation. She'll know the one.'

'Why don't you tell her the truth?'

'Please, Jock, don't ask. I need time to work this through.'

Since then I've been pacing the cell. I stand. I sit. I walk. I sit on the toilet. My nerves have made me constipated, or maybe it's the medication. Ruiz thinks I've been holding things back or being economical with the truth. Hindsight is an exact science. Right now my mistakes keep dividing inside my head, fighting for space with all the questions.

People talk about the sins of omission. What does that mean? Who decides if something is a sin? I know that I'm being semantic, but judging by the way people moralise and jump to conclusions, anyone would think that the truth is real and solid; that it's something that can be picked up and passed around, weighed and measured, before being agreed upon.

But the truth isn't like that. If I were to tell you this story tomorrow, it would be different than today. I would have filtered the details through my defences and rationalised my actions.

Truth *is* a matter of semantics, whether we like it or not.

I hadn't recognised Catherine from the drawing. And the body I saw in the morgue seemed more like a vandalised shopfront mannequin than a real human being. It had been five years. I told Ruiz as soon as I was sure. Yes, it could have been sooner, but he already knew her name.

Nobody likes admitting mistakes. And we all hate acknowledging the large gap between what we should do and what we actually do. So we alter either our actions or our beliefs. We make excuses, or redefine our conduct in a more flattering light. In my business it's called *cognitive dissonance*. It hasn't worked for me. My inner voice – call it my conscience or soul or guardian angel – keeps whispering, 'Liar, liar, pants on fire . . . '

Ruiz is right. I am in a shit-load of trouble.

I lie on the narrow cot, feeling the springs press into my back.

Summoning my sister's new boyfriend to a police station at six-thirty in the morning is an odd way to make somebody feel like part of the family. I don't know many criminal barristers. Usually I deal with Crown solicitors, who treat me like their new best friend or something nasty they stepped in, depending on what opinion I offer in court.

Simon arrives an hour later. There's no small talk about Patricia or appreciation for Sunday's lunch. Instead he motions for me to sit down and pulls up a chair. This is business.

The holding cells are on the floor below us. The charge room must be nearby. I can smell coffee and hear the tapping of computer keyboards. There are Venetian blinds at the windows of the interview room. The strips of sky are beginning to grow light.

Simon opens his briefcase and takes out a blue folder and a large legal notebook. I'm amazed at how he combines a Santa Claus physique with the demeanour of a lawyer.

189

'We need to make some decisions. They want to start the interviews as soon as possible. Is there anything you want to tell me?'

I feel myself blinking rapidly. What does he mean? Does he expect me to confess?

'I want you to get me out of here,' I say, a little too abruptly.

He begins by explaining that the Police and Criminal Evidence Act gives the police forty-eight hours in which to either charge a suspect or let them go, unless they've been granted leave by the courts.

'So I could be here for two days?'

'Yes.'

'But that's ridiculous!'

'Did you know this girl?'

'Yes.'

'Did you arrange to meet her on the night she died?'

'No.'

Simon is making notes. He leans over the notebook, scribbling bullet points and underlining some words.

'This is one of those no-brainers,' he says. 'All you have to do is provide an alibi for the thirteenth of November.'

'I can't do that.'

Simon gives me the weary look of a schoolteacher who hasn't received the answer he expects. Then he brushes a speck of fluff from his suit sleeve as if dismissing the problem. Standing abruptly, he knocks twice on the door to signal that he's finished.

'Is that all?'

'Yes.'

'Aren't you going to ask me if I killed her?'

He looks bemused. 'Save your plea for a jury and pray it never gets that far.'

The door closes after him but the room is still full of what he has left behind – disappointment, candour and the scent of aftershave. Five minutes later a WPC takes me along the corridor to the interrogation room. I have been in one before. Early in my career I sometimes acted as the 'responsible adult' when juveniles were being interrogated.

A table and four chairs take up most of the room. In the far corner is a large tape recorder, which is time-coded. There is nothing on the walls or the windowsill. The WPC stands immediately inside the door, trying not to look at me.

Ruiz arrives, along with a second detective who is younger and taller, with a long face and crooked teeth. Simon follows them into the interview room. He whispers in my ear, 'If I touch your elbow I want you to be quiet.'

I nod agreement.

Ruiz sits down opposite me, without bothering to remove his jacket. He rubs a hand across the whiskers on his chin.

'This is the second formal interview of Professor Joseph Paul O'Loughlin, a suspect in the murder of Catherine Mary McBride,' he says for the benefit of the tape. 'Present during the interview are Detective Inspector Vincent Ruiz, Detective Sergeant John Keebal and Dr O'Loughlin's legal representative, Simon Koch. The time is eight-fourteen a.m.'

A WPC checks the recorder is working. She nods to Ruiz. He places both his hands on the table and links his fingers together. His eyes settle on me and he says nothing. I have to admit it is a very eloquent pause.

'Where were you on the evening of November thirteenth this year?'

'I don't recall.'

'Were you at home with your wife?'

'No.'

'So you can recall that much?' he says sarcastically.

'Yes.'

'Did you work that day?'

'Yes.'

'What time did you leave the office?'

'I had a doctor's appointment at four o'clock.'

191

The questions go on like this, asking for specifics. Ruiz is trying to pin me down. He knows, as I do, that lying is a lot harder than telling the truth. The devil is in the detail. The more you weave into a story, the harder it is to maintain. It becomes like a straitjacket – binding you tighter, giving you less room to move.

Finally he asks about Catherine. Silence. I glance at Simon who says nothing. He hasn't said a word since the interview began. Neither has the younger detective, sitting to the side and slightly behind Ruiz.

'Did you know Catherine McBride?'

'Yes.'

'Where did you first meet her?'

I tell the whole story – about the self-mutilation and the counselling sessions; how she seemed to get better and how she eventually left the Marsden. It feels strange talking about a clinical case. My voice sounds vaguely strident, as though I'm trying too hard to convince them.

When I finish I open the palms of my hands to signal the end. I can see myself reflected in Ruiz's eyes. He's waiting for more.

'Why didn't you tell the hospital authorities about Catherine?'

'I felt sorry for her. I thought it would be cruel to see a dedicated nurse lose her job. Who would that benefit?'

'That's the only reason?'

'Yes.'

'Were you having an affair with Catherine McBride?'

'No.'

'Did you ever have sexual relations with her?'

'No.'

'When was the last time you spoke to her?'

'Five years ago. I can't remember the exact date.'

'Why did Catherine call your office on the evening she died?'

'I don't know.'

'We have other telephone records which indicate that she called the number twice the previous fortnight.'

'I can't explain that.'

'Your name was in her diary.'

I shrug. It's another mystery. Ruiz slaps his open palm on the table and everyone jumps, including Simon.

'You met her on that night.'

'No.'

'You lured her away from the Grand Union Hotel.'

'No.'

'You tortured her.'

'No.'

'This is horse-shit!' he explodes. 'You have deliberately withheld information and have spent the last three weeks covering your arse, misdirecting the investigation, trying to steer police away from you.'

Simon touches my arm. He wants me to be quiet. I ignore him.

'I didn't touch her. I haven't seen her. You have NOTHING!'

'I want to speak with my client,' says Simon more insistently.

To hell with that! I'm done with being polite. 'What possible reason would I have for killing Catherine?' I shout. 'You have my name in a diary, a telephone call to my office and no motive. Do your job. Get some evidence before you come accusing me.'

The younger detective grins. I realise that something is wrong. Ruiz opens a thin green folder which lies on the table in front of him. From it he produces a photocopied piece of paper which he slides across in front of me.

'This is a letter dated the nineteenth of April 1997. It is addressed to the senior nursing administrator of the Royal Marsden Hospital. In this letter, Catherine McBride makes an allegation that you sexually assaulted her in your office at the hospital. She says that you hypnotised her, fondled her breasts and interfered with her underwear—'

193

'She withdrew that complaint. I told you that.'

My chair falls backwards with a bang and I realise that I'm on my feet. The young detective is quicker than I am. He matches me for size and is bristling with intent.

Ruiz looks exultant.

Simon has hold of my arm. 'Professor O'Loughlin . . . Joe . . . I advise you to be quiet.'

'Can't you see what they're doing? They're twisting the facts—'

'They're asking legitimate questions.'

A sense of alarm spreads through me. Ruiz has a motive. Simon picks up my chair and holds it for me. I stare blankly at the far wall, numb with tiredness. My left hand is shaking. Both detectives stare at it silently. I sit and force my hand between my knees to stop the tremors.

'Where were you on the evening of November thirteenth?'

'In the West End.'

'Who were you with?'

'No one. I got drunk. I had just received some bad news about my health.'

That statement hangs in the air like a torn cobweb looking for something to cling to. Simon breaks first and explains that I have Parkinson's Disease. I want to stop him. It is *my* business. I'm not looking for pity.

Ruiz doesn't miss a beat. 'Is one of the symptoms memory loss?'

I'm so relieved that I laugh. I didn't want him treating me any differently. 'Exactly where did you go drinking?' Ruiz presses on.

'Different pubs and wine bars.'

'Where?'

'Leicester Square, Covent Garden . . . '

'Can you name any of these bars?'

I shake my head.

'Can anyone confirm your whereabouts?'

194

'No.'

'What time did you get home?'

'I didn't go home.'

'Where did you spend the night?'

'I can't recall.'

Ruiz turns to Simon. 'Mr Koch, can you please instruct your client—'

'My client has made it clear to me that he doesn't recall where he spent the night. He is aware that this does not help his situation.'

Ruiz's face is hard to read. He glances at his wristwatch, announces the time and then turns off the tape recorder. The interview is terminated. I glance from face to face, wondering what happens next. Is it over?

The young WPC comes back into the room.

'Are the cars ready?' asks Ruiz.

She nods and holds open the door. Ruiz strides out and the young detective snaps handcuffs on to my wrists. Simon starts to protest and is handed a copy of a search warrant. The address is typed in capital letters on both sides of the page. I'm going home.

My most vivid childhood memory of Christmas is of the St Mark's Anglican School nativity play in which I featured as one of the three wise men. The reason it is so memorable is that Russell Cochrane, who played the baby Jesus, was so nervous that he wet his pants and it leaked down the front of the Virgin Mary's blue robes. Jenny Bond, a very pretty Mary, was so angry that she dropped Russell on his head and swung a kick into his groin.

A collective groan went up from the audience, but it was drowned out by Russell's howls of pain. The entire production disintegrated and the curtain came down early.

The backstage farce proved even more compelling. Russell's father, a big man with a bullet-shaped head, was a police sergeant who sometimes came to the school to lecture us on road safety. He cornered Jenny Bond backstage and threatened to have her arrested for assault. Jenny's father laughed. It was a big mistake. Sergeant Cochrane handcuffed him on the spot and marched him along Stafford Street to the police station, where he spent the night.

Our nativity play made the national papers. 'Virgin Mary's Father Arrested', said the headline in the *Sun*. The *Star* wrote: 'Baby Jesus Kicked in the Baubles!'.

I think of it again because of Charlie. Is she going to see me in handcuffs, being flanked by policemen? What will she think of her father then?

The unmarked police car pulls up the ramp from the underground car park and emerges into daylight. Sitting next to me, Simon puts an overcoat over my head. Through the damp wool, I can make out the pyrotechnics of flashguns and TV lights. I don't know how many photographers and cameramen there are. I hear their voices and feel the police car accelerate away.

Traffic slows to a crawl in Marylebone Road. Pedestrians seem to hesitate and stare. I'm convinced they're looking at me – wondering who I am and what I'm doing in the back seat of a police car.

'Can I phone my wife?' I ask.

'No.'

'She doesn't know we're coming.'

'Exactly.'

'But she doesn't know I've been arrested.'

'You should have told her.'

I suddenly remember the office. I have patients coming today. Appointments need to be rescheduled. 'Can I call my secretary?'

Ruiz turns and glances over his shoulder. 'We are also executing a search warrant on your office.'

I want to argue but Simon touches my elbow. 'This is part

196

of the process,' he whispers, trying to sound reassuring.

The convoy of three police cars pulls up in the middle of our road, blocking the street in either direction. Doors are flung open and detectives assemble quickly, some using the side path to reach the back garden.

Julianne answers the front door. She is wearing pink rubber gloves. A fleck of foam clings to her hair where she has brushed her fringe to one side. A detective gives her a copy of the warrant. She doesn't look at it. She is too busy focusing on me. She sees the handcuffs and the look on my face. Her eyes are wide with shock and incomprehension.

'Keep Charlie inside,' I shout.

I look at Ruiz. I plead with him. 'Not in front of my daughter. *Please.*'

I see nothing in his eyes, but he reaches into his jacket pocket and finds the keys to the handcuffs. Two detectives take my arms.

Julianne is asking questions – ignoring the officers who push past her into the house. 'What's happening, Joe? What are you . . . ?'

'They think I had something to do with Catherine's death.'

'How? Why? That's ridiculous. You were helping them with their investigation.'

Something falls and smashes upstairs. Julianne glances upwards and then back to me. 'What are they doing in our house?' She is on the verge of tears. 'What have you done, Joe?'

I see Charlie's face peering out of the sitting room. It quickly disappears as Julianne turns. 'You stay in that room, young lady,' she barks, sounding more frightened than angry.

The front door is wide open. Anybody walking by can look inside and see what is happening. I can hear cupboards and drawers being opened on the floor above; mattresses are being lifted and beds dragged aside. Julianne doesn't know what to do. Part of her wants to protect her house from being vandalised, but mostly she wants answers from me. I don't have any.

The detectives take me through to the kitchen, where I find Ruiz peering out of the French doors at the garden. Men with shovels and hoes are ripping up the lawn. D.J. is leaning against Charlie's swing with a cigarette hanging from his mouth. He looks at me through the smoke; inquisitive, insolent. A faint hint of a smile creases the corners of his mouth – as though he's watching a Porsche get a parking ticket.

Turning away reluctantly, he lets the cigarette fall into the gravel where it continues to glow. Then he bends and slices open the plastic packing surrounding a radiator.

'We interviewed your neighbours,' explains Ruiz. 'You were seen burying something in the garden.'

'A bug-eyed goldfish.'

Ruiz is totally baffled. 'I beg your pardon?'

Julianne laughs at the absurdity of it all. We are living in a Monty Python sketch.

'He buried Charlie's goldfish,' she says. 'It's under the plum tree next to Harold the Hamster.'

A couple of the detectives behind us can't stifle their giggles. Ruiz has a face like thunder. I know I shouldn't goad him, but it feels good to laugh.

2

The mattress has compressed to the hardness of concrete beneath my hip and shoulder. From the moment I lie down the blood throbs in my ears and my mind begins to race. I want to slip into peaceful emptiness. Instead I chase the dangerous thoughts, magnified in my imagination.

By now Ruiz will have interviewed Julianne. He'll have asked where I was on 13 November. She'll have told him that I spent the night with Jock. She won't know that's a lie. She'll repeat what I told her.

Ruiz will also have talked to Jock, who will tell them that I left his office at five o'clock that day. He asked me out for a drink, but I said no. I said I was going home. None of our stories are going to match.

Julianne has spent all evening in the charge room, hoping to see me. Ruiz told her she could have five minutes but I can't face her. I know that's appalling. I know she must be scared, confused, angry and worried sick. She just wants an explanation. She wants to hear me tell her it's going to be all right. I'm more frightened of confronting her than I am of Ruiz. How can I explain Elisa? How can I make things right?

Julianne asked me if I thought it unusual that a woman I hadn't seen in five years is murdered and then the police ask me to help identify her. Glibly, I told her that coincidences were just a couple of things happening simultaneously. Now the coincidences are starting to pile up. What are the chances of Bobby being referred to me as a patient? Or that Catherine would phone my office on the evening she died? When do coincidences stop being coincidences and become a pattern?

I'm not being paranoid. I'm not seeing shadows darting in the corner of my eye or imagining sinister conspiracies. But something is happening here that is bigger than the sum of its parts.

I fall asleep with this thought and some time during the night I wake suddenly, breathing hard with my heart pounding. I cannot see who or what is chasing me, but I know it's there, watching, waiting, laughing at me.

Every sound seems exaggerated by the starkness of the cell. I lie awake and listen to the seesaw creaks of bedsprings, water dripping in cisterns, drunks talking in their sleep and guards' shoes echoing down corridors.

Today is the day. The police will either charge me or let me go. I should be more anxious and concerned. Mostly I feel remote and separate from what's happening. I pace out the cell, thinking how bizarre life can be. Look at all the twists and turns, the coincidences and bad luck, the mistakes and misunderstandings. I don't feel angry, or bitter. I have faith in the system. Pretty soon they're going to realise the evidence isn't strong enough against me. They'll have to let me go.

This sort of optimism strikes me as quite odd when I think about how naturally cynical I am concerning law and order. Innocent people get shafted every day. I've seen the evidence. It's incontrovertible. Yet I have no fears about this happening to me.

I blame my mother and her unwavering belief in authority figures such as policemen, judges and politicians. She grew up

200

in a village in the Cotswolds, where the town constable rode a bicycle, knew every local by name and solved most crimes within half an hour. He epitomised fairness and honesty. Since then, despite the regular stories of police planting evidence, taking bribes and falsifying statements, my mother has never altered her beliefs. 'God made more good people than bad,' she says, as though a headcount will sort everything out. And when this seems highly unlikely, she adds, 'They will get their comeuppance in Heaven.'

A hatch opens in the lower half of the door and a wooden tray is propelled across the floor. I have a plastic bottle of orange juice, some grey-looking sludge that I assume to be scrambled eggs and two slices of bread that have been waved over a toaster. I put it to one side and wait for Simon to arrive.

He looks very jolly in his silk tie printed with holly and silver bells. It's the sort of tie Charlie will give me for Christmas. I wonder if Simon has ever been married or had children.

He can't stay long; he's due in court. I see strands of his horsehair wig sticking out of his briefcase. The police have requested a blood and hair sample, he says. I have no problem with that. They are also seeking permission to interview my patients, but a judge has refused them access to my files. Good for him.

The biggest piece of news concerns two of the phone calls Catherine made to my office. Meena, bless her cotton socks, has told detectives that she talked to Catherine twice in early November.

I had totally forgotten about the search for a new secretary. Meena had placed an advertisement in the Medical Appointments section of the *Guardian*. It asked for experienced medical secretaries, or applicants with nursing training. We had over eighty replies. I start explaining this to Simon, getting more and more excited. 'Meena was coming up with a shortlist of twelve.'

'Catherine made the shortlist.'

'Yes. Maybe. She must have done. That would explain the call. Meena will know.' Did Catherine know she was applying to be *my* secretary? Meena must have mentioned my name. Maybe Catherine wanted to surprise me. Or perhaps she thought I wouldn't give her an interview.

Simon scissors his fingers across his tie, as if pretending to cut it off. 'Why would a woman who accused you of sexual assault apply to become your secretary?' He sounds like a prosecutor.

'I didn't assault her.'

He doesn't comment. Instead he looks at his watch and closes his briefcase. 'I don't think you should answer any more police questions.'

'Why?'

'You're digging yourself into a deeper hole.'

Simon shrugs on his overcoat and leans down to brush a smudge of dirt from the mirror-like surface of his black shoes. 'They have eight more hours. Unless they come up with something new, you'll be home by this evening.'

Lying on the bunk with my hands behind my head, I stare at the ceiling. Someone has scrawled in the corner: 'A day without sunlight is like . . . night'. The ceiling must be twelve feet high. How on earth did anyone get up there?

It is strange being locked away from the world. I have no idea what's been happening in the past forty-eight hours. I wonder what I've missed. Hopefully my parents have gone back to Wales. Charlie will have started her Christmas break; the boiler will be fixed; Julianne will have wrapped the presents and put them under the tree . . . Jock will have dusted off his Santa suit and done his annual tour of the children's wards. And then there's Bobby – what has he been doing?

Midway through the afternoon, I am summoned to the interview room again. Ruiz and the same detective sergeant are waiting. Simon arrives out of breath from climbing the stairs.

He's clutching a sandwich in a plastic prism and a bottle of orange juice.

'A late lunch,' he confesses apologetically.

The tape recorder is switched on.

'Professor O'Loughlin, help me out here.' Ruiz conspires to raise a polite smile. 'Is it true that killers often return to the scene of the crime?'

Where is he going with this? I glance at Simon who indicates I should answer.

'A "signature killer" will sometimes return, but more often than not it's an urban myth.'

'What's a "signature killer"?'

'Every killer has a behavioural imprint – it's like a criminal shadow that is left behind at a crime scene, a signature. It might be the way they tie a ligature or dispose of a body. Some feel compelled to return to the scene.'

'Why?'

'There are lots of possible reasons. Perhaps they want to fantasise and relive what they've done, or collect a souvenir. Some may feel guilty or just want to stay close.'

'Which is why kidnappers often help with the search?'

'Yes.'

'And arsonists help fight fires?'

I nod. The sergeant is pretending to be an Easter Island statue. Ruiz opens a folder and takes out several photographs.

'Where were you on Sunday November twenty-fourth?'

So this is it – this is what he's found.

'I was visiting my great auntie.'

A spark of excitement ignites in his eyes. 'What time was that?'

'In the morning.'

'Where does she live?'

'At Kensal Green Cemetery.'

The truth disappoints him. 'We have CCTV pictures of your car in the parking area.' He slides the photograph across the desk. I'm putting a box of leaves into Charlie's outstretched arms.

Ruiz pulls out another sheet of paper. 'Do you remember how we discovered the body?'

'You said a dog disturbed it.'

'The caller didn't leave a name or contact number. He phoned from a public phone box near the entrance to the cemetery. Did you see anyone in that vicinity?'

'No.'

'Did you use that phone box?'

Surely he's not suggesting that I made the call?

'You said the killer would know the area intimately.'

'Yes.'

'How would you describe your knowledge?'

'Detective Inspector, I think I see where you're going with this. Even if I did kill Catherine and then bury her by the canal, do you really think I'd bring my wife and daughter along to watch her being dug up?'

Ruiz slams the folder shut and snarls, 'I ask the fucking questions. You worry about answering them.'

Simon interrupts. 'Perhaps we should all cool down.'

Ruiz leans across the desk towards me, until I can see the capillaries beneath the skin of his nose. I swear he can breathe through those pores.

'Are you willing to talk to me without your lawyer present?'

'If you turn off the tape.'

Simon objects and wants to talk to me alone. Outside in the corridor we have a frank exchange of views. He tells me I'm being stupid. I agree. But if I can get Ruiz to listen, maybe I can convince him to look again at Bobby.

'I want it noted that I advised you against this.'

'Don't worry, Simon. Nobody's going to blame you.'

Ruiz is waiting for me. A cigarette is alight in the ashtray. He stares at it intently, watching it burn down. The grey ash forms a misshapen tower that will tumble with the slightest breath.

'I thought you were quitting.'

'I am. I like to watch.'

The ash topples and Ruiz pushes the ashtray to one side. He nods.

The room seems so much larger with just the two of us. Ruiz pushes back his chair and puts his feet on the table. His black brogues have worn heels. Above one sock, on the white of his ankle, there is a streak of black shoe polish.

'We took your photograph to every pub and wine bar in Leicester Square and Charing Cross,' he says. 'Not one barman or barmaid remembers you.'

'I'm easy to forget.'

'We're going out again tonight. Maybe we'll trigger someone's memory. Somehow I don't think so. I don't think you were anywhere near the West End.'

I don't respond.

'We also showed your photograph to the regulars at the Grand Union Hotel. Nobody remembers seeing you there. They remembered Catherine. She was dressed real nice, according to some of the lads. One of them offered to buy her a drink but she said she was waiting for someone. Was it you?'

'No.'

'Who was it?'

'I still think it was Bobby Moran.'

Ruiz lets out a low rumble that ends with a hacking cough. 'You don't give up, do you?'

'Catherine didn't die on the night she disappeared. Her body wasn't found for eleven days. Whoever tortured her took a long time to break her spirit – days perhaps. Bobby could have done it.'

'Nothing points to him.'

'I think he knew her.'

Ruiz laughs ironically. 'That's the difference between what

205

you do and what I do. You base your conclusions on bell curves and empirical models. A sob story about a lousy childhood and you're ready to put someone in therapy for ten years. I deal with facts and right now they're all pointing to you.'

'What about intuition? Gut instincts? I thought detectives used them all the time.'

'Not when I'm trying to get approval for a surveillance budget.'

We sit in silence, measuring the gulf between us. Eventually Ruiz speaks. 'I talked to your wife yesterday. She described you as being a little "distant" lately. You suggested the family go away on a trip . . . to America. It came up suddenly. She couldn't explain why.'

'It had nothing to do with Catherine. I wanted to see more of the world.'

'Before it's too late.' His voice softens. 'Tell me about your Parkinson's. Must be pretty gutting to get news like that – particularly when you've got a good-looking wife, a young daughter, a successful career. How many years are you going to lose? Ten? Twenty?'

'I don't know.'

'I reckon news like that would make a guy feel pretty pissed off with the world. You've worked with cancer patients. You tell me – do they get bitter and feel cheated?'

'Some of them do.'

'I bet some of them want to tear down the world. I mean, why should they get all the shitty luck, right? What are you going to do in a situation like that? Go quietly, or rail against the dying of the light? You could settle old scores and make amends. Nothing wrong with exacting a bit of rough justice if it's the only kind on offer.'

I want to laugh at his clumsy attempt at psychoanalysis. 'Is that what you'd do, Inspector?' It takes Ruiz a few moments to realise that I'm now scrutinising him. 'You think the vigilante spirit might take you?'

Doubt fills his eyes, but he won't let it stay there. He wants to move on; to change the subject, but first I want to set him straight about people with terminal illnesses or incurable diseases. Yes, some want to lash out in frustration at the sense of hopelessness and helplessness. But the bitterness and anger soon fade. Instead of feeling sorry for themselves, they face the fury of the ill wind and look ahead. And they resolve to enjoy every moment they have left; to suck the marrow out of life until it dribbles down their chin.

Sliding his feet to the floor, Ruiz puts both hands flat on the table and levers himself upwards. He doesn't look at me as he speaks. 'I want you charged with murder but the director of public prosecutions says I don't have enough evidence. He's right, but then so am I. I'm going to keep looking until we find some more. It's just a matter of time.' His eyes are gazing at something a great distance away.

'You don't like me, do you?' I ask.

'Not particularly.'

'Why?

'Because you think I'm a dumb, foul-mouthed plod who doesn't read books and thinks the theory of relativity has something to do with inbreeding.'

'That's not true.'

He shrugs and reaches for the door handle.

'How much of this is personal?' I ask.

His answer rumbles through the closing door. 'Don't flatter yourself.'

3

The same WPC who has shadowed me for the last forty-eight hours hands me my tennis racket and a parcel containing my watch, wallet, wedding ring and shoelaces. I have to count my money, including the loose change, and sign for it all.

The clock on the wall of the charge room says it's 9.45 p.m. What day is it? Wednesday. Seven days until Christmas. A small silver tree is perched on the front counter, decorated with a handful of baubles and a wonky star. Hanging on the wall behind it is a banner saying, 'Peace and Goodwill to All Men'.

The WPC offers to call me a cab. I wait in the reception area until the driver gives me a blast on the horn. I'm tired, dirty and smell of stale sweat. I should go home, yet when I slide on to the back seat of the cab I feel my courage leak away. I want to tell the driver to head in the opposite direction. I don't want to face Julianne. Semantics aren't going to wash with her. Only the unqualified truth.

I have never loved anyone as much as I love her – not until Charlie came along. There is no justification for cheating on her. I know what people will say. They'll call it classic mid-life paranoia. I hit my forties and, fearing my own mortality, had a one-night stand. Or they'll put it all down to self-pity. On the same day I learned of my progressive neurological disease I slept with another woman – getting my fill of sex and excitement before my body falls apart.

I have no excuses for what happened. It wasn't an accident or a moment of madness. It was a mistake. It was sex. It was tears, semen and someone other than Julianne.

Jock had just told me the bad news. I was sitting in his office, unable to move. A huge bloody butterfly must have flapped its wings in the Amazon because the vibrations knocked me down.

Jock offered to take me for a drink. I said no. I needed some air. For the next few hours I wandered around the West End, visiting bars and trying to feel like just another person having a few drinks to unwind.

First I thought I wanted to be alone. Then I realised that I really needed somebody to talk to. Somebody who wasn't part of my perfect life: somebody who didn't know Julianne, or Charlie, or any of my friends or family. So that's how I finished up on Elisa's doorstep. It wasn't an accident. I sought her out.

In the beginning we just talked. We talked for hours. (Julianne will probably say this makes my infidelity worse because it was more than just some insatiable male craving.) What did we talk about? Childhood memories. Favourite holidays. Special songs. Maybe none of these things. The words weren't important. Elisa knew I was hurting, but didn't ask why. She knew I would either tell her or I wouldn't. It made no difference to her.

I have very little memory of what happened next. We kissed. Elisa rolled me on top of her. Her heels bumped against my back. She moved so slowly as she took me inside her. I moaned as I came and the pain leaked away.

I spent the night. The second time *I* took her. I pushed Elisa down and drove into her violently, making her hips jerk and her breasts quiver. When it was over, white tissues, wet with sperm, lay on the floor like fallen leaves.

The strange thing is that I expected to be consumed by guilt or doubt. Feeling normal didn't even enter my calculations. I was convinced Julianne would see straight through me. She wouldn't need to smell it on my clothes, or see lipstick on my collar. Instead she would know intuitively, just as she seems to know everything else about me.

I have never regarded myself as a risk-taker, or someone who gets a thrill from living close to the edge. Once or twice at university, before I met Julianne, I had one-night stands. It seemed natural then. Jock was right – the left-wing girls were easier to bed. This was different.

The cabbie is pleased to be rid of me. I stand on the footpath and stare at my house. The only light is a glow from the kitchen window, down the side path.

My key slips into the lock. As I step inside I see Julianne silhouetted against a rectangle of light at the far end of the hall. She is standing in the kitchen doorway.

'Why didn't you call me? I would have picked you up . . .'

'I didn't want Charlie to come to the police station.'

I can't see the look on her face. Her voice sounds OK. I put down my tennis things and walk towards her. Her cropped dark hair is tousled and her eyes are pouchy from lack of sleep. As I try to put my arms around her she slips away. She can hardly bear to look at me.

This is not just about a lie. I have brought police officers into her house: opening cupboards, looking under beds, searching through her personal things. Our neighbours have seen me in handcuffs. Our garden has been dug up. She has been interviewed by detectives and asked about our sex life. She has waited for hours in a police station, hoping to see me, only to be turned away – not by the authorities but by me. All of this and not one phone call or message to help her understand.

I glance at the kitchen table and see a scattered pile of

newspapers. The pages are open at the same story. 'Psychologist Arrested in McBride Murder Probe', reads one headline. 'Celebrity Shrink Detained' says another. There are photographs of me sitting in the back seat of a police car with Simon's coat over my head. I look guilty. Put a coat over Mother Teresa's head and she would *look* guilty. Why do suspects do it? Surely it would be better to smile and wave.

I slump into a chair and look through the stories. One newspaper has used a telephoto shot of me perched on the roof of the Marsden, with Malcolm strapped in the harness in front of me. A second photo shows me covered in the coat. My hands are cuffed on my lap. The message is clear – I have gone from hero to zero.

Julianne fills the electric kettle and takes out two mugs. She is wearing dark leggings and an oversized sweater that I bought for her at Camden Market. I told her it was for me, but I knew what would happen. She always borrows my sweaters. She says she likes the way they smell.

'Where's Charlie?'

'Asleep. It's nearly eleven.'

When the water boils, she fills each mug and jiggles the tea bags. I can smell peppermint. Julianne has a shelf full of different herbal teas. She sits opposite me. Her eyes rest on me without any emotion. She slightly rotates her wrists, turning her palms face up. With that one small movement she signifies that she is waiting for me to explain.

I want to say it was all a misunderstanding but I'm afraid it will sound trite. Instead I stick to the story – or what I know of it. How Ruiz thinks I had something to do with Catherine's murder because my name was in her diary when they fished it out of the canal; and how Catherine came to London for a job interview to be *my* secretary. I had no idea. Meena arranged the shortlist. Catherine must have seen the advertisement.

Julianne is a step ahead of me. 'That can't be the only reason they arrested you?'

211

'No. The telephone records show that she called my office on the evening she was killed.'

'Did you speak to her?'

'No. I had an appointment with Jock. That's when he told me about . . . you know what.'

'Who answered the call?'

'I don't know. Meena went home early.'

I lower my eyes from her gaze. 'They've dredged up the sexual assault complaint. They think I was having an affair with her – that she threatened to destroy my career and our marriage.'

'But she withdrew the complaint.'

'I know, but you can see how it looks.'

Julianne pushes her cup to the centre of the table and slips off her chair. I feel myself relax a little because her eyes are no longer focused on me. Even without looking at her, I know exactly where she is – standing at the French windows, staring through her reflection at the man she thought she knew, sitting at the table.

'You told me you were with Jock. You said you were getting drunk. I knew you were lying. I've known all along.'

'I did get drunk, but not with Jock.'

'Who were you with?' The question is short, sharp and to the point. It sums up Julianne – spontaneous and direct, with every line of communication a trunk route.

'I spent the night with Elisa Velasco.'

'Did you sleep with her?'

'Yes.'

'You had sex with a prostitute?'

'She's not a prostitute any more.'

'Did you use a condom?'

'Listen to me, Julianne. She hasn't been a prostitute for years.'

'DID . . . YOU . . . USE . . . A . . . CONDOM?' Each word is clearly articulated. She is standing over my chair. Her eyes swim with tears.

'No.'

She delivers the slap with the force of her entire body. I reel sideways, clutching my cheek. I taste blood on the inside of my mouth and hear a high-pitched ringing inside my ears.

Julianne's hand is on my thigh. Her voice is soft. 'Did I hit you too hard? I'm not used to this.'

'I'm OK,' I reassure her.

She hits me again, this time even harder. I finish up on my knees, staring at the polished floorboards.

'You selfish, stupid, gutless, two-timing, lying bastard!' She is shaking her hand in pain.

I'm now an unmoving target. She beats me with her good fist, hammering on my back. She is screaming: 'A prostitute! Without a condom! And then you came home and you fucked me!'

'No! Please! You don't understand—'

'Get out of here! You are not wanted in this house! You will *not* see me. You will *not* see Charlie.'

I crouch on the floor, feeling wretched and pathetic. She turns and walks away, down the hallway to the front room. I pull myself up and follow her, desperate for some sign that this isn't the end.

I find her kneeling in front of the Christmas tree with a pair of garden shears in her hand. She has neatly lopped off the top third of the tree. It now looks like a large green lampshade.

'I'm so sorry.'

She doesn't answer.

'Please listen to me.'

'Why? What are you going to say to me? That you love me? That she meant nothing? That you *fucked* her and then you made *love* to me?'

That's the difficulty when arguing with Julianne. She unleashes so many accusations at once that no single answer satisfies them collectively. And the moment you start trying to

213

divide the questions up, she hits you again with a new series.

She is crying properly now. Her tears glisten in the lamplight like a string of beads draped down her cheeks.

'I made a mistake. When Jock told me about the Parkinson's it felt like a death sentence. Everything was going to change – all our plans. The future. I know I said the opposite. It's not true. Why give me this life and then give me this disease? Why give me the joy and beauty of you and Charlie and then snatch it away? It's like showing someone a glimpse of what life could be like and in the next breath telling them it can never happen.'

I kneel beside her, my knees almost touching hers.

'I didn't know how to tell you. I needed time to think. I couldn't talk to my parents or friends, who were going to feel sorry for me and give me chin-up speeches and brave smiles. That's why I went to see Elisa. She's a stranger, but also a friend. There's good in her.'

Julianne wipes her cheeks with the sleeve of her sweater and stares at the fireplace.

'I didn't plan to sleep with her. It just happened. I wish I could change that. We're not having an affair. It was one night.'

'What about Catherine McBride? Did you sleep with her?'

'No.'

'Well why did she apply to be your secretary? What would make her think you would ever give her a job after what she put us through?'

'I don't know.'

Julianne looks at her bruised hand and then at my cheek.

'What do you want, Joe? Do you want to be free? Is that it? Do you want to face this alone?'

'I don't want to drag you and Charlie down with me.'

My maudlin tone infuriates her. She bunches her fists in frustration.

'Why do you always have to be so fucking sure of yourself? Why can't you just admit you need help? I know you're sick. I know you're tired. Well, here's a news flash: we're all sick

214

and we're all tired. I'm sick of being marginalised and tired of being pushed aside. Now I want you to leave.'

'But I love you.'

'Leave!'

'What about us? What about Charlie?'

She gives me a cold, unwavering stare. 'Maybe I still love you, Joe, but at the moment I can't stand you.'

4

When it is over – the packing, the walking out the door and the cab-ride to Jock's doorstep – I feel like I did on my first day at boarding school. Abandoned. A single memory comes back to me, with all the light and shade of reality: I am standing on the front steps of Charterhouse as my father hugs me and feels the sob in my chest. 'Not in front of your mother,' he whispers.

He turns to walk away and says to my mother, 'Not in front of the boy,' as she dabs at her eyes.

Jock insists I'll feel better after a shower, a shave and a decent meal. He orders takeaway from his local Indian, but I'm asleep on the sofa before it arrives. He eats alone.

In the motley half-light leaking through the blinds I can see tin foil trays stacked beside the sink, with orange and yellow gravy erupting over the sides. The TV remote is pressing into my spine and the weekly programme guide is wedged under my head. I don't know how I managed to sleep at all.

My mind keeps flashing back to Julianne and the look she gave me. It went far beyond disappointment. Sadness is not a big enough word. It was as though something had frozen inside her. Very rarely do we fight. Julianne can argue with passion and emotion. If I try to be too clever or become insensitive she accuses me of arrogance and I see the hurt in her eyes. This time I saw only emptiness. A vast, windswept landscape that a man could die trying to cross.

Jock is awake. I can hear him singing in the shower. I try to swing my legs to the floor but nothing happens. For a fleeting moment I fear I'm paralysed. Then I realise that I can feel the weight of the blankets. Concentrating my thoughts, my legs grudgingly respond.

The *bradykinesia* is becoming more obvious. Stress is a factor in Parkinson's Disease. I'm supposed to get plenty of sleep, exercise regularly and try not to worry about things. Yeah, right!

Jock lives in a mansion block overlooking Hampstead Heath. Downstairs there is a doorman who holds an umbrella over your head when it rains. He wears a uniform and calls people 'Guv' or 'Madam'. Jock and his second wife used to own the entire top floor, but since the divorce he can only afford a one-bedroom apartment. He also had to sell his Harley and give her the cottage in the Cotswolds. Whenever he sees an expensive sports car he claims it belongs to Natasha.

'When I look back, it's not the ex-wives that frighten me, it's the mothers-in-law,' he says. Since his divorce he has become, as Jeffrey Bernard would say, a sort of roving dinner guest on the outside looking in, and a fly on the wall of other people's marriages.

Jock and I go a lot further back than university. The same obstetrician, in the same hospital, delivered us both on the same day, only eight minutes apart. That was on 18 August 1960, at Queen Charlotte's Maternity Hospital in Hammersmith. Our mothers shared a delivery suite and the OB had to dash back and forth between the curtains.

I arrived first. Jock had such a big head that he got stuck and they had to pull him out with forceps. Occasionally he still jokes about coming second and trying to catch up. In

217

reality, competition is never a joke with him. We were probably side-by-side in the nursery. We might have looked at each other, or kept each other awake.

It says something about the separateness of individual experience that we began our lives only minutes apart but didn't meet again until nineteen years later. Julianne says fate brought us together. Maybe she's right. Aside from being held upside down and smacked on the arse by the same doctor, we had very little in common. I can't explain why Jock and I became friends. What did I offer to the partnership? He was a big wheel on campus, always invited to the best parties and flirting with the prettiest girls. My dividend was obvious, but what did he get? Maybe that's what they mean when they say people just 'click'.

We long ago drifted apart politically, and sometimes morally, but we can't shake loose our history. He was best man at my wedding and I was best man at both of his. We have keys for each other's houses and copies of each other's wills. Shared experience is a powerful bond, but it's not just that.

Jock, for all his right-wing bluster, is actually a big softie, who has donated more money to charity than he settled on either of his ex-wives. Every year he organises a fundraiser for Great Ormond Street and he hasn't missed a London Marathon in fifteen years. Last year he pushed a hospital bed with a load of 'naughty' nurses in stockings and suspenders. He looked more like Benny Hill than Dr Kildare.

Jock emerges from the bathroom with a towel around his waist. He pads barefoot across the lounge to the kitchen. I hear the fridge door open and then close. He slices oranges and fires up an industrial-size juicer. The kitchen is full of gadgets. He has a machine to grind coffee, another to sift it and a third which looks like a cannon shell rather than a percolator. He can make waffles, muffins, pancakes or cook eggs in a dozen different ways.

I take my turn in the bathroom. The mirror is steamed up. I rub it with the corner of a towel, making a rough circle large enough to see my face. I look exhausted. Wednesday night's TV highlights are printed backwards on my right cheek. I scrub my face with a wet flannel.

There are more gadgets on the windowsill, including a battery-powered nasal hair trimmer that sounds like a demented bee stuck in a bottle. There are a dozen different brands of shampoo. It reminds me of home. I always tease Julianne about her 'lotions and potions' filling every available inch of our en suite. Somewhere in the midst of these cosmetics I have a disposable razor, a can of shaving foam and a deodorant stick. Unfortunately, retrieving them means risking a domino effect that will topple every bottle in the bathroom.

Jock hands me a glass of orange juice and we sit in silence staring at the percolator.

'I could call her for you,' he suggests.

I shake my head.

'I could tell her how you're moping around the place . . . no good to anyone . . . lost . . . desolate . . . '

'It wouldn't make any difference.'

He asks about the argument. He wants to know what upset her. Was it the arrest, the headlines or the fact that I lied to her?

'The lying.'

'I figured as much.'

He keeps pressing me for details. I don't really want to go there but the story comes out as my coffee grows cold. Perhaps Jock can help me make sense of it all.

When I reach the part about seeing Catherine's body in the morgue, I suddenly realise that he might have known her. He knew a lot more of the nurses at the Marsden than I did.

'Yeah, I was thinking that,' he says, 'but the photograph they put in the paper didn't ring any bells. The police wanted to know if you stayed with me on the night she died,' he adds.

'Sorry about that.'

'Where were you?'

I shrug.

'It's *true* then. You've been having a bit on the side.'

'It's not like that.'

'It never is, old son.'

Jock goes into his schoolboy routine, wanting to know all the 'sordid details'. I won't play along, which makes him grumpy.

'So why couldn't you tell the police where you were?'

'I'd rather not say.'

Frustration passes quickly across his face. He doesn't push any further. Instead he changes tack and admonishes me for not talking to him sooner. If I wanted him to provide me with an alibi, I should at least have told him.

'What if Julianne had asked me? I might have given the game away. And I could have told the police you were with me, instead of dropping you in the shit.'

'You told the truth.'

'I would have lied for you.'

'What if I *had* killed her?'

'I still would have lied for you. You'd do the same for me.'

I shake my head. 'I wouldn't lie for you if I thought you'd killed someone.'

His eyes meet mine and stay there. Then he laughs and shrugs. 'We'll never know.'

5

At the office I cross the lobby, aware that the security guards and receptionist are staring at me. I take the lift upstairs to find Meena at her desk and an empty waiting room.

'Where is everyone?'

'They cancelled.'

'Everyone?'

I lean over her desk and look down the appointments list for the day. All the names are crossed out with a red line. Except for Bobby Moran.

Meena is still talking. 'Mr Lilley's mother died. Hannah Barrymore has the flu. Zoe has to mind her sister's children . . . ' I know she's trying to make me feel better.

I point to Bobby's name and tell her to cross it out.

'He hasn't called.'

'Trust me.'

Despite Meena's best efforts to clean up, my office is still a mess. Evidence of the police search is everywhere, including the fine graphite powder they used to dust for fingerprints.

'They didn't take any of your files, but some of them were mixed up.'

I tell her not to worry. The notes cease to be important if I no longer have any patients. She stands at the door, trying to think of something positive to say. 'Did I get you into trouble?'

'What do you mean?'

'The girl who applied for the job . . . the one who was murdered . . . should I have handled it differently?'

'Absolutely not.'

'Did you know her?'

'Yes.'

'I'm sorry for your loss.'

This is the first time that anyone has acknowledged the fact that Catherine's death might have saddened me. Everybody else has acted as though I have no feelings one way or the other. Maybe they think I have some special understanding of grief or control over it. If that's the case, they're wrong. Getting to know patients is what I do. I learn about their deepest fears and secrets. A professional relationship becomes a personal one. It can be no other way.

I ask Meena about Catherine. How did she sound on the phone? Did she ask questions about me? The police took away her letters and job application but Meena has kept a copy of her CV.

She fetches it for me and I glance at the covering letter and the first page. The problem with curricula vitae is that they tell you virtually nothing of consequence about a person. Schools, exam results, tertiary education, work experience – none of it reveals an individual's personality or temperament. It is like trying to judge a person's height from their hair colour.

Before I can finish reading, the phone rings in the outer office. Hoping it might be Julianne, I pick up the call before Meena can patch it through. The voice on the line is like a force ten gale. Eddie Barrett lets loose with a string of colourful

222

invective. He is particularly imaginative when it comes to describing uses for my Ph.D. in the event of a toilet paper shortage.

'Listen, you over-qualified head-shrinker, I'm reporting you to the British Psychological Society, the Qualifications Board and the UK Registrar of Expert Witnesses. Bobby Moran is also going to sue you for slander, breach of duty and anything else he can find. You're a disgrace! You should be struck off! More to the point, you're an arsehole!'

I have no time to respond. Each time I sense a break in Eddie's diatribe, he simply rolls on through. Maybe this is how he wins so many cases – he doesn't shut up for long enough to let anyone else get a word in.

The truth is I have no defence. I have broken more professional guidelines and personal codes than I can list, but I would do the same again. Bobby Moran is a sadist and a serial liar. Yet at the same time I feel a terrible sense of loss. By betraying a patient's trust I have opened a door and crossed a threshold into a place that is supposed to be out of bounds. Now I'm waiting for the door to hit me in the arse.

Eddie hangs up and I stare at the phone. I press the speed-dial. Julianne's voice is on the answering machine. My guts contract. Life without her seems unthinkable. I have no idea what I want to say. I try to be cheerful because I figure Charlie might hear the message. I finish up sounding like Father Christmas. I call back and leave another message. The second one is even worse.

I give up and begin sorting out my files. The police emptied my filing cabinets, looking for anything hidden at the back of the drawers. I look up as Fenwick's head peers around the door. He is standing in the corridor, glancing nervously over his shoulder.

'A quick word, old boy.'

'Yes?'

'Terrible business, all this. Just want to say "Chin up" and all that. Don't let the rotters get you down.'

'That's very nice of you, Fenwick.'

He sways from foot to foot. 'Awful business. A real bugger. I'm sure you understand. What with the negative publicity and the like . . . ' He looks wretched.

'What's the matter, Fenwick?'

'Given the circumstances, old boy, Geraldine suggested it might be better if you weren't my best man. What would the other guests say? Awfully sorry. Hate kicking a man when he's down.'

'That's fine. Good luck.'

'Jolly good. Well . . . um . . . I'll leave you to it. I'll see you this afternoon at the meeting.'

'What meeting?'

'Oh dear, hasn't anyone told you? What a bugger!' His face turns bright pink.

'No.'

'Well, it's not really my place . . . ' He mumbles and shakes his head. 'The partners are having a meeting at four. Some of us – not me, of course – are a little concerned about the impact of all this on the practice. The negative publicity and the like. Never good news having the police raid the place and reporters asking questions. You understand.'

'Of course.' I smile through gritted teeth. Fenwick is already backing out of the door. Meena flashes him a look that sends him into full retreat.

There are no benign possibilities. My esteemed colleagues are to discuss my partnership – banishment being the issue. My resignation will be sought. A choice of words will be agreed and a chat with the chief accountant will wrap the whole thing up without any fuss. Bollocks to that!

Fenwick is already halfway down the corridor. I call after him: 'Tell them I'll sue the practice if they try to force me out. I'm not resigning.'

224

Meena gives me a look of solidarity. It is mixed with another expression that could be mistaken for pity. I'm not used to people feeling sorry for me.

'I think you should go home. There's no point in staying,' I tell her.

'What about answering the phone?'

'I'm not expecting any calls.'

It takes twenty minutes for Meena to leave, fussing over her desk and glancing fretfully at me as though she is breaking some secretarial code of loyalty. Once alone, I close the blinds, push the unsorted folders to one side and lean back in my chair.

What mirror did I break? What ladder did I walk under? I am not a believer in God or fate or destiny. Maybe this is the 'law of averages'. Maybe Elisa was right. My life has been too easy. Having won nearly every important toss of the coin, my luck has now run out.

The ancient Greeks used to say that Lady Luck was a very beautiful girl with curly hair who walked among people in the street. Perhaps her name was Karma. She is a fickle mistress, a prudent woman, a tramp and a Manchester United supporter. She used to be mine.

It rains on the walk to Covent Garden. In the restaurant, I shake out my coat and hand it to a waitress. Drops of water leak down my forehead. Elisa arrives fifteen minutes later, warmly wrapped in a black overcoat with a fur collar. Underneath she's dressed in a dark blue camisole with spaghetti straps and a matching mini skirt. Her stockings are seamed and dark. She uses a linen napkin to dry herself and runs her fingers through her hair.

'I never remember to carry an umbrella any more.'

'Why is that?'

'I used to have one with a carved handle. It had a stiletto blade inside the shaft . . . in case of trouble. See how well you taught me.' She laughs and reapplies her lipstick. I want

225

to touch the tip of her tongue with my fingers.

I cannot explain what it is like to sit in a restaurant with such a beautiful woman. Men covet Julianne, but with Elisa there is real hunger as their insides flutter and their hearts knock. There is something very pure, impulsive and innately sexual about her. It is as though she has refined, filtered and distilled her sexuality to a point where a man can believe that a single drop might be enough to satisfy him for a lifetime.

Elisa glances over her shoulder and instantly attracts a waiter's attention. She orders a salad niçoise and I choose the penne carbonara.

Normally I enjoy the confidence that comes with sitting opposite Elisa, but today I feel old and decrepit, like a gnarled olive tree with brittle bark. She talks quickly and eats slowly, picking at the seared tuna and slices of red onion.

Although I let her talk, I feel desperate and impatient. My salvation must start today. She is still watching me. Her eyes are like mirrors within mirrors. I can see myself. My hair is plastered to my forehead. I haven't slept for more than a few hours in what feels like weeks.

Elisa apologises for 'rabbiting on'. She reaches across the table and squeezes my hand. 'What did you want to talk to me about?'

I hesitate and then begin slowly – telling her about my arrest and the murder investigation. As I describe each new low point her eyes cloud with concern. 'Why didn't you just tell the police you were with me?' she asks. 'I don't mind.'

'It's not that easy.'

'Is it because of your wife?'

'No. She knows.'

Elisa shrugs her shoulders, neatly summing up her views on marriage. As a cultural institution she has nothing against it because it always provided some of her best customers. Married men were preferable to single men because they showered more often and smelled better.

'So what's stopping you telling the police?'

'I wanted to ask you first.'

She laughs at how old-fashioned that sounds. I feel myself blush.

'Before you say anything, I want you to think very carefully,' I tell her. 'I am in a very difficult position when I admit to spending the night with you. There are codes of conduct . . . ethics. You are a former patient.'

'But that was years ago.'

'It makes no difference. There are people who will try to use it against me. They already see me as a maverick because of my work with prostitutes and the TV documentary. And they're lining up to attack me over this . . . over you.'

Her eyes flash. 'They don't need to know. I'll go to the police and give a statement. I'll tell them you were with me. Nobody else has to find out.'

I try to muster all the kindness I have left, but my words still sting. 'Think for a moment what will happen if I get charged. You will have to give evidence. The prosecution will try everything they can to destroy my alibi. You are a former prostitute. You have convictions for malicious wounding. You have spent time in jail. You are also a former patient of mine. I met you when you were only fifteen. No matter how many times we tell them this was just one night, they'll think it was more . . . ' I run out of steam, stabbing my fork into my half-finished bowl of pasta.

Elisa's lighter flares. The flame catches in her eyes which are already blazing. I have never seen her so close to losing her poise. 'I'll leave it up to you,' she says softly. 'But I'm willing to give a statement. I'm not afraid.'

'Thank you.'

We sit in silence. After a while she reaches across the table and squeezes my hand again. 'You never told me why you were so upset that night.'

'It doesn't matter any more.'

227

'Is your wife *very* upset?'

'Yes.'

'She is lucky to have you. I hope she realises that.'

6

As I open the office door I'm aware of a presence in the room. The chrome-faced clock above the filing cabinet shows half past three. Bobby Moran is standing in front of my bookcase. He seems to have appeared out of thin air.

He turns suddenly. I don't know who is more startled.

'I knocked. There was no answer.' He drops his head. 'I have an appointment,' he says, reading my thoughts.

'Shouldn't that be with your lawyer? I heard you were suing me for slander, breach of confidentiality and whatever else he can dredge up.'

He looks embarrassed. 'Mr Barrett says I should do those things. He says I could get a lot of money.' He squeezes past me and stands at my desk. He's very close. I can smell fried dough and sugar. Damp hair is plastered to his forehead in a ragged fringe.

'Why are you here?'

'I wanted to see you.' There is something threatening in his voice.

'I can't help you, Bobby. You haven't been honest with me.'

'Are you always honest?'

'I try to be.'

'How? By telling the police I killed that girl?'

He picks up a smooth glass paperweight from my desk and weighs it in his right hand, then his left. He holds it up to the light. 'Is this your crystal ball?'

'Please, put it down.'

'Why? Scared I might bury it in your forehead?'

'Why don't you sit down?'

'After you.' He points to my chair. 'Why did you become a psychologist? Don't tell me, let me guess . . . A repressive father and an over-protective mother. Or is there a dark family secret? A relative who started howling at the moon or a favourite aunt who they had to lock away?'

I won't give him the satisfaction of knowing how close he is to the truth. 'I'm not here to talk about me.'

Bobby glances at the wall behind me. 'How can you hang that diploma? It's a joke! Until three days ago you thought I was someone completely different. Yet you were going to stand up in court and tell a judge whether I should be locked up or set free. What gives you the right to destroy someone's life? You don't know me.'

Listening to him I sense that for once I am talking to the real Bobby Moran. He lobs the paperweight on to the desk, where it rolls in slow-motion and drops into my lap.

'Did you kill Catherine McBride?'

'No.'

'Did you know her?'

His eyes lock on to mine. 'You're not very good at this, are you? I expected more.'

'This is not a game.'

'No. It's more important than that.'

We regard each other in silence.

'Do you know what a serial liar is, Bobby?' I ask eventually. 'It is someone who finds it easier to tell a lie rather than the truth, in any situation, regardless of whether it is important or not.'

'People like you are supposed to know when someone is lying.'

'That doesn't alter what you are.'

'All I did was change a few names and places – you got the rest of it wrong all by yourself.'

'What about Arky?'

'She left me six months ago.'

'You said you had a job.'

'I told you I was a writer.'

'You're very good at telling stories.'

'Now you're making fun of me. Do you know what's wrong with people like you? You can't resist putting your hands inside someone's psyche and changing the way they view the world. You play God with other people's lives . . . '

'Who are these "people like me"? Who have you seen before?'

'It doesn't matter,' Bobby says dismissively. 'You're all the same. Psychologists, psychiatrists, psychotherapists, tarot card readers, witch doctors—'

'You were in hospital. Is that where you met Catherine McBride?'

'You must think I'm an idiot.'

Bobby almost loses his composure but recovers himself quickly. He has almost no physiological response to lying. His pupil dilation, pore size, skin flush and breathing remain exactly the same. He's like a poker player who has no 'tells'.

'Everything I've done in my life and everyone I have come into contact with is significant – the good, the bad and the ugly,' he says with a note of triumph in his voice. 'We are the sum of our parts or the part of our sums. You say this isn't a game but you're wrong. It's good versus evil. White versus black. Some people are pawns and some are kings.'

'Which are you?' I ask.

He thinks about this. 'I was once a pawn but I reached the end of the board. I can be anything now.'

*　　*　　*

231

Bobby sighs and gets to his feet. The conversation has started to bore him. The session is only half an hour old but he's had enough. It should never have started. Eddie Barrett is going to have a field day.

I follow Bobby into the outer office. A part of me wants him to stay. I want to shake the tree and see what falls off the branches. I want the truth.

Bobby is waiting at the lift. The doors open.

'Good luck.'

He turns and looks at me curiously. 'I don't need luck.' The slight upturn of his mouth gives the illusion of a smile.

Back at my desk, I stare at the empty chair. An object on the floor catches my eye. It looks like a small carved figurine – a chess piece. Picking it up, I discover it's a wooden whale carved by hand. A key ring is attached with a tiny eyelet screw on the whale's back. It's the sort of thing you see hanging from a child's satchel or schoolbag.

Bobby must have dropped it. I can still catch him. I can call downstairs to the foyer and get the security guard to have him wait. I look at the clock. Ten minutes past four. The meeting has started upstairs. I don't want to be here.

Bobby's sheer size makes him stand out. He's a head taller than anybody else and pedestrians seem to divide and part to let him through. Rain is falling. I bury my hands in my over-coat. My fingers close around the smooth wooden whale.

Bobby is heading towards the underground station at Oxford Circus. If I stay close enough, hopefully I won't lose him in the labyrinthine walkways. I don't know why I'm doing this. I guess I want answers instead of riddles. I want to know where he lives and who he lives with.

Suddenly, he disappears from view. I suppress the urge to run forward. I keep moving at the same pace and pass an off-licence. I catch a glimpse of Bobby at the counter. Two doors further on I step inside a travel agency. A girl in a red skirt, white blouse and wishbone tie smiles at me.

'Can I help you?'

'I'm just looking.'

'To escape the winter?'

I'm holding a brochure for the Caribbean. 'Yes, that's right.'

Bobby passes the window. I hand her the brochure. 'You can take it with you,' she suggests.

'Maybe next year.'

On the pavement, Bobby is thirty yards ahead of me. He has a distinctive shape. He has no hips and it looks as though his backside has been stolen. He keeps his trousers pulled up high, with his belt tightly cinched.

Descending the stairs into the underground station, the crowd seems to swell. Bobby has a ticket ready. There is a queue at every ticket machine. Three underground lines cross at Oxford Circus – if I lose him now he can travel in any one of six different directions.

I push between people, ignoring their complaints. At the turnstile I place my hands on either side of it and lift my legs over the barrier. Now I'm guilty of fare evasion. The escalator descends slowly. A stale wind sweeps up from the tunnels, forced ahead of the moving engines.

On the northbound platform of the Bakerloo line, Bobby weaves through the waiting crowd until he reaches the far end. I follow him, needing to be close. At any moment I expect him to turn and catch sight of me. Four or five schoolboys, human Petri dishes of acne and dandruff, push along the platform, wrestling each other and laughing. Everyone else stares straight ahead in silence.

A blast of wind and noise. The train appears. Doors open. I let the crowd carry me forward into the carriage. Bobby is in my peripheral vision. The doors close automatically and the train jerks forward and gathers speed. Everything smells of damp wool and stale sweat.

Bobby gets off the train at Warwick Avenue. It has grown

dark. Black cabs swish past, the sound of their tyres louder than their engines. The station is only a hundred yards from the Grand Union Canal and perhaps two miles from where Catherine's body was found.

With fewer people around I have to drop further back. Now he's only a silhouette in front of me. I walk with my head down and collar turned up. As I pass a cement mixer on the footpath, I stumble sideways and put my shoe into a puddle. My balance is deserting me.

We follow Blomfield Road alongside the canal until Bobby crosses a footbridge at the end of Formosa Street. Spotlights pick out an Anglican church. The fine mist looks like falling glitter around the beams of light. Bobby sits on a park bench and looks at the church for a long time. I lean against the trunk of a tree, my feet growing numb with the cold.

What is he doing here? Maybe he lives nearby. Whoever killed Catherine knew the canal well: not just from a street map or a casual visit. He was comfortable here. It was his territory. He knew where to leave her body so that she wouldn't be found too quickly. He fitted in. Nobody recognised him as a stranger.

Bobby can't have met Catherine in the hotel. If Ruiz has done his job he will have shown photographs to the staff and patrons. Bobby isn't the sort of person you forget easily.

Catherine left the pub alone. Whoever she was supposed to meet had failed to show. She was staying with friends in Shepherd's Bush. It was too far to walk. What did she do? Look for a taxi. Or perhaps she started walking to Westbourne Park Station. From there it is only three stops to Shepherd's Bush. The walk would have taken her over the canal.

A London Transport depot is across the road. Buses are coming in and out all the time. Whoever she met must have been waiting for her on the bridge. I should have asked Ruiz which part of the canal they dredged to find Catherine's diary and mobile phone.

Catherine was five foot six and 134 pounds. Chloroform

takes a few minutes to act, but someone of Bobby's size and strength would have had few problems subduing her. She would have fought back or cried out. She wasn't the sort to meekly surrender.

But if I'm right and he knew her, he might not have needed the chloroform – not until Catherine realised the danger and tried to escape.

What happened next? It isn't easy carrying a body. Perhaps he dragged her on to the towpath. No, he needed somewhere private. Somewhere he'd prepared in advance. A flat or a house? Neighbours can be nosy. There are dozens of derelict factories along the canal. Did he risk using the towpath? The homeless sometimes sleep under the bridges or couples use them for romantic rendezvous.

The shadow of a narrow boat moves past me. The rumble of the motor is so low that the sound barely reaches me. The only light on the vessel is near the wheel. It casts a red glow on the face of the helmsman. I wonder. Traces of machine oil and diesel were found on Catherine's buttocks and hair.

I peer around the tree. The park bench is empty. Damn! Where has he gone? There is a figure on the far side of the church, moving along the railings. I can't be sure it's him. My mind sets off at a run but my legs are left behind. I finish up doing a perfect limp fall. Nothing is broken. Only my pride hurts.

I stumble onwards and reach the corner of the church where the iron railings take a 90-degree turn. The figure is staying on the path but moving much more quickly. I doubt if I can keep up with him.

What is he doing? Has he seen me? Jogging slowly, I carry on, losing sight of him occasionally. Doubt gnaws at my resolve. What if he's stopped up ahead? Perhaps he's waiting for me. The six lanes of the Westway curve above me, supported by enormous concrete pillars. The glow of headlights is too high to help me.

Ahead I hear a splash and a muffled cry. Someone is in the canal. Arms are thrashing at the water. I start running. There is the faint outline of a figure beneath the bridge. The sides of the canal are higher there. The stone walls are black and slick.

I try to shrug off my overcoat. My right arm gets caught in the sleeve and I swing it around until it comes loose. 'This way! Over here!' I call.

He doesn't hear me. He can't swim.

I kick off my shoes and leap. The cold slaps me so hard I swallow a mouthful of water. I cough it out through my mouth and nose. Three strokes. I'm with him. I slide my arm around him from behind and pull him backwards, keeping his head above the surface. I talk to him gently, telling him to relax. We'll find a place to get out. Wet clothes weigh him down.

I swim us away from the bridge. 'You can touch the bottom here. Just hold on to the side.' I scramble up the stone wall and pull him up after me.

It isn't Bobby. Some poor tramp, smelling of beer and vomit, lies at my feet, coughing and spluttering. I check his head, neck and limbs for any sign of trauma. His face is smeared with snot and tears.

'What happened?'

'Some sick fuck threw me in the canal! One minute I'm sleepin' and the next I'm flyin'.' He's resting on his knees, doubled over and swaying back and forth like an underwater plant. 'I tell yer, it ain't safe no more. It's like a fuckin' jungle . . . Did he take me blanket? If he took me blanket you can throw me back in.'

His blanket is still under the bridge, piled on a makeshift bed of flattened cardboard boxes.

'What about me teeth?'

'I don't know.'

He curses and scoops up his things, jealously clutching them to his chest. I suggest calling an ambulance and then the police

236

but he wants none of it. My whole body has started to tremble and I feel like I'm inhaling slivers of ice.

Retrieving my overcoat and shoes, I give him a soggy twenty pound note and tell him to find somewhere to dry out. He'll probably buy a bottle and be warm on the inside. My feet squelch in my shoes as I climb the stairs on to the bridge. The Grand Union Hotel is on the corner.

Almost as an afterthought, I lean over the side of the bridge and call out, 'How often do you sleep here?'

His voice echoes from beneath the stone arch. 'Only when the Ritz is full.'

'Have you ever seen a narrow boat moored under the bridge?'

'Nah. They moor further along.'

'What about a few weeks ago?'

'I try not to remember things. I mind me own business.'

He has nothing to add. I have no authority to press him. Elisa lives close by. I contemplate knocking on her door but I've brought her enough trouble already.

After twenty minutes I manage to hail a cab. The driver doesn't want to take me because I'll ruin the seats. I offer him an extra twenty quid. It's only water. I'm sure he's had worse.

Jock isn't home. I am so tired I can barely get my shoes off before collapsing into the spare bed. In the early hours I hear his key in the lock. A woman laughs drunkenly and kicks off her shoes. She comments on all the gadgets.

'Just wait till you see what I keep in the bedroom,' says Jock, triggering more giggles.

I wonder if he has any earplugs.

It is still dark as I pack a sports bag and leave a note taped to the microwave. Outside, a street-sweeping machine is polishing the gutters. There isn't a burger wrapper in sight.

On the ride through the city I keep looking out the rear window. I change cabs twice and visit two cash-point machines before catching a bus along the Euston Road.

I feel as though I'm slowly coming out of an anaesthetic. Over the past few days I have been letting details slip. Even worse, I have stopped trusting my instincts.

I am not going to tell Ruiz about Elisa. She shouldn't have to face a grilling in the witness box. I want to spare her that ordeal, if possible. And when this is all over – if nobody knows about her – I might still have a career that can be resurrected.

Bobby Moran had something to do with Catherine McBride's death. I'm convinced of it. If the police won't put him under the microscope then it's up to me. People normally need a motive to kill, but not to stay free. I *will* not let them send me to prison. I *will* not be separated from my family.

At Euston Station I do a quick inventory. Apart from a change of clothes, I have Bobby Moran's notes, Catherine McBride's CV, my mobile phone and a thousand pounds in cash. I forgot to bring a photograph of Charlie and Julianne.

I pay for the train ticket in cash. With fifteen minutes to spare, I have time to buy a toothbrush, toothpaste, a recharger for my mobile phone and one of those travelling towels that looks like a car chamois.

'Do you sell umbrellas?' I ask hopefully. The shopkeeper looks at me as though I've asked for a shotgun.

Nursing a takeaway coffee, I board the train and find a double seat facing forwards. I keep my bag beside me, covered by my overcoat.

The empty platform slides past the window and the northern suburbs of London disappear the same way. The train leans on floating axles as it corners at high speed. We tear past tiny stations with empty platforms where trains no longer seem to stop. One or two vehicles are parked in the long-stay car parks that look so far beyond the pale that I half expect to see a hose running from an exhaust pipe and a body slumped over a steering wheel.

My head is full of questions. Catherine applied to be my secretary. She phoned Meena twice and then took a train down to London, arriving a day early.

Why did she phone the office that evening? Who answered the call? Did she have second thoughts about surprising me? Did she want to cancel? Perhaps she'd been stood up and just wanted to go out for a drink. Maybe she wanted to apologise about causing me so much trouble.

All of this is supposition. At the same time, it fits the frame-work of detail. It can be built upon. All the pieces can be made to fit a story except for one – Bobby.

His coat smelled of chloroform. Bobby had machine oil on his shirt cuffs. Catherine's post-mortem mentioned machine oil. 'It's all about the oil,' Bobby told me. Did he know she had twenty-one stab wounds? Did he lead me to the place where she disappeared?

Perhaps he's using me to construct an insanity defence. By playing 'mad' he might avoid a life sentence. Instead they'll send him to a prison hospital like Broadmoor. Then he can astound some prison psychiatrist with his responsiveness to treatment. He could be out within five years.

I'm sounding more and more like him – fashioning conspir-acies out of coincidences. Whatever lies at the heart of this, I must not underestimate Bobby. He has played games with me. I don't know why.

My search has to start somewhere. Liverpool will do for now. I take out Bobby Moran's file and begin reading. Opening my new notebook, I make bullet points – the name of a primary school, the number of his father's bus, a club his parents used to visit . . .

These could be more of Bobby's lies. Something tells me they're not. I think he changed certain names and places, but not all of them. The events and emotions he described were true. I have to find the strands of truth and follow them back to the centre of the web.

7

The clock at Lime Street Station glows white with solid black hands pointing to eleven o'clock. I walk quickly across the concourse, past the coffee stand and closed public toilet. A gaggle of teenage girls, speaking at 110 decibels, communicate through a cloud of cigarette smoke.

It must be five degrees colder than in London, with a wind straight off the Irish Sea. I half expect to see icebergs on the horizon. St George's Hall is over the way. Banners snap in the wind, advertising the latest Beatles retrospective.

I walk past the large hotels on Lime Street and search the side streets for something smaller. Not far from the university I find the Albion. It has a worn carpet in the entrance hall and a family of Iraqis camped on the first-floor landing. Young children look at me shyly, hiding behind their mother's skirts. The men are nowhere to be seen.

My room is on the second floor. It is just large enough for a double bed and a wardrobe held shut with a wire hanger. The hand basin has a rust stain in the shape of a teardrop beneath the tap. The curtains will only half close and the windowsill is dotted with cigarette burns.

There have been very few hotel rooms in my life. I am grateful for that. For some reason loneliness and regret seem to be part of their décor.

I press the memory button on my mobile and hear the singsong tones of the number being automatically dialled. Julianne's voice is on the answering machine. I know she's listening. I can picture her. I make a feeble attempt to apologise and ask her to pick up the phone. I tell her it's important.

I wait . . . and wait . . .

She picks up. My heart skips.

'What is so important?' Her tone is harsh.

'I want to talk to you.'

'I'm not ready to talk.'

'You're not giving me a chance to explain.'

'I gave you a chance two nights ago, Joe. I asked you why you slept with a whore and you told me that you found it easier to talk to her than to me . . . ' Her voice is breaking. 'I guess that makes me a pretty lousy wife.'

'You have everything planned. Your life runs like clockwork – the house, work, Charlie, school; you never miss a beat. I'm the only thing that doesn't work . . . not properly . . . not any more . . . '

'And that's my fault?'

'No, that's not what I mean.'

'Well, pardon me for trying so hard. I thought I was making us a lovely home. I thought we were happy. It's fine for you, Joe, you have your career and your patients who think you walk on water. This is all I had – us. I gave up everything for this and I loved it. I loved you. Now you've gone and poisoned the well.'

'But don't you see – what I've got is going to destroy all that . . .'

'No, don't you dare blame a disease. You've managed to do this all by yourself.'

'It was only one night,' I say plaintively.

241

'No! It was someone else! You kissed her the way you kiss me. You fucked her! How could you?'

Even when sobbing and angry she manages to remain piercingly articulate. I am selfish, immature, deceitful and cruel. I try to pick out which of these adjectives doesn't apply to me. I fail. 'I made a mistake,' I say weakly. 'I'm sorry.'

'That's not enough, Joe. You broke my heart. Do you know how long I have to wait before I can get an AIDS test? Three months!'

'Elisa is clear.'

'And how do you know? Did you ask her before you decided not to use a condom? I'm going to hang up now.'

'Wait! Please! How's Charlie?'

'Fine.'

'What have you told her?'

'That you're a two-timing shit and a weak, pathetic, self-pitying, self-centred creep.'

'You didn't.'

'No, but I felt like it.'

'I'll be out of town for a few days. The police might ask you questions about where I am. That's why it's best if I don't tell you.'

She doesn't reply.

'You can get me on my mobile. Call me, please. Give Charlie an extra hug from me. I'll go now. I love you.'

I hang up quickly, afraid to hear her silence.

Locking the door on my way out, I push the heavy key deep into my trouser pocket. Twice on my way down the stairs I feel for it. Instead I find Bobby's whale. I trace its shape with my fingers.

Outside, an icy wind pushes me along Hanover Street towards the Albert Docks. Liverpool reminds me of an old woman's handbag, full of bric-a-brac, odds and ends and half finished packets of boiled sweets. Edwardian pubs squat beside mountainous cathedrals and art deco office blocks that can't decide which continent they should be on. Some of the more modern buildings have dated so quickly they look like derelict bingo halls only fit for the bulldozer.

The Cotton Exchange in Old Hall Street is a grand reminder of when Liverpool was the centre of the international cotton trade, feeding the Lancashire spinning industry. When the exchange building opened in 1906 it had telephones, electric lifts, synchronised electric clocks and a direct cable to the New York futures market. Now it houses, among other things, thirty million records of births, deaths and marriages in Lancashire.

A strange mixture of people queue at the indexes – a class of school children on an excursion; American tourists on the trail of distant relations; matronly women in tweed skirts; probate researchers and fortune hunters.

I have a goal. It seems fairly realistic. I queue at the colour-coded volumes where I hope to find the registration of Bobby's birth. With this I can get a birth certificate, which in turn will give me the names of his mother, father, their place of residence and occupations.

The volumes are stored on metal racks, listed by month and year. The 1970s and 1980s are arranged in quarters for each year, with surnames in alphabetical order. If Bobby has told the truth about his age, I might only have four volumes to search.

The year should be 1980. I can find no entry for a Bobby Moran or Robert Moran. I start working through the years on either side, going as far back as 1974 and forward to 1984. Growing frustrated, I look at my notes. I wonder if Bobby could have changed the spelling of his name or altered it entirely by deed poll. If so, I'm in trouble.

At the front information desk I ask to borrow a phone book. I can't tell if I'm charming people with my smile or frightening them. The Parkinson's mask is unpredictable.

Bobby lied about where he went to school, but perhaps he didn't lie about the name. There are two St Mary's in Liverpool – only one of them is a junior school. I make a note of the number and find a quiet corner in the foyer to make the call. The secretary has a Scouse accent and sounds like a character in a Ken Loach film.

'We're closed for Christmas,' she says. 'I shouldn't even be here. I was just tidying up the office.'

I make up a story about a sick friend who wants to track down his old mates. I'm looking for yearbooks or class photographs from the mid-eighties. She thinks the library has a cupboard full of that sort of thing. I should call back in the New Year.

'It can't wait that long. My friend is very sick. It's Christmas.'

'I might be able to check,' she says sympathetically. 'What year are you looking for?'

'I'm not exactly sure.'

'How old is your friend.'

'Twenty-two.'

'What is his name?'

'I think his name might have been different back then. That's why I need to see the photographs. I'll be able to recognise him.'

She is suddenly less sure of me. Her suspicion increases when I suggest coming to the school. She wants to ask the headmistress. Better still, I should put my request in writing and send it by post.

'I don't have time. My friend—'

'I'm sorry.'

'Wait! Please! Can you just look up a name for me? It's Bobby Moran. He might have worn glasses. He would have started in about 1985.'

She hesitates. After a long pause she suggests that I call her back in twenty minutes.

I go in search of fresh air. Outside, at the entrance to an alley, a man stands beside a blackened barrow. Every so often he yells, 'Roooooost chestnooooots', making it sound as plaintive as a gull's cry. He hands me a brown paper bag and I sit on the steps, peeling the sooty skin from the warm chestnuts.

One of my fondest memories of Liverpool is the food. The fish and chips and Friday night curries. The jam roly-poly, bread and butter pudding, treacle sponge, bangers and mash . . . I also loved the odd assortment of people – Catholics, Protestants, Muslims, Irish, African and Chinese – good grafters, fiercely proud and not afraid to wear their hearts and wipe their noses on the same sleeve.

The school secretary is less circumspect this time. Her curiosity has been sparked. My search has become hers.

'I'm sorry but I couldn't find any Bobby Moran. Are you sure that you don't mean Bobby Morgan? He was here from 1985 to 1988. He left in year three.'

'Why did he leave?'

'I'm not sure.' Her voice is uncertain. 'I wasn't here then. A family tragedy?' There is someone she can ask, she says. Another teacher. She takes the name of my hotel and promises to leave a message.

Back at the colour-coded volumes, I go through the names again. Why would Bobby change his surname by a single letter? Was he breaking with the past or trying to hide from it?

In the third volume I find an entry for Robert John Morgan. Born 24th September 1980 at Liverpool University Hospital. Mother: Bridget Elsie Morgan (née Aherne). Father: Leonard Albert Edward Morgan (merchant seaman).

I still can't be absolutely sure that it's Bobby but the chances are good. I fill out a pink application form to order a copy of his full birth certificate. The clerical officer behind the glass screen has an aggressive chin and flared nostrils. He pushes the form back towards me. 'You haven't stated your reasons.'

'I'm tracing my family history.'

'What about your postal address?'

245

'I'll pick it up from here.'

Without ever looking up at me, he thumps the applications with a fist-sized stamp. 'Come back in the New Year. We close from Monday for the holidays.'

'But I can't wait that long.'

He shrugs. 'We open until midday on Monday. You could try then.'

Ten minutes later I leave the exchange building with a receipt in my pocket. Three days. I can't wait that long. In the time it takes me to cross the pavement I make a new plan.

The offices of the *Liverpool Echo* look like a mirrored Rubik's cube. The foyer is full of pensioners on a day tour. Each has a souvenir bag and a stick-on nametag.

A young receptionist is sitting on a high stool behind a dark wooden counter. She is small and pale, with curry-coloured eyes. To her left is a metal barrier with a swipe-card entry that separates us from the lifts.

'My name is Professor Joseph O'Loughlin and I was hoping to use your library.'

'I'm sorry but we don't allow public access to the news-paper library.' A large bunch of flowers is sitting on the counter beside her.

'They're lovely,' I say.

'Not mine, I'm afraid. The fashion editor gets all the free-bies.'

'I'm sure you get more than your share.'

She knows I'm flirting, but laughs anyway.

'What if I want to order a photograph?' I ask.

'You fill out one of these forms.'

'What if I don't know the date, or the name of the photog-rapher?'

She sighs. 'You don't really want a photograph, do you?'

I shake my head. 'I'm looking for a death notice.'

'How recently?'

'About fourteen years.'

She makes me wait while she calls upstairs. Then she asks if I have anything official-looking, like a security pass or business card. She slides it into a plastic wallet and pins it to my shirt.

'The librarian knows you're coming. If anyone asks you what you're doing, say you're researching a story for the medical pages.'

I take the lift to the fourth floor and follow the corridors. Occasionally I glimpse a large open-plan newsroom through the swing doors. I keep my head down and try to walk with a sense of purpose. Every so often my leg locks up and swings forward as though in a splint.

The librarian is in her sixties, with dyed hair and half glasses that hang around her neck on a chain. She has a rubber thimble on her right thumb for turning pages. Her desk is surrounded by dozens of cacti.

She notices me looking. 'We have to keep it too dry in here for anything else to grow,' she explains. 'Any moisture will damage the newsprint.'

Long tables are strewn with newspapers. Someone is cutting out stories and placing them in neat piles. Another is reading each story and circling particular names or phrases. A third uses these references to sort the cuttings into files.

'We have bound volumes going back a hundred and fifty years,' says the librarian. 'The cuttings don't last that long. Eventually they fall apart along the edges and crumble into dust.'

'I thought everything would be on computer by now,' I say.

'Only for the past ten years. It's too expensive to scan all the bound volumes. They're being put on to microfilm.'

She turns on a computer terminal and asks me what I need.

'I'm looking for a death notice published around 1988. Leonard Albert Edward Morgan . . . '

'Named after the old king.'

247

'I think he was a bus conductor. He might have lived or worked in a place called Heyworth Street.'

'In Everton,' she says, flicking at a keyboard with two fingers. 'Most of the local buses either start or finish at the Pier Head or Paradise Street.'

I make a note of this on a pad. I concentrate on making the letters large and evenly spaced. It reminds me of being back in pre-school – tracing huge letters on cheap paper with crayons that almost rested on your shoulder.

The librarian leads me through the maze of shelves that stretch from the wooden floor to the sprinklers on the ceiling. Eventually we reach a wooden desk, scarred by cutting blades. A microfiche machine sits at the centre. She flicks a switch and the motor begins to hum. Another switch turns on the bulb and a square of light appears on the screen.

She hands me six boxes of film covering January to June 1988. Threading the first film on to the spools, she presses fast forward, accelerating through the pages and knowing almost instinctively when to stop. She points to the public notices and I make a note of the page number, hoping it will be roughly the same each day.

I trace my finger down the alphabetical listing, looking for the letter 'M'. Having satisfied myself there are no Morgans, I accelerate forward to the next day . . . and the next. The focus control is finicky and has to be constantly adjusted. At other times I have to pan back and forth to keep the newspaper columns on screen.

Having finished the first batch I collect another six boxes of microfiche from the librarian. The newspapers around Christmas have more pages and take longer to search. As I finish November 1988 my anxiety grows. What if it's not here? I can feel knots in my shoulder blades from leaning forward. My eyes ache.

The film rolls on to a new day. I find the death notices. For several seconds I carry on down the page before realising what

I've seen. I go back. There it is! I press my finger on the name as though frightened it might vanish.

Lenny A. Morgan, aged 55, died on Saturday December 10 from burns received in an explosion at the Carnegie Engineering Works. Mr Morgan, a popular bus conductor at the Green Lane Depot in Stanley, was a former merchant seaman and a prominent union delegate. He is survived by his sisters, Ruth and Louise, and sons Dafyyd, 19, and Robert, 8. A service will be conducted at 1 p.m. Tuesday at St James' Church in Stanley. The family requests that memorial tributes take the form of contributions to the Socialist Worker's Party.

I go back through papers for the week before. An accident like this must have been reported. I find the news story at the bottom of page five. The headline reads: 'Worker Dies in Depot Blast'.

A Liverpool bus conductor has died after an explosion at the Carnegie Engineering Works on Saturday afternoon. Lenny Morgan, 55, suffered 80 per cent burns to his body when welding equipment ignited gas fumes. The blast and fire severely damaged the workshop, destroying two buses.

Mr Morgan was taken to Rathbone Hospital where he died on Saturday evening without regaining consciousness. The Liverpool coroner has begun an investigation into what caused the explosion.

Friends and workmates paid tribute to Mr Morgan yesterday, describing him as extremely popular with the travelling public, who enjoyed his eccentricities. 'Lenny used to dress in a Santa hat and serenade the passengers with carols at Christmas,' said supervisor Bert McMullen.

At three o'clock I rewind the microfilm, pack it into boxes and thank the librarian for her help. She doesn't ask me if I found what I wanted. She's too busy trying to repair the spine of a bound volume that someone has dropped.

Despite looking through another two months of newspapers, I found no further references to the accident. There must have been an inquest. As I ride down in the lift I flick through my notes. What am I looking for? Some link to Catherine. I don't know where she grew up, but her grandfather certainly worked in Liverpool. My instincts tell me that she and Bobby met in care – either at a children's home or at a psych hospital.

Bobby didn't mention having a brother. Considering that Bridget was only twenty-one when she had Bobby, Dafyyd was either adopted or, more likely, Lenny had an earlier marriage that produced a son.

Lenny had two sisters but I only have maiden names, which makes it harder to find them. Even if they didn't marry, how many Morgans are likely to be in the Liverpool phone book? I don't want to have to go there.

Pushing through the revolving door, I'm so lost in thought I go round twice before finding the outside. Taking the steps carefully, I fix my bearings and head towards Lime Street Station.

I hate to admit it, but I'm enjoying this: the search. I'm motivated. I have a mission. Last-minute shoppers fill the footpaths and queue for buses. I'm tempted to find the number 96 and see where it takes me. Lucky dips are for people who like surprises. Instead I hail a cab and ask for the Green Lane Bus Depot.

8

A mechanic holds a carburettor in one blackened hand and gives me directions with the other. The pub is called the Tramway Hotel and Bert McMullen is usually at the bar.

'How will I recognise him?'

The mechanic chuckles and turns back to the engine, leaning inside the bowels of a bus.

I find the Tramway easily enough. Someone has scrawled graffiti on the blackboard outside: 'A beer means never having to say, "I'm thirsty".' Pushing through the door, I enter a dimly lit room with stained floors and bare wooden furniture. Red bulbs above the bar give the place a pink tinge like a Wild West bordello. Black and white photographs of trams and antique buses decorate the walls, alongside posters for 'live' music.

I take my time and count eight people, including a handful of teenagers playing pool in the back alcove near the toilets. I stand in front of the beer taps, waiting to be served by a barman who can't be bothered to look up from the *Racing Post*.

Bert McMullen is at the far end of the bar. His crumpled tweed jacket is patched at the elbows and adorned by various badges and pins, all related to buses. In one hand he holds a cigarette and in the other an empty pint glass. He turns the glass in his fingers, as if reading some hidden inscription etched into the side.

Bert growls at me. 'Who you gawpin' at?' His thick moustache appears to sprout directly from his nose and droplets of foam and beer are clinging to the ends of the grey and black hairs.

'I'm sorry. I didn't mean to stare.' I offer to buy him another pint. He half turns and examines me. His eyes, like watery glass eggs, stop at my shoes. 'How much did them shoes cost?'

'I don't remember.'

'Gimme an estimate.'

I shrug. 'A hundred pounds.'

He shakes his head in disgust. 'I wouldn't pick 'em up with two shitty sticks. You couldn't walk more 'an twenty mile in them things before they fall apart.' He's still staring at my shoes. He waves the barman over. 'Hey, Phil, get a load of these shoes.'

Phil leans over the bar and peers at my feet. 'What d'you call them?'

'Loafers,' I answer self-consciously.

'Gerraway!' Both men look at each other in disbelief. 'Why would you want to wear a shoe called a loafer?' says Bert. 'You got more bum than brains.'

'They're Italian,' I say, as if that makes a difference.

'Italian! What's wrong with English shoes? You a wog?'

'No.'

'You're wearing wog shoes.' Bert presses his face close to mine. I can smell baked beans. 'I reckon anyone who wears shoes like that hasn't done a proper day's work in his life. You got to wear boots, kid, with a steel cap in the toe and some grip on the bottom. Them shoes of yours wouldn't last a week in a real job.'

'Unless, of course, he works behind a desk,' says the barman.

Bert looks at me warily. 'Are you one of the overcoat gang?'

252

'What's that?'

'Never get your coat off.'

'I work hard enough.'

'Do you vote Labour?'

'I don't think that's any of your business.'

'Are you a Hail Mary?'

'Agnostic.'

'Ag-fucking-what?'

'Agnostic.'

'Jesus wept! OK, this is your last chance. Do you support the mighty Liverpool?' He crosses himself.

'No.'

He sighs in disgust. 'Get off home, yer Mam's got custard waiting.'

I look between the two of them. That's the problem with Scousers. You can never tell whether they're joking or being serious until they put a glass in your face.

Bert winks at the barman. 'He can buy me a drink, but he can't fiddle arse around. 'E's got five minutes before he can bugger off.'

Phil grins at me. His ears are laden with silver rings and dangling pendants.

The pub has tables are arranged along the walls, leaving a dance floor in the centre. The teenagers are still playing pool. The only girl among them looks underage and is dressed in tight jeans and a singlet top, revealing her bare midriff. The boys are trying to impress her but her boyfriend is easy to spot. Bulked up by weight training, he looks like an abscess about to explode.

Bert is watching the bubbles rise to the head of his Guinness. Minutes pass. I feel myself getting smaller and smaller. Finally he raises the glass to his lips and his Adam's apple bobs up and down as he swallows.

'I wanted to ask you about Lenny Morgan. I asked at the depot. They said you were friends.'

253

He shows no emotion.

I keep going. 'I know he died in a fire. I know you worked with him. I just want to find out what happened.'

Bert lights a cigarette. 'I can't see how it's any of your business.'

'I'm a psychologist. Lenny's son is in a spot of bother. I'm trying to help him.' As I hear the words I feel a pinprick of guilt. Is that what I'm trying to do? Help him?

'What's his name?'

'Bobby.'

'I remember him. Lenny used to bring him down the depot during the holidays. He used to sit up back and ring the bell to signal the driver. So what's he done?'

'He beat up a woman. He's about to be sentenced.'

Bert smiles sardonically. 'That sort of shit happens. You ask my old lady. I've hit her once or twice but she punches harder than I do. It's all forgotten in the morning.'

'This woman was badly hurt. Bobby dragged her out of a cab and kicked her unconscious in a busy street.'

'Was he shagging her?'

'No. He didn't know her.'

'Whose side are you on?'

'I'm assessing him.'

'So you're trying to get him banged up?'

'I want to help him.'

Bert snorts. Headlights from the road outside slide over the walls. 'It's all gin and oranges to me, son, but I can't see what Lenny has to do with it. He's been dead fourteen years.'

'Losing a father can be very traumatic. Perhaps it might help explain a few things.'

Bert pauses to consider this. I know he's weighing up his prejudices against his instincts. He doesn't like my shoes. He doesn't like my clothes. He doesn't like strangers. He wants to snarl and push his face into mine, but he needs a good enough reason. Another pint of Guinness has the casting vote.

'You know what I do every morning?' Bert says.

I shake my head.

'I spend an hour lying in bed, with my back so fucked up I can't even roll over to reach my fags. I stare at the ceiling and think about what I'm going to do today. Same as every day: I'm going to get up, hobble to the bathroom, then to the kitchen, and after breakfast I'm going to hobble down here and sit on this stool. Do you know why?'

I shake my head.

''Cos I've discovered the secret of revenge. Outlive the bastards. I'll dance on their graves. You take Maggie Thatcher. She destroyed the working class in this country. She closed down the mines, the docks and the factories. But she's rusting away now – just like those ships out there. She had a stroke not so long ago. Don't matter whether you're a destroyer or a dinghy – the salt always gets you in the end. And when she goes I'm gonna *piss* on her grave.'

He drains his glass as though washing away the bad taste in his mouth. I nod to the barman. He starts pouring another.

'Did Bobby look like his father?'

'Nah. He was a big pudding of a lad. Wore glasses. He worshipped Lenny; trailed after him like a puppy dog; running errands and fetching him cups of tea. When Lenny brought him to work, he'd sit outside of here and drink lemonade while Lenny had a few pints. Afterwards they'd cycle home.'

Bert is warming up. 'Lenny used to be a merchant seaman. His forearms were covered in tattoos. He was a man of very few words, but if you got him talkin' he'd tell you stories about his tattoos and how he got each one of 'em. Everybody liked Lenny. People smiled when they spoke his name. He was too nice a bloke. Sometimes folks can take advantage of that . . . '

'What do you mean?'

'You take his wife. I can't remember her name. She was some Irish Catholic shopgirl, with big hips and a ripcord in her knickers. I heard tell that Lenny only screwed her the

255

once. He was too much of a gentleman to say. She gets pregnant and tells Lenny the baby is his. Anyone else would have been suspicious, but straight away Lenny marries her. He buys a house – using up all the money he'd saved from going to sea. We all knew what his missus was like: a real Anytime Annie. Half the depot must have ridden her. We nicknamed her "number twenty-two" – our most popular route.'

Bert looks at me sadly, flicking ash from his sleeve. He explains how Lenny had started at the garage as a diesel mechanic and then taken a pay cut to go on the road. Passengers loved his funny hats and his impromptu songs. When Liverpool beat Real Madrid in the final of the European Cup in 1981, he dyed his hair red and decorated the bus in toilet paper.

Lenny knew about his wife's indiscretions, according to Bert. She flaunted her infidelity – dressing herself in mini skirts and high heels. Dancing every night at the Empire Ballroom and the Grafton.

Without warning, Bert windmills his arm as though wanting to punch something. His face twists in pain. 'He was too soft – soft in the heart, soft in the head. If it were raining soup Lenny would be stuck with a fork in his hand. Some women deserve a slap. She took everything . . . his heart, his house, his boy. Most men would have killed her. Most men weren't like Lenny. She sucked him dry. Drained his spirit. She spent a hundred quid a month more than he earned. He was working double shifts and doing the housework as well. I used to hear him pleading with her over the phone – "Are you staying in tonight, pet?" She just laughed at him.'

'Why didn't he leave her?'

He shrugs. 'Guess he had a blind spot. Maybe she threatened to take the kid. Lenny wasn't a wimp. I once seen him throw four hooligans off his bus because they were upsetting the other passengers. He could handle himself, Lenny. He just couldn't handle *her*.'

Bert falls silent. For the first time I notice how the bar has

256

filled up and the noise level has risen. The Friday night band is setting up in the corner. People are looking at me; trying to work out what I'm doing. There is no such thing as anonymity when you're the odd one out.

The red lights have started to sway and the wooden floorboards echo. I've been trying to keep up with Bert, drink for drink.

I ask about the accident. Bert explains that Lenny sometimes used the engineering workshop of a weekend to build his inventions. The boss turned a blind eye. The weekend buses were running, but the workshop was empty.

'How much do you know about welding?' Bert asks.

'Not much.'

He pushes his beer aside and picks up two coasters. Then he explains how two pieces of metal are joined together by using concentrated heat. Normally the heat is generated in two ways. An arc welder uses a powerful arc of electricity, with low voltage and high current generating temperatures of 11,000°F. Then you have oxy-fuel welders, where gases such as acetylene or natural gas are mixed with pure oxygen and burned to create a flame that can carve through metal.

'You don't muck around with this sort of equipment,' he says. 'But Lenny was one of the best welders I ever saw in me life. Fellas used to say he could weld two pieces of paper together.'

'We always took a lot of precautions in the workshop. All flammable liquids were stored in a separate room from the cutting or welding. We kept combustibles at least thirty-five feet away. We covered the drains and kept fire extinguishers nearby.

'I don't know what Lenny was building. Some people joked it was a rocket ship to send his ex-wife into outer space. The blast knocked an eight-ton bus on to its side. The acetylene tank blew a hole through the roof. They found it a hundred yards away.

257

'Lenny finished up near the roller doors. The only part of his body that hadn't been burned was his chest. They figure he must have been lying down when the fireball engulfed him because that part of his shirt was only slightly singed.

'A couple of the drivers dragged him clear. I still don't know how they managed it . . . what with the heat and all. I remember them saying afterwards how Lenny's boots were smoking and his skin had turned to crackling. He was still conscious but he couldn't speak. He had no lips. I'm glad I didn't see it. I'd still be having nightmares.' Bert puts his glass down and his chest heaves in a short sigh.

'So it was an accident?'

'That's what it looked like at first. Everyone figured a spark from the welder had ignited the acetylene tank. There might have been a hole in the hose, or some other fault. Maybe gas had accumulated in the tank he was welding.'

'What do you mean "at first"?'

'When they peeled off Lenny's shirt they found something written on his chest. They say every letter was inch-perfect – but I don't believe that, not when he was writing upside down and left to right. He'd used a welding torch to burn the word "SORRY" into his skin. Like I said, he was a man of very few words.'

9

I don't remember leaving The Tramway. Eight pints and then I lost count. The cold air hits me and I find myself on my hands and knees, leaving the contents of my stomach over the broken rubble and cinders of a vacant block.

It seems to be a makeshift car park for the pub. The country and western band is still playing. They're doing a cover of a Willie Nelson song about mothers not letting their children grow up to be cowboys.

As I try to stand something pushes me from behind and I fall into an oily puddle. The four teenagers from the bar are standing over me.

'Ya got any money?' asks the girl.

'Piss off!'

A kick is aimed at my head but misses. Another connects with my abdomen. My bowels slacken and I want to vomit again. I suck in air and try to think.

'Jesus, Baz, you said nobody gets hurt!' says the girl.

'Shut the fuck up! Don't use names.'

'Fuck you!'

'Leave it out, you two,' argues the one called Ozzie, who is left-handed and drinks rum and cola.

'Don't you start, dickhead.' Baz stares him down.

Someone takes my wallet out of my jacket.

'Not the cards, just the cash,' says Baz. He's older – in his early twenties – and has a swastika tattooed on his neck. He lifts me easily and pushes his face close to mine. I smell beer, peanuts and cigarette smoke.

'Hey, listen, toss-bag! You're not welcome here.'

Shoved backwards, I land against a wire fence topped with razor wire. Baz is toe-to-toe with me. He's three inches shorter and solid like a barrel. A knife blade gleams in his hand.

'I want my wallet back. If you give it to me, I won't press charges,' I say.

He laughs at me and mimics my voice. *Do I really sound that frightened?*

'You followed me from the pub. I saw you in there playing pool. You lost the last game on the black.'

The girl pushes her glasses up her nose. Her fingernails are bitten to the quick.

'What's he mean, Baz?'

'Shut up! Don't fucking use my name.' He shapes to hit her, but she shoots him a fierce glance. The silence lingers. I don't feel drunk any more.

I focus on the girl. 'You should have trusted your instincts, Denny.'

She looks at me, wide-eyed. 'How do you know my name?'

'You're Denny and you're underage – thirteen, maybe fourteen. This is Baz, your boyfriend, and these two are Ozzie and Carl—'

'Shut the fuck up!'

Baz shoves me hard against the fence. He can sense he's losing the initiative.

'Is this what you want, Denny? What's your mum going to say when the police come looking for you? She thinks you're staying at a girlfriend's house, doesn't she? She doesn't like you hanging out with Baz. She thinks he's a loser, a no-hoper.'

'Make him stop, Baz.' Denny covers her mouth.

'Shut the fuck up!'

No one says anything. They're watching me. I take a step forward and whisper to Baz. 'Use your grey cells, Baz. I just want my wallet.'

Denny interrupts, on the verge of tears, 'Just give him his fucking wallet. I want to go home.'

Ozzie turns to Carl. 'C'mon.'

Baz doesn't know what to do. He could carve me up like a wisp of smoke, but now he's on his own. The others are already disappearing, loose-limbed and hooting with laughter.

He pushes me hard against the fence, pressing the knife to my neck and his face next to mine. His teeth close around my earlobe. White heat. Pain. Ripping his head to one side, he spits hard into a puddle and shoves me away.

'There's a little souvenir from Bobby!'

He wipes blood from his mouth. Then he swaggers away and kicks at the door of a parked car. I'm sitting in water, braced against the fence, my wallet at my feet. In the distance I see navigation lights blinking from the top of industrial cranes on the far side of the Mersey.

Slowly, pulling myself upright, I try to stand. My right leg buckles and I fall to my knees. Blood leaks in a warm trail down my neck.

I stumble to the main road but there is no traffic. Glancing over my shoulder, I worry about them coming back. Half a mile down the road I find a mini-cab office with metal grilles over the door and windows. The inside is saturated with cigarette smoke and the smell of takeaway food.

'What happened to you?' asks a fat man behind the grille.

I catch a glimpse of my reflection in the window. The bottom part of my ear is missing and my shirt collar is soaked with blood.

261

'I got mugged.'

'Who by?'

'Kids.'

I open my wallet. The cash is still there . . . all of it.

The fat man rolls his eyes, no longer concerned about me. I'm just a drunk who got into a fight. He radios for a car and makes me wait outside on the footpath. I glance nervously up and down the street, looking for Baz.

A souvenir! Bobby has some charming friends. Why didn't they take the money? What was the point? Unless they were trying to warn me off. Liverpool is a big enough place to get lost and small enough to get noticed, particularly if you start asking questions.

Slumped on the back seat of an old Mazda 626, I close my eyes and let my heart slow. Sweat has cooled between my shoulder blades, making my neck feel stiff.

The mini-cab drops me at the University Hospital, where I wait for an hour to get six stitches in my ear. As the intern wipes the blood from my face with a towel, he asks if the police have been informed. I lie and say yes. I don't want Ruiz knowing where I am.

Afterwards, with a dose of paracetamol to dull the pain, I walk through the city until I reach Pier Head. The last ferry is arriving from Birkenhead. The engine makes the air throb. Lights leak towards me in a colourful slick of reds and yellows. I stare at the water and keep imagining I can see dark shapes. Bodies. I look again and they vanish. Why do I always look for bodies?

As a child I sometimes went boating on the Thames with my sisters. One day I found a sack containing five dead kittens. Patricia kept telling me to put the sack down. She was screaming at me. Rebecca wanted to see inside. She, like me, had never seen anything dead, except for bugs and lizards.

I emptied the sack and the kittens tumbled on to the grass. Their wet fur stood on end. I was attracted and repelled at

262

the same time. They had soft fur and warm blood. They weren't so different from me.

Later, as a teenager, I imagined that I would be dead by thirty. It was in the midst of the Cold War, when the world teetered on the edge of an abyss, at the mercy of whichever madman in the White House or the Kremlin had one of those 'I-wonder-what-this-button-does?' moments.

Since then my internal doomsday clock has swung wildly back and forth, much like the official version. Marrying Julianne made me hugely optimistic and having Charlie added to this. I even looked forward to graceful old age when we'd trade our backpacks for suitcases on wheels, playing with grandchildren, boring them with nostalgic stories, taking up eccentric hobbies . . .

The future will be different now. Instead of a dazzling road to discovery, I see a twitching, stammering, dribbling spectacle in a wheelchair. 'Do we really have to go and see Dad today?' Charlie will ask. 'He won't know the difference if we don't show up.'

A gust of wind sets my teeth chattering and I push away from the railing. I walk from the wharf, no longer worried about getting lost. At the same time I feel vulnerable. Exposed.

At the Albion Hotel the receptionist is knitting, moving her lips as she counts the stitches. Canned laughter emanates from somewhere beneath her feet. She doesn't acknowledge me until she finishes a row. Then she hands me a note. It has the name and telephone number of a teacher who taught Bobby at St Mary's school. The morning will be soon enough.

The stairs feel steeper than before. I'm tired and drunk. I just want to sink down and sleep.

I wake up suddenly, breathing hard. My hand slides across the sheets looking for Julianne. She normally wakes when I cry out in my sleep. She puts her hand on my chest and whispers that everything is all right.

263

Taking deep breaths, I wait for my heartbeat to slow and then slip out of bed, tiptoeing across to the window. The street is empty except for a newspaper van making a delivery. I touch my ear gingerly and feel the roughness of the stitches.

There is blood on my pillow.

The door opens. There is no knock. No warning footsteps. I'm positive that I locked it. A hand appears, red-nailed, long-fingered. Then a face coloured with lipstick and blusher. She is pale-skinned and thin, with short-cropped blonde hair.

'Shhhhhhhh!'

A person giggles behind her.

'For fuck's sake, will you be quiet?'

She's reaching for the light switch. I'm silhouetted against the window. 'This room is taken.'

Her eyes meet mine and she utters a single shocked expletive. Behind her, a large dishevelled man in an ill-fitting suit has his hand inside her top. 'You scared the crap out of me,' she says, pushing his hand away. He gropes drunkenly at her breasts again.

'How did you get into this room?'

She rolls her eyes apologetically. 'Made a mistake.'

'The door was locked.'

She shakes her head. Her male friend looks over her shoulder. 'What's he doing in *our* room?'

'It's *his* room, ya moron!' She hits him in the chest with a silver diamanté clutch bag and starts pushing him backwards. As she closes the door, she turns and smiles. 'You want some company? I can piss this guy off.'

She's so thin I can see the bones in her chest above her breasts. 'No thanks.'

She shrugs and hikes up her tights beneath her mini skirt. Then the door closes and I hear them trying to creep along the hall and climb to the next floor.

For a moment I feel a flush of anger. Did I really forget to lock the door? I was drunk, maybe even partly concussed.

It is just after six. Julianne and Charlie will still be sleeping. I take out my mobile and turn it on, staring at the glowing face in the darkness. There are no messages. This is my penance . . . to think about my wife and daughter when I fall asleep and when I wake.

Sitting on the windowsill, I watch the sky grow lighter. Pigeons wheel and soar over the rooftops. They remind me of Varanasi in India, where the vultures circle high over funeral pyres, waiting for the charred remains to be dumped in the Ganges. Varanasi is a sorry slum of a city, with crumbling buildings, cross-eyed children and nothing of beauty except the brightly coloured saris and swaying hips of the women. It appalled and fascinated me. The same is true of Liverpool.

I wait until seven before calling Julianne. A male voice answers. At first I think I've dialled the wrong number but then I recognise Jock's voice.

'I was just thinking about you,' he says in a booming voice. Charlie is in the background saying, 'Is that Dad? Can I talk to him? Please let me.'

Jock covers the receiver but I can still hear him. He tells her to fetch Julianne. Charlie complains, but obeys.

Meanwhile, Jock is full of chummy bonhomie. I interrupt him. 'What are you doing there, Jock? Is everything OK?'

'Your plumbing still sucks.'

What does he know about my fucking plumbing? He matches my coldness with his own. I can picture his face changing. 'Someone tried to break in. Julianne got a bit spooked. She didn't want to be on her own in the house. I offered to stay.'

'Who? When?'

'It was probably just some addict. He came through the front door. The plumbers had left it open. D.J. found him in the study and chased him down the street. Lost him near the canal.'

'Was anything taken?'

'No.'

I hear footsteps on the stairs. Jock puts his hand over the phone.

'Can I talk to Julianne? I know she's there.'

'She says no.'

I feel a flush of anger. Jock tries to banter again. 'She wants to know why you called her mother at three in the morning.'

A vague memory surfaces: dialling the number; her mother's icy rebuke. She hung up on me.

'Just let me talk to Julianne.'

'No can do, old boy. She's not feeling very well.'

'What do you mean?'

'Just what I said. She's feeling a bit off-colour.'

'Is anything wrong?'

'No. She's in good order. I've given her a full physical.' He's trying to wind me up. It's working.

'Give her the *fucking* phone—'

'I don't think you're in any position to give me orders, Joe. You're only makings things worse.'

I want to sink my fist into his 100-situps-a-day stomach. Then I hear a telltale click. Someone has picked up the phone in my office. Jock doesn't realise.

I try to sound conciliatory and tell him that I'll call later. He puts the phone down, but I wait, listening.

'Dad, is that you?' Charlie asks nervously.

'How are you, sweetheart?'

'Good. When are you coming home?'

'I don't know. I have to sort out a few things with Mummy.'

'Did you guys have a fight?'

'How did you know?'

'When Mum's angry at you I should never let her brush my hair.'

'I'm sorry.'

'That's OK. Was it your fault?'

'Yes.'

'Why don't you just say you're sorry? That's what you tell me to do when I have a fight with Taylor Jones.'

'I don't think that's going to be enough this time.'

I can hear her thinking about this. I can even picture her biting her bottom lip in concentration.

'Dad?'

'Yes.'

'Well . . . um . . . I want to ask you something. It's about . . . well . . . ' She keeps starting and stopping. I tell her to think of the whole question in her head and then ask me.

Finally it comes blurting out. 'There was this picture in the newspaper . . . someone with a coat over his head. Some of the kids were talking . . . at school. Lachlan O'Brien said it was you. I called him a liar. Then, last night, I took one of the newspapers from the bin. Mum had thrown them out. I sneaked them upstairs to my room—'

'Did you read the story?'

'Yes.'

My stomach lurches. How do I explain the concept of wrongful arrest and mistaken identity to an eight-year-old? Charlie has been taught to trust the police. Justice and fairness are important – even in the playground.

'It was a mistake, Charlie. The police made a mistake.'

'Then why is Mum angry at you?'

'Because I made another mistake. A different one. It has nothing to do with the police or with you.'

She falls silent. I can almost hear her thinking.

'What's wrong with Mummy?' I ask.

'I don't know. I heard her tell Uncle Jock she was late.'

'Late for what?'

'She didn't say. She just said she was late.'

I ask her to repeat the statement word for word. She doesn't understand why. My mouth is dry. It isn't just the hangover. In the background I can hear Julianne calling Charlie's name.

'I have to go,' whispers Charlie. 'Come home soon.'

She hangs up quickly. I don't have a chance to say goodbye. My first instinct is to call straight back. I want to keep calling until Julianne talks to me. Does 'late' mean what I think it means? I feel sick to the stomach: hopeless in the head.

I could be home in three hours if I caught a train. I could stand on the doorstep until she agrees to talk to me. Maybe that's what she wants – for me to come running back to fight for her.

We've waited six years. Julianne never stopped believing. I was the one who gave up hope.

10

A bell tinkles above my head as I enter the shop. The aromas of scented oils, perfumed candles and herbal poultices curl into my nostrils. Narrow shelves made of dark wood stretch from the floor to the ceiling. These are crammed with incense, soap, oils and bell jars full of everything from pumice stones to seaweed.

A large woman emerges from behind a partition. She wears a brightly coloured kaftan that starts at her throat and billows outwards over huge breasts. Strings of beads sprout from her skull and clack as she walks.

'Come, come, don't be shy,' she says, waving me towards her. This is Louise Elwood. I recognise her voice from the phone. Some people look like their voices. She is one of them – deep, low and loud. Bangles clink on her arms as she shakes my hand. At the centre of her forehead is a pasted red dot.

'Oh my, oh my, oh my,' she says, holding her hand beneath my chin. 'You are just in time. Look at those eyes. Dull. Dry. You haven't been sleeping well, have you? Toxins in the blood. Too much red meat. Maybe a wheat allergy. What happened to your ear?'

'An overzealous hairdresser.'

She raises an eyebrow.

'We spoke on the phone,' I explain. 'I'm Professor O'Loughlin.'

'Typical! Look at the state of you! Doctors and academics make the worst patients. They never take their own advice.'

She pirouettes with remarkable agility and bustles deeper into the shop. At the same time she keeps talking. There are no obvious signs of a man in her life. Photographs of children on the noticeboard are probably nieces and nephews. She has a Burmese (cat hair), a drawer full of chocolates (tinsel on the floor) and a taste for romance writers (*The Silent Lady* by Catherine Cookson).

Behind the partition is a small back room with just enough space for a table, three chairs and a bench containing a small sink. An electric kettle and a radio are plugged into the lone socket. The centre of the table has a women's magazine open at the crossword.

'Herbal tea?'

'Do you have coffee?'

'No.'

'Tea will be fine.'

She rattles off a list of a dozen different blends. By the time she's finished I've forgotten the first few.

'Camomile.'

'Excellent choice. Good for relieving stress and tension.' She pauses. 'You're not a believer, are you?'

'I have never been able to work out why herbal tea smells so wonderful but tastes so bland.'

She laughs. Her whole body shakes. 'The taste is subtle. It works in harmony with the body. Smell is the most immediate of all our senses. Touch might develop earlier and be the last to fade, but smell is hot-wired directly into our brains.'

She sets out two small china cups and fills a ceramic teapot with steaming water. The tea leaves are filtered twice through a silver sieve before she pushes a cup towards me.

'You don't read tea leaves then?'

'I think you're making fun of me, Professor.' She's not offended.

'Fifteen years ago you were a teacher at St Mary's.'

'For my sins.'

'Do you remember a boy called Bobby Morgan?'

'Of course I do.'

'What do you remember about him?'

'He was quite bright, although a little self-conscious about his size. Some of the other boys used to tease him because he wasn't very good at sports, but he had a lovely singing voice.'

'You taught the choir?'

'Yes. I once suggested singing lessons, but his mother wasn't the most approachable of women. I only saw her once at the school. She came to complain about Bobby stealing money from her purse to pay for an excursion to the Liverpool Museum.'

'What about his father?'

She looks at me quizzically. Clearly I'm expected to know something. Now she is trying to decide whether to continue.

'Bobby's father wasn't allowed at the school,' she says. 'He had a court order taken out against him when Bobby was in the second form. Didn't Bobby tell you any of this?'

'No.'

She shakes her head. Beads swing from side to side. 'I raised the alarm. Bobby had wet himself in class twice in a few weeks. Then he soiled his pants and spent most of the afternoon hiding in the boys' toilets. He was upset. When I asked him what was wrong he wouldn't say. I took him to the school nurse. She found him another pair of trousers. That's when she noticed the welts on his legs. It looked as though he'd been beaten.'

The school nurse followed the normal procedure and informed the deputy headmistress who, in turn, notified the

Department of Social Services. I know the process off by heart. A duty social worker would have taken the referral. It was then discussed with an area manager. The dominoes started falling – medical examinations, interviews, allegations, denials, case conferences, 'at risk' findings, interim care orders, appeals – each tumbling into the next.

'Tell me about the court order,' I ask.

She recalls only scant details. Allegations of sexual abuse, which the father denied. A restraining order. Chaperoning Bobby between classes.

'The police investigated but I don't know the outcome. The deputy headmistress dealt with the social workers and police.'

'Is she still around?'

'No. She resigned eighteen months ago; family reasons.'

'What happened to Bobby?'

'He changed. He had a stillness about him that you don't see in most children. A lot of the teachers found it very unnerving.' She stares into her teacup, tilting it gently back and forth. 'When his father died he became even more isolated. It was as though he was on the outside, with his face pressed against the glass.'

'Do you think Bobby was abused?'

'St Mary's is in a very poor area, Professor O'Loughlin. In some households just waking up in the morning is a form of abuse.'

I know almost nothing about cars. I can fill them with petrol, put air in the tyres and water in the radiator, but I have no interest in makes, models or the dynamics of the modern combustion engine. Usually I take no notice of other vehicles on the road but today it's different. I keep seeing a white van. I noticed it first this morning when I left the Albion Hotel. It was parked opposite. The other cars were covered in frost but not the van. The windscreen and back window had ragged circles of clear glass.

The same white van – or another one just like it – is parked on a delivery ramp opposite Louise Elwood's shop. The back doors are open. I can see hessian sacks inside, lining the floor. There must be hundreds of white vans in Liverpool: perhaps a whole fleet of them belonging to a courier company.

After last night I'm seeing phantoms lurking in every doorway and now sitting in cars. I walk across the market square, stopping at a department store window. Studying the reflection, I can see the square behind me. Nobody is following.

I haven't eaten. Seeking out warmth, I find a café on the first floor of a shopping arcade, overlooking the atrium. From my table I can watch the escalators.

H.L. Mencken – journalist, beer-drinker and sage – said that for every complex problem there is a solution that is simple, neat and wrong. I share his mistrust for the obvious.

At university I drove my lecturers to distraction by constantly questioning straightforward assumptions. 'Why can't you just accept things as they are?' they asked. 'Why *can't* the easy answer be right?

Nature isn't like that. If evolution had been about simple answers we would all have bigger brains and not watch *You've Been Framed*, or smaller brains and not invent weapons of mass destruction. Mothers would have four arms and babies would leave home after six weeks. We would all have titanium bones, UV-resistant skin, X-ray vision and the ability to have permanent erections and multiple orgasms.

Bobby Morgan – I'll call him by his real name now – had many of the hallmarks of sexual abuse. Even so, I don't want it to be true. I have grown to like Lenny Morgan. He did a lot of things right when he raised Bobby. People warmed to him. Bobby adored him.

Perhaps Lenny had two sides to his personality. There is nothing to stop an abuser being a safe, loving figure. It would certainly explain his suicide. It could also be the reason why Bobby needed two personalities to survive.

273

11

Social Services keep files on children who have been sexually abused. I once had full access to them but I'm no longer part of the system. The privacy laws are compelling.

I need help from someone I haven't seen in over a decade. Her name is Melinda Cossimo and I'm worried I might not recognise her. We arrange to meet in a coffee shop opposite the magistrates' court.

When I first arrived in Liverpool Mel was a duty social worker. Now she's an area manager (they call it a 'child protection specialist'). Not many people last this long in social services. They either burn out or blow up.

Mel was your original punk, with spiky hair and a wardrobe of distressed leather jackets and torn denim. She was always challenging everyone's opinions because she liked to see people stand up for their beliefs, whether she agreed with them or not.

Growing up in Cornwall, she had listened to her father, a local fisherman, pontificate on the distinction between 'men's work' and 'women's work'. Almost predictably, she became an ardent feminist and author of 'When Women Wear the Pants'

– her doctorate thesis. Her father must be turning in his grave.

Mel's husband Boyd, a Lancashire lad, wore khaki trousers, turtleneck sweaters and smoked roll-ups. Tall and thin, he went grey at nineteen but kept his hair long and tied back in a ponytail. I only ever saw it loose once, in the showers after we had played badminton.

They were great hosts. We'd get together most weekends for dinner parties at Boyd's run-down terrace, with its 'wind chime' garden and cannabis plants growing in an old fish-pond. We were all over-worked, under-appreciated and yet still idealistic. Julianne played the guitar and Mel had a voice like Joni Mitchell. We ate vegetarian feasts, drank too much wine, smoked a little dope and righted the wrongs of the world. The hangovers lasted until Monday and the flatulence until midweek.

Mel makes a face at me through the window. Her hair is straight and pinned back from her face. She's wearing dark trousers and a tailored beige jacket. A white ribbon is pinned to her lapel. I can't remember what charity it represents.

'Is this the management look?'

'No, it's middle-age,' she laughs, grateful to sit down. 'These shoes are killing me.' She kicks them off and rubs her ankles.

'Shopping?'

'An appointment in the children's court. An emergency care order.'

'Good result?'

'It could have been worse.'

I get the coffees while she minds the table. I know she's checking me out – trying to establish how much has changed. Do we still have things in common? Why have I suddenly surfaced? The caring profession is a suspicious one.

'So what happened to your ear?'

'Got bitten by a dog.'

'You should never work with animals.'

'So I've heard.'

Mel watches as my left hand tries to stir my coffee. 'Are you still with Julianne?'

'Uh-huh. We have Charlie now. She's eight. I think Julianne might be pregnant again.'

'Aren't you sure?' she laughs.

I laugh with her, but feel a pang of guilt.

I ask about Boyd. I picture him as an ageing hippy, still wearing linen shirts and Punjabi pants. Mel turns her face away, but not before I see the pain drift across her eyes like a cloud.

'Boyd is dead.'

Sitting very still, she lets the silence grow accustomed to the news.

'When?'

'Over a year ago. One of those big four-wheel drives, with a bullbar, went through a stop sign and cleaned him up.'

I tell her that I'm sorry. She smiles sadly and licks milk froth from her spoon.

'They say the first year is the hardest. I tell you, it's like being fucked over by fifty cops with batons and riot shields. I still can't get my head around the fact he's gone. I even blamed *him* for a while. I thought he'd abandoned me. It sounds silly, but out of spite I sold his record collection. It cost me twice as much to buy it back again.' She laughs at herself and stirs her coffee.

'You should have got in touch. We didn't know.'

'Boyd lost your address. He was hopeless. I know I could have found you.' She smiles apologetically. 'I just didn't want to see anyone for a while. It would just remind me of the good old days.'

'Where is he now?'

'At home in a little silver pot on my filing cabinet.' She makes it sound as though he's pottering around in the garden shed. 'I can't put him in the ground here. It's too cold. What if it snows? He hated the cold.' She looks at me mournfully. 'I know that's stupid.'

'Not to me.'

'I thought I might save up and take his ashes to Nepal. I could throw them off a mountain.'

'He was scared of heights.'

'Yeah. Maybe I should just tip them in the Mersey.'

'Can you do that?'

'Don't see how anyone could stop me.' She laughs sadly. 'So what brings you back to Liverpool? You couldn't get away from here fast enough.'

'I wish I could have taken you guys with me.'

'Down south! Not likely! You know what Boyd thought of London. He said it was full of people searching for something that they couldn't find elsewhere, not having bothered to look.'

I can hear Boyd saying exactly that.

'I need to get hold of a child protection file.'

'A red edge!'

'Yes.'

I haven't heard that term for years. It's the nickname given by social workers in Liverpool to child protection referrals because the initiating form has a dark crimson border.

'What child?'

'Bobby Morgan.'

Mel makes the connection instantly. I see it in her eyes. 'I dragged a magistrate out of bed at two in the morning to sign the interim care order. The father committed suicide. You must remember?'

'No.'

Her brow furrows. 'Maybe it was one of Erskine's.' Rupert Erskine was the senior psychologist in the department. I was the junior half of the team – a fact he pointed out at every opportunity. Mel had been the duty social worker on Bobby's case.

'The referral came from a schoolteacher,' she explains. 'The mother didn't want to say anything at first. When she saw the medical evidence she broke down and told us she suspected her husband.'

'Can you get me the file?'

I can see she wants to ask me why. At the same time, she realises it is probably safer to remain ignorant. Closed child-care files are stored at Hatton Gardens, the head office of the Liverpool Social Services Department. Files are held for eighty years and can only be viewed by an appropriate member of staff, an authorised agency or a court officer. All access becomes part of the record.

Mel stares at her reflection in her teaspoon. She has to make a decision. Does she help me or say no? She glances at her watch. 'I'll make a few phone calls. Come to my office at one-thirty.'

She kisses me on the cheek as she leaves. Another coffee is ordered for the wait. Down times are the worst. They give me too much time to think. That's when random thoughts bounce through my head like a ping-pong ball in a jar. Julianne is pregnant. We'll need a child gate at the bottom of the stairs. Charlie wants to go camping this summer. What's the connection between Bobby and Catherine?

Another van – but it's not white. The driver tosses a bundle of papers on to the pavement in front of the cafe. The front-page headline reads: 'Reward Offered in McBride Murder Hunt'.

Mel has a clean desk with two piles of paperwork on either side in haphazard columns. Her computer is decorated with stickers, headlines and cartoons. One of them shows an armed robber pointing a gun and saying, 'Your money or your life!' The victim replies, 'I have no money and no life. I'm a social worker.'

We're on the third floor of the Social Services department. Most of the offices are empty for the weekend. The view from Mel's window is of a half-built pre-fabricated warehouse. She has managed to get me three files, each held together by a loop of red tape. I have an hour before she gets back from shopping.

I know what to expect. The first rule of intelligent tinkering is to save all the parts. That's what the social services do. When they mess about with people's lives they make a careful note of every decision. There will be interviews, family assessments, psych reports and medical notes. There will be minutes of every case conference and strategy meeting, as well as copies of police statements and court rulings.

If Bobby spent time in a children's home or psych ward, this will have been recorded. There will be names, dates and places. With any luck I can cross-reference these with Catherine McBride's file and discover a link.

The first page of the file is a record of a telephone call from St Mary's School. I recognise Mel's handwriting. Bobby had 'displayed a number of recent behavioural changes'. Apart from wetting himself and soiling his pants, he had 'displayed inappropriate sexual behaviour'. He had removed his underpants and simulated sex with a seven-year-old girl.

Mel faxed through the information to the area manager. At the same time, she phoned the clerk in the area office and organised a check through the index files to see if Bobby, his parents or any siblings had ever come up on file. When this drew a blank, she started a new file. The injuries worried her most. She consulted with Lucas Dutton, the assistant director (children), who made the decision to launch an investigation.

The 'red edge' is easy to find because of the border. It records Bobby's name, date of birth, address and details of his parents, school, GP and known health problems. There are also details about the deputy headmistress of St Mary's, the original referrer.

Mel had organised a full medical examination. Dr Richard Legende found 'two or three marks about six inches long across both his buttocks'. He described the injuries as being consistent with 'two or three successive blows with a hard item such as a studded belt.'

Bobby had been distressed throughout the examination and

279

had refused to answer any questions. Dr Legende noted what appeared to be old scar tissue around the anus. 'Whether the injury was caused accidentally or by deliberate penetration is not clear,' he wrote. In a later report he hardened his resolve and described the scarring as being 'consistent with abuse'.

Bridget Morgan was interviewed. Hostile at first, she accused social services of being busybodies. When told of Bobby's injuries and behaviour, she began to qualify her answers. Eventually she began making excuses for her husband.

'He's a good man, but he can't help himself. He gets angry and loses his rag.'

'Does he ever hit you?'

'Yeah.'

'What about Bobby?'

'He gets the worst of it.'

'When he beats Bobby, what does he use?'

'A dog collar . . . He'll kill me if he knows I'm here . . . You don't know what he's like . . .'

When asked about any inappropriate sexual behaviour, Bridget categorically denied her husband could have done such a thing. Her protests became more strident as the interview went on. She became tearful and asked to see Bobby.

All allegations of sexual abuse have to be reported to the police. After being told this, Bridget Morgan grew even more anxious. Clearly distressed, she admitted to having concerns about her husband's relationship with Bobby. She wouldn't or couldn't elaborate.

Bobby and his mother were taken to Marsh Lane police station to be formerly interviewed. A strategy meeting was held at the station. Those present were Mel Cossimo, her immediate boss Lucas Dutton, Detective Sergeant Helena Bronte and Bridget Morgan. Having spent a few minutes alone with Bobby, Mrs Morgan accepted the need for an investigation.

Leafing through her police statement, I try to pick out the

crux of her allegations. Two years earlier she claimed to have seen Bobby sitting on her husband's lap, not wearing any underwear. Her husband had had only a towel around his waist and he appeared to be pushing Bobby's hand between his legs.

During the previous year she had often found that Bobby had no underwear on when he undressed to have a bath. When asked why, he'd said, 'Daddy doesn't like me wearing underpants.'

The mother also claimed that her husband would only take a bath when Bobby was awake and would leave the bathroom door open. He would often invite Bobby to join him, but the boy made excuses.

Although not a strong statement, in the hands of a good prosecutor it could be damning enough. The next statement I expect to find is Bobby's. It isn't there. I turn several pages and find that no mention is made of a formal statement, which could explain why Lenny Morgan was never charged. Instead there is a videotape and a sheaf of handwritten notes.

A child's evidence is crucial. Unless he or she admits to being molested, the chances of success are slim. The abuser would have to admit the crime, or the medical evidence would have to be incontrovertible.

Mel has a video and TV in her office. I slide the tape out of the cardboard sleeve. The label has Bobby's full name, as well as the date and place of the interview. As the first images flash on to the screen, the time is stamped in the bottom left hand corner.

A child protection evaluation is very different from a normal patient consultation because of the time constraints. It can often take weeks to establish the sort of trust that allows a child to slowly reveal his or her inner world. Evaluations have to be done quickly and the questions are therefore more direct.

The child-friendly interview room has toys on the floor and brightly coloured walls. Drawing paper and crayons have been left on the table. A small boy sits nervously on a plastic chair, looking at the blank piece of paper. He is wearing a school uniform with baggy shorts and scuffed shoes. He glances at the camera and I see his face clearly. He has changed a lot in fourteen years, but I still recognise him. He sits impassively, as if resigned to his fate.

There is something else. Something more. The details return like surrendered soldiers. I have seen this boy before. Rupert Erskine asked me to review a case. A young boy who wasn't responding to any of his questions. A new approach was needed. Perhaps a new face.

The video is still running. I hear *my* voice. 'Do you prefer to be called Robert, Rob or Bobby?'

'Bobby.'

'Do you know why you're here, Bobby?'

He doesn't answer.

'I have to ask you a few questions. Is that OK?'

'I want to go home.'

'Not just yet. Tell me, Bobby, you understand the difference between the truth and a lie, don't you?'

He nods.

'If I said that I had a carrot instead of a nose, what would that be?'

'A lie.'

'That's right.'

The tape continues. I ask non-specific questions about school and home. Bobby talks about his favourite TV shows and toys. He relaxes and begins doodling on a sheet of paper as he talks.

If he had three magic wishes what would they be? After two false starts and shuffling his choices, he came up with: 1) owning a chocolate factory; 2) going camping; and 3) building a machine that would make everybody happy. Who would he most like to be? Sonic the Hedgehog because 'he runs really fast and saves his friends'.

Watching the video, I can recognise some of the mannerisms and body language of the adult Bobby. He rarely smiled or laughed. He maintained eye contact only briefly.

I ask him about his father. At first Bobby is animated and open. He wants to go home and see him. 'We're making an invention. It's going to stop shopping bags from spilling in the boot of the car.'

Bobby draws a picture of himself and I get him to name the different body parts. He mumbles when he talks about his 'private parts'.

'Do you like it when you have a bath with your dad?'

'Yes.'

'What do you like about it?'

'He tickles me.'

'Where does he tickle you?'

'All over.'

'Does he ever touch you in a way that you don't like?'

Bobby's brow furrows. 'No.'

'Does he ever touch your private parts?'

'No.'

'What about when he washes you?'

'I suppose.' He mumbles something else that I can't make out.

'What about your mum? Does she ever touch your private parts?'

He shakes his head and asks to go home. He screws up the piece of paper and refuses to answer any more questions. He isn't upset or scared. It is another example of the 'distancing' that is common in sexually abused children who try to make themselves smaller and less of a target.

The interview ends and the outcome was clearly inconclusive. Body language and mannerisms weren't enough to formulate an opinion.

Turning back to the files, I piece together the history of what happened next. Mel recommended that Bobby be placed on the Child Protection Register – a list of all children in the area who were considered to be at risk. She applied for an interim custody order – getting a magistrate out of bed at two a.m.

Police arrested Lenny Morgan. His house was searched, along with his bus depot locker and a neighbouring garage he rented as a workshop. He maintained his innocence throughout. He described himself as a loving father who had never done anything wrong or been in trouble with the police. He claimed to have no knowledge of Bobby's injuries, but admitted to 'giving him a whack' when he dismantled and broke a perfectly good alarm clock.

I knew none of this. My involvement ended after a single interview. It was Erskine's case.

A child protection case conference was held on Friday 15 August. The conference was chaired by Lucas Dutton and included the duty social worker, consultant psychologist Rupert Erskine, Bobby's GP, the deputy headmistress of his school and Detective Sergeant Helena Bronte.

The minutes of the meeting indicate Lucas Dutton ran proceedings. I remember him. At my first case conference he shot me down in flames when I offered an alternative suggestion to his own. Directors are rarely questioned – especially by junior psychologists whose diplomas are fresh enough to smudge.

The police didn't have enough evidence to charge Lenny Morgan, but the criminal investigation continued. Based on the physical evidence and Bridget Morgan's statement, the conference recommended that Bobby be removed from his family and placed in foster care unless his father agreed to voluntarily stay away. Daily contact would be arranged but father and son were never to be left alone.

Bobby spent five days in foster care before Lenny agreed to leave the family home and live separately until the allegations were fully investigated.

The second case file begins with a contents page. I scan the list and continue reading. For three months the Morgan family was shadowed by social workers and psychologists, who tried discover exactly how it functioned. Bobby's behaviour was monitored and reviewed, particularly during the contact visits with his father. At the same time Erskine interviewed Bridget, Lenny and Bobby separately, taking detailed histories. He also spoke to the maternal grandmother, Pauline Aherne, and Bridget's younger sister.

Both seemed to confirm Bridget's suspicions about Lenny. In particular, Pauline Aherne claimed to have witnessed an example of inappropriate behaviour when father and son were wrestling at bedtime and she saw Lenny's hand inside Bobby's pyjamas.

When I compared her statement to Bridget's, I noticed how they used many of the same phrases and descriptions. This would have concerned me if it had been my case. Blood is thicker than water – never more so than in child custody cases.

Lenny Morgan's first wife had died in a car accident. A son from the first marriage, Dafyyd Morgan, had left home at eighteen without coming to the attention of Social Services.

Several attempts were made to find him. Child care workers traced his teachers and a swimming coach, who reported no cause for concern in his behaviour. Dafyyd had left school at fifteen and been apprenticed to a local building firm. He'd then dropped out and his last known address was a back-packer's hostel in South Australia.

The file contains Erskine's conclusions, but not his session notes. He described Bobby as 'anxious, fidgety, and tempera-mentally fragile', and displaying 'symptoms of post-traumatic stress disorder'.

'When questioned about any sexual abuse, Bobby became increasingly defensive and agitated,' Erskine wrote. 'He also seems defensive if anyone suggests his family is not ideal. It is as if he is working hard to hide something.'

Of Bridget Morgan he wrote: 'Her first concern is always for her son. She is particularly reluctant to allow any further

285

interviews with Bobby because of the anxiety these create. Bobby has apparently been wetting the bed and has had problems sleeping.'

Her concern was understandable. At a rough count, I estimated Bobby was interviewed more than a dozen times by therapists, psychologists and social workers. Questions were repeated and rephrased.

During free play sessions he was observed undressing dolls and naming body parts. None of these sessions were recorded, but a therapist reported that Bobby placed one doll on top of the other and made grunting noises.

Erskine included two of Bobby's drawings in the file. I hold them at arm's length. They're rather good in an abstract sort of way – a cross between Picasso and the Flintstones. The figures are robot-like, with skewed faces. Adults are drawn excessively large and children very small.

Erskine concluded:

There are several significant pieces of evidence which, in my opinion, strongly support the possibility of sexual contact between Mr Morgan and his son.

First, there is the evidence of Bridget Morgan, as well as that of the maternal grandmother, Mrs Pauline Aherne. Neither woman appears to have any reason to be biased or embellish their accounts. Both witnessed occasions when Mr Morgan exposed himself to his son and removed his son's underwear.

Secondly, there is the evidence of Dr Richard Legende, who found 'two or three strap marks about six inches long across both of the child's buttocks'. More perturbing was the evidence of scar tissue around the anus.

Added to this we have the behavioural changes in Bobby. He has displayed an unhealthy interest in sex, as well as a working knowledge far beyond that of a normal eight-year-old.

Based on these facts, I believe there exists a strong likelihood that Bobby has been sexually abused, most probably by his father.

There must have been another case conference in mid-November. I can find no minutes. The police investigation was suspended but the file left open.

The third file is full of legal documents – some of them bound in ribbon. I recognise the paperwork. Satisfied that Bobby was at risk, Social Services had applied for a permanent care order. The lawyers were set loose.

'What are you mumbling about?' Mel is back from her shopping, balancing two cups of coffee on a ledger. 'Sorry I can't offer you anything stronger. Remember when we used to smuggle boxes of wine in here at Christmas?'

'I remember Boyd getting drunk and watering the plastic plants in the foyer.'

We both laugh.

'Bring back any memories?' She motions to the files.

'Sadly.' My left hand is trembling. I push it into my lap. 'What did you make of Lenny Morgan?'

She sits down and kicks off her shoes. 'I thought he was a pig. He was abusive and violent.'

'What did he do?'

'He confronted me outside the court. I went to use a phone in the foyer. He asked me why I was doing this – as if it was personal. When I tried to get past him, he pushed me against the wall and put his hand around my throat. He had this look in his eyes . . . ' She shudders.

'You didn't press charges?'

'No.'

'He was upset?'

'Yes.'

'What about the wife?'

'Bridget. She was all fur coat and no knickers. A real social climber.'

'But you liked her?'

'Yes.'

'What happened about the care order?'

287

'One magistrate agreed with the application and two claimed there was insufficient evidence to sustain the argument.'

'So you tried to get Bobby made a ward of court?'

'You bet. I wasn't letting the father anywhere near him. We went straight to the county court and got a hearing that afternoon. The papers should all be there.' She motions towards the files.

'Who gave evidence?'

'I did.'

'What about Erskine?'

'I used his report.'

Mel is getting annoyed at my questions. 'Any social worker would have done what I did. If you can't get the magistrates to see sense, you go to a judge. Nine times out of ten you'll get wardship.'

'Not any more.'

'No.' She sounds disappointed. 'They've changed the rules.'

From the moment Bobby became a ward, every major decision on his welfare was made by a court instead of his family. He couldn't change schools, get a passport, join the army or get married without the court's permission. It also guaranteed that his father would never be allowed back into his life.

Turning the pages of the file, I come across the judgement. It runs to about eight pages, but I scan them quickly, looking for the outcome.

The husband and wife are each genuinely concerned about the welfare of the child. I am satisfied that they have in the past, in their own way, attempted to discharge their obligations as parents to the best of their ability. Unfortunately in the husband's case, his ability to properly and appropriately discharge his obligations to the child has, in my view, been adversely affected by the allegations hanging over his head.

*I have taken into consideration the countervailing evidence –
namely the husband's denials. At the same time, I am aware that
the child wishes to live with both his father and mother. Clearly,
the weight given to those wishes must be balanced against other
matters relevant to Bobby's welfare.*

*The child welfare guidelines and tests are clear. Bobby's interests
are paramount. This court cannot grant custody or access to a parent
if that custody or access would expose a child to an unacceptable
risk of sexual abuse.*

*I hope that, in due course, when Bobby has acquired a level of
self-protection, maturity and understanding, he will have an opportunity to spend time with his father. However, until that time arrives,
which I see regrettably as being some time in the future, he should
not have contact with his father.*

The judgement bears a court seal and is signed by Mr Justice
Alexander McBride, Catherine's grandfather.

Mel is watching me from the far side of the desk. 'Find
what you were looking for?'

'Not really. Did you ever have much to do with Justice
McBride?'

'He's a good egg.'

'I suppose you've heard about his granddaughter.'

'A terrible thing.'

She spins her chair slowly around and stretches out her legs
until her shoes rest on the wall. Her eyes are fixed on me.

'Do you know if Catherine McBride had a file?' I ask casually.

'Funny you should ask that.'

'Why?'

'I've just had someone else ask to see it. That's two interesting requests in one day.'

'Who asked for the file?'

'A homicide squad detective. He wants to know if *your* name
crops up in there.'

Her eyes are piercing. She is angry with me for holding something back. Social workers don't confide in people easily. They learn not to trust . . . not when dealing with abused children, beaten wives, drug addicts, alcoholics and parents fighting for custody. Nothing can be taken at face value. Never trust a journalist, or a defence lawyer, or a parent who is running scared. Never turn your back in an interview or make a promise to a child. Never rely on foster carers, magistrates, politicians or senior public servants. Mel had trusted me. I had let her down.

'The detective says you're a subject of interest. He says that Catherine made a sexual assault complaint against you. He asked if any other complaints had ever been made.'

This is Mel's territory. She has nothing against men, just the things they do.

'The sexual assault is a fiction. I didn't touch Catherine.'

I can't hide the anger in my voice. Turning the other cheek is for people who want to look the other way. I'm sick of being accused of something I haven't done.

On the walk back to the Albion Hotel, I try to put the pieces together. My stitched ear is throbbing but it helps focus my thoughts. It's like being able to concentrate with the TV turned up full volume.

Bobby was about the same age as Charlie when he lost his father. A tragedy like that can take a terrible toll, but more than one person is needed to shape a child's mind. There are grandparents, uncles, aunts, brothers, sisters, teachers, friends and a huge cast of extras. If I could call on all of these people and interview them, maybe I could discover what happened to him.

What am I missing? A child is made a ward of court. His father commits suicide. A sad story, but not unique. Children aren't made wards of court any more. The law changed in the early nineties. The old system was too open to abuse.

290

Precious little evidence was required and there were no checks and balances.

Bobby had shown all the signs of being sexually abused. Victims of child abuse find ways of protecting themselves. Some suffer from traumatic amnesia; others bury their pain in their unconscious minds or refuse to reflect on what has happened. At the same time, there are sometimes social workers who 'verify' rather than question allegations of abuse. They believe that accusers never lie and abusers always do.

The more Bobby denied anything had happened, the more people believed it had to be true. This one cast iron assumption underpinned the entire investigation.

What if we got it wrong?

Researchers at the University of Michigan once took a synopsis of an actual case involving a two-year-old girl and presented it to a panel of experts including eight clinical psychologists, twenty-three graduate students and fifty social workers and psychiatrists. The researchers knew from the outset that the child had *not* been sexually abused.

The mother alleged abuse based on her discovery of a bruise on her daughter's leg and a single pubic hair (that she thought looked like the father's) in the girl's nappy. Four medical examinations showed no evidence of abuse. Two lie detector tests and a joint police and Child Protection Service investigation cleared the father.

Despite this, three quarters of the experts recommended that the father's contact with the daughter be either highly supervised or stopped altogether. Several of them even concluded that the girl had been sodomised.

There is no such thing as presumed innocence in child abuse cases. The accused is guilty until proven otherwise. The stain is invisible, yet indelible.

I know all the defences to arguments like this. False accusations are rare. We get it wrong more times than we get it right.

Erskine is a good psychologist and a good man. He nursed his wife through MS until she died and he's raised a lot for a research grant in her name. Mel has passion and a social conscience that always puts me to shame. At the same time, she has never made any pretence of neutrality. She knows what she knows. Gut instinct counts.

I don't know where any of this leaves me. I'm tired and I'm hungry. I still don't have any evidence that Bobby *knew* Catherine McBride, let alone murdered her.

A dozen steps before I reach my hotel room I know something is wrong. The door is open. A wine dark stain leaks across the carpet, heading for the stairs. A potted palm lies on its side across the doorway. The clay pot must have broken in half when it sheared off the door handle.

A cleaner's trolley is parked in the stairwell. It contains two buckets, mops, scrubbing brushes and a collection of wet rags. The cleaning lady is standing in the middle of my room. The bed is upside down, littered with the remains of a broken drawer. The sink – wrenched from the wall – lies beneath a broken pipe and a steady trickle of water.

My clothes are scattered across the sodden carpet, interspersed with torn pages of notes and ripped folders. My sports bag is crammed inside the bowl of the toilet, decorated with a turd.

'There is nothing like having your room properly cleaned, is there?' I say.

The cleaning lady looks at me in disbelief.

Spearmint toothpaste spells out a message on the mirror that's full of local flavour: 'GO HOME OR GET BOXED'. Simple. Succinct. Precise.

The hotel manager wants to call the police. I have to open my wallet to change his mind. Picking through the debris, there isn't much worth salvaging. Gingerly, I lift a bundle of soggy papers smeared with ink. The only sheet legible is the last page of Catherine's CV. I had read the covering letter in

292

the office but got no further. Glancing down the page, I see a list of three character referees. Only one of them matters: Dr Emlyn R. Owens. She gives Jock's Harley Street address and phone number.

12

Maintenance work, leaves on the line, signal failures, point faults . . . pick any one of them, they all add up to the same thing – the train will be late arriving in London. The conductor apologises frequently over the tannoy, keeping everyone awake.

I buy a cup of tea from the dining car, along with a 'gourmet' sandwich which is evidence of how culinary words can be devalued. It tastes of nothing except mayonnaise. Random thoughts keep nudging away at my tiredness. Missing pieces. New pieces. No pieces at all.

There are little lies, so tiny that it doesn't much matter whether you do or you don't believe them. Other lies seem small, but have huge ramifications. And sometimes it isn't a case of what you say but what you don't say. Jock's lies are always close to the truth.

Catherine was having an affair with someone at the Marsden – a married man. She was in love with him. She reacted badly when he broke things off. On the night she died she arranged to meet someone. Was it Jock? Maybe *that's* why she called my office – because he didn't show up. Or maybe he *did* show.

He's not married any more. An old flame rekindled.

It was Jock who introduced me to Bobby. He said it was a favour for Eddie Barrett.

Jesus! I can't get my head around this. I wish I could go to sleep and wake up in a different body – or a different life. Any scenario would be better than this one. My best friend – I want to be wrong about him. We've been together from the very beginning. I used to think that sharing a delivery suite made us like brothers; non-genetic twins, who breathed the same air and saw the same bright light as we entered the world.

I don't know what to think any more. He has lied to me. He's in my house and he's taking advantage of everything that has happened. I have seen the way he looks at Julianne – with an emotion far baser than envy.

Everything with Jock is a contest. A duel. And he hates it most if he thinks you're not trying because it cheapens his victories.

Catherine would have been an easy conquest. Jock could always pick the vulnerable ones, although they didn't excite him as much as girls who were self-assured and cool. His affairs caused two divorces. He couldn't help himself.

Why would Catherine have stayed in touch with someone who broke her heart? And why would she list Jock as a referee on her CV?

Someone must have told her that I needed a secretary. It's too big a coincidence to think she happened to answer an advertisement and discover that she was applying to work for me. Perhaps Jock had started seeing her again. He wouldn't have to keep it a secret this time. Not unless he was embarrassed about the trouble Catherine caused me.

What am I missing?

She left the Grand Union Hotel alone. Jock hadn't turned up, or perhaps he'd arranged to meet her later. No! This is stupid! Jock isn't capable of torturing someone – forcing her to drive a knife through her own flesh. He can be a bully but he's not a sadist.

I'm going round in circles. What do I know to be true? He knew Catherine. He knew about her self-harm. He lied about knowing her.

A touch of fear passes across my consciousness like a slight fever. Aunt Gracie would have said that someone had walked across my grave.

Euston Station on a cold clear evening. The taxi queue stretches along the footpath and up the steps. On the ride to Hampstead, watching the red digits climb on the meter, I formulate a plan.

The doorman at Jock's mansion block has gone home for the evening, but the caretaker recognises my face and buzzes me through to the foyer.

'What happened to your ear?'

'Insect bite. Infected.'

The internal staircase is stained deep mahogany and the stair-rods gleam brightly as they reflect light from the chandeliers. Jock's flat is in darkness. I open the door and notice the blinking red light of the alarm. It isn't armed. Jock has trouble remembering the code.

I leave the lights off and walk through the flat until I reach the kitchen. The black and white marble tiles are like a giant chessboard. The light above the stove illuminates the floor and lower cabinets. I don't know why I'm frightened of turning on the overhead lights. I guess this feels more like a break-in than a house call.

First I try the drawer beneath the phone, looking for some evidence that he knew Catherine – an address book or a letter or an old telephone bill. I move to the wardrobe in the main bedroom where Jock has his shirts and suits and ties arranged by colour. A dozen shirts, still wrapped in plastic, are set out on separate shelves.

At the back of the wardrobe I find a box full of hanging files, including one for bills and invoices. The most recent phone bill is in a clear plastic sleeve. The service summary provides a breakdown of STD and international calls as well as calls to mobiles.

Scanning the first list, I look for any numbers with '0151' as the prefix – the code for Liverpool. I don't have any of Catherine's numbers.

Yes I do! Her CV!

I pull the still-damp pages from my jacket and spread them carefully on the rug. The ink has run into the corners but I can still read the address. I compare the numbers with the phone bill, running down the calls made on 13 November. The numbers jump out at me – two calls to Catherine's mobile. The second was at 5:24 p.m. and lasted for just over three minutes – too long for it to be a wrong number and long enough to make a date.

Something doesn't make sense. Ruiz has Catherine's phone records. He must know about these calls.

Ruiz's card is in my wallet but it has almost turned to pulp after my swim in the canal. At first I get his answering machine, but before I can hang up a gruff voice curses the technology and tells me to wait. I can hear him trying to turn the machine off.

'Detective Inspector Ruiz.'

'Ah, the professor returns.' He's reading Jock's number on a display window. 'How was Liverpool?'

'How did you know?'

'A little birdie told me you needed medical treatment. Suspected assaults have to be reported. How's the ear?'

'Just a touch of frostbite.'

I can hear him eating. Shovelling down a microwave curry or takeaway.

'It's about time you and I had another little chat. I'll even send a car to pick you up.'

'I'll have to take a raincheck on that.'

'Maybe we don't understand each other. At ten o'clock this morning a warrant was issued for your arrest.'

I glance down the hallway towards the door and wonder how long it would take for Ruiz to have someone kick it off its hinges.

'Why?'

'Remember I said to you I'd find something else? Catherine McBride wrote letters to you. She kept copies. We found them on her computer disk.'

'That's impossible. I didn't get any letters.'

'Well then, you won't mind coming in to explain them.'

'There must be some mistake. This is crazy.' For a moment I'm tempted to tell him everything – about Elisa and Jock and Catherine's CV. Instead I hold things back, bartering for information. 'You told me the last call Catherine made was to my office. But she must have made other calls that day. People must have called her. You have checked those, right? You didn't just drop everything when you saw my number on the list?'

Ruiz doesn't respond.

'There was someone else she knew from the Marsden. I think she was having an affair with him. And I think he contacted her that day – the thirteenth. Are you listening to any of this?'

I sound desperate. Ruiz isn't going to barter. He's sitting there with his crooked smile, thinking there's nothing new under the sun. Or maybe he's being sly. He's squeezing every drop out of me.

'You told me once that you collect bits of information until two or three pieces fit. Well, I'm trying to help you. I'm trying to find out the truth.'

After another age, Ruiz breaks his silence. 'You're wondering if I interviewed your friend Dr Owens about his relationship with Catherine McBride. The answer is yes. I talked to him.

I asked where he was that night and, unlike you, he could give me an alibi. Shall I tell you who he was with? Or perhaps, if I let you stumble around for long enough, you'll trip over the truth. Ask your wife, Professor.'

'What's she got to do with this?'

'She's his alibi.'

13

The black cab drops me on Primrose Hill Avenue and I walk the last quarter-mile. My mind is spinning, but a cold, overwhelming current of energy has swept away my tiredness.

My vain attempts to protect people from something I don't understand have been ridiculed. Someone, somewhere, is laughing at me. What a fool! All this time I've been operating under the misapprehension that tomorrow will be different. 'Wake up and smell the roses,' Jock's always telling me. OK, now I get it – every day is going to get worse.

At the end of my street I pause, straighten my clothes and move quickly along the footpath, wary of uneven paving stones. The upper floors of my house are in darkness, except for the main bedroom and a bathroom light on the first landing.

Something makes me stop. On the far side of the road, in the deeper shadows of the plane trees, I see the faint glow of a wristwatch held up to a face. The light goes out. Nobody moves. Whoever it belongs to must be waiting.

Crouching behind a parked car, I move from vehicle to vehicle, peering over the bonnets. I can just make out a figure in the shadows. Someone else is sitting in a car. The glow of a cigarette end lights up his lips.

Ruiz has sent them. They're waiting for me.

I retrace my steps, keeping to the shadows, until I turn the corner of my street and double back around the block. In the next road over I recognise the Franklins' house directly behind ours.

I jump a side gate and cross their garden, staying away from the rectangles of light shining from the windows. Daisy Franklin is in the kitchen stirring something on the stove. Two cats appear and disappear from under her skirt. Perhaps there's a whole family under there.

I head for a gnarled cherry tree in the back corner of the garden and lever myself upwards, swinging one leg over the fence. The other leg locks up and doesn't follow. All my weight is moving forwards and I deny gravity for only a split second, flapping my arms in slow-motion before crashing head-first into the compost heap.

Cursing, I crawl on my hands and knees, crushing snails under my palms, until I emerge from the fuchsias. Light spills out from the French doors. Julianne is sitting at the kitchen table, her newly washed hair wrapped in a towel.

Her lips are moving. She's talking to someone. I crane my neck to see who it is – leaning on a large Italian olive jar, which begins to topple until I rescue it with a bear hug.

A hand reaches across the table and the fingers mesh with hers. It's Jock. I feel sick. She pulls her hand away and slaps him on the wrist like she would a naughty child. Then she crosses the kitchen and bends to put coffee cups in the dish-washer. Jock watches her every movement. I want to stick needles in his eyes.

I've never been the jealous type, but I suddenly get a bizarre flashback to a former patient who was obsessed with losing his wife. She had a great figure and he kept imagining that men were staring at her breasts. Gradually, in his eyes, her

301

breasts grew bigger and her tops became smaller and tighter. Her every movement seemed provocative. All of this was nonsense, but not to him.

Jock is a breast man. Both his wives were surgically enhanced. Why be satisfied with nature's meagre bounty when you can be all that money can buy?

Julianne has gone upstairs to dry her hair. Jock fumbles in the pockets of his leather jacket. His shadow is framed in the French doors, just before he steps outside. Gravel crunches underfoot. A lighter flares. The cigar tip smoulders.

I kick his legs out from under him, sending him tumbling backwards, landing heavily in a shower of sparks.

'Joe!'

'Get out of my house!'

'Jesus! If there's a scorch mark on this jumper—'

'And stay away from Julianne!'

He edges away and tries to sit up.

'Stay down!'

'Why are you sneaking around out here?'

'Because the police are out front.' I make it sound so obvious.

He stares at his cigar and contemplates whether to light it again.

'You had an affair with Catherine McBride. Your name is on her fucking CV!'

'Steady on, Joe. I don't know what you're—'

'You told me that you didn't know her. You saw her that night.'

'No.'

'You arranged to meet her.'

'No comment.'

'What do you mean "no comment"?'

'Just that: no comment.'

'This is bullshit! You arranged to meet her.'

'I didn't show up.'

'You're lying.'

'All right, I'm lying,' he says sarcastically. 'Whatever you want to think, Joe.'

'Quit pissing about.'

'What do you want me to say? She was worth a poke. I arranged to meet her. I didn't show up. End of story. Don't preach to me. You screwed a hooker. You lost your chance to moralise.'

I swing a punch but this time he's ready. He sways to one side and then sinks his shoe into my groin. The pain comes as a shock and my knees buckle. My forehead is pressed against his chest as he stops me from falling.

'None of this matters, Joe,' he says in a soft voice.

Gasping for breath, I hiss, 'Of course it matters. They think I killed her.'

Jock helps me upright. I swat his hands away and step back.

'They think I had an affair with her. You could tell them the truth.'

Jock gives me a sly look. 'For all I know you were poking her as well.'

'That's bullshit and you know it!'

'You have to understand things from my point of view. I didn't want to get involved.'

'So you dump me even deeper in the shit.'

'You had an alibi – you just didn't use it.'

Alibis. That's what it comes down to. I should have been at home with my wife – my pregnant wife. She should have been *my* alibi!

It was a Wednesday night. Julianne had her Spanish class. She normally doesn't get home until after ten.

'Why didn't you keep your appointment with Catherine?'

There's a smile behind his eyes. 'I had a better offer.'

He's not going to tell me. He wants me to ask.

'You were with Julianne.'

'Yes.'

I feel something shift inside me. I'm scared now. 'Where did you see her?'

303

'Worry about your own alibi, Joe.'

'Answer the question.'

'We had dinner. She wanted to see me. She asked about your condition. She didn't trust you to tell her the truth.'

'And after dinner?'

'We came back here for coffee.'

'Julianne is pregnant.' I make it a statement, not a question.

I watch him contemplating another lie, but he decides against it. We now have a mutual understanding. All his mediocre lies and half-truths have diminished him.

'Yes, she's pregnant.' Then he laughs quietly. 'Poor Joe, you don't know whether to be happy or sad. Don't you trust her? You should know her better than that.'

'I thought I knew *you*.'

A toilet flushes upstairs. Julianne is getting ready for bed.

'These letters that Catherine wrote – were they to you?'

He gives me a searching look but doesn't answer.

'Why would Catherine write to me?'

Again he doesn't respond. I have to understand this now.

His silence infuriates me. I want to take one of his tennis rackets and break his kneecaps. I have it! The answer. Jock and I have the same initials – J. O. That's how she must have addressed the letters. She wrote them to Jock.

'You have to tell the police.'

'Maybe I should tell them where you are.'

He isn't joking. Inwardly, I want to kill him. I'm sick of the contest.

'Is this about Julianne? Do you think I've been keeping the seat warm all these years? Forget it! She's not going to come running to you if something happens to me. Not if you betray me. You'll never be able to live with yourself.'

'I live with myself now, that's the problem.' His eyes are shining and his oboe voice is wavering. 'You're a very lucky man, Joe, to have a family like this. It never worked out for me.'

'You couldn't stay with any woman long enough.'

'I didn't find the right one.'

Frustration is etched on his face. Suddenly it becomes clear to me. I see Jock's life for what it is – a series of bitter, repetitive disappointments, in which his mistakes and failings have been recast over and over because he could never break the mould.

'Get out of my house, Jock, and stay away from Julianne.'

He collects his things – a briefcase and a jacket – and turns towards me as he holds up the front door key, leaving it on the kitchen counter. I see him glance upstairs as if contemplating whether to say goodbye to Julianne. He decides against it and leaves.

As the front door closes behind him I feel a hollow, nagging doubt. The police are waiting outside. He could so easily tell them.

Before I can rationalise the danger, Julianne appears downstairs. Her hair is almost dry and she's wearing pyjama bottoms and a rugby jumper. Completely still, I watch her from the garden. She gets a glass of water and turns towards the French doors to check they're locked. Her eyes meet mine and show no emotion. She reaches down and picks up a ski jacket which is hanging on the back of a chair. Slipping it around her shoulders, she steps outside.

'What happened to you?'

'I fell over the fence.'

'I'm talking about your ear.'

'A dodgy tattooist.'

She's in no mood for glib asides. 'Are you spying on me?'

'No. Why?'

She shrugs. 'Someone has been watching the house.'

'The police.'

'No. Someone else.'

'Jock said somebody tried to break in.'

'D.J. scared him off.' She makes him sound like a guard dog.

The light behind her, shining through her hair, creates a soft halo effect. She's wearing the 'ugliest slippers in the world', which I bought her from a farm-stay souvenir shop. I can't think of anything to say. I just stand there, not knowing whether to reach out for her. The moment has passed.

'Charlie wants a kitten for Christmas,' she says, hugging the jacket around her.

'I thought that was last year.'

'Yes, but now she's stumbled on the perfect formula. If you want a kitten, ask for a horse.'

I laugh and she smiles, never taking her eyes off me. The next question is framed with her usual directness.

'Did you have an affair with Catherine McBride?'

'No.'

'The police have her love letters.'

'She wrote them to Jock.'

Her eyes widen.

'They had an affair when they were both at the Marsden. Jock was the married man she was seeing.'

'When did you find out?'

'Tonight.'

Her eyes are still fixed on mine. She doesn't know whether to believe me or not.

'Why didn't Jock tell the police?'

'I'm still trying to work that out. I don't trust him. I don't want him here.'

'Why?'

'Because he lied to me and he's kept details from the police and he arranged to meet Catherine on the night she died.'

'Surely you're not serious! This is Jock you're talking about. Your best friend—'

'With my wife as his alibi.' It sounds like an accusation.

Her eyes narrow to the points of knitting needles. 'An alibi

306

for what, Joe? Do you think he killed someone or do you think he's screwing me?'

'That's not what I said.'

'No. That's right. You never say what you mean. You couch everything in parenthesis and inverted commas and open questions.' She's on a roll. 'If you're such a brilliant psychologist, you should start looking at your own defects. I'm tired of propping up your ego. Do you want me to tell you again? Here's the list. You are *nothing* at all like your father. Your penis *is* the right size. You spend more than enough time with Charlie. You don't have to be jealous of Jock. My mother really *does* like you. And I don't blame you for ruining my black cashmere jumper by leaving tissues in your pockets. Satisfied?'

Ten years of potential therapy condensed to six bullet points. My God, this woman is good. The neighbourhood dogs start barking and it sounds like a muffled chorus of 'hear, hear!'.

She turns to go inside. I don't want her to leave so I start talking – telling her the whole story about finding Catherine's CV and searching Jock's apartment. I try to sound rational, but I'm afraid that I come across as though I'm clutching at straws.

Her beautiful face looks bruised.

'You met Jock that night. Where did you go?'

'He took me for supper in Bayswater. I knew you wouldn't tell me the truth about the diagnosis. I wanted to ask him.'

'When did you call him?'

'That afternoon.'

'What time did he leave here?'

She shakes her head sadly. 'I don't even recognise you any more. You're obsessed! I'm not the one who—'

I don't want to hear it. I blurt out: 'I know about the baby.'

She trembles slightly. It might be the cold. That's when I see the realisation in her eyes that we're losing each other. The pulse is getting weaker. She might want me but she doesn't need me. She is strong enough to cope on her own. She lived through the loss of her father; Charlie's meningitis scare when she was eighteen months old; a biopsy on her right breast. She is stronger than I am.

As I leave, breathing in the coldness of the air, I turn back to look at the rear of the house. Julianne has gone. The kitchen is in darkness. I can follow her progress as she moves upstairs, turning off the lights.

Jock has gone. Even if he tells Ruiz the truth, I doubt anyone will believe him. He will be seen as a friend trying to save my hide. I cross the Franklins' garden and slip down the side path. Then I walk towards the West End, watching my shadow appear and disappear beneath the streetlights.

A black cab slows as it passes. The driver glances at me. My hand pulls at the door handle.

Elisa doesn't see herself as a visionary and she dislikes being portrayed by journalists as some sort of evangelist who rescues girls from the streets. Nor does she see prostitutes as 'fallen women' or victims of a harsh society.

We all have undiscovered talents, but Elisa found a diamond in her hidden depths. Her reinvention came at her lowest point – six months after being released from prison. Out of the blue she left a message at the Marsden, simply giving her address and no other details. I don't know how she found me. She wore little make-up and her hair had been cut short. She looked like a junior executive in a dark skirt and jacket. She had an idea and wanted my opinion. As she talked I could sense the weather changing, not outside, but inside her head.

She wanted to set up a drop-in centre for young girls on the streets – giving advice about personal safety, health, accommodation and drug rehab programmes. She had some savings and had rented an old house near King's Cross station.

The drop-in centre proved to be just the start. Soon she had set up PAPT. I was always amazed at the people she could call upon for advice – judges, barristers, journalists, social workers and restaurateurs. I sometimes wondered how many were former clients. Then again, I helped her . . . and it had nothing to do with sex.

The 'inside out' house is in darkness. The Tudor beams glisten with frost and the small light above the doorbell flickers as I push the button. It must be after midnight and I can hear the buzzer echoing in the hall. Elisa isn't home.

I just need to put my head down for a few hours. Just to sleep. I know where Elisa hides her spare key. She won't mind. I can wash my clothes and I'll make her breakfast in the morning. That's when I'll tell her that I need her alibi after all.

Thumb and forefinger pinched together, I slide the key into the lock. Two turns. I swap keys. Another lock. The door opens. Mail spills out on the rug beneath the mail flap. She hasn't been home for a few days.

My footsteps echo on the polished floorboards. The lounge has the atmosphere of a boutique, with the embroidered pillows and Indian rugs. A light is flashing on her answering machine. The tape is full.

I see her legs first. She is sprawled on the Elizabethan love seat, with her ankles bound together with brown masking tape. Her torso is tilted back and her head is covered with a black plastic bin bag, secured with tape around her neck. Her hands are underneath her, tied behind her back. Her skirt is bunched up along her thighs and her stockings are laddered and torn.

In a heartbeat I am a doctor again, ripping plastic, feeling for a pulse, pressing my ear to her chest. Her lips are blue and her body is cold and stiff. Hair is stuck to her forehead. Her eyes are open, staring at me in wonder.

I feel a cold grinding in my chest as though a drilling machine is tunnelling through my insides. I see it all over again: the struggle and the dying; how she fought to get free. How much oxygen is in the bag? Ten minutes at most. Ten minutes to fight. Ten minutes to die. She sucked the plastic against her mouth as she twisted and kicked. There are CD cases on the floor and a trestle table is upside down. A framed photograph is lying face down, amid shattered glass. Her thin gold chain is broken at the clasp.

Poor Elisa. I can still feel the softness of her lips on my cheek when we said goodbye at the restaurant. She is wearing the same dark blue camisole and a matching mini skirt. It must have happened on Thursday, some time after she left me.

I walk from room to room, looking for evidence of a forced entry. The front door was locked from the outside. He must have taken a set of keys.

On the kitchen bench is a mug with a spoon full of coffee granules coagulated like dark toffee in the base. The kettle is lying on its side and one of the dining chairs has toppled over. A kitchen drawer is open. It contains neatly folded tea towels, a small toolbox, light fuses and a roll of black bin liners. The kitchen tidy is empty, with a fresh bag inside.

Elisa's coat is hanging on the edge of the door. Her car keys are on the table, next to her purse, two unopened letters and her mobile phone. The battery is dead. Where is her scarf? Retracing my steps, I find the scarf on the floor behind the chair. A single knot is pulled tight in the centre, forming a silken garrotte.

Elisa is far too careful to open the door to a stranger. Either she knew her killer or he was already inside. Where? How? The patio doors are made of reinforced glass and lead to a small brick courtyard. A sensor triggers the security lights.

The downstairs office is cluttered but tidy. Nothing obvious appears to have been taken, such as the DVD or Elisa's laptop.

Upstairs in the second bedroom, I check the windows again. Elisa's clothes are hanging undisturbed on racks. Her jewellery box, inlaid with mother of pearl, is in the bottom drawer of the vanity. Anyone looking would have found it soon enough.

In the bathroom the toilet seat is down. The bathmat is hanging on a drying rail, over a large blue towel. A new tube of toothpaste sits in a souvenir mug from the House of Commons. I stand on the lever of the pedal bin and the lid swings open. Empty.

I'm about to move on when I notice a dusting of dark powder on the white tiles beneath the sink. I run my finger over the surface, collecting a fine grey residue which smells of roses and lavender.

Elisa had a painted ceramic bowl of pot pourri on the windowsill. Perhaps she accidentally broke it. She would have swept up the debris in a dustpan and emptied it into the pedal bin. Then she might have emptied the pedal bin downstairs, but there's nothing in the kitchen tidy.

Looking closely at the window, I see splinters of bare wood at the edges where paint chips have been lost. The window had been painted shut and forced open. Levering my fingers under the base, I manage to do the same, gritting my teeth as the swollen wood screeches inside the frame.

Peering outside, I see the sewage pipes running down the outside wall and the flat roof of the laundry ten feet below. Wisteria has grown over the brick wall on the right side of the courtyard, making it easy to climb. The pipes would give someone a foothold to reach the window.

Projecting the scene against my closed lids, I see someone standing on the pipes, jemmying the window. He hasn't come to steal or vandalise. He knocks over the pot pourri as he squeezes through the opening and then has to clean up. He doesn't want it to look like a break-in. Then he waits.

The cupboard beneath the stairs has a sliding bolt. It's a storeroom for mops and brooms – big enough for someone to hide in, crouched down, staring through the gap where the hinges join the door.

Elisa arrives home. She picks up her mail from the floor and carries on to the kitchen. She drapes her coat over the door and tosses her things on the table. Then she fills the kettle and spoons coffee into a mug. One mug. He attacks her

311

from behind – wrapping the scarf around her neck, making sure the knot compresses her windpipe. When she loses consciousness he drags her into the lounge, leaving faint tracks against the grain of the rug.

He tapes her hands and feet, carefully cutting the tape and collecting any scraps that fall on the floor. Then he puts the plastic bin liner over her head. At some point she regains consciousness and sees only darkness. By then she is dying.

A jolt of rage forces my eyes open. I see my reflection in the bathroom mirror – a despairing face full of confusion and fear. Dropping to my knees, I vomit into the toilet, bashing my chin against the seat. Then I stumble out the door and into the main bedroom. The curtains are closed and the bedclothes are crumpled and unkempt. My eyes are drawn to a wastepaper bin. Half a dozen crumpled white tissues lie inside it. Memories swim to the surface – Elisa's weight on my thighs; our bodies together; brushing her cervix each time I moved.

Suddenly I scrabble in the bin, collecting tissues. My eyes are drawn around the room. Did I touch that lamp? What about the toothbrush or the door, the windowsill, the banister . . . ?

This is madness. I can't sterilise a crime scene. There will be traces of me all over this house. She brushed my hair. I slept in her bed. I used her bathroom. I drank wine from a wine glass, coffee from a coffee mug. I touched light switches; CD cases; dining chairs; we screwed on her sofa for God's sake!

The phone rings. My heart almost leaps out of my chest. I can't risk answering it. Nobody can know I'm here. I wait, listening to the ring and half expecting Elisa to suddenly stir and say, 'Can someone please get that? It could be important.'

The noise stops. I breathe again. What am I going to do? Call the police? No! I have to get out. At the same time, I can't leave her here. I have to tell someone.

My mobile starts to ring. I fumble through my jacket pockets and need both hands to hold it steady. I don't recognise the number.

'Is that Professor Joseph O'Loughlin?'

'Who wants to know?'

'This is the Metropolitan Police. Someone has called us about an intruder at an address in Ladbroke Grove. The informant gave this mobile as a contact number. Is that correct?'

My throat closes and I can hardly get the vowels out. I mumble something about being nowhere near that address. *No, no, that's not good enough!*

'I'm sorry. I can't hear you,' I mumble. 'You'll have to call back.' I turn off the phone and stare at the blank screen in horror. I can't hear myself thinking over the roar in my head. The volume has been steadily building until now it rattles inside my skull like a freight train entering a tunnel.

I have to get out. Run! Taking the stairs two at a time, I trip towards the bottom and fall. Run! Scooping up Elisa's car keys, I think only of fresh air, a place far away and the mercy of sleep.

14

An hour before daybreak the roads are varnished with rain and patches of fog appear and disappear between the drizzle. Stealing Elisa's car is the least of my worries. Working the clutch with a useless left leg is the more immediate problem.

Somewhere near Wrexham I pull into a muddy farm track and fall asleep. Images of Elisa sweep into my head like the headlights that periodically brush across hedgerows. I see her blue lips and her wide eyes; eyes that follow me still.

Questions and doubts go round in my head like there's a needle stuck in the groove. Poor Elisa.

'Worry about your own alibi,' was what Jock had said. What did he mean? Even if I could prove I didn't kill Catherine – which I now can't – they're going to blame me for this. They're coming for me now. In my mind I can picture policemen crossing the fields in a long straight line, holding Alsatians on leashes, riding horses, hunting me down. I stumble into ditches and claw my way up embankments. Brambles tear at my clothes. The dogs are getting closer.

There is a tap, tap, tapping sound on the window. I can see

nothing but a bright light. My eyes are full of grit and my body stiff with cold. I fumble for the handle and roll down the window.

'Sorry to wake you, mister, but yer blockin' the track.' A grizzled head under a woollen hat peers at me through the window. A dog is barking at his heels and I hear the throb of a tractor engine, parked behind me.

'You don't want to go falling asleep for too long out here. It's bloody cold.'

'Thanks.'

Light grey cloud, stunted trees and empty fields lie ahead of me. The sun is up but struggling to warm the day. I reverse out of the track and watch the tractor pass through a gate and bounce over puddles towards a half-ruined barn.

As the engine idles, I turn the heater up to full blast and call Julianne on the mobile. She's awake and slightly out of breath from her exercises.

'Did you give Jock Elisa's address?'

'No.'

'Did you ever mention her name to him?'

'What's this all about, Joe? You sound scared.'

'Did you say anything?'

' . . . I don't know what you're talking about. Don't get para-noid on me . . . '

I'm shouting at her, trying to make her listen, but she gets angry.

'Don't hang up! Don't hang up!'

It's too late. Just before the connection is cut off, I yell down the phone, 'Elisa is dead!'

I hit redial. My fingers are stiff and I almost drop the phone. Julianne picks up instantly. 'What do you mean?'

'Someone killed her. The police are going to think I did it.'

'Why?'

'I found her body. My fingerprints and God knows what else are all over her flat—'

315

'You went to her flat!' There is disbelief in her voice. 'Why did you go there?'

'Listen to me, Julianne. Two people are dead. Someone is trying to frame me.'

'Why?'

'I don't know. That's what I'm trying to work out.'

Julianne takes a deep breath. 'You're frightening me, Joe. You're sounding crazy.'

'Didn't you hear what I said?'

'Go to the police. Tell them what happened.'

'I have no alibi. I'm their only suspect.'

'Well, talk to Simon. Please, Joe.'

Tearfully, she hangs up and this time leaves the phone off the hook. I can't get through.

God's personal physician-in-waiting opens the door in his dressing gown. He has a newspaper in one hand and an angry scowl designed to frighten off uninvited guests.

'I thought you were the blasted carol singers,' he grumbles. 'Can't stand them. None of them can hold a tune in a bucket.'

'I thought the Welsh were supposed to be great choristers.'

'Another blasted myth.' He looks over my shoulder. 'Where's your car?'

'I parked around the corner,' I lie. I had left Elisa's Beetle at the local railway station and walked the last half-mile.

He turns and I follow him along the hallway towards the kitchen. His battered carpet slippers make slapping noises against his chalk-white heels.

'Where's Mum?'

'She was up and out early. Some protest rally. She's turning into a bloody leftie – always protesting about something.'

'Good for her.'

He scoffs, clearly not in agreement.

'The garden looks good.'

'You should see out back. Cost a bloody fortune. Your mother will no doubt give you the grand tour. Those bloody lifestyle programmes on TV should be banned. Garden "make-overs" and backyard "blitzes" – I'd drop a bomb on all of them.'

He isn't the slightest bit surprised to see me, even though I've turned up unannounced. He probably thinks that Mum mentioned it to him when he wasn't listening. He fills the kettle and empties the old tealeaves from the pot.

The tablecloth is dotted with flotsam gathered on various holidays, like a St Mark's Cross tea caddie and a jam pot from Cornwall. The Silver Jubilee spoon had been a present from Buckingham Palace when they were invited to one of the Queen's garden parties.

'Would you like an egg? There isn't any bacon.'

'Eggs will be fine.'

'There might be some ham in the fridge if you want an omelette.'

He follows me around the kitchen, trying to second-guess what I need. His dressing gown is tied at the waist with a tasselled cord and his glasses are clipped to the pocket with a gold chain so that he doesn't lose them. He knows about my arrest. Why hasn't he said anything? This is his chance to say, 'I told you so.' He can blame it on my choice of career and tell me that none of this would have happened if I'd become a doctor.

He sits at the table, watching me eat, occasionally sipping his tea and folding and unfolding the *Times*. I ask him if he's playing any golf. Not for three years.

'Is that a new Mercedes out front?'

'No.'

The silence seems to stretch out, but I'm the only one who finds it uncomfortable. He sits and reads the headlines, occasionally glancing at me over the top of the paper.

The farmhouse has been in the family since before I was

317

born. For most of that time, until my father semi-retired, it was our holiday house. He had other places in London and Cardiff. Elsewhere, teaching hospitals and universities would provide him with accommodation if he accepted visiting fellowships.

When he bought the farmhouse it had ninety acres, but he leased most of the land to the dairy farmer next door. The main house, built out of local stone, has low ceilings and strange angles, where the foundations have settled over more than a century.

I want to clean up before Mum gets home. I ask Dad if I can borrow a shirt and maybe a pair of trousers. He shows me his wardrobe. On the end of the bed is a man's tracksuit, neatly folded.

He notices me looking. 'Your mother and I go walking.'

'I didn't know.'

'It's only been the last few years. We get up early if the weather is OK. There are some nice walks in Snowdonia.'

'So I hear.'

'Keeps me fit.'

'Good for you.'

He clears his throat and goes looking for a fresh towel. 'I suppose you want a shower instead of a bath.' He makes it sound newfangled and disloyal. A true Welshman would use a tin tub in front of the coal fire.

I push my face into the jets of water, hearing it rush past my ears. I'm trying to wash away the grime of the past few days and drown out the voices in my head. This all began with a disease; a chemical imbalance; a baffling neurological disorder. It feels more like a cancer – a blush of wild cells that have infected every corner of my life, multiplying by the second and fastening on to new hosts.

I lie down in the guest bedroom and close my eyes. I just want a few minutes' rest. Wind beats against the windows. I can smell sodden earth and coal fires. I vaguely remember my father putting a blanket over me. Maybe it's a dream. My dirty clothes are hanging over his arm. He reaches down and strokes my forehead.

A while later I hear the ring of spoons in mugs and the sound of my mother's voice in the kitchen. The other sound – almost as familiar – is my father breaking ice for the ice bucket.

Opening the curtains, I see snow on the distant hills and the last of the frost retreating across the lawn. Maybe we'll have a white Christmas – just like the year Charlie was born.

I can't stay here any longer. Once the police find Elisa's body they will put the pieces together and come looking, instead of waiting for me to turn up somewhere. This is one of the first places they'll search.

Urine splatters into the bowl. My father's trousers are too big for me but I cinch in the belt, making the material gather above the pockets. They don't hear me padding along the hallway. I stand in the doorway watching them.

My mother, as always, is dressed to perfection, wearing a peach-coloured cashmere sweater and a grey skirt. She thickened around her middle after she turned fifty and has never managed to lose the weight.

She puts a cup of tea in front of my father and kisses him on the top of his head with a wet smacking sound. 'Look at this,' she says. 'My stockings have a ladder. That's the second pair this week.' He slips his hand around her waist and gives her a squeeze. I feel embarrassed. I don't remember ever seeing them share such an intimate moment.

My mother jumps in surprise and admonishes me for having 'crept up on her'. She begins fussing about what I'm wearing. She could easily take the trousers in, she says. She doesn't ask about my own clothes.

'Why didn't you tell us you were coming?' she asks. 'We've been worried sick, especially after all those ghastly *stories* in the newspapers.' She makes the tabloids sound as attractive as a soggy furball deposited on a carpet.

319

'Well, at least that's all over with now,' she says sternly, as if determined to draw a line under the whole episode. 'Of course, I'll have to avoid the bridge club for a while, but I daresay it will all be forgotten soon enough. Gwyneth Evans will be insufferably smug. She will think she's off the hook now. Her eldest boy, Owen, ran off with the nanny and left his poor wife with two boys to look after. Now the ladies will have something else to talk about.'

My father seems oblivious to the conversation. He is reading a book with his nose so close to the pages that it looks as though he's trying to inhale them.

'Come on, I want to show you the garden. It looks wonderful. But you must promise to come back in the spring when the blooms are out. We have our own greenhouse and there are new shingles on the stable roof. All that damp is gone. Remember the smell? There were rats nesting behind the walls. Awful!'

She fetches two pairs of Wellingtons. 'I can't remember your size.'

'These are fine.'

She makes me borrow Dad's Barbour and then leads the way down the back steps on to the path. The pond is frozen the colour of watery soup and the landscape is pearl grey. She points out the dry stone wall which had crumbled during my childhood but now stands squat and solid, pieced together like a three-dimensional jigsaw. A new greenhouse with glass panels and a framework of freshly milled pine backs on to the wall. Trays of seedlings cover trestle tables and spring baskets, lined with moss, hang from the ceiling. She flicks a switch and a fine spray fogs the air.

'Come and see the old stables. We've had all the junk cleared out. We could make it into a granny flat. I'll show you inside.'

We follow the path between the vegetable patch and the orchard. Mum is still talking, but I'm only half-listening. I can see her scalp beneath the parting of her grey hair.

'How was your protest meeting?' I ask.

'Good. We had over fifty people.'

'What was it all about?'

'We're trying to stop that blasted wind farm. They want to build it right on the ridge.' She points in the general direction. 'Have you ever heard a wind turbine? The noise is monstrous. Blades flashing around. The air screaming in pain.'

Standing on tiptoes, she reaches above the stable door to get the key from its hiding place.

The tightness in my chest returns. 'What did you say?'

'When?'

'Just then . . . "the air screaming in pain".'

'Oh, the windmills; they make such a horrible sound.'

She has the key in her hand. It is tied to a small piece of carved wood. Unconsciously, my hand flashes out and grips her wrist. I turn it over and the pressure makes her fingers open.

'Who gave you that?' My voice is trembling.

'Joe, you're hurting me.' She looks at the keyring. 'Bobby gave me that. He's the young man I've been telling you about. He fixed the stone wall and the shingles on the stable. He built the greenhouse and did the planting. Such a hard worker. He took me to see the windmills . . . '

For a brief moment I feel myself falling, but nothing happens. It's like someone has tilted the landscape and I'm leaning into it, clutching the doorframe.

'When?'

'He stayed with us for three months over the summer—'

'What did he look like?'

'How can I put it politely? He's very tall, but perhaps a little overweight. Big-boned. Sweet as can be. He only wanted room and board.'

The truth isn't a blinding light or a cold bucket of water in the face. It leaks into my consciousness like a red wine stain on a pale carpet, or a dark shadow on a chest X-ray. Bobby knew things about me; things I dismissed as coincidences. Tigers and

321

lions; Charlie's painting of the whale; Aunt Gracie . . . He knew things about Catherine and how she died. A mind-reader. A stalker. A medieval conjurer who disappears and reappears in a puff of smoke.

But how did he know about Elisa? He saw us having lunch together and then followed her home. No. I saw him that afternoon. He turned up for his appointment. That's when I lost him, by the canal – close to Elisa's house.

'*No comprenderas todavia lo que comprenderas en el futuro.*' You do not understand yet what you will understand in the end . . .

Moving suddenly, I stumble and land awkwardly on the path. Scrambling upwards, I set off in a limping run towards the house, ignoring my mother's questions about not seeing the stable.

Bursting through the door, I ricochet off the laundry wall, upsetting a washing basket and a box of detergent on a shelf. A pair of my mother's knickers catches on the toe of my boot. The nearest telephone is in the kitchen. Julianne answers on the third ring. I don't give her time to speak.

'You said someone was watching the house.'

'Hang up, Joe, the police are trying to find you.'

'Did you see someone?'

'Hang up and call Simon.'

'Please Julianne!'

She recognises the desperation in my voice. It matches her own.

'Did you see anyone?'

'No.'

'What about the person D.J. chased out of the house – did he get a good look at him?'

'No.'

'He must have said something. Was he big, tall, overweight?'

'D.J. didn't get that close.'

'Do you have someone in your Spanish class called Bobby or Robert or Bob? He's tall, with glasses.'

322

'There *is* a Bobby.'

'What's his last name?'

'I don't know. I gave him a lift home one night. He said he used to live in Liverpool—'

'Where's Charlie? Get her out of the house! Bobby wants to hurt you. He wants to punish me . . . '

I try to explain but she keeps asking me why Bobby would do such a thing? It's the one question I can't answer.

'Nobody is going to hurt us, Joe. The street is crawling with police. One of them followed me around the supermarket today. I shamed him into carrying my shopping bags . . . '

Suddenly I realise that she's probably right. She and Charlie are safer at the house than anywhere else because the police are watching them . . . waiting for me.

Julianne is still talking. 'Call Simon, please. Don't do anything silly. '

'I won't.'

'Promise me.'

'I promise.'

Simon's home number is written on the back of his business card. When he answers I can hear Patricia in the background. He's sleeping with my sister. Why does that seem strange?

His voice drops to a whisper and I can hear him taking the phone somewhere more private. He doesn't want Patricia to hear the conversation.

'Did you have lunch with anyone on Thursday?'

'Elisa Velasco.'

'Did you go home with her?'

'No.'

He takes a deep breath. I know what's coming.

'Elisa was found dead at her flat. She was suffocated with a bin liner. They're coming for you, Joe. They have a warrant. They want you for murder.'

My voice is high-pitched and shaking. 'I know who killed

her. He's a patient of mine – Bobby Morgan. He's been watching me . . . '

Simon isn't listening. 'I want you to go to the nearest police station. Give yourself up. Call me when you get there. Don't say anything unless I'm with you—'

'But what about Bobby Morgan?'

Simon's voice is more insistent. 'You *have* to do as I say. They have DNA evidence, Joe. Traces of your semen and strands of your hair; your fingerprints were in the bedroom and bathroom. On Thursday afternoon a cab driver picked you up less than a mile from the murder scene. He remembers you. You flagged him down outside the same pub where Catherine McBride went missing—'

'You wanted to know where I spent the night of the thirteenth. I'll tell you. It was with Elisa.'

'Well, your alibi is dead.'

The statement is so blunt and honest I stop trying to convince him. The facts have been laid out, one by one, revealing how hopeless my position is. Even my denials sound hollow.

My father is standing in the doorway, dressed in his tracksuit. Behind him, through the open curtains of the lounge, two police cars have pulled into the drive.

Book Three

In the real dark night of the soul it is always three o'clock in the morning, day after day.

F. Scott Fitzgerald
The Crack-up

1

Three miles is a long way when you're running in Wellington boots. It is even further when your socks have slipped down and gathered in a ball beneath your arches, making you run like a penguin.

Scrambling along muddy sheep tracks and jumping between rocks, I follow a partly frozen stream cutting through the fields. In spite of the boots I manage to keep up a good pace and only occasionally glance behind me. Right now, I'm doing everything automatically. If I stop for anything I'm finished.

My childhood holidays were spent exploring these fields. I used to know every copse and hillock; the best fishing spots and hiding places. I kissed Ethelwyn Jones in the hayloft of her uncle's barn on her thirteenth birthday. It was my first kiss with tongues and I got an instant hard-on. She leaned right into it and let out a scream, biting down hard on my bottom lip. She wore braces and had a mouth like Jaws in the James Bond films. I had a blood blister on my lip for a fortnight, but it was worth it.

When I reach the A55 I slip beneath the concrete pylons of a bridge and carry on along the stream. The banks grow steeper and twice I slide sideways into the water, breaking thin ice at the edges.

I reach a waterfall about ten feet high and drag myself upwards using tufts of grass and rocks as handholds. My knees are muddy and trousers wet. Ten minutes further on, I duck under a fence and find a track marked for ramblers.

My lungs have started to hurt but my mind is clear. As clear as the cold air. As long as Julianne and Charlie are safe, I don't care what happens to me. I feel like a rag that has been tossed around in a dog's mouth. Someone is playing with me, ripping me to shreds: my family, my life, my career . . . Why? This is all bullshit. It's like trying to read mirror writing – everything is back to front.

A hundred yards on – over a farm gate – I reach the road to Llanrhos. The narrow blacktop has hedgerows down either side, broken by farm gates and pot-holed tracks. Staying close to the ditch along one side, I head towards a church spire in the distance. Patches of mist have settled in the low ground like pools of spilled milk. Twice I leap off the road when I hear a vehicle coming. The second is a police van, with dogs barking from behind the mesh-covered windows.

The village seems deserted. The only places open are a café and an estate agent with a 'back in ten minutes' sign on the door. There are coloured lights in some of the windows and a Christmas tree in the square, opposite the war memorial. A man walking a dog nods hello to me. My teeth are clenched so hard that I can't reply.

I find a park bench and sit down. Steam is rising off my oilskin jacket. My knees are covered in mud and blood. The palms of my hands are scratched and my fingernails are bleeding. I want to close my eyes to think but I need to stay alert.

The houses around the square are like storybook cottages, with picket fences and wrought iron arbours. They have Welsh names written in flowery script beside each front door. At the

328

top of the square, white streamers are threaded through the railings of the church and soggy confetti clings to the steps.

Welsh weddings are like Welsh funerals. They use the same cars, florists and church halls, with their ancient tea urns operated by the same ample-breasted women wearing spacious floral dresses and support hose.

The cold leaks into my limbs as the minutes tick by. A battered Land Rover turns into the square and crawls slowly around the park. I watch and wait. Nobody is following. Stiff-legged, I stand. My sweat-soaked shirt clings to the small of my back.

The passenger door groans with age and neglect. I slide into the seat. A large pillow of foam covers the rusting springs and torn vinyl. The engine is so badly tuned that it sets off a thousand rattles and clinks as my father struggles to find first gear.

'Damn machine! Hasn't been driven in months.'

'What about the police?'

'They're searching the fields. I heard them say they'd found a car at the station.'

'How did you get away?'

'I told them I had surgery. I took the Merc and swapped it for the Land Rover. Thank God it started.'

Each time we hit a puddle, water spouts like a fountain from a hole in the floor. The road twists and turns, dipping and rising through the valley. The sky is clearing to the west and the shadows of clouds sweep across the landscape on a freshening breeze.

'I'm in a lot of trouble, Dad.'

'I know.'

'I didn't kill anyone.'

'I know that too. What does Simon say?'

'I should give myself up.'

'That sounds like good advice.'

In the same breath he accepts that it won't happen and nothing he can say will change things. We're driving along the

329

Vale of Conwy towards Snowdonia. Fields have given way to sparse woodland, with thicker forests in the distance.

The road loops through the trees and a large manor house is visible on a ridge overlooking the valley. The iron gates are closed and a 'For Sale' sign is propped against them.

'That used to be a hotel,' he says without taking his eyes off the road. 'I took your mother there on our honeymoon. It was very grand in those days. People came to tea dances of a Saturday afternoon and the hotel had its own band . . . '

Mum has told me the story before, but I've never heard it from my father.

' . . . we borrowed your uncle's Austin Healey and went touring for a week. That's when I found the farmhouse. It wasn't for sale back then, but we stopped to buy apples. We were stopping quite often because your mother was sore. She had to sit on a pillow over the rough roads.'

He's giggling now and I realise what he means. This is more information than I really require about my mother's sexual initiation, but I laugh along with him. Then I tell him the story of my friend Scot, who knocked his new bride unconscious on a dance floor in Greece during their wedding reception.

'How did he do that?'

'He was trying to show her "the flip" and he dropped her. She woke up in hospital and didn't know what country she was in.'

Dad laughs and I laugh too. It feels good. It feels even better when we stop laughing and the silence isn't awkward. Dad glances at me out of the corner of his eye. He wants to tell me something but doesn't know how to start.

I remember when he gave me the 'coming of age' speech. He told me he had something important to tell me and took me for a walk in Kew Gardens. This was such an unusual event – spending time together – that I felt my chest swell with pride.

Dad made several attempts to start his speech. Each time he became tongue-tied he seemed to lengthen his stride. By the time he reached the bit about intercourse and taking precautions I was sprinting alongside him, trying to catch the words and stop my hat from falling off.

Now he nervously drums his fingers on the steering wheel as though trying to send me the message in Morse Code. Clearing his throat unnecessarily, he begins telling me a convoluted story about choices, responsibility and opportunities. I don't know where he's going with this.

Finally he starts telling me about when he studied medicine at university.

' . . . after that I did two years of behavioural science. I wanted to specialise in educational psychology . . . '

Hold on! Behavioural science? Psychology? He glances at me balefully and I realise that he's not joking.

' . . . my father discovered what I was doing. He was on the university board and was a friend of the Vice Chancellor. He made a special trip to see me and threatened to cut off my allowance.'

'What did you do?'

'I did what he wanted. I became a surgeon.'

Before I can ask another question he raises a hand. He doesn't want to be interrupted.

'My career was mapped out for me. I had my placements, tenures and appointments handed to me. Doors were opened. Promotions were approved . . . ' His voice drops to a whisper. 'I guess what I'm trying to say is that I'm proud of you. You stuck to your guns and did what you wanted. You succeeded on your own terms. I know I'm not an easy man to love, Joe. I don't give anything in return. But I *have* always loved you. And I will always be here for you.'

He pulls off the road into a lay-by and leaves the engine running as he gets out and retrieves a bag from the back seat.

'This is all I managed to bring,' he says, showing me the contents. There is a clean shirt, some fruit, a thermos, my shoes and an envelope stuffed with £50 notes.

'I also picked up your mobile.'

'The battery is dead.'

'Well, take mine. I never use the damn thing.'

He waits for me to slide behind the wheel and tosses the bag on the passenger seat.

'They'll never miss the Land Rover . . . not for a while. It's not even registered.'

I glance at the bottom corner of the windscreen. A beer bottle label is stuck to the glass. He grins. 'I only drive her around the fields. Decent run will do her good.'

'How will you get home?'

'Hitchhike.'

I doubt if he's thumbed a ride in his entire life. What do I know? He's been full of surprises today. He still looks like my father, but at the same time he's different.

'Good luck,' he says, shaking my hand through the window. Maybe if we'd both been standing it would have been a hug. I like to think so.

I wrestle the Land Rover into gear and pull on to the asphalt. I can see him in the rear mirror, standing at the edge of the road. I remember something he told me when Aunt Gracie died and I was hurting inside.

'Remember, Joseph, the blackest hour of your life only lasts for sixty minutes.'

The police will track me on foot along the stream. The road-blocks will take longer to organise. With any luck I will be outside any cordon they throw up. I don't know how much time this gives me. By tomorrow my face will be all over the newspapers and on TV.

My mind seems to be speeding up as my body slows down. I can't do what they expect. Instead I have to bluff and double bluff. This is one of those he-thinks-that-I-think-that-he-thinks scenarios, where each participant is trying to guess the other's next move. I have two minds to consider. One belongs to a deeply pissed-off policeman who thinks I've played him like a fool, and the other to a sadistic killer who knows how to reach my wife and daughter.

The engine of the Land Rover cuts out every few seconds. Fourth gear is almost impossible to find and, when I do, I have to hold it in place with one hand on the gearstick.

I reach over the back seat and feel for the mobile phone. I need Jock's help. I know I'm taking a risk. He's a lying bastard but I'm running out of people to trust.

He answers and fumbles the phone. I can hear him cursing. 'Why do people always call when I'm taking a piss?' I picture him trying to balance the phone under his chin and zip up his fly.

'Have you told the police about the letters?'

'Yeah. They didn't believe me.'

'Convince them. You must have something from Catherine that can help prove you were sleeping with her.'

'Yeah. Sure. I kept Polaroids so I could show my wife's divorce lawyers.'

God he can be a smug bastard. I don't have time for this. Yet I'm smiling to myself. I was wrong about Jock. He's not a killer.

'The patient you referred to me, Bobby.'

'What about him?'

'How did you meet him?'

'Like I told you – his solicitor wanted neurological tests.'

'Who suggested my name – was it you or Eddie Barrett?'

'Eddie suggested you.'

Rain has started spitting down. The wipers have only one speed – slow.

'There is a cancer hospital in Liverpool called the Clatterbridge. I want to know if they have any record of a patient by the name of Bridget Morgan. She may be using her maiden name, Bridget Aherne. She has breast cancer. Apparently it's well advanced. She might be an outpatient, or be in a hospice. I need to find her.'

333

I'm not asking as a favour. He either does this or our long association is irredeemably ended. Jock fumbles for an excuse but can't find one. Mostly he wants to run for cover. He has always been a coward unless he can physically intimidate someone. I won't give him the chance to wheedle out. I know that he's lied to the police. I also have too many details about the assets he kept hidden from his ex-wives.

His voice is sharp. 'They're going to catch up with you, Joe.'

'They catch up to all of us,' I say. 'Call me on this number as soon as you can.'

2

In the third form, during a holiday in Wales, I took some matches from the china bowl on the mantelpiece to make a campfire. It was near the end of a dry summer and the grass was brittle and brown. Did I mention the wind?

My smouldering bundle of twigs sparked a grass fire that destroyed two fences, a 200-year-old hedgerow and threatened a neighbouring barn full of winter-feed. I raised the alarm, screaming at the top of my lungs as I ran home with blackened cheeks and smoky hair.

I crawled into the far corner of the loft in the stables, wedging myself against the sloping roof. I knew my father was too big to reach me. I lay very still, breathing in the dust and listening to the sirens of the fire engines. I imagined all sorts of horrors. I pictured entire farms and villages ablaze. They were going to send me to jail. Carey Moynihan's brother had been sent to borstal because he set fire to a train carriage. He came out meaner than when he went in.

I spent five hours in the loft. Nobody shouted or threatened me. Dad said I should come out and take my punishment like a man. Why do young boys have to act like men? The look of disappointment on my mother's face was far more painful than the sting of my father's belt. What would the neighbours say?

Prison seems much closer now than it did then. I can picture Julianne holding up our baby across the table. 'Wave to Daddy,' she tells him (it's a boy, of course) as she tugs down her skirt self-consciously, aware of the dozens of inmates staring at her legs.

I picture a red brick building rising out of the asphalt. Iron doors with keys the size of a man's palm. I see metal landings, meal queues, exercise yards, swaggering guards, nightsticks, pisspots, lowered eyes, barred windows and a handful of snapshots taped to a cell wall.

What happens to someone like me in jail?

Simon is right. I can't run. And just like I learned in third form, I can't hide for ever. Bobby wants to destroy me. He doesn't want me dead. He could have killed me a dozen times over but he wants me alive so I can *see* what he's doing and *know* that it's him.

Will the police keep watching my home or will they call off the surveillance to focus on Wales? I don't want that. I need to know that Julianne and Charlie are safe.

The phone rings. Jock has an address for a Bridget Aherne at a hospice in Lancashire.

'I talked to the senior oncologist. They give her only weeks.'

I can hear him unwrapping the plastic from a cigar. It's early. Maybe he's celebrating. Both of us have settled for an uneasy truce. Like an old married couple, we recognise the half-truths and ignore the irritations.

'There's a photograph of you in today's papers,' he says. 'You look like a banker rather than a "Most Wanted".'

'I don't photograph well.'

'Julianne gets a mention. They describe her as being "overwrought and emotional when visited by reporters".'

'She told them to fuck off.'

'Yeah, that's what I figured too.'

I can hear him blowing smoke. 'I got to hand it to you, Joe. I always took you for a boring fart. Likeable enough, but virtuous. Look at you now! Two mistresses and a wanted man.'

'I didn't sleep with Catherine McBride.'

'Shame. She was good in the sack.' He laughs wryly.

'You should listen to yourself sometimes, Jock.'

To think I once envied him. Look at what he's become: a crude parody of a right-wing, middle-class chauvinist and bigot. I no longer trust him, but I need another favour.

'I want you to stay with Julianne and Charlie – just until I sort this out.'

'You told me not to go near her.'

'I know.'

'Sorry, I can't help you. Julianne isn't returning my calls. I figure you must have told her about Catherine and the letters. She's pissed off at both of us now.'

'At least call her; tell her to be careful. Tell her to let no one into the house.'

3

The Land Rover has a top speed of forty and a tendency to oversteer into the centre of the road. It looks more like a museum piece than a motor car and people honk when they overtake as if I'm driving for charity. This could be the most perfect getaway vehicle ever conceived because nobody expects a wanted man to escape so slowly.

I use the back roads to reach Lancashire. A mouldy road map from the glove compartment, circa 1965, keeps me on track. I pass through villages with names like Puddinglake and Woodplumpton. On the outskirts of Blackpool, at a near-deserted petrol station, I use the restroom to clean up. I sponge the mud from my trousers and hold them under the hand dryer, before changing my shirt and washing the cuts on my hands.

The Squires Gate Hospice is fixed to a rocky headland as though rusted there by the salt air. The turrets, arched windows and slate roof look Edwardian, but the out-buildings are newer and less intimidating.

Flanked by poplar trees, the driveway curves around the front of the hospital and emerges into a parking area. I follow the signs to the palliative care ward on the ocean-side. The corridors are empty and the stairways almost tidy. A black nurse with a shaved head sits behind a glass partition staring at a screen. He is playing a computer game.

'You have a patient called Bridget Aherne.'

He looks down at my knees, which are no longer the same colour as the rest of my trousers.

'Are you family?'

'No. I'm a psychologist. I need to speak to her about her son.'

His eyebrows arch. 'Didn't know she had a son. She doesn't get many visitors.'

I follow his smooth, rolling walk along the corridor, where he turns beneath the staircase and takes me through double doors leading outside. A loose gravel pathway dissects the lawn where two bored-looking nurses share a sandwich on a garden seat.

We enter a single-storey annexe nearer to the cliffs and emerge into a long shared ward with maybe a dozen beds, half of them empty. A skinny woman with a smooth skull is propped up on pillows. She is watching two young children who are scribbling on drawing paper at the end of her bed. Elsewhere, a one-legged woman in a yellow dress sits in a wheelchair in front of a television with a crocheted blanket on her lap.

At the far end of the ward, through two doors, are the private rooms. He doesn't bother to knock. The room is dark. At first I don't notice anything except the machines. The monitors and dials create the illusion of medical mastery: as though everything is possible if you calibrate the machinery and press the right buttons.

A middle-aged woman, with sunken cheeks, is lying at the centre of the web of tubes and leads. She has a blonde wig, pendulous breasts and tar-coloured lesions on her neck. A pink chemise covers her body, with a tattered red cardigan hanging

339

over her shoulders. A bag of solution drips along tubing that snakes in and out of her body. There are black lines around her wrists and ankles – not dark enough to be tattoos and too uniform to be bruises.

'Don't give her any cigarettes. She can't clear her lungs. Every time she coughs it shakes the tubes loose.'

'I don't smoke.'

'Good for you.' He takes a cigarette from behind his ear and transfers it to his mouth. 'You can find your own way back.'

The curtains are drawn. Music is coming from somewhere. It takes me a while to realise there is a radio playing softly on the bedside table, next to an empty vase and a copy of the Bible.

She's asleep. Sedated. Morphine, perhaps. A tube sticks out of her nose and another comes from somewhere near her stomach. Her face is turned towards the respirator.

I lean my shoulder against the wall and rest my head.

'This place gives you the creeps,' she says, without opening her eyes.

'Yes.'

I sit down on a chair so she doesn't have to turn her head to see me. Her eyes open slowly. Her face is whiter than the walls. We stare at each other in the semi-darkness.

'Have you ever been to Maui?'

'It's in Hawaii.'

'I know where it fucking is.' She coughs and the bed rattles. 'That's where I should be now. I should be in America. I should have been born American.'

'Why do you say that?'

'Because the Yanks know how to live. Everything is bigger and better. People laugh about it. They call them arrogant and ignorant, but the Yanks are just being honest. They eat little countries like this for breakfast and shit them out before lunch.'

'Have you ever been to America?'

She changes the subject. Her eyes are puffy and dribble has leaked from the corner of her mouth. 'Are you a doctor or a priest?'

'A psychologist.'

She laughs sarcastically. 'No point getting to know me. Not unless you like funerals.'

The cancer must have struck quickly. Her body hasn't had time to waste away. She is pale, with a neat chin, graceful neck and flaring nostrils. If it weren't for her surroundings and the harshness of her voice, she would still be an attractive woman.

'The problem with cancer is that it doesn't feel like cancer, you know. A head cold feels like a cold. And a broken leg feels like a broken leg. But with cancer, you don't know unless you have X-rays and scans. Except for the lump, of course. Who can forget the lump? Feel it!'

'That's OK.'

'Don't make a fuss. You're a big boy. Have a feel. You're probably wondering if they're real. Most men do.'

Her hand shoots out and closes around my wrist. Her grip is surprisingly strong. I fight the urge to pull away. She puts my hand under her chemise. My fingers fold into the softness of her breast. 'Just there. Can you feel it? It used to be the size of a pea – small and round. Now it's the size of an orange. Six months ago it spread to my bones. Now it's in my lungs.'

My hand is still on her breast. She brushes it over the nipple, which hardens under my palm. 'You can fuck me if you like.' She's serious. 'I'd like to feel something other than this . . . this decay.'

The look of pity on my face infuriates her. She thrusts my hand away and wraps her cardigan tightly around her chest. She won't look at me.

'I need to ask you a few questions.'

'Forget it! I don't need any of your buck-up-now speeches. I'm not in denial and I've stopped making bargains with God.'

'I'm here about Bobby.'

341

'What about him?'

I haven't planned what I'm going to ask her. I'm not even sure what I'm looking for.

'When was the last time you saw him?'

'Six, maybe seven years ago. He was always in trouble. Wouldn't listen to anyone. Not me, anyway. Give a kid the best years of your life and he'll always be ungrateful.' Her sentences are ragged and short. 'So what has he done now?'

'He's been convicted of a serious assault. He kicked a woman unconscious.'

'A girlfriend?'

'No, a stranger.'

Her features soften. 'You've talked to him. How is he?'

'He's angry.'

She sighs. 'I used to think they gave me the wrong baby at the hospital. It didn't feel like mine. He looked like his father, which was a shame. I couldn't see any of me in him, except his eyes. He had two left feet and a round loaf of a face. He could never keep anything clean. He had to put his hands into things, open them up, find out how they worked. He once ruined a perfectly good radio and leaked battery acid all over my best rug. Just like his father . . . '

She doesn't finish the statement, but starts again. 'I never felt what a mother is supposed to feel. I guess I'm not maternal, but that doesn't make me cold, does it? I didn't want to get pregnant and I didn't want to inherit a stepson. I was only twenty-one, for Christ's sake!'

She arches a pencil-thin eyebrow. 'You're itching to get inside my head, aren't you? Not many people are interested in what someone else is thinking or what they have to say. Sometimes people act like they're listening, when really they're waiting for their turn, or getting ready to jump in. What are you waiting to say, Mr Freud?'

'I'm trying to understand.'

'Lenny was like that; always asking questions; wanting to

342

know where I was going and when I was coming home.' She mimics his pleading voice. '"Who are you with, petal? Please, come home. I'll wait up for you." It was so pathetic! No wonder I got to thinking is this the best I can do. I wasn't going to lie next to his sweaty back for the rest of my life.'

'He committed suicide.'

'I didn't think he had it in him.'

'Do you know why?'

She doesn't seem to hear me. Instead she stares at the curtains. The window must look directly over the ocean.

'You don't like the view?'

She shrugs. 'There's a rumour going around that they don't bother burying us. They throw us off the cliff instead.'

'What about your husband?'

She doesn't look at me. 'He called himself an inventor. What a joke! Do you know that if he made any money – fat chance of that – he was going to give it away? "To enrich the world," he said. That's what he was like: always rambling on about empowering the workers and the proletariat revolution, making speeches and moralising. Communists don't believe in heaven or hell. Where do you think he is?'

'I'm not a religious person.'

'But do you think he might have gone somewhere?'

'I wouldn't know.'

Her armour of indifference shows a weakness. 'Maybe we're all in hell and we just don't realise it.' She pauses and half closes her eyes. 'I wanted a divorce. He said no. I told him to get himself a girlfriend. He wouldn't let me go. People say I'm cold, but I *feel* more than they do. I knew how to find pleasure. I knew how to use what I was given. Does that make me a slut? Some people spend their entire lives in denial, or making other people happy, or collecting points they think can be redeemed in the next life. Not me.'

'You accused your husband of sexually abusing Bobby.'

She shrugs. 'I just loaded the gun. I didn't fire it. People

343

like you did that. Doctors, social workers, schoolteachers, lawyers, do-gooders . . . '

'Did we get it wrong?'

'The judge didn't think so.'

'What do you think?'

'I think that sometimes you can forget what the truth is if you hear a lie often enough.' She reaches up and pushes the buzzer above her head.

I can't leave yet. 'Why does your son hate you?'

'We all end up hating our parents.'

'You feel guilty.'

She clenches her fists and laughs hoarsely. A chrome stand holding a morphine drip swings back and forth. 'I'm forty-three years old and I'm dying. I'm paying the price for anything I've done. Can you say the same?'

The nurse arrives, looking pissed off at being summoned. One of the monitor leads has come loose. Bridget holds up her arm to have it reconnected. In the same motion she dismissively waves her hand. The conversation is over.

It has grown dark outside. I follow the path lights between the trees until I reach the car park. Taking the thermos from the bag, I swig from it greedily. The whisky tastes fiery and warm. I want to keep drinking until I can't feel the cold or notice my arm trembling.

4

Melinda Cossimo answers the door reluctantly. Visitors this late are rarely good news for a social worker, particularly on a Sunday. Weekends are when family tensions are inclined to simmer and anger boil over. Wives get beaten and children run away from home. Social workers look forward to Mondays.

I don't give her time to speak. 'The police are looking for me. I need your help.'

She blinks at me wide-eyed, but looks almost calm. Her hair is swept up and pinned high on her head with a large tortoise-shell clip. Wispy strands have escaped to stroke her cheeks and neck. As the door closes, she motions me onwards, telling me to march straight up the stairs to the bathroom. She waits outside the door while I pass her my clothes.

I protest about not having the time, but she doesn't react to the urgency in my voice. It won't take long to wash a few things, she says.

I stare at the naked stranger in the mirror. He has lost weight. That can happen when you don't eat. I know what Julianne would say: 'Why can't I lose weight that easily?' The stranger in the mirror smiles at me.

I come downstairs wearing a robe and hear Mel hang up the phone. By the time I reach the kitchen she has opened a bottle of wine and is filling two glasses.

'Who did you call?'

'Nobody important.'

She curls up in a large armchair, with the stem of her wine glass slotted between the first and second fingers of her outspread palm. Her other hand rests on the back of an open book, lying facedown across the armrest. The reading lamp above her casts a shadow beneath her eyes and gives her mouth a harsh downward curve.

This has always been a house I associate with laughter and good times, but now it seems too quiet. One of Boyd's paintings hangs above the mantelpiece and another is on the opposite wall. There is a photograph of him and his motorbike at the Isle of Man TT track.

'So what have you done?'

'The police think I killed Catherine McBride, among others.'

'Among others?' One eyebrow arches like an oxbow.

'Well, just *one* "other". A former patient.'

'You're going to tell me that you've done nothing wrong.'

'Not unless being foolish is a crime.'

'Why are you running?'

'Because someone wants to frame me.'

'Bobby Morgan.'

'Yes.'

She raises her hand. 'I don't want to know any more. I'm in enough trouble for showing you the files.'

'We got it wrong.'

'What do you mean?'

'I just talked to Bridget Morgan. I don't think Bobby's father abused him.'

'She told you that!'

'She wanted out of the marriage. He wouldn't give her a divorce.'

346

'He left a suicide note.'

'One word.'

'An apology.'

'Yes, but for what?'

Mel's voice is cold. 'This is ancient history, Joe. Leave it alone. You know the unwritten rule – never go back, never re-open a case. I have enough lawyers looking over my shoulder without another bloody lawsuit . . . '

'What happened to Erskine's notes? They weren't in the files.'

She hesitates. 'He might have asked to have them excluded.'

'Why?'

'Perhaps Bobby asked to see his file. He's allowed to do that. A ward can see the write-ups by the duty social worker and some of the minutes of the meetings. Third-party submissions like doctor's notes and psych reports are different. We need to get permission from the specialist to release them.'

'Are you saying that Bobby saw his file?'

'Maybe.' In the same breath she dismisses the idea. 'It's an old file. Things get misplaced.'

'Could Bobby have removed the notes?'

She whispers angrily, 'You can't be serious, Joe! Worry about yourself.'

'Could he have seen the video?'

She shakes her head, refusing to say anything more. I can't let it go. Without her help, my frail improbable theory goes south. Talking quickly, as though afraid she might stop me, I tell her about the chloroform, the whales and the windmills: how Bobby has stalked me for months, infiltrating the lives of everyone around me.

At some point she puts my washed clothes in the dryer and refills my wine glass. I follow her to the kitchen and shout over the whine of the blender as it pulverises warm chickpeas. She puts a dollop of humus on slices of toast, seasoned with crushed black pepper.

347

'So that's why I need to find Rupert Erskine. I need his notes or his memories.'

'I can't help you any more. I've done enough.' She glances at the clock on the stove.

'Are you expecting someone?'

'No.'

'Who did you call earlier?'

'A friend.'

'Did you call the police?'

She hesitates. 'No. I left instructions with my secretary. If I didn't call her back in an hour she had to contact the police.'

I glance at the same clock, counting backwards. 'Christ, Mel!'

'I'm sorry. I have my career to think about.'

'Thanks for nothing.' My clothes aren't quite dry, but I wrestle on the trousers and shirt. She grabs at my sleeve. 'Give yourself up.'

I brush her hand aside. 'You don't understand.'

My left leg is swinging as I try to move quickly. My hand is on the front door.

'Erskine. You wanted to find him.' She blurts it out. 'He retired ten years ago. Last I heard he was living near Chester. Someone from the department contacted him a while back. We had a chat . . . caught up.'

She remembers the address – a village called Hatchmere. Vicarage Cottage. I scribble the details on a scrap of paper balanced on the hallway table. My left hand refuses to budge. My right hand will have to do.

All mornings should be so bright and clear. The sun angles through the cracked back window of the Land Rover, fracturing into a disco ball of beams. With two hands on the handle, I force a side window open and peer outside. Someone has painted the world white; turned colour into monochrome.

Cursing the stiffness of the door, I shove it open and swing

348

my legs outside. The air smells of dirt and wood smoke. Scooping a handful of snow, I rub it into my face, trying to wake up. Then I undo my fly and pee on the base of a tree, painting it a darker brown. How far did I travel last night? I wanted to keep going but the headlights on the Land Rover kept cutting out and plunging me into darkness. Twice I nearly finished up in a ditch.

How did Bobby spend the night? I wonder if he's looking for me or watching Julianne and Charlie? He's not going to wait for me to figure this out. I need to hurry.

Hatchmere lake is fringed with reeds and the water reflects the blueness of the sky. I stop at a red and white painted house and ask for directions. An old lady, still in her dressing gown, answers the door and mistakes me for a tourist. She starts giving me the history of Hatchmere, which segues into her own life story about her son who works in London and her grandchildren whom she only sees once a year.

I keep thanking her and backing away. She stands at her front gate as I struggle to start the Land Rover. That's just what I need. She's probably an expert on cribbage, crosswords and remembering licence plates. 'I never forget a number,' she'll say as she rattles it off to police.

The engine kindly turns over and fires, belching smoke from the exhaust. I wave and smile. She looks concerned for me.

Vicarage Cottage has Christmas lights strung over the windows and doors. Parked on the front path are a handful of toy cars, circled like wagons around an old milk crate. Hanging diagonally across the path is a rust-stained bed sheet with two ends tied to a tree. A boy squats underneath with a plastic ice-cream bucket on his head. He points a wooden stick at my chest.

'Are you a Slytherin?' he says with a lisp.

'Pardon?'

'You can only come in here if you're from Gryffindor.' The freckles on his nose are the colour of toasted corn.

A young woman appears at the door. Her blonde hair is sleep-tossed and she's fighting a cold. A baby is perched on her hip, sucking on a small piece of toast.

'You leave the man alone, Brendan,' she says, smiling at me tiredly.

Stepping around the toys, I reach the door. I can see an ironing board set up behind her.

'I'm sorry about that. He thinks he's Harry Potter. Can I help you?'

'Hopefully, yes. I'm looking for Rupert Erskine.'

A shadow crosses her face. 'He doesn't live here any more.'

'Do you know where I might find him?'

She swaps her baby on to her opposite hip and does up a loose button on her blouse. 'You'd be better asking someone else.'

'Would one of the neighbours know? It's very important that I see him.'

She bites her bottom lip and looks past me towards the church. 'Well, if you want to see him you'll find him over there.'

I turn to look.

'He's in the cemetery.' Realising how blunt the statement sounds, she adds, 'I'm sorry if you knew him.'

Without making a conscious decision I find myself sitting down on the steps. 'We used to work together,' I explain. 'It was a long time ago.'

She glances over her shoulder. 'Would you like to come in and sit down?'

'Thank you.'

The kitchen smells of sterilised bottles and porridge. There are crayons and pieces of paper spread over the table and chair. She apologises for the mess.

'What happened to Mr Erskine?'

'I only know what the neighbours told me. Everyone in the village was pretty shook up by what happened. You don't expect that sort of thing – not round these parts.'

'What sort of thing?'

'They say he came across someone trying to rob the place, but I don't see how that explains anything. What sort of burglar ties an old man to a chair and tapes his mouth? He lived for two weeks. Some folks say he had a heart attack, but I heard he died of dehydration. It was the hottest fortnight of the year . . . '

'When was this?'

'August just gone. I reckon some folks are feeling guilty because nobody noticed him missing. He was always pottering in the garden and taking walks by the lake. Someone from the church choir knocked on the door and a man came to read the gas meter. The front door was unlocked, but nobody thought to go inside.' The baby is squirming in her arms. 'Are you sure you won't have a cup of tea? You don't look too good.'

I can see her lips moving and hear the question, but I'm not really listening. The ground has dropped away beneath me like a plunging lift. She's still talking, ' . . . a really nice old man, people say. A widower. You probably know that already. Don't think he had any other family . . . '

I ask to use her phone and need both hands to hold the receiver. The numbers are barely legible. Louise Elwood answers. I have to stop myself from shouting.

'The deputy headmistress at St Mary's – you said that she resigned for family reasons.'

'Yes. Her name was Alison Gorski.'

'When was that?'

'About eighteen months ago. Her mother died in a house fire and her father was badly burned. She moved to London so she could nurse him. I think he's in a wheelchair.'

'How did the fire start?'

'They think it was a case of mistaken identity. Someone put a petrol bomb through the letterbox. The newspapers thought it might have been an anti-Jewish thing, but there was never anything more said.'

A rush of fear becomes liquid on my skin. My eyes fix on the young woman who is watching me anxiously from beside the stove. She is frightened of me. I have brought something sinister into her house.

I make another call. Mel picks up immediately. I don't give her time to speak. 'The car that hit Boyd: what happened to the driver?' My voice sounds strident and thin.

'The police have been here, Joe. A detective called Ruiz—'

'Just tell me about the driver.'

'It was a hit and run. They found the four-wheel drive a few blocks away.'

'And the driver?'

'They think it was probably a teenage joy-rider. There was a thumbprint on the steering wheel but it matched nothing on file.'

'Tell me exactly what happened.'

'Why? What's this got to do—'

'Please, Mel.'

She stumbles over the first part of the story, trying to remember whether it was seven-thirty or eight-thirty that evening when Boyd went out. It upsets her to think she could have forgotten a detail like this. She worries that Boyd might be growing fainter in her memories.

It was bonfire night. The air was laced with gunpowder and sulphur. Neighbourhood kids, giddy with excitement, had gathered round bonfires built from scrap wood on allotments and waste ground. Boyd often went out of an evening for tobacco. He went to his local for a quick pint and picked up his favourite blend from an off-licence on the way. He wore a fluorescent vest and a canary yellow helmet. His grey pony-tail hung down his back. He paused at an intersection on Great Homer Street.

Perhaps he turned at the last moment, when he heard the car. He might even have seen the driver's face in that fraction of a second before he disappeared beneath the bullbar. His body was dragged for a hundred yards beneath the chassis, caught in the twisted frame of the motorbike.

'What's going on?' asks Mel. I imagine her wide red mouth and timid grey eyes.

'Lucas Dutton: where is he now?'

Mel answers in a calm, quavering voice. 'He works for some government advisory body on teenage drug use.'

I remember Lucas. He dyed his hair; played golf off a low handicap; collected matchbooks and blends of Scotch. His wife was a drama teacher; they drove a Skoda and went on holidays to a caravan in Bognor; they had twin girls . . .

Mel is demanding an explanation but I talk over her. 'What happened to the twins?'

'You're scaring me, Joe.'

'What happened to them?'

'One of them died last Easter of a drug overdose.'

I am ahead of her now, reading a list of names: Justice McBride, Melinda Cossimo, Rupert Erskine, Lucas Dutton, Alison Gorski – all were involved in the same child protection case. Erskine is dead. The others have all lost someone close to them. What has this got to do with me? I only interviewed Bobby the once. Surely that isn't enough to explain the wind-mills, the Spanish lessons, the Tigers and Lions . . . Why did he spend months living in Wales, landscaping my parents' garden and fixing the old stables?

Mel is threatening to hang up on me. I can't let her go. 'Who put together the legal submission for the care order?'

'I did, of course.'

'You said Erskine was on holiday. Who signed off on the psych report?'

She hesitates. Her breathing changes. She is about to lie. 'I don't remember.'

More insistent this time: 'Who signed the psych report?'

She speaks straight through me, directly into the past. 'You did.'

'How? When?'

'I put the form in front of you and you signed. You thought it was a foster parent authorisation. It was your last day in Liverpool. We were having farewell drinks at the Windy House.'

I moan inwardly, the phone still to my ear. 'My name was in Bobby's files?'

'Yes.'

'You took it out of the folders before you showed them to me?'

'It was a long time ago. I thought it didn't matter.'

I can't answer her. I let the phone fall from my hand. The young mother is clutching her baby tightly in her arms, jiggling him up and down to calm his cries. As I retreat down the steps, I hear her calling her older son inside. Nobody wants to be near me. I am like an infectious disease. An epidemic.

5

George Woodcock called the ticking of the clock a mechanical tyranny that turned us into servants of a machine that we created. We are held in fear of our own monster – just like Baron von Frankenstein.

I once had a patient, a widower living alone, who became convinced that the ticking of a clock above his kitchen table sounded like human words. The clock would give him short commands. 'Go to bed!' 'Wash the dishes!' 'Turn off the lights!' At first he ignored the sound, but the clock repeated the instructions over and over, always using the same words. Eventually he began to follow the orders and the clock took over his life. It told him what to have for dinner and what to watch on TV; when to do the laundry; which phone calls to return . . .

When he first sat in my consulting room, I asked him whether he wanted a tea or a coffee. He didn't reply at first. He nonchalantly wandered over to the wall clock and after a moment he turned and said that a glass of water would be fine.

Strangely, he didn't want to be cured. He could have removed all clocks from his house or gone digital, but there was something about the voices that he found reassuring and even comforting. His wife, by all accounts, had been a fusspot and a well-organised soul, who hurried him along, writing him lists, choosing his clothes and generally making decisions for him.

Instead of wanting me to stop the voices, he needed to be able to carry them with him. The house already had a clock in every room, but what happened when he went outside?

I suggested a wristwatch, but for some reason these didn't speak loudly enough or they babbled incoherently. After much thought, we went shopping at Gray's Antique Market and he spent more than an hour listening to old-fashioned pocket watches, until he found one that quite literally spoke to him.

The clock I hear ticking could be the knocking of the Land Rover's engine. Or it could be the doomsday clock – seven minutes to midnight. My perfect past is fading into history and I can't stop the clock.

Two police cars pass me on the road out of Hatchmere, heading in the opposite direction. Mel must have finally given them Erskine's address. They can't know about the Land Rover – not yet, at least. The little old lady with the photographic memory will tell them. With any luck she'll recount her life story first, giving me time to get away.

I keep glancing in the rear mirror, half expecting to see flashing blue lights. This will be the opposite of a high-speed police chase. They could overtake me on bicycles unless I can find fourth gear. Maybe we'll have one of those O.J. Simpson moments, a slow-motion motorcade, filmed from the news helicopters.

I remember the final scene of *Butch Cassidy and the Sundance Kid*, when Redford and Newman keep wisecracking as they go out to face the Mexican army. Personally, I'm not quite as fearless about dying. And I can't see anything glorious about a hail of bullets and a closed coffin.

* * *

Lucas Dutton lives in a red brick house in a suburban street, where the corner shops have disappeared and been replaced by drug dealers and brothels. Every blank wall is covered in spray paint. Even the folk art and Protestant murals have been spoiled. There is no sense of colour or creativity. It is mindless, malicious vandalism.

Lucas is perched on a ladder in the driveway, unbolting a basketball hoop from the wall. His hair is even darker, but he's thickened around the waist and his forehead is etched with frown lines that disappear into bushy eyebrows.

'Do you need a hand?'

He looks down and takes a moment to put a name to my face.

'These things are rusted on,' he says, tapping the bolts. Descending the ladder, he wipes his hands on his shirtfront and shakes my hand. At the same time he glances at the front door, betraying his nerves. His wife must be inside. They will have seen the news reports or heard the radio.

I can hear music coming from an upstairs window: something with lots of thumping bass and shuffling turntables. Lucas follows my eyes.

'I tell her to turn it down but she says that it has to be loud. Sign of age, I guess.'

I remember the twins. Sonia was a good swimmer – in the pool, in the sea, she had a beautiful stroke. I was invited to a barbecue one weekend when she must have been about nine. She announced that she was going to swim the Channel one day.

'It'll be much quicker to take the tunnel,' I'd told her.

Everyone had laughed. Sonia had rolled her eyes. She didn't like me after that.

Her twin sister Claire was the bookish one, with steel-framed glasses and a lazy eye. She spent most of the barbecue in her room, complaining that she couldn't hear the TV because everyone outside was 'gibbering like monkeys'.

Lucas is folding up the ladder and explaining that 'the girls don't use the hoop any more'.

'I was sorry to hear about Sonia,' I say.

He acts as though he doesn't hear me. Tools are packed away in a toolbox. I'm about to ask him what happened when he starts telling me that Sonia had just won two titles at the national swimming championships and had broken a distance record.

'Yet even after all that training, all those early morning laps, mile after mile, she knew she wasn't going to be good enough. There is a fine line between being good and being great . . .'

I let him talk because I sense he's making a point. The story unfolds. Sonia Dutton, not quite twenty-three, dressed up for a rock concert. She went with Claire and a group of friends from university. Someone gave her a white pill imprinted with a shell logo. She had always been so careful about medication and health supplements. She danced all night until her heartbeat grew rapid and her blood pressure soared. She felt faint and anxious. She collapsed in a toilet cubicle.

Lucas is still crouched over the toolbox as though he's lost something. His shoulders are shaking. In a rasping voice, he describes how Sonia spent three weeks in a coma, never regaining consciousness. Lucas and his wife argued over whether to turn off her life-support. He was the pragmatist. He wanted to remember her gliding through the water, with her smooth stroke. His wife accused him of giving up hope; of thinking only of himself; of not praying hard enough for a miracle.

'She hasn't said more than a dozen words to me since – not all together in a sentence. Last night she told me that she saw your photograph on the news. I asked her questions that she answered. It was the first time in ages . . . '

'Who gave Sonia the tablet? Did they ever catch anyone?'

Lucas shakes his head. Claire gave them a description. She looked at mugshots and a police line-up.

'What did she say he looked like?'

'Tall, skinny, tanned . . . he had slicked-back hair.'

'How old?'

'Mid-thirties.'

He closes the toolbox and flips the metal catches, before glancing despondently at the house, not yet ready to go inside. Chores like the basketball hoop have become important because they keep him busy and out of the way.

'Do you remember Bobby Morgan?'

'Yes.'

'When was the last time you saw him?'

'Fourteen . . . fifteen years ago. He was only a kid.'

'Not since then?'

He shakes his head and then narrows his eyes as if something has just occurred to him. 'Sonia knew someone called Bobby Morgan. It could have been the same person. He worked at the swimming centre.'

'You never saw him?'

'No.' He sees the curtains moving in the lounge. 'I wouldn't stick around if I were you,' he says. 'She'll call the police if she sees you.'

The toolbox is weighing down his right hand. He swaps it over and glances up at the basketball hoop. 'Guess that'll have to stay there a bit longer.'

I thank him and he hurries inside. The door shuts and the silence amplifies my steps as I walk away. I used to think Dutton was conceited and dogmatic, unwilling to listen or alter his point of view when it came to case conferences. He was the sort of autocratic, nit-picking public servant who is brilliant at making the trains run on time but fails miserably when it comes to dealing with people. If only his staff could be as loyal as his Skoda – starting first time on cold mornings and reacting immediately to every turn of the steering wheel. Now he has been diminished, lessened, beaten down by circumstances.

The man who gave Sonia the tainted white tablet doesn't sound like Bobby but eyewitness accounts are notoriously unreliable. Stress and shock can alter perceptions. Memory is flawed. Bobby is a chameleon, changing colours, camouflaging himself, moving backwards and forwards, but always blending in.

There is a poem that Aunt Gracie used to recite to me – a politically incorrect piece of doggerel called Ten Little Indian Boys. It started off with ten little Indian boys going out to dine, but one chokes himself and then there were nine. All nine little Indian boys stay up late, but one oversleeps and then there are eight . . .

Indian boys are stung by bees, eaten by fish, hugged by bears and chopped in half until only one remains, left alone. I feel like that last little Indian boy.

I understand what Bobby is doing now. He is trying to take away what each of us holds most dear – the love of a child, the closeness of a partner, the sense of belonging. He wants us to suffer as he suffered, to lose what we most love, to experience *his* loss.

Mel and Boyd had been soulmates. Anyone who knew them could see that. Jerzy and Esther Gorski had survived the Nazi gas chambers and settled in north London, where they raised their only child, Alison, who became a schoolteacher and moved to Liverpool. Firemen discovered Jerzy's body at the bottom of the stairs. He was still alive, despite the burns. Esther suffocated in her sleep.

Catherine McBride, a favoured granddaughter in a well-connected family – wayward, spoiled and smothered, she had never lost the heart of her grandfather, who doted on her and forgave her indiscretions.

Rupert Erskine had no wife or children. Perhaps Bobby couldn't discover what he held most dear or perhaps he knew all along. Erskine was a cantankerous old sod, about as likeable as a carpet burn. We made excuses for him because it can't have been easy looking after his wife for all those years. Bobby didn't give him any latitude. He left him alive long enough – tied to a chair – to regret his limitations.

There might be other victims. I don't have time to find them all. Elisa is my failure. I didn't discover Bobby's secret soon enough. Bobby has grown more sophisticated with each death but I am to be the prize. He could have taken Julianne or Charlie from me, but instead he has chosen to take it all – my family, friends, career, reputation and finally my freedom. And he wants me to *know* that he's responsible.

The whole point of analysis is to understand, not to take the essence of something and reduce it to something else. Bobby once accused me of playing God. He said people like me couldn't resist putting our hands inside someone's psyche and changing the way they view the world.

Maybe he is right. Maybe I've made mistakes and fallen into the trap of not thinking hard enough about cause and effect. And I know it isn't good enough, in the wash-up, to make excuses and say, 'I meant well.' That's what they told Gracie when they took her baby away. I've used the same words. 'With the best possible intentions . . . ' and 'with all the goodwill in the world . . . '

In one of my first cases in Liverpool I had to decide if a mentally handicapped twenty-year-old, with no family support and a lifetime of institutionalised care, could keep her unborn child.

I can still picture Sharon with her summer dress stretched tightly over the swell of her pregnancy. She had taken great care, washing and brushing her hair. She knew how important the interview was for her future. Yet despite her efforts, she had forgotten little things. Her socks were the same colour but different lengths. The zipper at the side of her dress was broken. A smudge of lipstick stained her cheek.

'Do you know why you're here, Sharon?'
'Yes, sir.'

'We have to decide whether you can look after your baby. It's a very big responsibility.'

'I can. I can. I'll be a good mother. I'm going to love my baby.'

'Do you know where babies come from?'

'It's growing inside me. God put it there.' She spoke very reverentially and rubbed her tummy.

I couldn't fault her logic. 'Let's play a "what if" game, OK? I want you to imagine that you're bathing your baby and the telephone rings. The baby is all slippery and wet. What do you do?'

'I . . . I . . . I . . . put my baby on the floor, wrapped in a towel.'

'While you are on the telephone, someone knocks on the front door. Do you answer it?'

She momentarily looked unsure. 'It might be the fire brigade,' I added. 'Or maybe it's your social worker.'

'I'd answer the door,' she said, nodding her head forcefully.

'It turns out to be your neighbour. Some young boys have thrown a rock through her window. She has to go to work. She wants you to sit inside her flat and wait for the glaziers to come.'

'Those little shits – they're always throwing rocks,' Sharon said, bunching her fists.

'Your neighbour has satellite TV: movie channels; cartoons; daytime soap operas. What are you going to watch while you're waiting?'

'Cartoons.'

'Will you have a cup of tea?'

'Maybe.'

'Your neighbour has left you some money to pay the glazier. Fifty quid. The job is only going to cost forty-five, but she says you can keep the change.'

Her eyes lit up. 'I can keep the money?'

'Yes. What are you going to buy?'

'Chocolate.'

'Where are you going to buy it?'

'Down the shops.'

'When you go to the shops, what do you normally take?'

'My keys and my purse.'

'Anything else?'

She shook her head.

'Where is your baby, Sharon?'

A look of panic spread across her face and her bottom lip began to tremble. Just when I thought she was going to cry, she suddenly announced, 'Barney will look after her.'

'Who's Barney?'

'My dog.'

A couple of months later, I sat outside the delivery suite and listened to Sharon sobbing as her baby boy was swaddled in a blanket and taken away from her. It was my job to transfer the boy to a different hospital. I strapped him in a carrycot on the back seat of my car. Looking down at the sleeping bundle, I wondered what he'd think, years from then, about the decision I had made for him? Would he thank me for rescuing him or blame me for ruining his life?

A different child has come back. His message is clear. We have failed Bobby. We failed his father – an innocent man, arrested and questioned for hours about his sex life and the length of his penis. His house and workplace were searched for child pornography that didn't exist and his name put on a central index of sex offenders despite him never having been charged, let alone convicted.

This indelible stain was going to blot his life for ever. All his future relationships would be tainted. Wives and partners would have to be told. Fathering a child would become a risk. Coaching a kids' soccer team would be downright reckless. Surely this is enough to drive a man to suicide.

Socrates – the wisest of all Greeks – was wrongly convicted of corrupting the youth of Athens and sentenced to death.

363

He could have escaped but he drank the poison. Socrates believed that our bodies are less important than our souls. Maybe he had Parkinson's.

I share the blame for Bobby. I was part of the system. Mine was the cowardice of acquiescence. Rather than disagree I said nothing. I went along with the majority view. I was young, just starting my career, but that is no excuse. I acted like a spectator instead of a referee.

Julianne called me a coward when she threw me out. I know what she means now. I have sat in the grandstand, not wanting to get drawn into my marriage or my disease. I kept my distance, scared of what might happen. I have let my own state of mind absorb me. I was so worried about rocking the boat, I failed to spot the iceberg.

6

Three hours ago I came up with a plan. It wasn't my first. I worked my way through about a dozen, looking at all the fundamentals, but each had a fatal flaw. I have enough of those already. My ingenuity has to be tempered by my physical limitations. This meant jettisoning anything that requires me to abseil down a building, overpower a guard, short-circuit a security system or crack open a safe.

I also shelved any plan that didn't have an exit strategy. That's why most campaigns fail. The players don't think far enough ahead. The end game is the boring bit, the mopping-up operation, without the glamour and excitement of the principal challenge. Therefore, people get frustrated and only plan so far. From then on they imagine winging it, confident in their ability to master their retreat as skilfully as their advance.

I know this because I have had people in my consulting room who cheat, steal and embezzle for a living. They own nice houses, send their children to private schools and play off single figure handicaps. They vote Tory and view law and order as an important issue because the streets just aren't safe any more. These people rarely get caught and hardly ever go to prison. Why? Because they plan for every outcome.

I am sitting in the darkest corner of a car park in Liverpool. On the seat beside me is a waxed paper shopping bag with a pleated rope handle. My old clothes are inside it and I'm now wearing new charcoal grey trousers, a woollen jumper and an overcoat. My hair is neatly trimmed and my face is freshly shaved. Lying between my legs is a walking stick. Now that I'm walking like a cripple I might as well get some sympathy for it.

The phone rings. I don't recognise the number on the screen. For a split second I wonder whether Bobby could have found me. I should have known it would be Ruiz.

'You surprise me, Professor O'Loughlin.' His voice is all gravel and phlegm. 'I figured you for the sort who would turn up at the nearest police station with a team of lawyers and a PR man.'

'I'm sorry if I disappoint you.'

'I lost twenty quid. Not to worry – we're running a new book. We're taking bets on whether you get shot or not.'

'What are the odds?'

'I can get three to one on you dodging a bullet.'

I hear traffic noise in the background. He's on a motorway.

'I know where you are,' he says.

'You're guessing.'

'No. And I know what you're trying to do.'

'Tell me.'

'First you tell me why you killed Elisa.'

'I didn't kill her.' Ruiz draws deeply on a cigarette. He's smoking again. I feel a curious sense of achievement. 'Why would I kill Elisa? That's where I spent the night on the thirteenth of November. She was my alibi.'

'That's unfortunate for you.'

'She wanted to give a statement, but I knew you wouldn't believe her. You'd drag up her past and humiliate her. I didn't want to put her through it all again . . . '

He laughs the way Jock often does, as though I'm soft in the head.

'We found the shovel,' he says. 'It was buried under a shit-load of leaves.'

What's he talking about? Think! There was a shovel leaning on Gracie's grave.

'The boys and girls at the lab did us proud again. They matched the soil samples found on the shovel with those taken from Catherine's grave. And then they matched the finger-prints on the handle with yours.'

When does this end? I don't want to know any more. Instead I talk over Ruiz, trying to keep the desperation out of my voice. I tell him to go back to the beginning and look for the red edge.

'His name is Bobby Morgan – not Moran. Read the case notes. All the pieces are there. Put them together . . . '

He's not listening to me. It's too big for him to comprehend.

'Under different circumstances I might admire your enthu-siasm, but I have enough evidence already,' he says. 'I have motive, opportunity and physical evidence. You couldn't have marked your territory any better if you'd pissed in every corner.'

'I can explain—'

'Good! Explain it to a jury! That's the beauty of our legal system – you get plenty of chances to state your case. If the jury don't believe you, you can appeal to the High Court and then the House of Lords and the European Court of Human Sodding Rights. You can spend the rest of your life appealing. It obviously helps pass the time when you're banged up for life.'

I press the 'end call' button and turn off the phone.

Leaving the car park, I descend the stairs and emerge on street level. I dump my old clothes and shoes in a rubbish bin, along with the holdall and the soggy scraps of paper from my hotel room. As I head along the street, I swing my cane in what I hope is a jaunty, cheerful way. The shoppers are out and every store is bedecked with tinsel and playing Christmas carols. It makes me feel homesick. Charlie loves that sort of stuff – the department store Santas, window displays and watching old Bing Crosby movies set in Vermont.

As I'm about to cross the road, I spot a poster on the side of a newspaper van. 'MANHUNT FOR CATHERINE'S KILLER'. My face is underneath, pinned beneath the plastic ties. Instantly I feel like I'm wearing a huge neon sign on my head with the arrow pointing downwards.

The Adelphi Hotel is ahead of me. I push through the revolving door and cross the foyer, fighting the urge to quicken my stride. I tell myself not to walk too quickly or hunch over. Head up. Eyes straight ahead.

It's a grand old railway hotel, dating back to a time when steam trains arrived from London and steam ships left for New York. Now it looks as tired as some of the waitresses, who should be at home putting curlers in their hair.

The business centre is on the first floor. The secretary is a skinny thing called Nancy, with permed red hair and a red cravat around her neck that matches her lipstick. She doesn't ask for a business card or check if I have a room number.

'If you have any questions, just ask,' she says, keen to help.

'I'll be fine. I need to check my e-mails.' I sit at a computer terminal and turn my back to her.

'Actually, Nancy, you could do something for me. Can you find out if there are any flights to Dublin this afternoon?'

A few minutes later she rattles off a list. I choose the late afternoon shuttle and I give her my credit card details.

'Can you also see about getting me to Edinburgh?' I ask.

She raises an eyebrow.

'You know what head offices are like,' I explain. 'They can never make a decision.'

She nods and smiles.

'And see if there's a sleeper available on the Isle of Man ferry.'

'The tickets are non-refundable.'

'That's OK.'

In the meantime, I search for the e-mail addresses of all the major newspapers and gather the names of news editors, chief reporters and police roundsmen. I start typing an e-mail using my right hand, pressing one key at a time. I tuck my left hand under my thigh to stop it trembling.

I start with proof of my identity – giving my name, address, National Insurance number and employment details. They can't think this is a hoax. They have to believe that I am Joseph O'Loughlin – the man who killed Catherine McBride and Elisa Velasco.

It is just after 4.00 p.m. Editors are deciding the running order for stories in the first edition. I need to change tomorrow's headlines. I need to knock Bobby off his stride – to keep him guessing.

Up until now he's always been two, three, four steps ahead of me. His acts of revenge have been brilliantly conceived and clinically executed. He didn't simply apportion blame. He turned it into an art form. But for all his genius, he is capable of making a mistake. Nobody is infallible. He kicked a woman unconscious because she reminded him of his mother.

To whom it may concern:

This is my confession and testament. I, Joseph William O'Loughlin, do solemnly, sincerely and truly affirm that I am the man responsible for the murders of Catherine McBride and Elisa Velasco. I apologise to those who grieve at their loss. And for those of you who thought better of me, I am genuinely sorry.

I intend to give myself up to the police within the next 24 hours. At that point I will not seek to hide behind lawyers or to excuse the suffering I have caused. I will not claim there were voices inside my head. I wasn't high on drugs or taking instructions from Satan. I could have stopped this. Innocent people have died. My every hour is long with guilt.

I list the names, starting with Catherine McBride. I put down everything I know about her murder. Boyd Cossimo is next. I describe Rupert Erskine's last days; Sonia Dutton's overdose; the fire that killed Esther Gorski and crippled her husband. Elisa comes last.

I do not plead any kind of mitigation. Some of you may wish to know more about my crimes. If so, you must walk in my shoes, or find someone who has done so. There is such a person. His name is Bobby Moran (aka Bobby Morgan) and he will appear at the Central Criminal Court in London tomorrow morning. He, more than anyone, understands what it means to be both victim and perpetrator.

Sincerely yours,
Joseph O'Loughlin.

I have thought of everything, except what this will mean to Charlie. Bobby was a victim of a decision made beyond his control. I'm doing the same thing to my daughter. My finger hovers over the send button. I have no choice. The e-mail disappears into the labyrinth of the electronic post office.

Nancy thinks I'm mad but has made my travel arrangements, booking flights to Dublin, Edinburgh, London, Paris and Frankfurt. In addition there are first-class seats on trains to Birmingham, Newcastle, Glasgow, London, Swansea and Leeds. She has also managed to hire me a white Vauxhall Cavalier, which is waiting downstairs.

Everything has been paid for with a debit card that doesn't require authorisation from a bank. The card is linked to a trust account set up by my father. Inheritance tax is another of his pet hates. I'm assuming Ruiz will have frozen all my accounts but he can't touch this one.

The lift doors open and I set out across the foyer, staring straight ahead. I bump into a potted palm and realise that

I'm drifting sideways. Walking has become a constant assortment of adjustments and corrections, like landing a plane.

The hire car is parked outside. As I walk down the front steps of the hotel I keep expecting to feel a hand on my shoulder or to hear a shout of recognition or alarm. My fingers fumble with the keys. Black cabs are queued in front of me but one of them eases out of my way. I follow the stream of traffic, glancing in the mirrors and trying to remember the quickest way out of the city.

Stopped at a red light, I look beyond the stream of pedestrians at the multi-storey car park. Three police cars are blocking the entry ramp and another is on the pavement. Ruiz is leaning on an open door, talking on the radio. He has a face like thunder.

As the lights change to green, I imagine him looking up and me saluting him like a World War I flying ace in a crippled plane, living to fight another day.

One of my favourite songs is on the radio — 'Jumpin' Jack Flash'. At university I played bass guitar for a band called the Screaming Dick Nixons. We weren't as good as the Rolling Stones but we were louder. I knew nothing about playing the bass guitar but it was the easiest instrument to fake. Mostly my ambition was to get laid but that only ever happened to our lead singer, Morris Whiteside, who had long hair and a crucifixion scene tattooed on his torso. He's now a senior accountant working for Deutsche Bank.

I head west towards Toxteth and park the Cavalier in a vacant plot, among the cinders and weeds. A handful of teenagers watch me from the shadows beside a boarded-up community hall. I'm driving the sort of fancy car they normally only see on bricks.

I phone home. Julianne answers. Her voice sounds close, crystal clear, but already starting to shake. "Thank God! Where have you been? Reporters keep ringing the doorbell. They say you're dangerous. They say the police are going to shoot you.'

I try to steer the conversation away from firearms. 'I know who did this. Bobby is trying to punish me for something that happened a long time ago. It isn't just me. He has a list of names—'

'What list?'

'Boyd is dead.'

'How?'

'He was murdered. So was Erskine.'

'My God!'

'Are the police still watching the house?'

'I don't know. There was someone in a white van yesterday. At first I thought D.J. had come to finish the central heating but he's not due until tomorrow.'

I can hear Charlie singing in the background. A rush of tenderness catches in my throat.

The police will be trying to trace this call. With mobile phones, they have to work backwards, identifying which towers are relaying the signals. There are probably half a dozen transmitters between Liverpool and London. As each one is ticked off, the search area narrows.

'I want you to stay on the line, Julianne. If I don't come back, just leave the line open. It's important.' I slide the phone under the driver's seat. The car keys are still in the ignition. I close the car door and walk away, head down, retreating into the darkness, wondering if he's watching me still.

Twenty minutes later, on a railway platform that looks abandoned and burned out, I step gratefully on to a suburban train. The carriages are almost empty.

Ruiz will know about the ferry, train and airline bookings by now. He'll realise I'm trying to stretch his resources but he will have to check them anyway.

The express to London leaves from Lime Street Station. The police will search each carriage but I'm hoping they won't stay on the train. Edgehill is one stop further, which is where I board a train to Manchester just after 10.30 p.m. After

372

midnight I catch another, this one bound for York. I have a three-hour wait until the Great North Eastern Express leaves for London, sitting in a poorly lit ticket hall, watching the cleaners compete to do the least work.

I pay for the tickets with cash and choose the busiest carriage. Staggering drunkenly along the aisles, I topple into people and mumble apologies.

Only children stare at drunks. Adults avoid eye contact, hoping that I keep moving and choose somewhere else to sit. When I fall asleep, leaning against a window, the entire carriage lets out a silent collective sigh.

7

The train journeys of my youth were to and from boarding school, when I'd gorge myself on bags of sweets and chewing gum, which weren't allowed at Charterhouse. Sometimes I think Semtex would have been more acceptable than bubblegum. One of the seniors, Peter Clavell, swallowed so much that it clogged his intestines and doctors had to remove the blockage through his rectum. Not surprisingly, gum wasn't so popular after that.

My father's back-to-school pep-talk normally boiled down to a seven-word warning: 'Don't let me hear from the headmaster.' When Charlie started school I promised that I'd be a different sort of parent. I sat her down and gave her a talk best saved for secondary school, or perhaps even university. Julianne kept giggling, which set Charlie off.

'Don't be scared of maths,' I finished up saying.

'Why?'

'Because a lot of girls are scared of numbers. They talk themselves out of being good at things.'

'OK,' Charlie replied, having absolutely no idea what I was talking about.

I wonder if I'm going to get to see her start secondary school. For weeks I've been worried about this disease denying me things. Now it pales into insignificance when set alongside murder.

As the train pulls into King's Cross I walk slowly through the carriages, studying the platform for any sign of the police. I fall into step with an elderly woman pulling a large suitcase. As we reach the barrier I offer to help her and she nods gratefully. At the ticket booth I turn to her. 'Where's your ticket, Mum?'

She doesn't bat an eyelid as she hands it to me. I give both tickets to the guard and give him a weary smile.

'Don't you hate these early starts?' he says.

'I'll never get used to them,' I reply as he hands me the stubs.

Weaving my way through the crowded concourse, I pause at the entrance to WH Smith where the morning papers are stacked side by side. KILLER CONFESSES – "I KILLED CATHERINE" screams the headline in the *Sun*.

The broadsheets are reporting rising interest rates and a threatened strike by postal workers. Catherine's story – my story – is beneath the fold. People reach past me and pick up copies. Nobody makes eye contact. This is London, a city where people walk bolt upright with fixed expressions as though ready to face anything and avoid everything. They have somewhere else to be. Don't interrupt. Just keep moving.

Finding a rhythm to my stride, I weave my way through Covent Garden, past the restaurants and expensive boutiques. Reaching the Strand, I turn left and follow Fleet Street until the gothic façade of the Old Bailey comes into view.

A courthouse has stood on this site for nearly five hundred years and even before that, in medieval times, they held public executions here every Monday morning.

I take up position over the road, tucked against a wall in an alley that runs down towards the Thames. There are brass

375

plates on nearly every doorway. I glance occasionally at my watch, to give the impression of waiting for someone. Men and women in black suits and gowns glide past me, clutching box files and bundles of paper tied with ribbon.

At half past nine the first of the news crews arrives – a cameraman and sound recordist. Others join them. Some of the stills photographers carry stepladders and milk crates. The reporters stick together in the background – sipping take-away coffee, swapping gossip and misinformation.

Shortly before ten, I notice a cab pull up on my side of the road. Eddie Barrett gets out first, looking like Danny DeVito with hair. Bobby is behind him, at least two heads taller but still having somehow managed to find a suit that looks too big for him.

Both are less than fifteen feet away from me. I lower my head and blow into my hands. Bobby's overcoat pockets are bulging with paper and his eyes are watery blue. The warmth of the cab meets the coldness of the air and fogs up his glasses. He pauses to wipe them clean. His hands are steady. The reporters have spotted Eddie and are waiting for him with cameras poised and TV lights at the ready.

I see Bobby lower his head. He is too tall to hide his face. Reporters are firing questions at him. Eddie Barrett puts his hand on Bobby's arm. Bobby pulls away as though scalded. A TV camera is right in his face. Flashguns flare. He wasn't expecting this. He doesn't have a plan.

Barrett is trying to hustle him up the stone steps and through the arches. Photographers are jostling each other and one of them suddenly tumbles backwards. Bobby is standing over him, his fist raised. Bystanders grab at his shoulders and Eddie swings his briefcase like a scythe, clearing a path in front of them. The last thing I see as the doors close is Bobby's head above the throng.

I allow myself a fleeting smile, but nothing more. I can't afford to get my hopes up. Nearby, a gift shop window is

376

crammed with marshmallow Santas and Christmas crackers in red and green. There are reindeer clocks with noses that glow in the dark. I use the reflection in the glass to watch the courthouse steps.

I can picture the scene inside. The press bench will be packed and the public gallery standing room only. Eddie loves working a crowd. He will ask for an adjournment due to my unprofessional conduct and claim his client has been denied natural justice because of my malicious allegations. A new psych report will have to be commissioned, which could take weeks. Blah, blah, blah . . .

There is always a chance the judge might say no and sentence Bobby immediately. More likely, he will grant the adjournment and Bobby will walk free – even more dangerous than before.

Rocking back and forth on my heels, I have to remind myself of the rules. Avoid standing with my feet too close together. Consciously lift feet to avoid shuffling and foot drag. Don't instinctively pivot. My favourite suggestion for breaking a 'frozen pose' is to step over an imaginary obstacle in front of me. I have visions of looking like Marcel Marceau.

I walk to the end of the block, turn and come back again, never taking my eye off the photographers still milling outside the court entrance. Suddenly, they surge forward, cameras raised. Eddie must have had a car waiting. Bobby comes out in a half crouch, pushing through the mêlée and falling on to the back seat. The car door closes as the flashguns continue firing.

I should have seen this coming. I should have been prepared. Limping on to the road, I wave both arms and a walking stick at a black cab. It swerves out of my way and swings past, forcing a line of traffic to brake hard. A second cab has an orange beacon. The driver either stops or runs me over.

He doesn't bat an eyelid when I tell him to follow that car. Maybe cab drivers hear that all the time.

The silver sedan carrying Bobby is ahead of us, sandwiched between two buses and a line of cars. My driver manages to nudge into gaps and dodge between lanes, never losing touch. At the same time I notice him sneaking glances at me in the rear mirror. He looks away quickly when our eyes meet. He is young, perhaps in his early twenties, with rust-coloured hair and freckles on the back of his neck. His hands uncurl and flutter on the steering wheel.

'You know who I am.'

He nods.

'I'm not dangerous.'

He looks into my eyes, trying to find some reassurance. My face can't give him any. My Parkinson's mask is like cold chiselled stone.

8

This stretch of the Grand Union Canal is graceless and untidy, with the asphalt towpath pitted and broken. A rusting iron fence leans at a precarious angle, separating the terraced back gardens from the water. A graffiti-daubed caravan, missing a door, sits on bricks instead of wheels. A half-buried child's tricycle sprouts from a vegetable patch.

Bobby hasn't looked over his shoulder since the car dropped him at Camley Street, behind St Pancras Station. I know the rhythm of his walk now. He passes the Lock Keeper's cottage and keeps going. The gas works cast a shadow over the abandoned factories that lie along the south bank. A redevelopment sign announces a new industrial estate.

Four narrow boats are moored against a stone wall on the curve. Three are brightly painted in reds and greens. The fourth has a tug-style bow, with a black hull and a maroon trim to the cabin.

Bobby steps lightly on board and appears to knock on the deck. He waits for several seconds and then unlocks the sliding hatch. He pushes it forward and unlatches the door below. He steps down into the cabin, out of sight. I wait on the edge of

379

the towpath, hidden by a bramble that is trying to swallow a fence. A woman in a grey overcoat pulls at a dog lead, dragging the animal quickly past me.

Five minutes pass. Bobby emerges and glances in my direction. He slides the hatch closed and steps ashore. Reaching into his pocket, he counts loose change in his hand. Then he sets off along the path. I follow at a distance until he climbs a set of steps on to a bridge. He turns south towards a garage.

I return to the boat. I need to see inside. The lacquered door is closed, but not locked. The cabin is dark. Curtains are drawn across the window slits and portholes. Two steps lead me down into the galley. The stainless steel sink is clean. A lone cup sits draining on a tea towel.

Six steps further is the saloon. It looks more like a workshop than a living area, with a bench down one side. My eyes adjust to the light and I see a pegboard dotted with tools – chisels, wrenches, spanners, screwdrivers, metal cutters, planes and files. There are boxes of pipes, washers, drill bits and waterproof tape on shelves. The floor is partly covered with drums of paint, rust proofing, epoxy, wax, grease and machine oil. A portable generator squats under the bench. An old radio hangs on a cord from the ceiling. Everything has its proper place.

On the opposite wall there is another pegboard, but this one is clear. The only attachments are four leather cuffs – two near the floor and a matching set near the roof. My eyes are drawn to the floor. I don't want to look. The bare wood and skirting boards are stained by something deeper than the darkness.

Reeling backwards, I strike the bulkhead and emerge into a cabin. Everything seems slightly askew. The mattress is too large for the bed. The lamp is too large for the table. The walls are covered in scraps of paper but it's too dark for me to see them properly. I turn on a lamp and my eyes take a moment to adjust.

380

Suddenly I'm sitting down. Newspaper cuttings, photographs, maps, diagrams and drawings cover the walls. I see images of Charlie on her way to school, playing soccer, singing in the school choir, shopping with her grandmother, on a merry-go-round, feeding the ducks. Others show Julianne at her yoga class, at the supermarket, painting the garden furniture, answering the door . . . Looking closer, I recognise receipts, ticket stubs, soccer newsletters, business cards, photocopies of bank statements and telephone bills, a street map, a library card, a reminder for school fees, a parking notice, registration papers for the car . . .

The small bedside table is stacked high with ring-bound notebooks. I take the top one and open it. Neat, concise handwriting fills each page. The left-hand margin logs the time and date. Alongside are details of my movements, including places, meetings, duration, modes of transport, relevance. It is a 'how to' manual of my life. How to be me!

There is a sound on the deck above my head. Something is being dragged and poured. I switch off the light and sit in darkness, trying to breathe quietly. Someone swings through the hatch into the saloon. He moves through to the galley and opens cupboards. I lie on the floor, squeezed between the bulkhead and the end of the bed, feeling my pulse throbbing at the base of my jaw.

The engine starts up. The pistons rise and fall, then settle into a steady rhythm. I see Bobby's legs through the portholes and feel the boat pitch as he steps along the sides, casting off the lines.

I glance to the galley and saloon. If I move quickly I might be able to get ashore before he comes back to the wheelhouse. I try to stand and knock over a rectangular frame leaning against the wall. As it topples, I manage to catch it with one hand. The painting is frozen momentarily in the light leaking through the curtains: a beach scene, bathing sheds, ice-cream stalls and a Ferris wheel. On the horizon, Charlie's stout, grey whale.

I fall backwards with a groan, unable to make my legs obey me. They belong to someone else.

The narrow boat rocks again as the footsteps return. He has cast off the bowline. The engine is put into gear and we swing away from the mooring. Water slides along the hull. Pulling myself upwards, I ease the curtain open a few inches and lift my face to the porthole. I can only see the treetops.

There is a new sound – a whooshing noise, like a strong wind. All the oxygen seems to disappear from the air. Fuel runs along the floor and soaks into my trousers. Varnished wood crackles as it burns. Fumes sting my eyes and the back of my throat. On my knees, I crawl down the boat into the gathering smoke.

Pulling myself through the U-shaped galley, I reach the saloon. The engine is close by. I can hear it thudding on the far side of the bulkhead. My head hits the stairs and I climb upwards. The hatchway is locked from the outside. I slam my shoulder against it. Nothing moves. My hand feels heat through the door. I need another way out.

The air feels like molten glass in my lungs. I can't see a thing but I can feel my way. On the benches in the workroom my fingers close around a hammer and a sharp, flat chisel. I retreat along the boat, away from the seat of the blaze, rico-cheting off walls and hammering on the portholes with the hammer. The glass is reinforced.

Against the bulkhead in the cabin there is a small storage door. I squeeze through it, flopping like a stranded fish until my legs follow me. Oily tarpaulins and ropes snake beneath me. I must be in the bow. I reach above my head and feel the indentation of a hatch. Running my fingers around the edge, I search for a latch, then try wedging the chisel into a corner and swinging the hammer, but the angle is all wrong.

The boat has started to list. Water has invaded the stern. I lie on my back and brace both my feet against the underside of the hatch. Then I kick upwards . . . once, twice, three times. I'm screaming and cursing. The wood splinters and gives way. A square of blinding light fills the hold. I glance back as the petrol in the cabin ignites and a ball of orange flame erupts towards me. At the same moment, I drag myself upwards into daylight, rolling over and over. Fresh air embraces me for a split second and then water wraps itself around me. I sink slowly, inexorably, screaming inside my head, until I settle in the silt. I don't think about drowning. I'll just stay down here for a while where it's cool and dark and green.

When my lungs start to hurt, I reach upwards, grasping for handfuls of air. My head breaks the surface and I roll on to my back, sucking greedily. The stern of the boat has slipped under. Drums in the workroom are exploding like grenades. The engine has stopped but the boat is turning slowly away from me.

I wade towards the bank with mud sucking at my shoes and pull myself upwards using handfuls of reeds. I ignore the outstretched hand. I just want to lie down and rest. My body twists. My legs bump over the edge of the canal. I am sitting on the deserted towpath. Giant cranes are silhouetted against grey clouds.

I recognise Bobby's shoes. He reaches under my arms and grabs me around the chest. I'm being lifted. His chin digs into the top of my head as he carries me. I can smell petrol on his clothes or maybe on mine. I don't cry out. Reality seems far away.

A scarf loops around my neck and is pulled tight, with a knot pressing into my windpipe. The other end is tied to something above me, forcing me up on to my toes. My legs jerk like a marionette because I can't get any purchase on the ground to stop myself choking. I squeeze my fingers inside the scarf and hold it away from my throat.

We are in the courtyard of an abandoned factory. Wooden

palletes are stacked against a wall. Sheets of roofing iron have fallen in a storm. Water leaks down the walls, weaving a tapestry of black and green slime. Bobby shifts away from me. His face is damp with sweat.

'I know why you're doing this,' I say.

He doesn't answer. He strips off his suit jacket and rolls up the sleeves of his shirt as if there is business to be taken care of. Then he sits on a packing crate and takes out a white hand-kerchief to clean his glasses. His stillness is remarkable.

'You won't get away with killing me.'

'What makes you think I want to kill you?' He hooks his glasses over his ears and looks at me. 'You're a wanted man. They'll probably give me a reward.' His voice betrays him. He isn't sure. In the distance I can hear a siren. The fire brigade is coming.

Bobby will have read the morning papers. He *knows* why I confessed. The police will have to re-open every case and examine the details. They will cross-reference the times, dates and places, putting my name into the equation. And what will they discover? That I couldn't have killed all of them. Then they'll begin to wonder why I confessed. And maybe – just maybe – they'll put Bobby's name into the same equation. How many alibis can he have tucked away? How well did he cover his tracks?

I have to keep him off-balance. 'I visited your mother yesterday. She asked about you.'

Bobby stiffens slightly and the pattern of his breathing quickens.

'I don't think I've met Bridget before, but she must have been very beautiful once. Alcohol and cigarettes aren't very kind to the skin. I don't think I met your father either, but I think I would have liked him.'

'You know nothing about him.' He spits the words.

'Not true. I think I have something in common with Lenny . . . and with you. I need to take things apart – to understand

384

how they work. That's why I came looking for you. I thought you might help me figure something out.'

He doesn't answer.

'I've got most of the story now – I know about Erskine and Lucas Dutton, Justice McBride and Mel Cossimo. But what I can't fathom is why you punished everyone except the person you hate the most.'

Bobby is on his feet, blowing himself up like one of those fish with the poisonous spikes. He shoves his face close to mine. I can see a vein, a faint blue pulsing knot above his left eyelid.

'You can't even say her name, can you? She says you look like your father but that's not entirely true. Every time you look in the mirror you must see your mother's eyes . . . '

A knife is gripped between his fingers. He holds the point of the blade against my bottom lip. If I open my mouth it will draw blood. I can't stop now.

'Let me tell you what I've worked out so far, Bobby. I see a small boy, suckled on his father's dreams but polluted by his mother's violence . . . ' The blade is so sharp I don't feel a thing. Blood is leaking down my chin and dripping on to my fingers, still pressed against my neck. ' . . . he blames himself. Most victims of abuse do. He thought of himself as a coward – always running, tripping, mumbling excuses; never good enough, always late, born to disappoint. He thinks he should have been able to save his father, but he didn't understand what was happening until it was too late.'

'Shut the fuck up! You were one of them. *You* killed him! You mind-fucker!'

'I didn't know him.'

'Yeah, that's right. You condemned a man you didn't know. How arbitrary is that? At least I choose. You haven't got a clue. You haven't got a heart.'

Bobby's face is still inches from mine. I see hurt in his eyes and hatred in the curl of his lips.

'So he blames himself, this boy, who is already growing too

quickly and becoming awkward and uncoordinated. Tender and shy, angry and bitter – he can't untangle these feelings. He hasn't the capacity to forgive. He hates the world, but no more than he hates himself. He cuts his arms to rid himself of the poison. He clings to memories of his father and of how things used to be. Not perfect, but OK. Together.

'So what does he do? He withdraws from his surroundings and becomes isolated, making himself smaller, hoping to be forgotten, living inside his head. Tell me about your fantasy world, Bobby. It must have been nice to have somewhere to go.'

'You'll only try to spoil it.' His face is flushed. He doesn't want to talk to me, but at the same time he's proud of his achievements. This is something *he* has made. A part of him does want to draw me into his world – to share his exhilaration.

The blade is still pressing into my lip. He pulls it away and waves it in front of my eyes. He tries to make it look practised but fails. He isn't comfortable with a knife.

My fingers are growing numb holding the scarf away from my windpipe. And the lactic acid is building in my calves as I balance on my toes. I can't hold myself up much longer.

'How does it feel to be omnipotent, Bobby? To be judge, jury and executioner, punishing all those who deserve to be punished? You must have spent years rehearsing all of this. Amazing. But who were you doing it for, exactly?'

Bobby reaches down and picks up a plank. He mumbles at me to shut up.

'Oh, that's right, your father. A man you can hardly remember. I bet you don't know his favourite song or what movies he liked or who his heroes were. What did he carry in his pockets? Was he left- or right-handed? Which side did he part his hair?'

'I told you to SHUT YOUR MOUTH!'

The plank swings in a wide arc, striking me across the chest. Air blasts out of my lungs and my body spins, tightening the scarf like a tourniquet. I kick my legs to try to spin back. My mouth is flapping like the gills of a stranded fish.

Bobby tosses the plank aside and looks at me as if to say, 'I told you so.'

My ribs feel broken, but my lungs are working again. 'Just one more question, Bobby. Why are you such a coward? I mean, it's pretty obvious who deserved all this hatred. Look at what she did. She belittled and tormented your dad. She slept with other men and made him a figure of pity, even to his friends. And then, to top it all off, she accused him of abusing his own son . . . '

Bobby has turned away from me but even the silence is speaking to him.

'She ripped up the letters he wrote to you. I bet she even found the photographs you kept and destroyed them. She wanted Lenny out of her life and out of yours. She hated hearing his name . . . '

Bobby is growing smaller, as if collapsing from the inside. His anger has turned to grief.

'Let me guess what happened. She was going to be the first. You went looking for her and found her easily enough. Bridget had never been the shy, retiring type. Her stilettos made big footprints.

'You watched her and waited. You had it all planned . . . every last detail. Now was the moment. The woman who had destroyed your life was just a few feet away, close enough for you to put those fingers around her throat. She was right there, *right there*, but you hesitated. You couldn't do it. You were twice her size. She had no weapon. You could have crushed her so easily.'

I pause, letting the memory live in his mind. 'Nothing happened. You couldn't do it. Do you know why? You were scared. When you saw her again you became that little boy, with his trembling bottom lip and his stutter. She terrified you then, and she terrifies you now.'

387

Bobby's face is twisted in self-loathing. At the same time, he wants to wipe me from his world.

'Someone had to be punished. So you found your child protection files and the list of names. And you set about punishing all those responsible, by taking away what each of them loved most. But you never lost the fear of your mother. Once a coward, always a coward. What did you think when you discovered she was dying? Has her cancer done the job for you, or has it robbed you?'

'Robbed me.'

'She's dying a terrible death. I've seen her.'

He explodes. 'It's not enough. She is a MONSTER!' He kicks at a metal drum, sending it spinning across the court-yard. 'She destroyed my life. She *made* me into this.'

Spittle hangs from his lips. He looks at me for validation. He wants me to say, 'You poor bastard. It *is* all her fault. It's no wonder you feel like this.' I can't give him that. If I sanction his hatred there is no way back.

'I'm not going to give you any bullshit excuses, Bobby. Terrible things happened to you. I wish it could have been different. But look at the world around you – there are children starving in Africa; jets are being flown into buildings; bombs are being dropped on civilians; people are dying of disease; prisoners are being tortured; women are being raped . . . Some of these things we can change, but others we can't. Sometimes we just have to accept what happened and get on with our lives.'

He laughs bitterly. 'How can you say that?'

'Because it's true. You know it is.'

'I'll tell you what's true.' He is staring at me unblinkingly. His voice is a low rumble. 'There is a lay-by on the coast road through Great Crosby – about eight miles north of Liverpool. It's on the dual carriageway, set back from the road. If you drive in there after ten o'clock at night, you will sometimes see another car parked up. You put on your indicator – either

388

left or right, depending on what you want – and you wait for the car in front to respond with the same indicator. Then you follow it.'

His voice is ragged. 'I was six when she first took me to the lay-by. I just watched the first time. It was in a barn some-where. She was laid out on a table like a smorgasbord. Naked. There were dozens of hands on her. Anyone could do what they wanted. She had enough for all of them. Pain. Pleasure. It was all the same to her. And every time she opened her eyes she looked directly at me. 'Don't be selfish, Bobby,' she said. 'Learn to share.'

He rocks slightly, back and forth, staring straight ahead, picturing the scene in his mind. 'Private clubs and swingers bars were too middle class for my mother. She preferred her orgies to be anonymous and unsophisticated. I lost count of how many people shared her body. Women and men. That's how I learned to share. At first they took from me, but later I took from them. Pain and pleasure – my mother's legacy.'

His eyes are brimming with tears. I don't know what to say. My tongue has grown thick and prickly. My peripheral vision has started to fail because I can't get enough oxygen to my brain.

I want to say something. I want to tell him that he isn't alone. That a lot of people fret through the same dreams, yell into the same emptiness and walk past the same open windows and wonder whether to jump. I know he's lost. He's damaged. But he still has choices. Not every abused child turns out like this.

'Let me down, Bobby. I can't breathe properly.'

I can see the back of his square neck and his badly trimmed hair. He turns in slow motion, never looking at my face. The blade sweeps above my head and I collapse forwards, still clutching the remnants of the scarf. The muscles in my legs go into spasm. I taste concrete dust, mingled with blood. There are more loose planks leaning against one wall and industrial

389

sinks against another. Where is the canal from here? I have to get out.

Lifting myself on to my knees, I start crawling. Bobby has disappeared. Metal shavings dig into my hands. Broken concrete and rusting drums are like an obstacle course. As I reach the entrance I can see a fire engine beside the canal and the flashing lights of a police car. I try to shout but no sound emerges.

Something is wrong. I've stopped moving. I turn to see Bobby standing on my coat.

'Your fucking arrogance blows me away,' he says, grasping my collar and lifting me to my feet. 'You think I'd fall for your cereal box psychology. I've seen more therapists, counsellors and psychiatrists than you've had crappy birthday presents. I've been to Freudians, Jungians, Adlerians, Rogerians – you name it – and I wouldn't give any of them the steam off my piss on a cold day.' He puts his face close to mine once more. 'You *don't* know me. You think you're inside my head. Shit! You're not even close!' He places the blade under my ear. We're breathing the same air.

A flick of his wrist and my throat will open like a dropped melon. That's what he's going to do. I can feel the metal against my neck. He is going to end this now.

At that moment I picture Julianne looking at me across her pillow, with her hair mussed up from sleep. And I see Charlie in her pyjamas, smelling of shampoo and toothpaste. I wonder if it's possible to count the freckles on her nose. Wouldn't it be a terrible thing to die without trying?

Bobby's breath is warm on my neck – the blade is cold. His tongue comes out, wetting his lips. There is a moment of hesitation – I don't know why.

'I guess we both underestimated each other,' I say, inching my hand inside my coat pocket. 'I knew you wouldn't let me go. Your kind of vengeance isn't negotiable. You've invested too much in it. It's the reason you get up in the morning. That's why I had to get off that wall.'

390

He wavers, trying to work out what he hasn't prepared for. My fingers close around the handle of the chisel.

'I have a disease, Bobby. Sometimes I have difficulty walking. My right hand is OK, but see how my left arm trembles.' I hold up the limb that no longer feels as if it belongs to me. It draws his gaze like a birthmark on someone's face or a disfiguring burn.

With my right hand I drive the chisel through my coat into Bobby's abdomen. It strikes his pelvic bone and twists, puncturing the transverse colon. Three years at medical school are never wasted.

Still holding my collar, he falls to his knees. I swing around and hit him as hard as I can with my fist, aiming for his jaw. He puts his arm up, but I still manage to connect with the side of his head, throwing him backwards. Everything has slowed down. Bobby tries to stand but I move forward a pace and catch him under the chin with a clumsy but effective kick that snaps his head back.

For a moment I stare at him, crumpled on the ground. Then, crablike, I scuttle across the courtyard. Once I get my legs moving they still do the job. It might not be pretty but I've never been Roger Bannister.

A police dog handler is searching for a scent along the canal bank. He sees me coming and takes a step back. I keep going. It takes two of them to hold me. Even then I want to keep running.

Ruiz has me by the shoulders. 'Where is he?' he yells. 'Where's Bobby?'

9

Aunt Gracie made the best milky tea. She would always put
an extra scoop of tealeaves in the pot and another slurp of
milk in my cup. I don't know where Ruiz managed to find
such a brew, but it helps to wash the taste of blood and petrol
from my mouth.

Sitting in the front seat of a squad car, I hold the cup with
both hands in a vain attempt to stop them trembling.

'You should really get that seen to,' Ruiz says. My bottom
lip is still bleeding. I touch it gingerly with my tongue.

Ruiz takes the cellophane off a packet of cigarettes and
offers me one.

I shake my head. 'I thought you'd given up.'

'I blame you. We chased that stolen bloody hire car for near
on fifty miles. Found two fourteen-year-olds and a kid of eleven
inside it. We also staked out the railway stations, airports, bus
terminals . . . I had every officer in the north-west looking for
you.'

'Wait till you get my invoice.'

He regards his cigarette with a mixture of affection and
distaste. 'Your confession was a nice touch. Very creative. I

had the press hyenas sniffing everything except my arse —
asking questions, talking to relatives, stirring up the silt. You
gave me no choice.'

'You found the red edge?'

'Yeah.'

'What about the other names on the list?'

'We're still looking into them.'

He leans against the open door, studying me thoughtfully.
The glint of sunlight off the canal picks up the Tower of Pisa
pin on his tie. His distant blue eyes have fixed on the ambulance parked a hundred feet away, framed against the factory
wall.

The pain in my chest and throat is making me feel light-
headed. I wince as I pull a rough grey blanket around my
shoulders. Ruiz tells me how he spent all night checking the
details from the child protection file. He ran the names through
the computer and pulled up the unsolved deaths.

Bobby had worked in Hatchmere as a council gardener up
until a few weeks before Rupert Erskine died. He and
Catherine McBride attended the same group therapy sessions
for self-mutilators at an outpatients clinic in West Kirkby in
the mid-nineties.

'What about Sonia Dutton?' I ask.

'Nothing. He doesn't match the description of the pusher
who sold her the drug.'

'He worked at her swimming club.'

'I'll check it out.'

'How did he get Catherine to come to London?'

'She came for the job interview. You wrote her a letter.'

'No I didn't.'

'Bobby wrote it for you. He stole stationery from your
office.'

'How? When?'

Ruiz can see I'm struggling. 'You mentioned the word
Nevaspring sewn into Bobby's shirt. It's a French company

that delivers water coolers to offices. We're checking the CCTV footage from the medical centre.'

'He made deliveries—'

'Walked right past security with a bottle over his shoulder.'

'That explains how he managed to get into the building when he arrived late for several of his appointments.'

Across the waste ground, visible above the broken fence, Bobby is lying on a stretcher. A paramedic holds a transfusion bottle above his head.

'Is he going to be OK?' I ask.

'You haven't saved the taxpayer the cost of a trial, if that's what you're asking.'

'No.'

'You're not feeling sorry for him, are you?'

I shake my head. Maybe one day – a long while from now – I'll look back at Bobby and see a damaged child who grew into a defective adult. Right now, after what he did to Elisa and the others, I'm happy to have half killed the bastard.

Ruiz watches as two detectives climb into the back of the ambulance and sit either side of Bobby. 'You told me that Catherine's killer was going to be older . . . more practised.'

'I thought he would be.'

'And you said it was sexual.'

'I said her pain aroused him, but the motive wasn't clear. Revenge was one of the possibilities. You know, it's strange, but even when I was sure it was Bobby, I still couldn't picture him being there, making her cut herself. It was too sophisticated a form of sadism. But then again, he infiltrated all those lives – my life. He was like a piece of scenery that nobody notices because we concentrate on the foreground.'

'You saw him before anyone else did.'

'I tripped over him in the dark.'

The ambulance pulls away. Water birds lift out of the reeds. They twist and turn across the pale sky. Skeletal trees stretch upwards as if trying to pluck the birds from the air.

Ruiz gives me a ride to the hospital. He wants to be there when Bobby gets out of surgery. We follow the ambulance along St Pancras Way and turn into the accident and emergency bay. My legs have seized up almost completely now the adrenalin has drained out of them. I struggle to get out of the car. Ruiz commandeers a wheelchair and pushes me into a familiar white-tiled public hospital waiting room.

As usual, the Detective Inspector gets off on the wrong foot by calling the triage nurse 'sweetheart' and telling her to get her 'priorities sorted'. She takes her annoyance out on me, shoving her fingers between my ribs with unnecessary zeal. I feel like I'm going to pass out.

The young doctor who stitches up my lip has bleached hair, an old-fashioned feather-cut and a necklace of crushed shells. She has been on holiday somewhere warm and the skin on her nose is pink and peeling.

Ruiz has gone upstairs to keep tabs on Bobby. Not even an armed guard outside the surgery and a general anaesthetic is insurance enough for him to relax. Maybe he's trying to make amends for not believing me sooner. I doubt it.

Lying on a gurney, I try to keep my head still as I feel the needle slide into my lip and the thread tug at the skin. Scissors snip the ends and the doctor takes a step back, appraising her handiwork.

'And my mother told me I'd never be able to sew.'

'How does it look?'

'You should have waited for the plastic surgeon but I've done OK. You'll have a slight scar, just there.' She points to the hollow beneath her bottom lip. 'Guess it'll match your ear.' She tosses her latex gloves into a bin. 'You still need an X-ray. I'm sending you upstairs. Do you need someone to push you or can you walk?'

'I'll walk.'

She points to the lift and tells me to follow the green line to Radiology on the fourth floor. Half an hour later, Ruiz finds me in the waiting room. I'm hanging around for the radiologist to confirm what I already know from viewing the X-rays: two fractured ribs but no internal bleeding.

'When can you make a statement?'

'When they strap me up.'

'It can wait till tomorrow. Come on, I'll give you a lift home.'

A twinge of regret elevates me above the pain. Where is home? I haven't had time to contemplate where I'll spend tonight, and the night after that. Sensing my quandary, Ruiz murmurs, 'Why don't you go and listen to her? You're supposed to be good at that sort of thing.' In the same breath he adds, 'There's no frigging room at my place!'

Downstairs, he continues bossing people around until my chest is strapped and my stomach is rattling with painkillers and anti-inflammatories. I float along the corridor, following Ruiz to his car.

'There is one thing that puzzles me,' I say as we drive north towards Camden. 'Bobby could have killed me. He had the blade at my throat, yet he hesitated. It was as though he couldn't cross that line.'

'You said he couldn't kill his mother.'

'That's different. He was scared of her. He had no trouble with the others.'

'Well, he doesn't have to worry about Bridget any more. She died at eight o'clock this morning.'

'So that's it. He has no one left.'

'Not quite. We found his half-brother. I left a message for him, telling him Bobby was in hospital.'

Uneasiness washes over me, inching upwards like an incoming tide. 'Where did you find him?'

'He's a plumber in north London. Dafyyd John Morgan.'

Ruiz is shouting into the two-way radio. He wants cars sent to the house. I'm shouting too – trying to reach Julianne on a mobile, but the line is engaged. We're five minutes away but the traffic is murder. A truck has run a red light at a five-way intersection, blocking Camden Road.

Ruiz is weaving on to the pavement, forcing pedestrians to scatter. He leans out of the window. 'Dumbassfuck! Dickhead! Go, go! Just fucking move!'

This is taking way too long. He has been inside my house – inside my walls. I can see him standing in my basement, laughing at me. And I remember his eyes when he watched the police digging up the garden, the lazy insolence and his half-smile.

Now it makes sense. The white van that followed me in Liverpool; it was a plumber's van. Magnetic mats were taken off the doors, making it look nondescript. The fingerprint on the stolen four-wheel drive didn't belong to Bobby. And the drug dealer who gave Sonia Dutton the adulterated Ecstasy matched the description of D.J., Dafyyd – one and the same.

At the narrow boat, Bobby knocked on the deck before opening the hatch. It wasn't his boat. The workroom was full of tools and plumbing equipment. They were D.J.'s diaries and notes. Bobby torched the boat to destroy the evidence.

I can't sit here waiting. The house is less than a quarter of a mile away. Ruiz tells me to wait but I'm already out of the door, running along the street, dodging between pedestrians, joggers, mothers with toddlers, nannies with prams. Traffic is backed up in both directions as far as I can see. I hit 'redial' on the mobile. The line is still engaged.

There had to be two of them. How could one person have done it all? Bobby was too easy to recognise. He stood out in a crowd. D.J. had the intensity and the power to control people. He didn't look away.

When it came to the moment of truth, Bobby couldn't kill me. He couldn't make that leap because he'd never done it before. Bobby could do the planning but D.J. was the foot soldier. He was older, more practised, more ruthless.

I vomit into a rubbish bin and keep running, passing the local off-licence, the betting shop, a pizzeria, discount store, pawnbroker, bakery and the Rag and Firkin pub. Nothing is coming quickly enough. My legs are slowing down.

I round the final corner and see the house ahead of me. There are no police cars. A white van is parked out front with the sliding side door open. Hessian sacks cover the floor . . .

I fall through the front gate and up the steps. The phone is off the hook.

I scream Charlie's name but it comes out as a low moan. She is sitting in the living room, dressed in jeans and a sweat-shirt. A yellow Post-It note is stuck to her forehead. Like a new puppy, she throws herself at me, crushing her head to my chest. I almost black out with the pain.

'We were playing a game of "Who Am I?",' she explains. 'D.J. had to guess he was Homer Simpson. What did he choose for me?'

She lifts her face to mine. The note is curling at the edges but I recognise the small, neat print.

YOU'RE DEAD.

I find enough air to speak. 'Where's Mum?'

The urgency in my voice frightens her. She takes a step back and sees the bloodstains on my shirt and the sheen of sweat. My bottom lip is swollen and the stitches are crusted with blood.

'She's downstairs in the basement. D.J. told me to wait here.'

'Where is he?'

'He's coming back in a minute, but he said that ages ago.'

I push her towards the front door. 'Run, Charlie!'

'Why?'

'RUN! NOW! Keep running!'

The basement door is shut and wet paper towels have been pushed into the doorjamb. There is no key in the lock. I turn the handle and gently pull it open.

Dust is swirling in the air – the sign of leaking gas. I can't

398

yell and hold my breath at the same time. Halfway down the steps, I stop to let my eyes adjust to the light. Julianne is slumped on the floor beside the new boiler. She's lying on her side, with her right arm under her head and her left reaching out as though pointing to something. A dark fringe has fallen over one eye.

Crouching next to her, I slip my hands under her arms and drag her backwards. The pain in my chest is unbelievable. White dots dance in front of my eyes like angry insects. I still haven't taken a breath but the time is close. I take the stairs one at a time, dragging Julianne upwards and sitting down heavily after each exertion. One step, two steps, three steps . . .

I hear Charlie coughing behind me. She takes hold of my collar, trying to help me, pulling when I pull.

Four steps, five steps . . .

We reach the kitchen and Julianne's head bounces off the floor as I set her down. I'll apologise later. Hauling her over my shoulder, I roar in pain, and totter down the hallway. Charlie is ahead of me.

What is the trigger? A timer or a thermostat; the central heating; a refrigerator; the security lights?

'Run, Charlie. Run!'

When did it grow dark outside? Police cars fill the street with flashing lights. I don't stop this time. I scream one word, over and over. I cross the road, dodge the cars and get to the far end of the street before my knees buckle and Julianne falls on to the muddy grass. I kneel beside her.

Her eyes are open. The blast begins as a tiny spark in the midst of her deep brown corneas. The sound arrives a split second later, along with the shock wave. Charlie is thrown backwards. I try to shield them both. There is no orange ball like you see in the movies, only a cloud of smoke and dust. Debris rains down and I feel the warm breath of fire drying the sweat on my neck.

The blackened van lies upside down in the middle of the

street. Chunks of roofing and ribbons of gutters are draped over trees. Rubble and splintered wood covers the road.

Charlie sits up and looks at the desolation. The note is still stuck to her forehead, blackened at the edges but still legible. I pull her against my chest, holding her close. At the same time, my fingers close around the yellow square of paper and crush it within my fist.

Epilogue

The nightmares of my recent past still see me running – escaping the same monsters and rabid dogs and Neanderthal second-row forwards – but now they seem more real. Jock says it is a side effect of the Levodopa, my new medication.

The dosage has halved in the past two months. He says I must be under less stress. What a comedian! He phones me every day and asks if I fancy a game of tennis. I tell him no and he tells me a joke. 'What's the difference between a nine months pregnant woman and a *Playboy* centrefold?'

'I don't know.'

'Nothing, if her husband knows what's good for him.'

This is one of the cleaner ones and I risk telling Julianne. She laughs, but not as loudly as I do.

We're living in Jock's flat while we decide whether to rebuild or buy a new place. This is Jock's way of trying to make amends, but he hasn't been forgiven. In the meantime, he's moved in with a new girlfriend, Kelly, who hopes to be the next Mrs Jock Owens. She will need a harpoon gun or a cast-iron pre-nup to get him anywhere near an altar.

Julianne has thrown away all his gadgets and the out-of-date frozen meals in the freezer. Then she went out and bought fresh sheets for the beds and new towels.

Her morning sickness is over, thankfully, and her body is getting bigger each day (everything except her bladder). She is convinced we're having a boy, because only a man could cause her so much grief. She always looks at me when she says this. Then she laughs, but not as loudly as I do.

I know she's watching me closely. We watch each other. Maybe it's the disease she's looking for, or perhaps she doesn't trust me entirely. We had an argument yesterday – our first since nursing things back together. We're going to Wales for a week and she complained that I always leave my packing until the last possible minute.

'I never forget anything.'

'That's not the point.'

'What is the point?'

'You should do it earlier. It's less stressful.'

'For who?'

'For you.'

'But I'm not the one who is getting stressed.'

After tiptoeing around her for five months, grateful for her forgiveness, I decided to draw a line in the sand. I asked her: 'Why do women fall in love with men and then try to change them?'

'Because men need help,' she replied, as if this was common knowledge.

'But if I become the man you want, I won't be the man I am.'

She rolled her eyes and said nothing, but since then she's been less prickly. This morning she came and sat on my lap, putting her arms around my neck and kissing me with the sort of passion that marriage is supposed to kill. Charlie said 'Yuck!' and hid her eyes.

'What's wrong?'

'You guys are French kissing.'

402

'What do you know about French kissing?'

'It's when you slobber over each other.'

I rubbed my hand across Julianne's stomach and whispered, 'I want our children never to grow up.'

Our architect has arranged to meet me at the hole in the ground. The only thing left standing is the staircase, which goes nowhere. The force of the blast sent the concrete floor of the kitchen through the roof and blew the boiler into a yard two streets over. The shockwave shattered almost every window in the block and three houses have had to be demolished.

Charlie says she saw someone at a first floor window just before the blast. Anyone on that floor would have been vaporised, say the experts, which might explain why they didn't find so much as a fingernail or a fibre or a stray tooth. Then again, I keep asking myself, why would D.J. stick around once the gas had been turned on and the timer set to fire the boiler? He had plenty of time to get out, unless he planned this as a 'final' act in every sense of the word?

Charlie doesn't understand that he could have done these things. She asked me the other day if I thought he was in heaven. I felt like saying, 'I just hope he's dead.'

His bank accounts haven't been touched in two months and nobody has seen him. There is no record of him leaving the country, applying for a job, renting a room, buying a car or cashing a cheque.

Ruiz has pieced together the early facts. D.J. was born in Blackpool. His mother, a sewing machinist, married Lenny in the late sixties. She died in a car accident when D.J. was seven. His grandparents (her parents) raised him until Lenny remarried. Then he fell under Bridget's spell.

I suspect that he experienced everything Bobby did, although no two children react the same way to sexual abuse or to sadism. Lenny was the most important figure in both their lives and his death lay at the heart of everything.

D.J. finished his apprenticeship in Liverpool, becoming a master plumber. He joined a local firm where people remember him more with apprehension than fondness. At a bar one night he drove a broken bottle into a woman's face because she didn't laugh at the punchline of his joke.

He disappeared in the late eighties and reappeared in Thailand, running a bar and a brothel. Two teenage junkies who tried to smuggle of kilo of heroin out of Bangkok told police they had met their supplier in D.J.'s bar, but he skipped the country before anyone could link him to the bust.

He turned up in Australia, working his way down the east coast on building sites. In Melbourne he befriended an Anglican minister and became the manager of a homeless shelter. For a while he seemed to have mended his ways. No more sucker punches, broken noses or snapping ribs with his boots.

Appearances can be deceptive. The police in Victoria are now investigating the disappearance of six people from the hostel over a four-year period. Many of their welfare cheques were still being cashed up until eighteen months ago when D.J. appeared in the UK again.

I don't know how he found Bobby, but it can't have been too hard. Given the difference in their ages when D.J. left home, they must have been virtually strangers. Yet they discovered a shared desire.

Bobby's fantasies of revenge were just that – fantasies – but D.J. had the experience and the lack of empathy to make them come true. One was the architect, the other the builder. Bobby had the creative vision, D.J. had the tools. The end result was a psychopath with a plan.

Catherine was probably tortured and killed on the narrow boat. Bobby had watched me for so long, he knew exactly where to bury the body. He also knew that ten days later I'd be at the cemetery. One of them must have phoned the police from the call box near the gates. And leaving the shovel resting on Gracie's grave was a touch of the macabre with an explosive outcome.

Other small pieces have fallen into place as the weeks have passed. Bobby learned about our plumbing problems from my mother. She is notorious for boring people with stories of her children and grandchildren. She even showed him the photo albums and the building plans we submitted to the council for the renovations.

D.J. dropped leaflets through every letterbox in the street. Each small job provided another reference and helped convince Julianne to hire him. Once inside it was easy, although he almost came unstuck when Julianne caught him in my study one afternoon. That's when he made up the story of disturbing an intruder and chasing him out. He'd gone into the study to check to see if anything had been taken.

Bobby goes on trial at the end of next month. He hasn't entered a plea, but they expect it to be 'not guilty'. The case, though strong, is circumstantial. None of the physical evidence puts a murder weapon in his hand – not for Catherine or Elisa or Boyd or Erskine or Sonia Dutton or Esther Gorski.

Ruiz says it will be over after that, but he's wrong. This case will never be closed. People tried to shut this away years ago and look what happened. Ignore our mistakes and we are doomed to repeat them. Don't stop thinking of the white bear.

The events leading up to Christmas have almost become a surreal blur. Rarely do we talk about it, but I know from experience that it will come out one day. Sometimes, late at night, I hear a car door slam or heavy steps on the footpath and my mind won't be still. I have feelings of sadness, depression, frustration and anxiety. I am easily startled. I imagine people are watching me from doorways and parked cars. I can't see a white van without trying to make out the driver's face.

These are all common reactions to shock and trauma.

405

Maybe it's good that I know these things, but I would prefer to stop analysing myself.

I still have my disease, of course. I am part of a study being conducted at one of the research hospitals. Fenwick put me on to it. Once a month I drive to the hospital, clip a card to my shirt pocket and flip through the pages of *Country Life* while waiting my turn.

The head technician always offers me a cheery, 'How are you today?'

'Well, since you ask, I have Parkinson's Disease.'

He smiles wearily, gives me an injection and runs a few tests on my co-ordination, using video cameras to measure the degree and frequency of my tremors.

I know it will get worse. But what the hell! I'm lucky. A lot of people have Parkinson's. Not all of them have a beautiful wife, a loving daughter and a new baby to look forward to.